PARRISH FOR THE DEFENSE

BY HILLARY WAUGH

PARRISH
FOR THE DEFENSE

Hillary Waugh

DOUBLEDAY & COMPANY, INC.
GARDEN CITY, NEW YORK
1974

ISBN: 0-385-07302-x
Library of Congress Catalog Card Number 78–186047
Copyright © 1974 by Hillary Waugh
All Rights Reserved
Printed in the United States of America
First Edition

To Diana

MY APPRECIATION
TO ATTORNEY RICHARD L. HERSHATTER
FOR HIS GUIDANCE
IN THE LEGAL ASPECTS OF THIS BOOK.

PARRISH FOR THE DEFENSE

CHAPTER 1

The five-piece orchestra at the Madison Summer Club didn't play Rock. There were no electric guitars, lighting effects, or giant speakers. The music did not shatter the eardrums.

There was a piano, alto sax, drums, and two muted trumpets. The musicians wore black tie and short hair, with only one pair of sideburns. They were plump, portly, gray, and balding men in late middle age and the songs they played were from the Big Band era of the thirties.

It was what the customers wanted; the Fox-Trot, now and then a waltz, the traditional "Stardust" with the lights down low and, for the frisky, an occasional jitterbug number and a conga line. The club members attending the dance were of that era. They were the ones who had fox-trotted, jitterbugged, clung together through "Stardust," done the conga, and thrilled to the music of the past. This was a Hallowe'en dance for the over-thirty crowd, for the parents of the youth generation. This was for people who wanted to sway, not writhe, who wanted to be able to talk against the music. These were people who could let themselves go on Hallowe'en costumes, but not on the dance floor. Not any more. They had achieved a dignity in life; they had positions to maintain. Besides, their bones and muscles weren't what they used to be.

The decor of the club's ballroom was simple: candlelit pumpkins on the tables, black and orange streamers across the ceiling, giant black paper cats around the walls, and that spooky violet lighting that made the teeth glow.

It was the First Annual Summer Club Hallowe'en Costume Ball, a unique post-season event in the barnlike clubhouse. It was an experiment, for the Summer Club, as its name implied, specialized in tennis courts, swimming pool and beach privileges. Most of its members originally belonged to the town's summer population, the vacationers who flocked to Madison to escape the heat and grime of the city. Now, with the flight to the suburbs, a good majority of the members were year-round residents. But the expense of heating the club for winter use hadn't yet been managed and a roaring blaze in the great ballroom fireplace was all that could be provided against the October chill. The rest of the heat had to be generated by *la danse*.

There was warmth to spare. The event was over-subscribed and an enthusiastic success. It was a club of people who loved good times, who enjoyed the challenge and the foolishness of a costume party, the dressing up, the pre-party dinners, the imagination of costume designing or the status of a high-priced ready-made one. Madison was a town of the well-to-do and those who belonged to the club made up a roster of the top income earners, the coupon clippers, the cream of the leisured upper middle class.

So they had gathered, laughing, chatting, dancing, drinking, for a final fling. It was BYOB with the club providing setups and ice. The bar had been put in mothballs after Labor Day and all had lain dormant until now, when it had come alive with witches and goblins and the revels of Satan on All Hallows E'en. Except that if Satan were abroad, he lurked under the semblance of gentility that lay beneath the appearances of Satan that served as costumes. He lurked behind the laughter, the poses, the antics; below the lilt of song and the quest for prizes.

Corey Clifford won the award for the most ghoulish costume. He came in a hideous blue-white beard and red-stained shirt, with three bloody female heads tied to his belt by their hair. The heads were *papier-mâché*, but so realistic that, from a few feet away, they gave one a start. But that was Corey Clifford. He was a painter and sculptor and had the most *terrific* imagination. Everyone knew Corey would win. They didn't know what he'd come up with but they knew he'd win.

Sally Whittaker took the prize for the most beautiful costume. She wore a filmy, frilly, off-the-shoulder, knee-length gown of black and eerie green. The skirt gave a contrasting effect of rags and tatters, yet had a swirling, wraithlike aura. Her accessories were a witch's cap, black eye-mask, and a knobby broomstick. It was a costume she'd designed herself and it set off her figure to perfection. With

2

her lush blonde hair, twinkling eyes and pert face, she was enough to give even a Satan wayward thoughts. As George Bakewell was heard to remark, but not to his wife, "She can haunt my house any time."

Sally's husband, Jerry, a popular local internist, played his role in lower key. He dressed in a skeleton costume and clued it to his profession by clipping an X-ray negative on his back and painting an outsized thermometer on his front.

The First Selectman was there, lean and gray, the first Democrat in over a century. He gave out champagne prizes with gentle, joking remarks and Sally Whittaker, for one, gave him a kiss. George Bakewell, in turn, gave Sally a kiss when she came back with the bottle. "At least our table got one winner," he said, and popped the cork at Sally's behest. George and his wife were among those who had hosted pre-dance dinner parties and sixteen people were in his group.

The orchestra returned, the lights went down, and the music started again. The song was "Blue Moon" and couples moved onto the dim floor. George Bakewell grabbed Sally, but her husband didn't mind. Jerry downed his champagne and picked Nolene Shedd for a partner. He'd danced once with Sally, once with Cindy Magnuson, once with Eunice Oliver, and the rest of the time he had watched. He was a good-looking man of thirty-six, youthful and vigorous, carrying ten more pounds than he had when he and Sally had married six years before. He was the kind of man who appealed to women. He had the looks and the charm. And he had that other quality which enhanced those values, the quality of not trying to use his charms for such a purpose. So, if his costume didn't do for him what Sally's did for her, they still made a handsome couple together—the handsomest at the table.

After Nolene he danced with Alice Noyes and the sequence was a rarity. He wasn't that keen about dancing. Besides, the music was before his time. He didn't know "Moon over Miami"; he was only two years old when it had been a hit. And "The Beer Barrel Polka"? He had a vague recollection of it from his childhood. However, he did feel it fitting to dance once with every girl at the table.

The party grew noisier as the evening progressed. Alcohol, that ice-melting ice-breaker, did ease the tensions of the workaday world, did make the revelers feel more comfortable in their costumes, did make them talk a little louder, dance a little faster, and drink a little more recklessly.

3

It was a good party. It was a great party. They should do this every Hallowe'en. The club should open its doors just that one last time on the final Saturday of October. Let's have another costume ball. And let's get that same dance band back. Except maybe we should have one that plays the music of the forties instead of the thirties. Sure, there's that camp thing about the Big Band era, but the younger members of the club don't relate to the Big Band era. They were in diapers back then. Some weren't even born. Only the fifty-year-olds go for that stuff these days, except as some kind of a fad. They're the only ones who can get genuinely nostalgic. So maybe next year we ought to update the music a little. But other than that, it was a great party. It really was great.

That was the consensus, for the dance floor was still crowded when, at two minutes after one, the band swung into "Goodnight, Sweetheart." After, there was laughter and whooping in the chill night air and the sound of a hundred cars. Neighbors had to resign themselves to a twenty-minute noise break while the partyers cleared the area.

But who could get angry at such good spirits? The middle-agers needed their fun and, after all, it was harmless pleasure. They weren't vandalizing property or shouting obscenities. They were just being unquiet.

Inside the clubhouse, the five portly musicians put away their instruments, wiped the sweat from their faces, quaffed provided beer, and collected their pay. When was the last time they had played together? Back in the fifties, wasn't it? They'd gathered for a reunion—the same old five who had played together in high school.

And they weren't bad, if they did say so themselves. They weren't bad at all. It hadn't taken them long to get the rust out of their fingers and tongues and brains and brush up on their old arrangements.

They drove back to New Haven together in one car, talking and laughing. It was like the old days except the car now was a two-year-old Cadillac and not an eight-year-old Ford. Those were the days, though; drive forty miles for an engagement, play till one or two, drive home again, get up and go to school and then, maybe, do the same thing the next night. Now, perhaps once a year, like tonight, to retaste one's youth was all right. But not much more than once. You can't afford it any more. Twenty-five bucks apiece for

4

four hours' work? Guys who are making fifteen to thirty thousand dollars a year? But it's fun to forget the insurance business, or the brokerage business, or retail clothing for a few practice sessions and one evening of playing together.

The club lights were out now. The place was quiet. The night was blacker and the town grew still. All the little Trick and Treaters, the tiny ghosts and elves and hobgoblins were long in bed. And the big ghosts and skeletons and Bluebeards who had danced out their frenetic passions to love song music were on their way.

Now the hours before dawn belonged to the souls of the dead, the wings of the devil, and the faces of evil. The restless whirling of their frenzies would be the *Danse Macabre*.

CHAPTER 2

The apparitions of evil still had two hours before the cock crowed when a Madison policeman named Jack Falmouth drove slowly through the dark center of town. The road had a divider to channel traffic, and shops lined the sidewalks on either side—the ubiquitous liquor and drug stores, the banks, the gas stations, shoe and clothing stores, the movie theater; all of which were to be found in the central area of any town. But Madison, Connecticut, had its distinguishing characteristics as well. There were four real estate firms on that two-hundred-yard strip of U. S. Route 1. There were two travel agencies and a number of specialty shops—gifts, jewelry, women's fashions. There was a ski shop, a music center and, on the second floor at the corner, a dance studio.

One could tell a lot about a town from its main street shops, Jack Falmouth reflected as his eyes ceaselessly swept the dark, empty surroundings. These shops spelled Madison, bespoke a small town, well-to-do. They were its signature, its pedigree, the essence that made Madison unlike any other small town in the world, just as a person is unlike any other person in the world.

You would not find their like in Clinton, the next town up the line. That was blue-collar territory with a cosmetic factory its dominant feature. The factory stamped its impress not only on the nature of the inhabitants, but the nature of the stores.

Nor would you find them in Guilford, back to the west, which was more of a bedroom for New Haven's elite. Yale professors, intellectuals, and Democratic liberals were encroaching upon the rock-ribbed Republican natives in Guilford. But not in Madison. (That Democratic First Selectman was a fluke, after all.)

Madison was an entity of and in itself. This was a town of little industry and little interest in industry. Its newcomers were predominantly the wealthy retired, with older couples outnumbering the younger, and women outnumbering the men by as much as two to one. For those who had the money and who wanted to escape the frenzy of modern life without moving far from the population centers, Madison formed a satisfying eye in the hurricane.

The town was not, of course, quite such a heaven to someone like Jack Falmouth. He was twenty-nine years old and the police department paid him $8,600 a year. His wife was a schoolteacher which helped their income but, on the debit side, that meant paying a woman to mind two younger children during the day. However, he had little to complain about. He had bought in one of those few areas in town where the lots were small and the houses modest, and he and his family survived in reasonable comfort. Less lucky members of the force had had to cross into Clinton to find housing they could afford.

But Madison was a good town. It offered the opportunities of Long Island Sound to the south and woods and farms to the north. The people were solid. "Stuffy" might be applied to some of them, "Conservative" to more, and "WASP" to still more, but they were reliable and responsible, and that was to the town's credit.

True, the crime rate was up and Charlie Hallock and Ed DuBois, the police force's two detectives, were working hard on some serious robberies—$21,000 worth of jewels being the most recent and most severe—but these thefts were believed to be the work of out-of-towners. Locally there had been a bomb scare the past week and they'd had to close the schools for the day, but there'd been a rash of scares all around and the other towns had had more than one.

6

Even Hallowe'en had been no problem. In fact, things were so well under control that the police could spare a man for traffic duty at the big Hallowe'en costume ball at the Summer Club. Jack himself, working the twelve-to-eight shift, had handled departing traffic when the dance had ended. Now it was half past four and he, Jim Leech, and Ken Woolson were cruising the town in Madison's three police cars.

Falmouth turned right at the corner and his reflections were broken by the police radio coming to life. Grace Felton was on the town hall communications desk and she had a hoarse, sexless voice. Leech always claimed she sounded like a horn in search of a fog, but Woolson said she sounded like Mammy Yokum being humped by a goat.

"Cars seven-one, seven-two and seven-three," she rasped in her laryngeal tones, "there's a report of a death at Doctor Gerald Whittaker's house, twenty-two River Edge Farms Road. He says it's his wife. Please confirm."

Jack Falmouth gripped the wheel. Dr. Whittaker's wife—Sally Whittaker—was dead? It was like a kick in the belly.

He forgot the jokes about Grace Felton's voice. He forgot what a good town Madison was. He forgot everything except the DOA. If it had been some old biddy it would have been routine. But Mrs. Whittaker? That cute blonde with the ready smile, the bright eyes, the nifty figure!

Of course it wouldn't be natural circumstances. Not someone her age. Why, he'd seen her just that night—coming out of the parking lot after the dance. The doctor was driving his big white Cadillac and seemed in good spirits. Sally was beside him, in shadow, so all he got of her was that she was wearing something fluffy and gauzy under a laxly closed mink. There was another couple in the back seat whom the patrolman didn't know. The doctor had been smiling and said, "Hello, Jack," in passing. And Jack had responded, "Hi, Doc."

Suicide was Jack's first thought. There were more suicides in Madison than people knew about. Because you didn't advertise them. The obits read, "Died suddenly." That was enough. It wouldn't help to add, "By his (or her) own hand."

You couldn't tell about suicides—incipient suicides. Just because Sally had been to a dance three and a half hours before and had sat, blonde and gorgeous, in a big Cadillac beside a man as handsome as the doctor, that didn't prove anything at all.

7

Like the woman with the husband and children loading the car for a picnic. She stepped into the closet and blew her head off with a shotgun. And the husband and children called and the husband came back and couldn't find her—until he saw the blood coming out from under the door.

So you just didn't know. And when you'd been a policeman long enough and had seen enough, you didn't get surprised at anything.

Jack Falmouth picked up his mike and muttered mechanically, "Seven-one, on my way." He circled in the shopping center lot and touched his siren into a low, warning growl as he turned onto Route 1 again and sped back.

There was no traffic so he didn't hit the siren button again. No point in waking people, although Jack felt like sounding the alarm as loud as he could. Mrs. Whittaker dead? So pretty, so alluring, so very well formed, so—what would you say? So outstanding! Mrs. Whittaker with her mink coat over her slacks in the supermarket. Jack's wife, Muriel, thought it was terrible. She said it was conspicuous consumption. But not Jack. He knew different. It wasn't studied and for effect, it was natural. It was flair. It was style. It was Sally.

Jack's thoughts turned to Dr. Whittaker as he raced west down the highway toward the scene. He was a hell of a handsome guy, the doctor. But no airs; a regular joe. He was a good golfer too, Jack had heard, one of the better players in the club. Golf wasn't Jack's game so he didn't know what the doctor's handicap was, or how handicaps were arrived at or what they actually meant. But he'd heard remarks and he'd seen Whittaker's name in the weekly *Shore Line Times* and the daily New Haven *Register*.

He was a good doctor too. Muriel swore by him. But Jack would expect women to swear by someone like Whittaker even if he were a quack. However, Jack had been a patient too and was also convinced the doctor had a thorough grounding in his field.

The doctor's offices were in the small new building right there in the center of town, in with the real estate offices and the gift shops and fancy fashions. He'd come a long ways in the six years he'd been in Madison. Jack could remember his first office, off a side street in back of things, with his wife as his receptionist.

They'd bought the subdivision house on River Edge Farms Road before they even got to town. They'd bought it when it was still under construction, that spring before they were married. It was a big house, expensive for a doctor just getting started, but it had been a good choice for he'd done well. He belonged in a house like that. It was a fitting home for one who had an office in the newest building in town, who had a receptionist and nurse and the most modern medical equipment a doctor could ask for.

Falmouth slowed and bore left onto the blacktop of Neck Road. Leech and Woolson had responded to the call but there was no sign of them yet. The night was soft and silent and no sirens wailed in the distance. Leech and Woolson had no more urge to disturb the sleeping citizenry than did Falmouth.

Neck Road was not in sight of Long Island Sound but it was near. It paralleled the shore, ejecting roadway feelers to cottage-clad beaches a quarter of a mile away. The homes along Neck Road were modest, the earlier houses, the property of working people rather than the well-to-do.

It was off this road, opposite to the shore, that River Edge Farms Road formed a circle. Nineteen homes were spaced around its perimeter with nine more grouped in its interior. These were among the expensive dwellings in town, in the sixty-five-thousand-dollar category. This was one of Madison's comfortable subdivisions and if the acreage was less than two to a house, it was because two-acre zoning only applied north of the turnpike. The homes were well spaced nevertheless, and the location was closer to the center of town—always a consideration.

Jack Falmouth, entering onto River Edge Farms Road, turned left at the junction. He knew where Gerald Whittaker lived, as he knew where everyone of repute in Madison lived—and many who were not in repute. In fact, Jack Falmouth knew the homes of an amazing number of people. Some were the ones who'd had run-ins with the police: the drunkards, the fighters, the hollerers, the trouble-makers. And, of course, he well knew where lived the ones who got into more serious trouble, the felons (for even Madison had felons), the vandals, the thieves, the car stealers, the troublemaking kids, the whores (for there were those too). And he knew the houses of the victims, those who had been robbed, or were bothered by prowlers or unneighborly neighbors. And others he knew about just because a policeman came to know who bought what big house or was remodeling what old one.

The Whittaker residence was two-floored and spacious, larger than a childless couple required but fitting as a sign of status. A light

9

over the door cast a welcome along the path and over the still-green, leaf-covered grass around the front yard maples. All the downstairs lights were on and those in the master bedroom as well.

"I saw her alive tonight," Jack Falmouth thought to himself as he turned onto the drive to the right of the house. "It was only three and a half hours ago. And now she's dead. It doesn't seem real."

CHAPTER 3

A floodlamp over the garage doors illuminated the blacktop and patio lights gleamed in the rear. All the other homes were black but the Whittaker house was ablaze, as if the light would stamp out reality, would drive off death. These were the futile lights, the late night lights that shined on horrors. Jack knew them well.

He crossed the lawn and stamped cold morning dew from his shoes when he pressed the illuminated button beside the screen door. He waited, his mind in neutral, ready to handle whatever state the doctor was in, whatever state the body was in.

The doctor opened the inside door almost immediately and did not seem distressed. His pajamas were smeared with blood, but his gray-flecked hair was combed, his face composed, and he seemed as much in command of himself as when giving out medical advice. He pushed open the screen and said, "Oh, it's you, Jack. Come in."

When the doctor stepped back into the light, the policeman could see that the pajama stains were from wiping his hands, that the pinkness of blood remained on his palms and that the crevices around his nails were etched in red. That meant a lot of gore, and Jack thought of the woman who had blown off her head in the closet.

The front hall was paved with slate, with a staircase on the left, a sunken living room on the right, and a blazing chandelier suspended from the roof beams overhead. Falmouth took it all in. He not only noticed the blood around the doctor's fingernails, but the marble bust on the phone table beside the staircase. He not only noted the lighted breakfast nook at the back, with a floodlit patio beyond the glass, but the Chinese print on the wall of the coat closet and the fact the doctor was barefoot. It was so quick and automatic that the doctor thought he had all of the patrolman's attention. "She's in there," he said, and indicated the living room. Jack stepped to the entrance and turned.

The room was the essence of Sally. She had decorated the whole house, but this was her showplace: the enormous, shaggy apricot rug on the parquet floor, the great, hot-yellow couch with its multi-colored throw cushions by the distant fireplace; the white leather chairs, brass and glass coffee table, the vibrant geometric paintings on the off-white walls. There was the bric-a-brac, the Spanish break-front, the *intime* corner with the fragile Victorian chairs.

It was an expensive room, a careful room. It was to be admired, not used, and the Whittaker parties were held in another part of the house, in what they called the "wreck room." There, the furniture was wood and heavy; round tables and low-backed armchairs, built-in bar and a pool table. That was a knockabout room, a room to exist in. The front room was where Sally had lived.

And it was the room where Sally had died.

She lay in the center of the rug, her feet toward him, and she wore a blue miniskirted dress so short it just covered her hips. Her legs and feet were bare, the soles slightly soiled, and she was positioned on her side with her right knee flexed. The rest of her was hideous. It lay in a great dark pool, her body battered, her head smashed.

It wasn't just a bloody death, it had been a fighting death and the scene was a shambles. Chairs had been upended and lamps broken. Blood was everywhere; in splotches and spatters on the white leather of an upset chair, on the shade of a fallen lamp, the brass and glass of the coffee table. It speckled the near parts of the couch and sprinkled the scattered cushions. Sally had sought every hope of escape.

The weapon that had bludgeoned her was not in sight, but Jack could guess what it was. The poker in the fireplace stand was missing. It was the kind of weapon that could have wrought such damage and Jack was appalled, not so much by the scene as by the kind of creature who could have done it.

He turned to the doctor, stunned and disbelieving. Only a few hours before, Whittaker and his wife had been dancing at the Summer Club. They had been to a party together. "Was it you?" he said aghast.

Dr. Whittaker shook his head slowly. He was not upset by the question, or surprised. He looked in shock himself. "I was asleep," he said slowly. "I heard her cry out. I heard the pounding. I came down and found her." He choked back a sob.

Jack took another look, this time noting what he should have seen the first time. Her wristwatch, bracelet and rings were in place. She hadn't been robbed—at least of personal jewelry. If that had been the motive, the robber hadn't had time to steal them.

Falmouth glanced again at the doctor beside him, white and haggard now, staring at his wife and wiping his hands mindlessly on the soiled top of his pajamas. Falmouth noted the bright red patches of blood on the pajama knees. He noted too that the blood on the doctor's pajamas was not spattered as was the blood on the furniture.

But it was not for him to investigate the crime. Sergeant Charlie Hallock and Ed DuBois were the detectives on the force. His role was to protect the scene. They would take it from there.

"I'd like to use your phone, Doctor," he said and turned to the hall table.

CHAPTER 4

State's Attorney Vincent Masters stretched lazily in bed and looked at his watch. It was nine-fifteen, time to get up if he were going to ten o'clock Mass. He didn't really believe skipping Mass was any sin and he certainly didn't get anything out of the service, but Adele liked it and didn't like going alone. Besides, it set a good example for Judy. And, of course, when one was state's attorney for the county of New Haven, one was not completely his own man. He had obligations to his office as well as to himself.

He swung his feet over the side of the bed and rubbed sleep from his eyes. He was a good-looking, dark-haired man standing a little over six feet, with a reasonably trim figure for a man of thirty-eight who didn't exercise. It was diet that did it and he was conscious of everything that went into his mouth. Not that he was vain, but a man had a responsibility to do the best he could in this world and that included doing right by his body and mind as well as obeying the law and making a contribution to the world he lived in.

Adele had let him sleep and that was good. He was really more tired than he realized. He'd been state's attorney for four years now, with two full-time and four part-time assistant state's attorneys, but never had he been working harder than now, starting the tight security murder trial of two Black Panthers. Tuesday through Friday were the trial days, but preparation was a full-time job even though the case had been readied months ago. There were so many things to keep on top of when a case was big, like the Panther one. But now it was Sunday, trial proceedings were under control, and he'd had nine hours' sleep. He could enjoy church and could, with a clear conscience, even watch football in the afternoon.

There was a clatter on the stairs and Judy, who was nine, burst into the room. "Are you awake, Daddy?" she asked, and said he was wanted on the telephone.

The bedroom extension hadn't rung, which meant Adele had turned off the bell for him. He told Judy her coming made sure he was awake and tried to swat her on the bottom, but he wasn't quick enough. He picked up the phone.

The caller was a reporter from the *Journal Courier*, New Haven's morning daily, who'd been assigned to the Whittaker murder story, and could Masters give him anything on it?

"Me?" Masters scratched his hair. "I haven't even heard about it. What happened?"

The reporter was vague. Outside of the victim's name and the name of the town, he was informationless.

Masters called Bill Coyne's number in Clinton. Coyne was the county detective attached to the state's attorney's office who would work on the case with the Madison police. Coyne's mother answered in her squeaky tin voice and said she didn't know where her William was. He was gone when she woke up.

Masters thought of trying the Madison force but decided the hell with it. Everybody would be at the scene except the cop on the desk, who wouldn't know any more than the reporter. Don't look for trouble, Masters, he told himself. That was his bad habit—jumping in at the first word. It was a thing with him, that passion for a neat, orderly universe with everything in its place. It was one of the reasons he was a state's attorney. Most lawyers who accepted the appointment were older men who'd made their money. It wasn't the kind of job to attract the young. The work was hard and thankless and the pay was nothing compared to what a good lawyer could make on his own.

Only somebody like Vincent Masters, who was dedicated to law and order and the belief that quick, sure punishment of wrongdoers was the best way to maintain law and order, would voluntarily take such a job so early in life. Not that he was trying to be noble. It was this passion he had to put the cups and saucers back on the shelf, to glue broken pieces together, to make everything right. It was something he chastised himself about because he felt it abnormal. Like now. What could he do about this murder in Madison right this moment? Why should he be calling Coyne; worrying the case? Coyne would be in touch as soon as he had something to tell him. Maybe he'd have the murderer in tow and the whole thing wrapped up.

"Get some breakfast, Masters," he told himself. "Go to church, relax, and wait. Maybe nobody will bother you until the football games are over."

Masters wasn't that lucky. Coyne phoned in at quarter of ten, just as the state's attorney and his family were leaving for church. Coyne had a high, tenor voice, a remarkable quality for he was a huge man, three inches over six feet, broad of beam and padded with fat. Everything about him was outsized, a giant among pygmies. He was Irish, reddish-haired, pushing fifty and, for the most part, easygoing. There was talk that he had almost killed a man in his youth and he had reformed his hell-raising ways thereafter. Whatever the case, he kept himself under rigid control and displayed a tenacity and skill that his size and manner concealed.

He reported that both Charlie Hallock and he had interviewed Dr. Whittaker at the scene and each had obtained the same story. The Whittakers had gone to the Yale-Dartmouth game with friends from Trumbull, had brought them back to a dinner party and the costume dance. The Trumbull friends and two other couples returned for a nightcap after the dance and remained till two-thirty.

"Whittaker," Coyne continued in his thin tenor, "says he retired immediately and went to sleep while his wife was still downstairs. He knew nothing more until her screams woke him up at quarter past four. He went out into the upstairs hall calling her name and when he got to the head of the stairs, suddenly a man ran out the front door and disappeared."

"Could Dr. Whittaker identify the man?"

"No, he could not identify the man," Coyne said, a distinct note of testiness in his voice. Coyne liked to tell a story through before answering questions and if things didn't go his way, he tended to pout.

"Yes, I see. Go on, Bill."

"Dr. Whittaker maintains he could not identify the man because a chandelier blocked part of his view and the man never showed his face. He had dark hair, a scarf high around his neck, wore dark pants and a lighter shade sport coat, no hat, no overcoat. Dr. Whittaker says he called to the man to stop, but the man ignored him. The doctor ran down to the door and looked out, but the figure had disappeared. He went to the living room and found his wife on the floor with her skull crushed. He knelt beside her and tried to cradle her but realized she was dead, so he desisted and telephoned a lawyer,

15

name of Edward Balin, who is a friend of his, and asked what he should do—"

"He called a lawyer?" Masters said in surprise.

"That's what I said," Coyne replied huffily. Masters had interrupted again. "He asked the lawyer what he should do and the lawyer told him to call the police. This he did at four twenty-five. As for the lawyer, he appeared on the scene himself at twenty minutes of five, before the detectives got there."

Now Coyne was through and, since they would no longer interrupt a train of thought, he was eager for questions.

Masters had only a few. "What about a murder weapon?"

"None at the scene, but we think it was the fireplace poker. It's missing."

"Why did Whittaker call a lawyer instead of the police?"

Coyne grunted. "He says he'd never called the police before in his life and it didn't occur to him now. He wanted help, so he called a friend he thought could help."

"Was the house locked?"

"Yeah. All except the front door. We can't tell about that on accountta it's one of those where the lock has to be reset every time the door is opened."

"You think the doctor did it?"

Coyne grunted once more. "Hard to say. The lawyer kept advising him not to answer questions and he kept saying he had to. He's been co-operative and he won't shake on his story."

After the questions, Coyne went into the minutiae of his report: He had arrived on the scene at five-twenty, just as Dr. Elizabeth Allen, the medical examiner, was leaving. The body was removed at six-fifteen and would be autopsied at Yale-New Haven. He had called Dr. Marvin Liebman, pathologist, regarding the desirability of establishing the time of death and Liebman had left at once for the hospital. Meanwhile, the house was being fingerprinted and photographed, neighbors interviewed, and a search of the area would be undertaken in an effort to find the murder weapon.

Masters listened to the overdetailed recital impatiently. Already his family had gone on ahead. But Coyne didn't like being interrupted, or hurried. His hypersensitive ego needed constant nourishment and if he felt slighted he would sulk, he would become antagonistic, and his work would suffer. So Masters waited him out, gave him the required pat on the back, and managed to be only fifteen minutes late joining Adele and Judy in their pew.

He got another call after church, this time from Lou Savitt, the county coroner. "It looks like we've got a live one," Savitt said with relish. He was a lawyer with a small practice but good connections, and the coroner's position was gravy. Since his job was to assess results rather than do the digging, he thoroughly enjoyed his work. And never more than when a big case came along. The main thrust of his efforts was determining responsibility in automobile fatalities, and what was that compared to a real life murder?

Savitt didn't know what had been going on in Madison but he could report on other areas. The autopsy would be that afternoon and the state's chief medical examiner himself would come down from Hartford to conduct it.

"Why him?" Masters wanted to know. "If the woman was beaten to death, anybody can do the autopsy."

Savitt wouldn't wait to explain the necessity. "This murder victim is no ordinary housewife, Vince. She's high society: and I mean high Philadelphia society. They've got more money than the treasury, my friend, and when they speak, kingdoms tremble. I mean they've got power. They've been on the phone to me once already and I don't know who else they're contacting, but they aren't wasting any time. I hear they're coming up."

"I see," Masters said without Savitt's enthusiasm.

"And here's something else," Savitt went on conspiratorially. "This is confidential. We're not letting it out to the papers, but Mrs. Whittaker was wearing a minidress when she was killed, and nothing else. I mean *nothing* else. No pants, no slip, no bra. Not a damned stitch. The hospital called me when they undressed her."

The poker was found at noon. It was fifty feet into the deep grass on a slope separating the Whittakers' small back yard from a large marsh. It was discovered by one of six auxiliary policemen combing the area. Caked on the handle were quantities of dried blood, hair and bits of flesh, skin and bone.

Meanwhile, a group of the curious patrolled the background, its members coming and going in a continuous shift, its numbers remaining relatively constant. Most were elderly neighbors, but two were reporters.

17

Out front, traffic on River Edge Farms Road was unusually heavy, and cars crept by in a constant stream while families peered at the murder house as if the Mark of Cain had been added. The house, however, was locked, sealed, guarded and empty. The body was gone and the doctor was gone. William and Nolene Shedd, one of the couples at the Whittakers' nightcap party, had taken him in. Meanwhile, four other families, two of them patients, were awaiting a chance.

Empty as it might be, the house was still scarred by crime and, much like a house that had burned, would be a long time recovering. Only here it wasn't smoke damage that had to be eradicated. Here it was the signs of crime and its investigation. Here it was the deep wide bloodstain on the apricot rug, the spatters and flecks on the furniture, the masking tape outlining the body's position, the broken lamp and upset furniture, the fingerprint powder that dirtied everything that could retain the oily pattern of a print.

In New Haven that afternoon, Dr. Elliot Grove, the newly appointed state medical examiner, did a careful autopsy, an event witnessed by Detective Sergeant Charlie Hallock and County Detective Bill Coyne. In addition to the damage to her head, Sally Whittaker had suffered a broken arm and broken collarbone fighting off her attacker. What was equally interesting was that, despite her scanty clothing, there had been no sex.

The poker was undergoing laboratory analysis but it was a formality. Everyone knew it was the murder weapon. But who had wielded it?

That was the question everyone was asking. The detectives asked it, reporters asked it, and the people in the streets asked it. It was a horror story that shocked and frightened the people of Madison. What was especially shocking was the doctor's tale of a strange intruder. Such a thing could happen in Madison? What kind of an age were we living in when decent, law-abiding people could not enjoy safety? If it could happen to a young and attractive woman like Mrs. Whittaker, it could happen to anyone.

CHAPTER 5

Melody Stevens parted the slats of the motel blind and looked out. The rain gave the blackness an inky quality and the lights gleamed like empty beacons—the slash of neon advertising the motel, the blurry name of the diner across the way, the streetlights, the rotating red and white beacon on the police car roof.

They were still out there, waiting and silent. She couldn't see them well and she couldn't be sure how many. About a dozen, she guessed; men in raincoats, short, tall, dumpy or lean, grouped together in one black glob, except for the one in front whose raincoat was yellow. Him she could see quite distinctly, hands pushed deep into wet pockets, legs braced, rain hat shielding a hawklike face. He was too far away and the light too bad for her to read his expression, but she could feel his hate.

She looked around for the policeman. He had a yellow rain cape too, and a big hand lantern. He was not out in the rain, but back in the car. The cluster of people were not troublesome now. Earlier, when the crowd was larger, the people yelled and called and threw bricks and cans and bottles. Some of the missiles had chipped the masonry of the motel and broken one of the windows. Then the police had gotten hard-nosed and driven the people back. There were no more rocks but there was a lot of name-calling. Then she and Cleve and the guards were safely inside the motel, shepherded from the limousine by grim-faced patrolmen. It was a job they did not like.

The yelling and the name-calling kept up for a while. The names weren't bad but if the words did not hurt, the venom did. She thought she was used to hate. She sampled it so often. Anyone near Cleveland Parrish was a recipient. He generated so much of it.

19

When the rain started in earnest, the shouting faded and people drifted away. All except the hard-core dozen who were out there now, waiting and watching.

Melody let the blind go, fumbled for a cigarette from her bag and lighted it. What were they waiting for anyway? Maybe they knew Cleveland Parrish was supposed to leave tonight. Maybe they were waiting for him to reappear. But they weren't going to do anything. There was the patrolman in his car with the blinking light. There were the bodyguards.

She took a nervous drag on the cigarette and looked around at the impersonal, the bleak, the despairingly empty room and she felt again that agonizing pain of loneliness. It almost made her scream. She clenched her fists, crushing the cigarette, and closed her eyes tight. It was the hate, she told herself. That God damned implacable hatred that the walls couldn't keep out. It was the rain too, the black, shivering rain; and the room—the God damned never ending succession of motel rooms and hotel rooms, of clerks and maids and bellhops, all of them sterilely polite, looking upon her as a job or a tip.

She turned and viewed herself in the dresser mirror. She was thirty-two years old, an ash blonde with a willowy body and a damned well-put-together face. There were darker eyebrows, the real color of her hair; brown, well-spaced eyes, broad cheekbones, a classic nose, small mouth, the lips a trifle thin perhaps, and a good chin. She had a lot going for her, God damn it. She was a Phi Beta Kappa out of Vassar with a master's from Columbia. She was secretary to one of the most glamorous lawyers and exciting legal minds in the country, for which she was paid a munificent amount in straight salary and God knew how much more in expenses and extras. But of course she wasn't just any old secretary. She was Cleveland Parrish's private, confidential secretary. She was his right arm, his Girl Friday, his aid, his comforter, his mistress. He needed her. She was the only thing in the whole God damned world he did need.

But she got these pangs; a real, sharp, violent pain that almost made her cry out, and they were coming more often. Not every day, not every week, not even every month. But once in a while something would happen, the combination of forces would click into place, and it was as if a secret door in her mind would trigger open for a moment and show her the terrible darkness beyond. She didn't know what the pain really was, except it seemed to be linked with fear and loneliness.

Yet how could she be lonely? She had everything. She had a great job, an exciting, demanding job. She was always where the action was —sometimes, as those silent men outside reminded her, the kind of action she didn't desire. And she was needed. Cleve depended upon her. He couldn't move without her.

Was it the hate then? Was it the way hate cut her off from other people—cut her and Cleve off, she meant, for the hate was only incidentally directed at her. Cleve was the one those men outside hated. He was the one who had just got that young black acquitted of the cop-killing charge. And those men outside thought the black man had done it. In fact, Melody herself thought he had. He had the sullen, dull, insensitive look of a killer about him. He had the background too. But Cleve had raised a reasonable doubt and the conscientious jurors, so carefully picked by Cleve, had let him go.

But those rednecks outside, waiting and hating, they weren't persuaded. There was no reasonable doubt in their mindless minds. But they couldn't touch that surly, sullen black kid. The police had whisked him away fast. They didn't want any lynchings in the state of Tennessee. Not in this day and age. Better to let the kid get away with a murder than have the state get a bad name.

So the haters gathered to give their due to the man who had got the nigger off, the man who had been paid fifty thousand dollars by those nigger groups and those nigger-loving groups to get the cop-killer sprung. If they couldn't lynch the kid, maybe they could lynch his lawyer.

But, of course, they couldn't touch the lawyer. With Cleve's money and his power he was invulnerable to the likes of them. So all they could do was stand in the rain and vent their impotent hatred.

Except that the hate wasn't impotent. Maybe it was to Cleve. He was insensitive to intangibles. He was oblivious of them. But Melody could feel it and respond to it. And she was a recipient as well as he. Because she went with him. If Cleve Parrish were ever strung up by his heels as Mussolini had been, she would be strung up beside him, just like Clara Petacci.

Melody pulled herself together, put out the cigarette she had broken, picked up the newspaper she had listlessly been reading, tossed it back on the bed and opened the connecting door to the next room. Cleve was sitting on the foot of the bed with his back to her. A card table was in front of him, the other three men had pulled up chairs, and a poker game was in progress. One of the men was a sheriff whose name she didn't remember. Another was a local plainclothesman assigned to protect Cleveland Parrish, and the third was a private detective hired for the same purpose. Tennessee didn't want lawyers lynched either. Nor did Cleve himself. The private detective was in his own employ.

The poker game was penny-ante. Professional cops couldn't play for Parrish's stakes. Even so, the lawyer played to win pennies with the same dedication as when playing for hundred-dollar bills. Cleveland Parrish was dedicated not to stakes but to winning.

He had his coat and tie off, his shirt and collar unfastened. He was a husky man of forty-four, just under six feet tall with a broad build, graying hair, a ruddy complexion and a still handsome face. The looks were going a little. Lines were deepening, and good living was turning hard muscle into fat so that his face was taking on a blowsy look. He was getting a paunch but it wasn't much yet, and his big-boned frame would take a heavy overlay of fat before it really began to show. If his looks were starting to go, his voice had lost nothing. He was a baritone and had he not gone into law, he could have gone into opera. He had even taken singing lessons while at law school. But he wasn't interested in singing, he was interested in breath control and voice control. He wanted to sway juries by tone and inflection, by resonance and power, not merely with words. His voice was a weapon and he had developed it as such. Now the desired effect came forth as easily as the desired word.

Cleveland Parrish tossed a dime into the pot from the loose coins in front of him and turned. "Still raining out?" he asked Melody. Cleve Parrish's poker technique was guilelessness, a lack of tension, an apparent lack of concern. He didn't affect the unchanging expression that betrayed no clue. His manner was relaxed, conversational, smiling and friendly. In five-card draw, which was his game, and which the men were now playing, he would look at his cards once, arrange his hand like an amateur bridge player sorting by suits, fold it together and place it face down. When he asked for cards, he would peel the proper number of discards from the top of his pack, look at the new cards and lay them in their stead. He never worried the cards, he never mulled over them, he never took peeks. All he ever touched were his chips or his coins. Those he did fondle, all the while talking of other things, looking around the room, seeming genuinely to treat poker as only a game. And when he made his move, be it call, raise, check, or fold, it was done the moment his turn came up, always with the same tempo, the same motions, the same casual-sounding voice inflection.

"It's raining," she said dully and detoured around the group. The ceiling light was on and gave the room a barren glare. There was the sour smell of cigar smoke overlaying the haze of the cigarettes and a charred brown stub lay in a tin tray beside the sheriff. He was an obese man with a large fold of stomach hanging over his belt, a tall, heavy-featured man, who eyed her above the top of his cards and carefully laid them down at her approach. "And up a nickel," he said throatily, watching her as he pushed the coins forward.

Melody noticed that the other two also concealed their hands when she went by and she wondered. Did they really think she was Cleve's confederate, preparing to signal what they had? They hated Cleve's guts; that was obvious. Just as much as the people outside. But he'd conned them into playing poker to pass the time. Maybe they thought they could take a little something out of his hide for getting the black kid off. But judging from the distribution of coins around the table, they were losing there too.

She went to the window and peeked through the blind again. She didn't know really why she had come in. It was a man's room, a smelly kind of tobacco and spittoon room, cold and bare of the qualities of man that made him attractive to women. This room only held the unattractive qualities of manness; their clannishness, their smelliness, their oafishness, sweatiness, messiness. It was a Keep Out room, a Men Only room, and should a woman open the door, it was only the premises she entered. It wasn't their minds. In their minds she didn't exist. Even in Cleve's mind she didn't exist and she felt lonelier there than in her own room.

She wanted to tell Cleve about the dozen people standing in the rain, not because he cared, but because she wanted to slip inside someone's ken for a bit, in out of the cold. But she didn't. If Cleve wanted the information, he'd ask her. Meanwhile, his mind was on other things and she had been his faithful secretary long enough to know her duties. You waited to be asked; you waited to be told. Even when they bedded down together, it was more on orders than invitation. She was a capable, affirmative girl, once thought to have a mind of her own, but for six years now she had done little more than say, "Yes, sir," to Cleveland Parrish. Nor did it end with business hours. Since he was keeping her, she had developed into a yes-girl nearly full time.

But he had been good to her. He was kind, he was even-tempered, he did not browbeat her. He expected his way in all things and it was true that those who worked for him jumped when he said jump, but she couldn't fault him for that. And if he didn't propose marriage, she couldn't fault him for that either. He cared for her; more than for any other woman, and she was realist enough not to expect more than that from any man.

And she cared for him too, even if she didn't swoon. He was an exciting man to be around. Sparks flew. And he was good in bed too, a fact which surprised her. His demanding, self-seeking nature was bent on his own gratification, yet he did, unaccountably, excite her. He aroused her without trying and she wasn't sure whether it was an unconscious talent he had, whether it was the sheer animal magnetism of his super-maleism, or, possibly, it was her own response to his response. Only in bed could she know she affected him. It was the only evidence she had that anybody affected him, that he wasn't total and utter master of himself and all his surroundings.

There was a debit side, however. No words of fondness, let alone of passion, passed between them in these interludes. Though she gained her own satisfactions from them, she couldn't hide from the fact that this was not much different than any other task she undertook to fulfill his needs. It was for him. Very little of it could be called "for them."

But he was what she had and if his monopoly of her life kept her from other males, kept her from the possibilities of marriage, she was a willing participant. There were no strings tying her.

Melody, however, was sufficiently chary not to want to abandon the sure thing for the will-o'-the-wisp, and she was cynic enough to realize how slight the chances of marriage were. In her three career years before she went with Parrish she had discovered how scarce marriageable men were and how eager the rest were bent on everything except marriage.

If this, therefore, was not the best of all possible worlds, Melody found it a sufficiently satisfactory one. There were only those pangs of aloneness to cope with and she could bear them if she had to. So long as their coming was seldom and their duration brief.

She turned around. The plainclothesman had anted his fifteen cents and the private detective was tossing in his hand and getting out. Parrish added fifteen cents and said, "Five and ten to raise. You know, Sheriff, if this rain keeps up we can go the night. You got a wife holding supper for you?"

24

The sheriff appeared not to hear. He plucked his lip and gazed at the small collection of coins in the center of the table. He picked up his hand and held it close, fanning the cards just enough to read the markings. He looked at Parrish, but the lawyer was turning to the private detective and saying, "How about you, Bill? You got a wife?"

Bill said, "Yes, sir."

"Well, I'm sorry to have to keep you like this. But it's better here than at the airport."

The sheriff finally said, "I'm going to call," and pushed a dime into the pot.

Bill threw in his hand and the sheriff looked at Parrish. The lawyer turned over his cards. "Jacks over twos."

The sheriff grinned and laid down three sixes. "Well, I guess I got a little back," he said and drew in the coins.

Parrish agreed. "Yeah. That was pretty good." He took a cigarette from a pack in his shirt pocket and Melody came over to light it. The act reminded him of her presence and he said, "Anybody want some coffee or sandwiches? My secretary can go to that place across the street."

Nobody did. The cards were shuffled, coins were anted, Parrish cut and the sheriff dealt. Melody, for lack of anything else to do, decided to take a shower.

CHAPTER 6

The phone rang as she started for the door and she picked it up. It was Pete Tucker, Parrish's personal pilot, chauffeur and handyman, calling from the airport. "Melody," he said, his voice cool, "it's clear in New York. You can tell the old man he can leave any time."

She accepted the message with equal coolness. Pete didn't like her and she didn't like him. She muffled the phone against her hip and relayed the news.

Parrish, his cards stacked in front of him, looked around and said that was excellent. "Last hand, gentlemen. It looks as if the Great Rainmaker is going to let me out of here after all. No tears, I'm sure you'll make do."

Melody told Pete they'd be right out and put down the phone. There was a breeziness about Pete that she didn't like. It was his calling Parrish "the old man"; it was his calling her "Melody." He was an able pilot but he was an ordinary garage mechanic type with an impossible wife and three monstrous children; whereas she was Cleveland Parrish's right arm. She felt she deserved respect according to her station. Were she Mrs. Parrish in name as well as being, he'd address her that way! But because her title was only "secretary" he couldn't seem to recognize any distinction between her role and his. She knew she could be accused of snobbery for letting it rankle her but a single girl, alone in the world, had to fight for her place in the sun and guard it jealously.

She brought in her suitcase from the other room as the last hand ended. The private detective named Bill collected a preciously small kitty and Parrish tucked the cards back into their little box for Melody to keep. His suitcase was ready in the closet and Parrish had the private detective fetch it. He himself shrugged into a raincoat and straightened it over his bulky form. Melody said, "There're still a dozen people hanging around outside."

"Jerks," Parrish answered.

The sheriff parted the blinds and said sourly, "They won't be no trouble." Now that the game was over he was aware of his duty once more and the onerous charge of protecting the hide of a man who, in his eyes, made a mockery of Tennessee justice and spit in the face of every Tennessee law enforcement officer. That black son of a bitch had sure as hell cold-bloodedly killed that cop and Parrish had roared into town on his figurative black charger and spirited the cop-killer away.

The plainclothesman took his own look out the window. He was taciturn and it was hard to tell whether he hoped there'd be trouble or not.

The sheriff went out first and the policeman left the patrol car to meet him. The small group of people, clustered seventy feet away, shifted position uneasily.

The plainclothesman went next, crossing to an unmarked police car three doors back. Someone in the huddled group called, "Traitor!"

The car edged forward and the sheriff, standing with the patrolman, snarled in reply, "Go on home."

The detective opened the car door when it stopped. Melody slipped into the back seat, followed by the lawyer. Parrish, settling beside her, looked at the rain. "Maybe we can get into New York, but did Pete make sure we can get out of here?"

The hired guard climbed in next to Parrish and the sheriff got in front. The patrolman returned to his car and swung around to lead the way. The angry men edged closer and their voices grew louder, cursing Cleveland Parrish and the protective police. A rock thudded against the hood of the car.

The squad car sounded a siren and circled back. The group was moving in now and Melody could see the flash of brandished clubs. Another rock struck the window beside the sheriff, flaring it with cracks.

"Get down," Cleve told Melody and pushed her to the floor of the car. Bill, the hired detective, had his gun out. "You'd better get down too, sir," he said, depressing the door lock and keeping himself between the lawyer and the window.

"You aren't kidding." Parrish bent over Melody.

The attackers tried to get close, shouting epithets, hurling chunks of asphalt. The squad car, siren screaming, headed into their midst, scattering them. It screeched into a semicircle and went out the drive. The plainclothesman behind the wheel of the other car, didn't let the men regroup. He stepped on the gas, cutting a tight circle inside. The demonstrators couldn't close in. One struck the car with his club, the others could only reach it with rocks and shouts. One chunk of stone crashed against the door and another cracked the rear window.

Then the car broke onto the highway behind the police car, its own siren keening through the black, sticky night.

They rocketed past other vehicles, the two cars in procession, and Parrish sat back on the seat, helping Melody up. He took a cigarette from a gold case and said to no one in particular, "Nice town. Nice people."

Bill gave him a light and there was silence for a moment. The sheriff, looking out the window at the cars they passed, finally answered, "They got a grudge, mister."

Parrish laughed with an edge of bitterness. "So why don't they take it out on the jury? The jury set Turner free."

The sheriff didn't reply. Parrish put his hand on Melody's knee and took deep drags on his cigarette. Melody tensed inwardly. Bill, the detective, was noticing and she knew what he could read from it. It wasn't that she was ashamed of being Cleve's mistress. It was his methods. She knew it wasn't affection that made him place his hand there. It was ownership. It made her a thing, a nobody. She was only a chattel. She turned and stared out the window as a rush of tears filled her eyes.

The airport was five miles out of town, a small field with two paved runways crisscrossing into the prevailing winds. There was a corrugated metal hangar with a wooden control tower beside it and a concrete apron all around.

It was still raining and no one was in sight. The silver twin-engined Beechcraft stood outside the hangar bathed in yellow light from floodlamps surrounding the apron. At least there was no welcoming committee of hate-filled citizens on hand, waiting to throw more rocks and shout more names.

The ride out had been a quiet one. It was a carful of five dissimilar people. The sheriff and the plainclothesman had a certain rapport, and certainly there was understanding between Parrish and Melody, but there was nothing to talk about between the two groups, nor to the

28

hired bodyguard who was in the lawyer's employ. The sheriff's contempt for the lawyer was ill concealed and, while Parrish did not show it, he had no more use for the sheriff. By the lawyer's standards, the sheriff was an uninteresting clod who could only gain fascination should he be accused of a major crime and have the wherewithal to hire Parrish for his defense.

Now the lead police car drove through the hangar doorway to the dry interior and Parrish's car followed. When they got out, Parrish did not remark on the absence of angry townspeople. The trial that saw the Turner youth freed was now history and forgotten. Parrish had no further interest in Tennessee and his only concern was how fast he and Melody could get back to New York.

Pete Tucker, Parrish's pilot, was in a small coffee shop in a corner of the hangar, where a wan girl read a newspaper behind the counter. When the newcomers crowded in, Pete turned from a plate of spaghetti and said, "Well, here comes the army."

The remark was ignored. The sheriff, in the lead, looked around, took a seat and beckoned the girl peremptorily. "Coffee and doughnuts," he told her and turned to the lawyer. "Well, Counselor, you reckon you'll be safe here, or do you want us to put you on the plane?"

But Parrish had passed by and was talking to the pilot. "When can we go, Pete?"

"Whenever you like, Mr. Parrish. As long as the windshield wipers work I can take her out of here."

"But you can't even see out there. Don't they have any runway lights?"

"Yeah. They'll turn them on when we want to go."

"There's nobody in the tower."

"Yeah, I know. The airport's closed. But the tower operator's here. I told him you'd be wanting to take off as soon as we got an all clear from New York."

"We can get into New York?"

"Any time."

"All right. We might as well start."

"Aren't you going to want something to eat first? It'll take three hours."

"New York might get socked in again."

Tucker shook his head. "It's clearing."

Parrish was persuaded. He took the counter stool beside the pilot. "Melody, better get yourself something. You too, Bill."

The sheriff and the plainclothesman were already having coffee and the girl jotted down the other orders. Melody took a seat dutifully beside Parrish, away from Tucker. She settled for a bowl of soup.

"Hey, Counselor," the sheriff called down the row. "Do you think it's safe to leave you here, or do you want us to tuck you nice and snug aboard the plane?"

Parrish said coldly, "That's your job, isn't it?" He picked up the paper the countergirl had been reading and, turning away from the sheriff, skimmed the front page. The paper was that morning's, dated Monday, November 2, and near the bottom was a one-column headline: "SOCIETY MATRON SLAIN IN CONN."

That was the kind of story his antennae homed in on and he read it rapidly:

MADISON, Conn., Nov. 1—Mrs. Sally Demarest Whittaker, of the Philadelphia Demarests, was brutally slain in her home early this morning following a Hallowe'en party. Her body was found by her husband, Gerald Whittaker, popular Madison doctor, who was awakened by her cries and surprised a mysterious intruder fleeing the scene. According to his lawyer, Edward Balin, who Whittaker called to the scene, the doctor was unable to identify the stranger or give any reason for the attack.

Police have ruled out burglary as a motive but refuse further comment, although they admit they are following a number of leads.

Mrs. Whittaker was the daughter of Mr. and Mrs. Howard Demarest of Villanova, Pa.; granddaughter of the late Senator Edward Demarest, grandniece and great grandniece of two of Pennsylvania's governors, the descendant of numerous of that state's public figures. She was a graduate of Barnard College in New York.

Dr. Whittaker, an internist, graduated from Yale University and Columbia Medical School. They have no children.

Parrish tore the item from the paper and handed it to Melody. "Keep track of this case," he said. "I want everything written about it."

She skimmed the item. "You want everything? You mean I should get the Madison newspapers?"

"I'm talking about New York. New York papers. Keep a file on what the New York papers do with it. I want to see the coverage it gets."

"You think it's going to be a lot?"

"A society matron with a Philadelphia Main Line background? I think it's going to be big."

Melody glanced at the item again and tucked it in her purse. "Madison, Connecticut? I never heard of it."

"Probably nobody has. But you notice it made the Tennessee newspapers."

CHAPTER 7

The rain had stopped when Cleveland Parrish and his party left the coffee shop and looked out the big hangar doors. The sky was black, the air was moist and had a clean, washed smell.

Parrish, flanked by his pilot and his secretary, stood and eyed the wet, shiny plane. Bill, the detective, hung back to one side. The sheriff, the plainclothesman and the patrolman clustered in another group, waiting out their job.

"Is she gassed?" Parrish asked the pilot.

"Gassed and ready, boss."

"You're sure it's still clear in New York?"

"Clear and getting clearer."

There was a light in the nearby tower and the runway lights came on. Parrish said, "All right then, let's go."

Tucker started for the plane and the lawyer paid off Bill, taking thirty dollars out of a large billfold. He shook hands and told the detective he'd done a fine job. "I've got your card," he said. "I'll be glad to recommend you to my friends."

Bill was appreciative. He bordered on the obsequious. Parrish had that way with him. He was the dispenser, not the receiver. He helped, yet needed no help in return.

Turning from the detective, he went to the policemen, chuckling jovially, and shook hands all around. "Well, I guess you're glad to see me go. I expect I've stuck you with a warmed-over supper. Too bad we couldn't have continued that poker game, though. We could have put in a night."

The three policemen accepted the handshakes but did not respond to the affected camaraderie. A man they believed had slain a cop had gone free because of Parrish and they couldn't take it in the same "that's the way the ball bounces" manner as the attorney. That court case—that was no motel poker game.

The sheriff muttered a good-by. His glance took in Melody and she could feel the chill. He might not quite pray to God that the plane would crash, but if it happened, he might permit himself a small smile.

Parrish was seemingly unaware of the cold politeness surrounding the men, but Cleveland Parrish was an able actor and no one knew, whether he roared with laughter or foamed with rage, what he was really feeling and what he was really thinking. He took Melody by the arm and strode across the apron toward the door of the plane that Pete Tucker held open. They boarded and Pete pulled in the steps, locked them in, and went forward to the pilot's compartment.

The interior of the craft had been specially designed for Parrish. There was a small galley at the rear, a daybed on the left of the aisle, with a table and chair against the pilot's partition. On the right there were four swivel chairs with folding tables between.

Parrish and Melody took seats near the door and the big man stretched his legs. He peered out the window at the hangar and the departing policemen and said, "I'm glad to get the hell out of this frigging town."

Melody glanced out and swung the seat away. "I expect the feeling is mutual. In fact, they wish you'd never come."

Parrish laughed. "What the hell difference does the verdict make? They'll never see Turner again. He's probably over the border by now."

"He really killed that cop, didn't he?"

Parrish spread his hands grandly. "How the hell should I know? He claimed he didn't, and the jury agreed with him."

"There was a lot of evidence against him."

"Circumstantial. Purely circumstantial."

"But a lot of it all the same."

"That's right," Parrish grinned. "That's what makes it interesting. That's the kind of case I really like to get my teeth into—one of those lost cause things. That's where the challenges lie. A case like that would be almost worth taking for nothing, just because of the challenge."

"And the publicity."

"Oh, hell, there wasn't all that much publicity about it."

"Only across the country."

"Sure, but little items. I like the real *cause célèbre*. Suppose Turner had been accused of murdering that society matron in Madison, Connecticut, instead of a red-necked cop in a backwater town in Tennessee! Can you imagine the coverage that trial would get?"

The prop on the left-hand motor twisted and whined and exploded into sound and vibration. Parrish waved at the open door to the pilot's compartment and Melody went to shut it. The sound diminished markedly. The cabin had been heavily padded and soundproofed and, with all the doors closed, one could speak in almost conversational tones.

The second motor started and, after a minute of warm-up and engine testing, the plane began to taxi. Parrish and Melody fastened their seat belts and faced forward for the takeoff. They stayed that way after the plane left the ground and while it climbed to altitude even though Tucker switched off the "Fasten Seat Belts" and "No Smoking" signs. Parrish never completely trusted planes, much as he enjoyed the time they saved. Though he could pretty well relax flying straight and level, when it came to climbs and turns, he wanted to be seated face forward with the security of a taut belt across his lap. Despite the thousands of miles he had logged, Cleveland Parrish could never shake the idea that man had no business in the air and that planes had a natural inclination to dive into the ground, which inclination could be overcome only by the sheer domination and total attention of the pilot.

So he faced straight forward, concentrating on the shape of Melody's head, her neck and the arrangement of her hair. Only occasionally did he peer out the window at the blackness that enveloped them. Rain streaked the panes and the little plane bounced through squalls of rough air.

Finally, however, Parrish could sense them leveling off. It would be a three-hour trip and they'd set down at Teterboro between ten-thirty and eleven. That was enough for him to know. He wasn't concerned with their altitude or ground speed or the terrain they were passing over. That was for the pilot to ponder. Just so long as he could be assured the weather was safe.

He pushed aside the belt, swung his seat out and put one foot on the daybed. A magazine rack was beside him on the inside of the door. He pulled out the three magazines that were there and thumbed through them. They contained nothing of interest and he stuck them back. He shifted restlessly. The trial was over, the pressure was off. For once he had no work to do on a flight, nothing to occupy his mind and make him forget he wasn't on the ground. He looked at Melody as she turned in her seat. She smiled and said, "You want some coffee?"

"No."

He continued to look at her, the well-boned face, the neat, attended hair, her form, not buxom but lithe, the very good legs. She felt the power of his gaze and turned again. "How about something to eat?"

He shook his head. "Didn't you get enough back at the airport?"

"Oh, I did. I thought you might be hungry."

He beckoned. "C'mere."

"What?" She got up, puzzled.

He pulled her down onto his lap. One big hand enveloped her breast.

"Cleve! What are you doing?"

He grinned at her. "What the hell do you think I'm doing?" He squeezed her and slid his hand to the blouse buttons at her throat.

"Cleve! For God's sake. Not here!"

"What's the matter? Haven't you ever been laid in an airplane before?"

"No. And I don't want to start now!"

He pulled her closer. "We've got three hours, kid. What the hell better way is there to spend our time?"

He was holding her roughly, fumbling with her buttons. She said desperately, "But Pete might come back."

"He's flying the goddam plane. He can't leave the controls."

"It's got automatic pilot. He might open the door for God's sake!"

Parrish's voice was husky now, his actions fevered. "So what if he does? You think he's never seen a cunt before?"

Melody blinked away tears and silently whispered, "Oh, please, dear God."

34

Parrish had her blouse open. His moist lips were on her throat, his hand pushing inside her bra, feeling for and finding a nipple. "I'll make you like it," he whispered. "Don't I always?"

"But Pete's there. Please, Cleve. I'm too nervous."

"Relax, baby. Pete minds his own business. He knows his place and he stays in it."

She was going to have to go through with it. But if Pete, who held her in such contempt, should open that door— She wanted anything but that. Perhaps if it were dark he wouldn't be able to see what was going on. "Can we have the lights off?" she pleaded.

"What for?" Parrish growled. "I want to see what I'm doing."

"Just to help me relax. Please, Cleve."

"I'll relax you."

"Please. I'm so nervous about Pete I won't be any good for you. Please make it dark."

Parrish let her off his lap and went forward, grumbling. She thought he was going to the light switches and waited, cringing beside the daybed, for darkness.

Instead, he opened the pilot's door and leaned inside for a moment. He closed it and turned around. "You can forget about Pete," he announced. "I told him not to open the door until I tell him to." He gestured impatiently. "Hurry up. Get your clothes off. I want you."

CHAPTER 8

The funeral was Tuesday afternoon at two o'clock in the DeWitt parlors in Madison. The home was a converted Victorian mansion full of small downstairs rooms, which were convenient in that the casket could be in one, the family in another, and friends in the other two. The difficulty was the size of the rooms, for the largest could seat no more than forty and what could one do with the three hundred people who filed in for the Sally Whittaker service?

When the first arrivals mounted the steps at an unheard-of quarter past one, and the first room began to fill, Mr. Paradise vetoed his assistant's suggestion that chairs be put in the casket room. That was where the mourners would be received and where, when Mr. Paradise was an apprentice, an elderly lady had fallen over a chair and broken her hip. Mr. Paradise would have no clutter around the bier.

But all these people!

Mr. Paradise made a bold decision. All the chairs would be removed and everyone would stand.

So it was that, when the service started, the only seated people were the members of the family in the small side room looking in at the casket. In the other two rooms, stifling and sardined, were the nearly three hundred mourners who had come to pay their final respects to the murder victim.

The service was conducted by Dr. Jonas Fothergill, an elderly Episcopal priest who, since Sally and Jerry hadn't set foot inside a church since their wedding, had been imported from Pennsylvania by her parents. Dr. Fothergill had baptized Sally and it was under his auspices that she had received whatever of religious education she had had. (The education consisted of Sunday School through sixth grade and enforced church attendance till college.)

36

Fothergill didn't really know much about Sally Demarest (Whittaker, that is). She had been young, blonde, and saucy. Maybe irreverent was a better term. She would attend church with her parents and elder sister, and she would sit there very dutifully, because she was being made to go, but she didn't like it. Not for a minute. And he could stand in the pulpit and know it.

Charlotte would sit attentively, would say the prayers, sing the hymns and kneel on the cushions with all the sobriety of her parents. Charlotte was a real believer. Not Sally. She was three beats slower than the rest of the congregation getting down on her knees and she had a distracting way during the prayers of looking around with cool detachment at all the bowed heads. And she had a habit of deciding to read her program calendar just as he was reaching the climax of his sermon. It wasn't a studied insult, he was sure. It was that her interest operated in inverse proportion to his enthusiasm.

She wouldn't call him Father. The rest of the family did, even Mr. Demarest. So did the whole congregation, excepting the lay leaders, who called him Jonas. But Sally called him Mister Fothergill. She wouldn't even call him Doctor. He asked her about that once, why she was reluctant to address him as Father. Her reply was she felt it would be hypocritical (rather a misuse of the term, he thought) because he wasn't her father. When he explained he represented her spiritual father, she answered very seriously, "I don't think the Pope in Rome would agree with you."

He pursued her no further after that, believing that Time would bring her into the fold. But Time had run out and she had never returned. He was supposed to speak of her knowingly and affectionately. But he didn't know her and he couldn't summon up any more affection for her than for a Hottentot princess. She was as strange to him as that. However, he had been a minister for so many years that talking came easily. One only need think of God and let the Master take over.

Jerry Whittaker, listening to the words, tried to put some meaning into them, tried to evoke some expected emotion. He and she were supposed to be a beautiful couple, popular and well suited, one of the happily married pairs. Shouldn't there be some tears from the bereft husband?

He glanced sideways at Sally's parents, seated on his left. Their eyes were dry too, focused unblinkingly on Dr. Fothergill, standing

37

beside the end of the coffin, facing the doorway to the side family room. They had not only come into town, they had taken over the funeral arrangements. It was they who had ordered the mahogany casket and summoned the family priest. Through it all, they had hardly addressed him, the bereaved spouse. It was as if they, alone, had suffered loss.

All except for Sally's sister, Charlotte. She was seated behind, sniffling quietly into a handkerchief while her husband patted her arm. Jerry's own sister was back there too, but not his brother.

He would have liked his mother present, but she was too ill. His father was there, though, Charles Zacharias Whittaker, the stalwart one. His hand was on Jerry's arm, while Fothergill talked of Sally's charity and kindliness, trying to communicate strength and human fellowship. Jerry respected his father and his rigid, God-fearing ways, but human fellowship was one emotion that didn't come through.

Zacharias Whittaker squeezed his son's arm as the service came to an end. He was feeling anything but stalwart. Those elegant Demarests on Jerry's other side with their stiff, haughty ways. This was the second time in his life he had met them, the first being at the wedding. The wedding had been as frighteningly elegant as the service now. The coffin was the most beautiful Zacharias had ever seen. And the flowers! There were banks upon banks. Was that their doing, or were they tokens of love from the many friends of Sally and Jerry?

The service was over. Everyone in the family room was rising now. Zack had to go in and stand beside Jerry and shake the hands of the mourners. He wished his wife, Janet, could have been there. He wouldn't feel so alone, so conscious of his poor quality clothes. What was a druggist with a run-down store doing with these well-to-do people?

He looked around for his daughter as he followed Jerry through the doorway. Arnold, his other son, with a drugstore in West Haven, hadn't come. Maybe he was busy. Maybe he couldn't get away.

His daughter came to him as they lined up by the bier and that was better. Son on one side, daughter on the other. Now he could face the crowd that was starting to queue and move through the family room. Zacharias had never seen so many people at a funeral before. It would be a long, unnerving process. He hoped Jerry could stand it. He turned and whispered, "Trust in God," and Jerry, tight-lipped, nodded.

It was well after three when Mr. Paradise closed the door on the last of the visitors and his assistants lifted the heavy casket off its supports and put it and some of its flowers into the hearse for the drive to Pennsylvania. Sally Whittaker would be buried in the family plot.

Her husband, her parents, and Dr. Fothergill rode behind in a black limousine for graveside services the next morning. Her husband's father went back to the drugstore.

CHAPTER 9

Walter Costaine lifted the bottle of rye off the bed table and checked the contents. They'd done quite a job on it last night, Jackie mostly. She was in the shower now and the noise of cascading water sounded in the room with him. The walls of the crumby motel were like cheesecloth.

He poured an inch of the remaining rye into a water glass and sipped. Pretty early in the morning for something like that, but he felt the need.

A day-old newspaper was on the other bed, the one that was made, and he reached across from where he sat to pick it up. Sally Whittaker's picture was on the front page and he studied it once again. It was the portrait photo she had posed for six months ago, a beautiful thing. He had gone over the proofs with her and both had opted for that one. He'd wanted a copy for himself but she only laughed. No way. Well, he had it now.

The shower stopped and Walter tucked the paper under the bed between his legs. He lay back on the wrinkled sheets, adjusted a pillow under his head, and sipped more of the raw, burning rye. He needed time to think.

Jackie came into the room toweling herself, letting him watch her. She went to the small mirror over the bureau and looked at her teeth. "I don't know why I don't have them all pulled. You think I ought to, Walter?"

If she thought he was going to pay for dental surgery, she was out of her tree. "Keep them as long as you can," he advised. "Nothing's as good as your own teeth."

"Yeah, but look how rotten they are. My dentist—"

He looked at his watch. "I don't want to rush you, Jackie, but what time do you have to be at work?"

She turned around and posed without the towel. "I could take the morning off. I don't really feel like selling dry goods today. You got some rye left and we could ball it for a while."

The idea should have appealed to him more than it did. Jackie was young and her flesh had good tone even if she was potbellied and saggy. He should be getting the hots for her. But there was that disturbing newspaper under the bed and he wasn't sure yet what he ought to do about it.

"You're sweet." He got off the bed and kissed her. She melted in his arms and he slid his hands over her back. "But why don't we save it for tonight?" he went on, putting his forehead against hers and smiling. "I'll meet you at your place at half past five and we'll have a bite of supper—?"

He'd never taken her out two days running and she recognized the significance of the suggestion. Maybe she was making more headway than she'd believed. She giggled. "Sure, honey. That'd be great." She let him go and started for her clothes. Maybe there was more to the relationship than a possible denture bill. In any case, it would be best not to talk about her teeth for a while.

They left the room together. It was number one in a bank of six, adjacent to the office where the neon sign said, East River Motel. Costaine had been occupying it, when he was in town, since early summer.

His car was a late model Comet angled in front and he drove past the office through the entry gate and turned east on Route 1 for Madison and the shop where Jackie worked. She left him with a warm, clinging kiss and a happy wave of the hand. Her future was looking up.

He watched the swing of her hips as she went through the front door of the store but his thoughts were of Sally Whittaker. Well, what the hell was he going to do now, go back to the motel and get sloppy on rye, or was he going to make a hard and fast decision for once? If he was going to do it at all, he'd better do it now. The longer he waited the funnier it'd seem. And he couldn't go back and drink a lot of rye first. They'd smell it on his breath.

He swung the car around and headed back from the center of town to the patch of village green, the yellow, monstrously shaped town hall, and the small police department building adjacent. He parked in one of the slots opposite the town hall entrance and sat through two cigarettes. He wished he had the rye bottle with him but he was glad he didn't. He'd kill it for sure.

At last he had enough of what it took to open the door and step out into the cold November air. He buttoned the top button of his coat, pulled his felt hat tighter and cocked the brim. He told himself he was a member of the country club set and he had nothing to fear from the police. They would be deferential. He was the one in command, not they.

He went up the steps of the small building marked Police, and opened the door. The anteroom was cramped, with a tiny counter ahead. The officer behind the counter was the only person in sight, and he looked up with a quiet face. The police weren't ogres after all.

"Could I see the chief? I mean, is the chief here?"

The officer smiled at Costaine appraisingly. "Something I can do for you?"

"No, it's the chief." Costaine didn't mean to be so nervous. "I think I ought to see the chief."

There was no problem. The officer asked Costaine's name and left the cubicle behind the counter. The chief came back with him, a mild, gray-headed man with an uninquisitive air.

"Yes, Mr. Costaine?" he said. "May I help you?"

Costaine blurted it out. "The Sally Whittaker case—you know— the murder? Last Saturday night? She was supposed to come to my motel room after the party. Only she never showed up!"

CHAPTER 10

The story broke with giant headlines on Thursday and Melody hurried into Cleve's inner sanctum with the papers that morning. "Cleve," she said with a certain awe, "you hit it. You said it would be big! Look!"

Cleve took the news calmly. "Of course. It figures."

"But this Walter Costaine! He's been having an affair with Sally Whittaker for six months. Six months! And his wife threw him out of the house because of it? And Dr. Whittaker—he knew it was going on? You didn't expect that, did you?"

Parrish was blasé. "I knew it would be something like that."

"'In a prepared statement,'" she said, quoting one of the stories, "'Costaine said that, upon his return from a six weeks' business trip to Italy, he attended the now notorious costume dance at the Summer Club dressed, "perhaps appropriately," as Satan. He danced with Sally Whittaker and, before her husband broke in angrily, he made a date to meet Sally at his motel room as soon after the dance as she could get away.

"'Her failure to appear didn't surprise him, he said, until he learned the reason was murder. Thereafter, he spent two tormented days wrestling with his conscience, trying to determine whether he should withhold this vital piece of information, or sacrifice Sally's reputation.'"

Cleve laughed at that. "I'll bet it broke his heart."

"But this means the doctor did it, doesn't it?"

"Never leap to conclusions, pet. Don't forget the 'mysterious stranger.'"

Melody scoffed and Parrish laughed again. The news was making

42

him happy. She said, "You still want me to keep a file?" and he nodded.

"You act as if you saw the whole thing coming. You didn't and you know it."

Daniel F. Price, a lanky young man with red curly hair and a crooked grin came in without knocking. He was a private detective with the Webster-Smith Detective Agency, which Cleve customarily employed for his research, and Dan was the man he worked with most.

Price, who was almost tall enough to duck through the door, came in, patting Melody on the fanny. He was one year younger but he affected the Big Brother approach. Had he his own way, things would not have been so platonic for she was the kind of female he could work up a full head of steam over. But, though he couldn't prove it, he suspected she was Cleve's girl and that made her hands-off. No sane man poached on Cleve's preserve.

He put a folder on Cleve's desk and slid into one of the handsome leather client chairs, stretching out his long thin legs. He wore narrow, highly polished loafers, argyle socks (knitted for him by a girl he had no intention of marrying) gray pants, plain tie and plaid jacket. The pistol on his hip hardly showed and if it weren't for that, no one would have believed him a private detective. His clothes and his infectious grin gave him the look of a Columbia grad student who wasn't trying very hard.

Parrish showed Melody the name on the folder and she did a double take. "Edward Balin?" she said. "You mean the lawyer Doctor Whittaker called when he found his wife was dead?"

"The same. Stick around. You might find this interesting." Cleve opened the folder while Melody sank into another chair and he proceeded to read through a comprehensive report on the New Haven lawyer that went into far greater detail than anything he could have learned from *Martindale-Hubbell*, the national directory of lawyers. On a separate sheet was a history of Petrie, Balin, Dormer, French and Farrell, the corporation law firm for which he worked. A final page listed a number of important cases the firm had handled, all of the information meticulously typed by a girl in the Webster-Smith office who, unlike the elegant Miss Stevens, was a secretary Dan Price *did* make out with.

Cleveland Parrish read through the report carefully, passing the

43

sheets to Melody as he finished. He looked up and Price said, "Satisfactory?"

The lawyer creased the folder at the last page. "This list of important cases handled by the firm. I want to know which ones Balin was responsible for."

"All of them."

"These were his cases? Does he handle all the important work?"

"Hell no. Not even most." Price waved at the page. "That list is only his cases, not the firm's cases. I thought you just wanted to know about *him*. If you want a complete list—"

"No, this is what I want. Any of these cases landmark cases?"

Price shook his head. "He's one of those solid, reliable, stodgy, capable lawyers. He's not going to break new ground. He wouldn't know how. He doesn't have the temperament. Safe and sane. That's Balin."

"All right. That's what I need to know."

Price uncoiled himself and rose to his full six feet five. "O.K., Mr. Parrish. Anything else while I'm here?"

There was nothing and he departed without question.

Melody didn't watch him go. She finished the report and stared at Cleve. "I don't get it."

He grinned. "You will. Take a letter."

She swung her steel swivel secretary's chair closer to the desk and opened her double-columned note pad.

Parrish tilted back and half closed his eyes. "To Edward Balin, law firm of Petrie, Balin, Dormer, French and Farrell, Union Trust Company Building, New Haven, Connecticut. Dear Mr. Balin. I have been approached and presently am in negotiation with a large publishing firm which is interested in putting out a comprehensive law textbook for student and layman alike. The book, which is aimed at being the definitive work on law as of the present date, would cover all aspects of the field: criminal law, corporation law, maritime law, etc.

"New paragraph. Naturally, while I would expect to write the chapter on my own specialty, which is criminal law, I could not write about the other fields this book would encompass. My task is therefore that of editor or anthologist. It falls to me to line up top men in the other areas of law and persuade them to contribute to the success of this book.

"New paragraph. I have been much impressed with your work in

44

the field of corporate law as evidenced in particular by blank, blank and blank." Parrish tilted his chair forward and indicated the folder. "Melody, in that report is a list of the most important cases this Edward Balin has had. Look them up and go over them. Pick the three that impress you most and put them in the blanks in order of preference. To go on with the letter: blank, blank and blank. Period. Would you be willing to lend your efforts to this enterprise by writing a chapter on corporation law? Needless to say, you will be paid for this work. There will be a fee of five hundred dollars for the chapter, plus a share of the royalties which we can expect, if the book has the success we anticipate, may well amount to several thousand dollars.

"New paragraph. I know that to a man in your position, the money is of no consequence. I know too that a man with your prestige is not going to have that prestige enhanced by appearing in the book. Rather, the book would be enhanced by your appearance. So my real appeal to you is to ask you to consider what a contribution your work will make to law school students and law laymen everywhere, to whom this book will be their Bible.

"New paragraph. If you would do me the favor of saying you will be willing to write such a chapter, I shall consider myself greatly in your debt. Period. Formal closing. End of letter. Read it back. Let me hear how it sounds."

Melody read it back while he listened with closed eyes, fingertips together, a faint smile on his lips. She finished and he nodded in satisfaction. "Yes, that should do the trick."

"What are you up to? You don't have any arrangement with any publisher."

"Relax. If Balin says yes, there's time enough to have the deal fall through. If he says no, it doesn't matter."

"He won't say no. Not with all the lures you've thrown in. You've got enough bait in there to hook a school of Balins. The question is, what do you want of him?"

Cleveland Parris chuckled. "The best lure is the last one."

"Which?"

"Where I say, 'I shall consider myself greatly in your debt.'"

CHAPTER 11

Melody opened the shower door and listened. Yes, it was the phone. She muttered an oath, shut off the water, and stepped from the tub, pulling off her cap and snatching a towel.

There were twin beds in the next room and she kneeled across the nearer to reach the phone on the table between. The voice on the other end was the operator saying there was a collect call, and she knew what that meant even before she heard, "From Mrs. Sheppard Stevens."

"I'll accept the charges," she said flatly and made herself comfortable. It wasn't that she objected to paying for her mother's calls. The family wasn't that well off. Her father was a truck farmer in Massachusetts and they couldn't even afford a phone when she was growing up. What bugged her was that her mother, frugal as she was with her own funds, felt no compunction to keep her calls short if Melody was paying the bill.

She couldn't be blamed, of course. Melody was the goddess of the Stevens clan, the one who was in New York making all that money and enjoying the exciting existence that went with being secretary to that brilliant Mr. Parrish. Melody had the glamor job. Melody went places and did things. She wasn't like her siblings, all married and settled down, leading drab, ordinary lives fixing cars, struggling to make a go of the sports shop or the antique business, or as a young engineer.

Melody's folks were short on formal education, nor did they miss it. Farming was Shep Stevens' life and a farmer didn't need book learning to make the crops grow. All a farmer needed were strong sons to help him in the fields.

So, of course, his first child was a daughter, which his foolish wife named Melody after a song that had been popular. Shep Stevens believed in good solid respectable names that people could understand, and if it had been a boy, Shep would have done the naming. But girl children were handier in a kitchen than behind a plow and his wife could name her what she chose.

Two boys had followed, Shep Junior and Joe, and they were able to pull their weight for they were big and strapping. Sonny, as young Shep was nicknamed, could do more in the fields and barn at nine than Melody could at eleven. Melody had tried. Shep had seen to that, but she was reed thin, like her ma, and she didn't have the strength.

The boys made up for it, though, and old Shep could even welcome another girl when Lisa was born six years behind Melody. Now the kitchen could stand more help.

At the end, a year later, came Gary, the baby of the family and the pet. He was the brightest of the boys and the one Shep ultimately came to lavish education on. Nor did Gary have to work the farming stint that had been demanded of his brothers. Shep had seen, from the older boys' disinterest, that his farming way of life was not to be a legacy and he was no longer trying to force it.

Sonny went to trade school and was now an automobile mechanic. Joe had a sporting goods store, Lisa married a young man in the antique business, and Gary went to college where he majored in engineering and was regarded as the boy with the bright, promising future.

Melody had gone through college too, but it had been through scholarships, work and self-denial. Shep had given her little more than disapproval. He had the full family to support and he couldn't see how a college degree would enhance a girl's ability to keep house, cook meals and rear children.

As it turned out, Melody hadn't opted for keeping house, cooking meals and rearing children, and Shep grudgingly had to admit that education hadn't hurt her any. But when Gary's turn came due, he didn't have to work his way. Shep had sold off the farm, except for the house and six acres, and had gotten a pretty good price for it. He could put his son through college and have enough left over to retire in modest comfort, him and Ma. In fact, he had enough so that Lottie could have paid for her own New York phone calls— at least if she didn't ramble on so. But she'd struggled too long and the habit was too deeply ingrained. If she paid for the calls, she'd never go over three minutes.

Besides, Melody could afford it. She was rich. Despite Shep's hopes for Gary, Melody was the one who had already achieved success, had already made her mark. She was the one Lottie bragged about, the one even Shep could feel pride over. Yes, sir, right from the start and it was no surprise to the home folks that she was where she was. Why, all through school everybody knew she'd achieve great things, and it was no surprise to the home folks that she was where she was.

Nor could Lottie swallow her pleased smile when neighbors asked what the children were doing. There's Sonny and Joe and Lisa—and Gary with that engineering firm in Mansfield. As for Melody, well, you've heard of Cleveland Parrish, haven't you? You know, that big lawyer who's on television and everything? Well, Melody is his private secretary. I mean she's not just a secretary, doing typing and dictation. I mean she'll hire somebody else for little jobs like that. She's his assistant. That kind of secretary. He takes her with him everywhere he goes. Did you know he has his own plane? Specially designed. And his car is specially designed too!

Lottie's voice came on the wire with its familiar whine. Melody didn't think of it as a whine. It was only her mother's voice. But the whine was there, developing over the grinding years. A lifetime of long hours had ingrained drudgery too deeply, had given her voice the dreary note of resignation that stems from exhaustion.

"Hello, Ma," Melody answered back. If company had been present, she would have said, "Mother," but her natural response was the childhood one. So it was Ma and Pa and usually Sonny, though Shep Junior was thirty years old now and even Ma and Pa had come to call him Shep.

"Hope I didn't interrupt your supper," Lottie said and, with that token amenity out of the way, started explaining how frantic she was to reach her and how she almost called her at the office.

Melody made proper noises and looked at the clock. Cleve would be picking her up at seven-fifteen for dinner with a client and already it was twenty of. If she knew her mother, she'd have to work to get her off the phone by seven.

"You'll never guess the terrible thing that happened," her mother was saying, and something about her voice told Melody this wasn't one of the minor disasters that made delicious gossip, but a matter of some consequence. She went on, "Gary's been fired."

"Gary?" Melody responded in shock and alarm. He had two young children and a third one due. "What happened?"

Lottie didn't know the details. Priscilla had called from Mansfield that morning. Gary had received his pink slip the previous afternoon. Retrenchment was the explanation. Business was off. Several engineers were being let go. And since he was twenty-five and had only been with the firm a little over two years—

It was a blow, Lottie said. Neither she nor Pa could explain it. There were any number of other engineers not nearly as talented whom they could have fired.

Melody agreed and then, to forestall a ten-minute monologue extolling Gary's virtues, asked, "What's Gary going to do?"

Lottie didn't know yet. Nobody did. They were still numb.

"There's unemployment insurance, Ma," Melody volunteered.

Lottie wasn't listening. "He won't be able to meet the payments on the house," she wailed. "And Priscilla's—the baby's due in two months. That's going to cost money. I don't know what we're going to do."

Melody didn't know either. "He can sell the house," she suggested. "He won't have much equity, but he might get something."

"But where will they live?"

"They can move in with you and Pa. There's no reason for him to stay in Mansfield any longer."

"Yes, but the baby and all?"

Melody's voice sharpened. This was no time to throw up roadblocks. "You don't have any choice, Ma. You and Pa can't meet his mortgage payments and nobody knows where Gary's next job will take him."

She stressed again the need to sell, for the sudden fear assailed her that the family might think Big Rich Sister Melody could be tapped for support. She'd help, but not with mortgage payments.

Ma's thoughts weren't about the house, but the impending baby, and it appeared the family would not be looking to her for provender. Melody breathed easier and looked at the clock. It was nearly six-fifty. She got to her feet and toweled herself while she talked. "Engineering jobs are scarce," she was explaining. "It's nothing against Gary. There just isn't enough work to go around."

"I know," her mother agreed. "That's what Pa and me was talking about. There's nothing around here and we were wondering about New York."

49

New York? That was the source of a new fear and Melody stepped on the idea fast. "There's no work for engineers in New York," she said bluntly. "They're all on welfare. Gary should look anywhere but in New York. In fact, he ought to think about finding another kind of job." An idea came to her. "What about Joe? Could he use Gary in the store?"

Joe couldn't, Ma said. The store really wasn't doing very well.

"Well, there are other jobs. It doesn't have to be engineering, Ma. It can be something else."

"That's what we were thinking," her ma answered. "We were thinking Gary should get some other kind of job. It shouldn't be hard with all his ability. And he wouldn't be fussy. He'd take almost anything. We were thinking, Pa and me, that you might find him something down where you are."

So that was the purpose of the phone call! God, her parents were naïve. New York wasn't the kind of place where an older sister could job hunt for her young brother. Especially when she had no idea what his qualifications were. Employers in New York wouldn't be impressed by the fact Gary's mother thought him the key to the universe. "I can't get him a job," she said flatly. "New York people won't buy a pig in a poke. What he's got to do is look around home."

"We were thinking you might know somebody who might need some help. Gary can do anything."

"I don't know anybody. Honest."

"How about your boss? Maybe he could use somebody. How about a chauffeur?"

"He's got a chauffeur, Ma, for Pete's sake."

"But maybe he could let that chauffeur go. Nobody can drive a car better than Gary, and you know it. Besides, he's your brother."

"Now, Ma, listen. Not only does Mr. Parrish already have a chauffeur, that chauffeur is an expert mechanic and an airplane pilot to boot."

"Well, maybe Mr. Parrish—"

They were after her to find him work and the arm twisting would get severe if she didn't stop it fast. "Forget it, Ma," she said firmly. "I can't go to Mr. Parrish and beg him to give Gary a job. That's all there is to it."

There was a momentary side conversation and Melody's father

came on the line. "Melody," he said rebukingly, "is what Ma tells me true? You won't help out your kin?"

She trembled. She was helpless against her father. It was so hard to justify herself to him. "Pa," she said desperately, "I'd do anything for Gary and Priscilla and you know it. All I'm saying is I can't ask Mr. Parrish to give him a job. Mr. Parrish only hires people who are exceptionally qualified in whatever it is he wants them to do. What could Gary do for him except maybe shine his shoes?"

"Gary would be a good valet, Melody."

"Pa, please." Melody half sobbed. "If Mr. Parrish wanted a valet, he'd *have* a valet."

Her father would make her ask, though. She was sure of it. The thought of Gary as Cleve's valet made her shudder.

On top of the rest, it was five minutes of seven.

"Gary's out of a job," her father said sternly. "You live in a city of eight million people. You work for a man who's got a lot of influence. I cannot believe that if you put your mind to it you couldn't find your brother a job."

At least he was off the valet kick. Meanwhile, what could she say if she didn't want to disappoint her father still another time, if she didn't want to keep Cleve waiting, if she wanted to get out from under the squeeze and get a chance to think? "I'll see what I can do, Pa," she promised. "I'll ask around. I'll see what I can do."

"That's what I thought you'd say," answered her father, and Melody, putting down the phone, muttered, "That's what you knew I'd say."

CHAPTER 12

Parrish's letter to Edward Balin arrived in the offices of Petrie, Balin, Dormer, French and Farrell the following Monday and the embossed Cleveland Parrish envelope caused a stir. How the hell did the unknown firm of Petrie, Balin, Dormer, French and Farrell rate recognition from a big wheel like Cleveland Parrish? How come it was addressed to Ed? Maybe somebody outgoing and aggressive like Max Dormer. Max got his name in the papers more than the rest. Max had an eye for publicity. But Ed Balin? He didn't even know what publicity was. He didn't know anything except the case in front of him. Steady Eddie.

Edward Balin unsealed the letter himself. His secretary, Miss Simpkins, usually handled such matters, but a letter from Cleveland Parrish? It must be important and it must be personal. To read a letter from Cleveland Parrish without Mr. Balin's permission would be akin to dipping into his diary.

So Ed Balin, alone in his office, slit the envelope and withdrew the letter, aware that his partners, that the whole office staff, was a hive of curiosity. He read the magic words and he smiled. He beamed. Mr. Parrish wanted him!? Of all the law firms in the country specializing in corporation law—of all the lawyers in the field, some of them famous, much sought after—? And Cleveland Parrish had picked him—Edward Balin! Cleveland Parrish had *found* him. Cleveland Parrish was impressed by his work in *Wells, Inc.* v. *McCormick Tool;* in *Rossamond & Tweed* v. *United States;* and *New Haven Shipping* v. *Allied Lines.* Well, he'd always thought he'd handled those rather well. Thorough preparation was the key, he always said. But he'd never dreamed such cases would come to the notice of someone like Cleveland Parrish. He'd have to revise his estimate of the man. Parrish didn't live in his own private world of criminal law after all—caring nothing for law itself, only using it to make himself rich. Parrish was alert to what else was going on in the field. He was conversant with all the aspects of law. He even knew what the little man was doing. No wonder the publishing house had turned to Cleveland Parrish to edit this law book. It wasn't just the drawing power of his name, it was his immense knowledge of the subject and the men in the field.

And Cleveland Parrish had picked him!

Edward Balin read the letter twice more, savoring the words. He laid it on his blotter and tipped back his chair. The grin on his face wouldn't go away. Max Dormer thought himself such a hotshot? He believed he was the best lawyer in the firm, eh? Balin couldn't wait to see his face. Of course he couldn't flaunt the letter, wave it under everybody's nose. He'd have to let them know what it said but he'd have to be modest about it. "A letter from Cleveland Parrish? Nothing to get excited about. He was just asking me to do him a small favor. He needs someone to help him with a book on law he's writing. After all, I daresay I *do* know more about corporation law than he does." (Pause here for the laugh.) And when they saw the cases that had impressed Parrish!

The thing to do was dictate a reply to Miss Simpkins and give her the letter. Oh, if she wants to let the others see it, it's all right. It's nothing personal, after all.

And the chapter. Let's see, how would he start it? "For all that corporation law sounds unglamorous, especially when contrasted with criminal law—" That's not so good. Too negative. Better would be something to the effect that all the challenge and excitement of criminal law can be found in corporation law. The difference is it's subtler. It is for the connoisseur rather than the man in the street— That would be the kind of approach—unless Parrish would feel he was drawing invidious comparisons.

Well, no point in thinking about that now. The main thing was to call in Miss Simpkins, dictate a reply and give her the letter for the files. He pressed the buzzer and straightened his face. He had to be very businesslike now, affect an, "Oh, dear, I suppose I must," attitude.

Miss Simpkins came in tingling with curiosity. Mr. Balin handed her the letter, then went and looked out the window while she read it. The pesky grin was threatening to break out again.

"Oh, Mr. Balin! Isn't that wonderful!"

"Oh, is it?" he said, half turning. "Well, yes." He resumed his interest in the street below. "I suppose it does speak well for the firm." He had the grin under control now and returned to his seat.

"You're going to do it, aren't you, Mr. Balin?"

"Do it? Oh, the chapter? Hmm, well—"

"To have your name in a book like that? Oh, Mr. Balin, I'd be so proud!"

He couldn't help smiling, but it was permissible now. "Oh, I suppose I have to. I'm busy, of course, but he knows that. Everyone he'd approach would be busy. Of course I'll do it." He laughed lightly. "But it'll mean extra work for you. You'll have to type it."

She didn't mind at all. She'd be honored to death.

He dictated an appropriate reply and she departed with the letter. In a few minutes it'd be all over the office. How jealous his partners would be. Perhaps he merited a higher salary. Not everyone got plaudits from his peers like that. And it would boost the prestige of the firm. His fame would bring in business. Very definitely he was entitled to a larger share in things.

He drew over a foolscap pad and wrote at the top, "Corporation Law," and, underneath, in bold letters, "By Edward H. Balin." He sat back and thought about good opening sentences. Of course the deal wasn't set and he was wise enough to know nothing counts until the ink is dry on the contract. But the book idea was a good one and the choice of Parrish to edit it was superior. If the rest of his choices were as astute as—well, let's be modest. Let's say, if Parrish probed as deeply for good, if little-known, talent in the other fields, it would be a valuable tome. The deal would go through all right. Balin had no doubt about that. So it wouldn't hurt to plan a little what he would say.

Old Brock Petrie, white-haired and senior, came into the office. "What's this, Edward? Somebody wants you to contribute a chapter to a law book they're writing?"

"Yes, that's right." (Somebody? Petrie knew damned well who that somebody was.)

"You're going to do it?"

"Yes. I thought it would help the firm."

"I daresay you'll help the author more than the firm. I hope you make sure you get what's coming to you."

Always the put-down, Balin thought. That was old Petrie. He couldn't stand anyone else having any success. "They won't cheat me, Brock. I'll have *you* go over the contract." (That ought to fix him.)

Max Dormer came in. "Well, we've got a goddam author in our midst. Where did Parrish get your name, out of a hat?"

He's jealous, Balin thought and couldn't quite conceal his smile. Well, let him find out what the back seat was like.

The buzzer on his desk sounded and Balin pressed the button. "Yes?"

Miss Simpkins told him Dr. Whittaker was on the phone.

Balin excused himself and picked up the receiver. Let Max and old Brock stand there with their noses out of joint. "Yes, Jerry?"

"Ed," Whittaker said wildly, "I've been arrested!"

Balin's first thought was, Traffic violation. Then, because Whittaker was a doctor, Malpractice. Except Jerry wasn't the type.

"Arrested? What for?"

"Murder! They're trying to say I killed Sally!"

Balin was stunned. He had somehow forgotten that Sally's death wasn't natural, that it didn't end with her funeral, that Jerry faced more than the normal pangs and problems of readjustment. He hadn't seen Jerry since the funeral. He'd scarcely thought of him. Now he felt shaken and guilty. Here he'd been, preening himself over his own good fortune, and his friend was suffering from bad fortune. First Jerry had lost his wife. Now he was being put in jail.

Balin asked where he was being held and said he'd be right over. He stumbled past the other lawyers into the anteroom for his coat.

CHAPTER 13

Jerry Whittaker's father, Charles Zacharias Whittaker, had never been known by anything but his middle name, not as a child, and certainly not in his gray-haired, arthritic later life. The name Zacharias became his quiet integrity, his puritanical allegiance to the virtues of honesty, hard work and fear of God.

He had been a druggist throughout. Whittaker's Drug Store on Elm Street, a mile from the center of New Haven. It was a small store, dispensing pharmaceuticals and nostrums to a small neighborhood. There had once been a soda fountain but he had removed it upon taking over. While it had brought in business, he felt it induced idleness and self-indulgence in the young.

Had he more business sense, or more interest in selling than in merely providing, he could have developed Whittaker's Drug Store into a bag of gold. But the attitude that had closed the fountain affected the rest of the enterprise. It was Zacharias' view that a shopper entered a store with specific purchases in mind. To encourage him to spend more than he had intended, or buy something not in the shopping plan was, to Zacharias, a near neighbor to robbery. He believed he was enough of a sinner already and did not want knowingly to lengthen the period he would spend in hell.

Zacharias thought deeply about such matters in his little prescription room with the glass window to the store. It was a quiet comforting place for thought. There he could weigh God's purposes as he weighed his ingredients.

Right now, as he prepared Mrs. Chitters' prescription, he was glad his business was slow. It had been hard enough facing customers after Jerry's arrest, but now, two days ago, a grand jury had indicted him for murder and that made it doubly hard. Not that

56

customers asked about him, for they didn't. It was because they avoided his eye, because they were excessively polite, almost apologetic. Business had never been good but it was hurting more since Jerry's arrest. Customers were going elsewhere to supply their needs. That way they wouldn't have to look upon the hurt in the old man's eye or feel they should say something sympathetic. But he didn't mind. He'd rather stay out of sight in the prescription room and let young Leslie Guggins, the attractive black girl who worked for him, handle the customers.

He labeled the prescription and pushed it through the slot in the glass so Leslie could get it when Mrs. Chitters returned. He looked out into the store. One woman was there, that new one in the neighborhood whose name he didn't know, buying some toilet article and quizzing Leslie. She knew he was back there but she wasn't looking. Nor did she talk loud enough for Zacharias to hear. She must be pumping Leslie for gossip. Leslie looked cool and reserved and her replies appeared brief. He hoped Leslie wasn't a talebearer but he realized, though she had worked for him nearly a year, he didn't know much about her. She was honest and neat and careful, and got along with the customers. That was what mattered. But how much did she tell about the Whittaker family, about Janet's increasingly infrequent turns behind the counter and the increasing trips to the living quarters upstairs that he had to make? Had he told her about his daughter, Dorothy, married to a struggling minister in Pennsylvania, living poor as the proverbial church mouse? She knew about Jerry, the doctor, of course. Everybody did, even before the murder. Zacharias couldn't help but talk about him. But did she know about Arnold, the other son, a druggist in West Haven—and that he hadn't come to Sally's funeral? And did she tell?

A man came through the door and shut it carefully against the outside chill. It was thin-haired, beady-eyed Martin Wraxler, and Zacharias' heart stopped for a moment as it inevitably did when Martin Wraxler appeared. Wraxler always closed the door carefully, even though it had a spring. It was as if he wanted to conserve every bit of heat. It was as if he already owned the store. But he didn't yet, and Zacharias hoped he never would.

Twenty thousand dollars was his offer—an incredible figure. Why, Zacharias could have sold it six years before for sixty. That was what he'd been offered and the man would have gone higher. Much higher. But Zacharias was only sixty-three back then and he wouldn't have known what to do with himself without the store. And he had hopes that Arnold might be interested. No, he wasn't about to sell out back then.

Now it was different. It was harder and harder to hold his hand steady. And there was Janet's illness. He'd be glad to sell the store for sixty thousand dollars. He'd sell it for fifty. But Martin Wraxler would only offer twenty. And Martin Wraxler wouldn't take no for an answer. He kept coming back and repeating the offer, asking if Mr. Whittaker was ready to sell yet. It was as if it were only a matter of time and Martin Wraxler had all the time in the world.

Of course the business had gone downhill in those intervening six years. The neighborhood was getting seedy and so was the store. There was more shoplifting. Much more shoplifting. Especially with the kids. He'd had to move the candy counter over where Leslie could keep an eye on it and she had to guard against those kids sneaking magazines out under their jackets. All in all, it wasn't fun having a store any more. If Martin Wraxler were to offer him forty thousand, he'd be tempted.

Wraxler had seen him in the prescription room. He was ignoring Leslie and coming to the rear counter. Zacharias had no choice but to go out and see what he wanted. Wraxler smoothed his hand over the scant strands of hair that crossed the top of his scalp and gave a half smile of greeting.

Wraxler was always smoothing those strands of hair, seeking reassurance of their presence, and even his small smiles were full of teeth. It wasn't that his teeth protruded, it was that they were long and prominent, thrusting against his lips so as to burst through crookedly at every chance. He had a narrow, hawklike nose, his cheeks were sallow and bore a beard stubble as black as his hair. Zacharias thought him as lean and hungry as Cassius, but it was difficult for Zacharias to view anyone who would offer only twenty thousand for his store with a charitable eye.

"How's Jerry?" said Wraxler in an undertone when Zacharias appeared behind the counter. Martin was trying to be sympathetic but he had never met Jerry and Zacharias didn't like unscrupulous men like Martin Wraxler referring to his son the doctor in such a familiar manner.

"He's well," Zacharias answered in a monotone. Whether one liked what another said or not, one never forgot manners.

"A shame," Wraxler went on, shaking his head. "A terrible shame. He had such a fine future."

"He still has. This will soon be over."

"Yes, I'm sure. I want to say you have my sympathy. You and Mrs. Whittaker." Martin changed the subject and asked for bunion pads and stomach pills—(hardly enough to make the visit necessary). He waited till Zacharias had rung up the sale and was giving him change before he spoke again. "Will you be needing money?"

Zacharias, thinking the conversation concluded, started a little. "Money? What for?"

Wraxler shrugged. "Why, I don't know. Under the circumstances— with Jerry coming to trial— Sometimes it's good to have a little extra."

Zacharias wasn't sure just what Martin meant. He could guess but he wasn't certain. "Are you in the lending business, Mr. Wraxler?"

Wraxler smiled and his mouthful of cramped teeth showed to the gums, top and bottom. "Not lending business, Zack. Buying. I just want you to remember. I'm still interested in the store any time you want to sell."

Zacharias shook his head. "You don't have the price."

"Twenty thousand dollars is a lot of money."

"Chicken feed." Zacharias could still say it boldly, but not with the contempt he could once produce.

CHAPTER 14

Edward Balin entered the Empire State Building elevator with sweat soaking into his undershirt. He was sure in the hours after Jerry's indictment he had taken leave of his senses. Jerry had been so frantic, so stricken with despair, so pathetically helpless against movements of justice about which he knew nothing. "The plea date is December second," Jerry had cried. "It gives us no time to get ready!"

It was easy for Balin to explain that the plea date was only a formality, but difficult to explain that it couldn't be "us," that Edward Balin could not be Jerry's defense attorney.

Jerry almost frothed at the blow. He accused Balin of deserting him, of believing him guilty. It was so hard to get through to the distraught doctor that he was the wrong kind of attorney, that a specialist in criminal law was necessary.

Jerry didn't know any, of course, and Balin was little better off. He had a nodding acquaintance with a few, but they were young lawyers who helped defend the raft of arrested criminals who appeared in court every day. These were lawyers who sat down with assistant state's attorneys to go over the defendant's arrest record, study the amount of evidence against him, and try to reach an accommodation as to what the defendant should plead to. How could they hope to inflame the passions of a jury, or put across the idea of Whittaker's innocence?

Then Balin's mouth had popped open. In his pocket he was carrying a third letter from Cleveland Parrish that had arrived that day. In the state he was in, Balin was suddenly convinced that this extraordinary correspondence was an Act of God. It was too providential to permit any other explanation. Cleveland Parrish was fated to be Whittaker's attorney!

Whittaker had been less enthusiastic. He couldn't afford the likes of Cleveland Parrish.

But Balin had conviction. Parrish was noble, he said, as he himself had discovered. Parrish had always supported the little guy, the alleged rioters, alleged spies. Surely, defending that hippie and his girl friend against the charge of murdering her parents must have brought him a meager sum. But it had brought him vast publicity. And certainly the Whittaker slaying was another nationwide murder case. It was meant to be, Balin had assured the doctor. Cleveland Parrish would rush to the rescue.

But now, as the elevator climbed to the seventy-fifth floor, Balin's euphoria had become a nightmare. How could he have all but guaranteed Jerry a Parrish defense? What possessed him to think a coincidental request for an article was an Act of God? The spy, the Weathermen bombing, the Tennessee black who allegedly killed a cop—there were Commie groups, civil liberties groups, or black power groups anteing up his fee. Whittaker was nothing but a WASP, a cipher. And his wife wasn't killed defending Women's Lib, she was killed, probably, for defending her own chastity—such as it was, and who the hell cares about *that* any more? Certainly not Cleveland Parrish. Defending Jerry Whittaker would be akin to pitching pennies to a man of Parrish's reputation.

But Edward Balin, in his distress, had promised to try for the brass ring.

The seventy-fifth floor gave no sense of its height when Balin stepped from the elevator. There were no windows, only halls and office doors. The one for Cleveland Parrish was down a south-side hall and his name and profession were painted in gold letters on pebbled glass. It was like the door to many law offices except that this office looked down upon the Manhattan executive suites of all the great companies of the world from an aerie half again as high. It was a typical Parrish touch.

In front of the door, Edward Balin trembled and mopped his brow before daring to turn the knob. Caesar was crossing the Rubicon.

Inside was a spacious reception room in paneled mahogany with formal, expensive waiting room furniture, a couch, matching chairs, a table with recent magazines. Behind a fence and gate was the lawyer's secretary and Balin was instantly awed. She was stunning, poised, confident and at home.

The nameplate on her desk said Miss Stevens, the "Miss" being a surprise for one so beautiful, and she was rattling the keys of her electric typewriter in a way that said she had talent as well as looks. Balin, reflecting upon the difficulties his firm had in attracting girls who were merely skillful, decided that wealth and fame had their concomitant benefits.

He gave her his name and half his nervousness vanished when Miss Stevens flashed him a smile worthy of visiting potentates. When Parrish's "Send him in" sounded equally welcoming over the intercom, he almost felt as if he belonged.

The inner office gave views south and west through large windows. Downtown Manhattan, the Battery and the bay were at Cleveland Parrish's back, the Hudson and New Jersey on his left. The other walls were lined with bookcases and boasted a library of tomes. It was an impressive display and reinforced Balin's persuasion that Parrish was not merely a flamboyant entrepreneur, he was a knowledgeable, dedicated man.

Behind his desk Parrish came to his feet. "Mr. Balin, I can't tell you what a pleasure this meeting is!"

There were handshakes, the offer and refusal of a drink and the most aromatic cigar Balin had ever smelled. By the time he was ensconced in a deep leather chair, Balin's cup was running over. What a fine person Cleveland Parrish was, so renowned, yet so unassuming; so able, yet so generous.

Parrish, emphasizing again his pleasure at the meeting, picked up Balin's last letter and sat back. "You have a way, Mr. Balin. No matter how busy I might have been, I would have made time to meet the author of a letter like this." He smiled. "This problem you mention does not, I gather, have to do with the chapter I might be asking you to write?"

"Oh, no, sir."

Parrish laughed and said he didn't think so, which was what made it intriguing. He couldn't imagine what it might be. "I trust none of the corporations you represent is in need of a criminal lawyer?"

Balin wasn't alert to the humor. "Oh, no, nothing like that, sir," he said, overanxious to reassure.

"What then?" Parrish had a waiting grin.

Balin's nervousness returned tenfold. He cleared his throat and cleared it again. He was certain he would stutter. "I wonder—if you —you've heard of the—ah—Whittaker murder case?"

"Whittaker?" Parrish assumed a reflective pose. "Whittaker?"

"Gerald Whittaker. A doctor. Accused of slaying his wife, Sally, with a poker, the first of this month."

"Oh, yes," Parrish said slowly. "Of course. How stupid." He laughed. "I try to keep up on all the serious crimes. It's a thing with me. But there're so many. It took me a moment. I remember it now. It's up in your state, isn't it?"

"Yes."

Parrish was all innocence. "But what has this to do with you? Or, more particularly, with me?"

"Jerry Whittaker is a friend of mine. So was his wife."

"Oh." Parrish let the word hang.

Balin swallowed. He began to understand what it was to die. "So I was wondering if you'd consider defending him."

"I see." Parrish was dead sober now.

"I'm persuaded he's an innocent man," Balin went on quickly, "a victim of a most unfortunate set of circumstances. I don't want to presume upon our friendship, Mr. Parrish, but if you would only talk to him, I think you'll believe in his innocence too."

Parrish looked at the lawyer guilelessly. "Is that supposed to make a difference? I've defended guilty people too, you know."

Balin swallowed and fumbled and went paler. "The trouble is—I'm afraid—he doesn't have a great deal of money. I'm afraid your fees are beyond his means."

The guilelessness was replaced by sterner stuff. "That puts matters in a different light, doesn't it?"

Balin's undershirt began to feel sticky again. "But he's innocent. That's what counts. I mean, in that position it's especially important that he have the best attorney possible."

"Any man," Parrish reminded him, "in any kind of legal situation, should have the best attorney possible." He paused and added, "If I had a problem in corporation law, for instance, I'd go to you."

Balin's spine tingled. It was egocentric, of course, but he was thinking of Jerry too. If he could command such respect from this well-known attorney, he ought to be able to influence him in this worthy cause. "And I," he said with more confidence, "needing help in a criminal case, naturally turn to you."

Parrish acknowledged the compliment with a nod. "What can I say?" he smiled. "Whether I can help him or not I don't know. I would have to talk to him."

"That can be arranged."

"There would be expenses. Are you trying to tell me the man, a doctor, is penniless?"

"Oh, no," Balin quickly assured him. "He makes a very comfortable income. I only meant he doesn't have the kind of wealth most of your clients have. Money is a concern to him."

Parrish said he would be glad to at least talk to Dr. Whittaker and see what could be arranged. He rose to end the interview. Balin pumped his hand and said how good it was of him and when would he want to see him?

Parrish said he'd check his schedule and be in touch. He saw Balin to the outer door, treating him with warm regard. Miss Stevens, the secretary, also had a ready smile, and Edward Balin floated into the hall. His instincts told him this was no final parting. They would see more of each other. Much, much more.

Cleveland Parrish closed the door behind the departing attorney and said to Melody, "Tell Pete Tucker to have the car ready for Monday morning. He's taking me to New Haven."

"You're going to defend Dr. Whittaker?"

"That's right. Bread cast upon the waters."

She gestured at the scrapbook on the table beside her desk. "What about these clippings on the case? You want me to keep on collecting them?"

"From now on, only the ones that mention me."

CHAPTER 15

Cleveland Parrish rode to New Haven in a mauve custom-built Cadillac equipped with phone, dictaphone, bar, icebox and television. It took an hour and forty minutes, door to door, for time was important to Cleve Parrish and Pete Tucker drove with a heavy foot. En route Cleve dictated nine letters, phoned three clients and two would-be clients. Spare time was his enemy and he fled it as from death.

When they turned off the Oak Street Connector into New Haven traffic, Cleve Parrish called Balin himself. He was in town, he said, and would let Balin know the results of the meeting as soon as it was over.

It was a courtesy call, but Balin was hoping for more. "You're on Church Street," he said. "I'm just past the green, across from the courthouse. I can be outside waiting. I'll show you where the jail is." Balin was dreaming of climbing into Parrish's special car (there'd been pictures of it in a magazine) while the office force peered from the windows.

Parrish would have none of it. "Not necessary," he said. "My driver's had two days to find out where the jail is."

"But I can introduce you to people there—Captain O'Rourke, who's in charge—introduce you to Jerry—"

"No need. I know my way around jails."

"Perhaps it would be good if I were present at the interview. You know, we may be working together on this."

"Not permitted. When I talk to a client, I talk to him privately."

"Oh." Balin sensed he had overstepped. "I wouldn't want to interfere."

"Thank you, Mr. Balin. I'll let you know when I'm through."

Parrish hung up and decided that Balin was going to be a pain in the ass. Well, into each case some goddam rain must fall.

The State Correctional Center, formerly the county jail, was out Whalley Avenue a half dozen blocks from the center of town, and was a red brick building of sundry parts put together in the decade before the Civil War. There were spacious grounds in front but the entrance drive to the check-in office was down a side street. When the big car let him out in front of the steps, Parrish gazed around in distaste. The building looked like what it was meant to be, a place to incarcerate human beings and do it with a minimum of waste space, waste effort and disguise. It was not a playground for the naughty; it was not a rest camp or a rehabilitation center; it was a jail. What rehabilitation efforts went on behind its walls were incidental to its main function: to pen the criminally inclined so they could do no harm. Though the approach of the jail authorities was up-to-date, the building itself stood as a relic of another era and another view of crime and punishment.

Inside, Parrish presented his card, gave Whittaker's name, and was let through the buzzer lock to the inside hall. He signed the book and was taken to the visitors' room outside the wire-meshed meeting room. The escorting guard banged on the cell block door and hollered, "Whittaker!" to the guard inside; then he departed, locking the lawyer in.

Parrish looked around at the green-tinted concrete and the black-painted metal, the starkness and the rude appurtenances. It was a far cry from the softness of his own environment and it made him uneasy. Jail, he knew, would drive him insane, and he couldn't understand how others could endure it phlegmatically, coming out little changed. Locked in a room like this made his heart beat faster, the sweat begin to bead under his arms and around his groin.

The prisoner was brought in at last, behind the meshed screen. Doors were unlocked and locked again, permitting Parrish to join him, and Parrish was cold and formal in his manner. Intimidate the client and start the relationship on a proper basis. He shook hands and waited, sizing up the other man while the guard withdrew. He noted the toll jail had exacted from the doctor; the drawn, chalk face, the growing agony lines around the mouth, the dull, lackluster eyes. Whittaker was like himself, Parrish reflected. Captivity was driving him to equal despair.

The last door clanged, the last lock caught, and they were alone together, lawyer and client, the helper and the helpless, the knight and the quest. Now, for Parrish, the heart slowed, the sweat dried, walls disappeared, sounds ceased, time vanished, and nothing existed except the man facing him and the problem that enveloped him. This was what made the rest bearable. He let compassion enter his voice. "I hear you want my help, Doctor. Sit down."

Whittaker obeyed. "Ed said you were interested," he mumbled.

So it was like that, was it? Parrish permitted a short laugh. "Well that shows how mixed up a message can get. I am here because your friend, Mr. Balin, has prevailed upon me to hear your story. He has hopes that I will handle your defense. Is that your hope?"

Whittaker nodded. "I didn't mean," he said quickly. "I thought you were eager to help me. It's not all that easy a case—"

"I'll decide how easy or hard the case is, Doctor. But I'm not going to decide that until I hear it. Do you want to tell it to me?"

Whittaker licked his lip. "Yes," he said fervently.

Parrish decided the man was sufficiently submissive. He sat down, opened a notebook and said, "Tell me about the grand jury hearing."

Whittaker blinked. "The hearing? I thought you'd want to know what happened the night she died."

"I know what happened. Your wife was murdered." Parrish scribbled a heading on his pad. "I want to know why the grand jury thinks you killed her."

Everything was topsy-turvy and Whittaker shifted in his seat. "Well, I called my lawyer when I found she was dead, and he told me to call the—"

Parrish pinned him with an icy eye. "Don't you understand English, Doctor? I want to know about the hearing. Who came, who spoke, who said what!"

Whittaker, chastened, responded meekly. "What I mean is, the first witness was the policeman who came that night."

"We can skip him. Go on."

"Then there was Dr. Allen. She's the medical examiner for Guilford and Madison—"

"And she testified your wife was dead. Go on."

"And the state medical examiner—"

"Who did the autopsy and said the wounds were neither accidental nor self-inflicted. Did he say whether the killer was left- or right-handed?"

67

"He said it was impossible to tell."

Parrish had him get on with it. There was the man, Whittaker said, who had found the poker, the detective who had taken pictures and drawn maps. "Then they read my statement—the one I signed about what happened that night, about how I woke up hearing her screams—"

"I'm not interested in that. What else?"

Whittaker was crestfallen, but he managed to continue. Next had come Walter Costaine's wife, Barbara. She told the jury about Walter's womanizing, day after day, year after year. Then she related how she trailed him and learned about Sally, how she reported it to Jerry and brought him with her to the East River Motel to catch the couple coming out of a room together.

"There was a fight," Jerry continued. "She said Walter knocked me down. What happened was, I tripped. That's how he gave me the black eye. I tripped and was—"

Parrish cut him off. "I've told you not to bother me with your version. Tell me her version."

The doctor swallowed. It was so difficult. "If I could just—"

"Don't you understand English? What did she tell the grand jury?"

Whittaker regained control. Barbara, he went on, claimed she had brought him to the motel in hopes he'd put an end to the affair. When this didn't work and when Walter refused her ultimatums, she had no choice but to throw him out. This had been in early July.

Costaine himself was the next witness. He confessed to having slept with Sally since the preceding May and freely admitted his wife had thrown him out of the house because of it. He swore that until the night of the dance he hadn't seen Sally for two months, but that nothing had changed between them and both had agreed to a liaison at his motel room as soon after the dance as possible. Needless to say, she had not appeared.

Parrish, taking notes, asked, "He testify to anything else?"

"He said I cut in when they were dancing and I was sore and dragged Sally away and Sally said to him, loud and clear, 'See you later.'"

Another who testified was Nellie Burr, a part-time maid, who said the Whittakers fought all the time. On one occasion she heard Jerry strike Sally and many other times heard Sally call him "impotent."

The Bakewells also testified. They admitted the "Battling Whittakers," as they were known, were not speaking to each other at the pre-dance dinner, and George confirmed Sally's "See you later" remark.

"Was there anyone else?"

Whittaker nodded and his face had become white. "There was a pathologist," he whispered and stopped.

"And?"

"He took Sally's temperature at the hospital."

"What about it?"

Whittaker's voice dropped so low Parrish had to lean forward to hear. "The pathologist said she died at three o'clock."

Parrish made a note and looked up. Whittaker had his fists to his head. "He's lying," he cried out. "He's lying or he's crazy. Because I heard her screaming at quarter past four. I heard the pounding."

Parrish was unimpressed. "Was there anything else?"

Whittaker sank back and let his hands drop helplessly. "That was all. I got sent out of the room and the next I knew, I was called in front of the judge and told I'd been indicted for murdering my own wife! With a goddam poker, for Christ's sake!"

Parrish folded his notebook and put it away. He tilted back his chair and regarded the nervous, sweating man across the table from him. "And what, exactly, do you want from me?" he asked.

Whittaker looked up at him slowly. "Why, I want you to defend me." He spread his hands. "What else?"

Parrish rocked back and forth in the tilted chair, a slight, bemused smile toying with his lips. Whittaker grew palpably nervous under such idle scrutiny. The perspiration began to bead more quickly on his face. He said, his voice timid, "Will you?"

"That depends," Parrish remarked, continuing his rocking. He brought the chair to rest and grew straighter. "How much money have you got?"

CHAPTER 16

"Money?" Whittaker looked blank.

"Money," Parrish repeated. "The green stuff; the root of all evil; what makes the world go around. How much have you got?"

The doctor wet his lips. His face was the color of white clay. "I don't know," he said hoarsely. "A couple of thousand dollars, I guess."

"A couple of what?" Parrish's voice affected overwhelming incredulity.

"It may be more," Whittaker hastened to amend. "There's my checking account. There're a couple hundred in that. And there are the patients' bills." His speech quickened as he sought to improve his assets. "There's quite a lot in due bills. There might be three or four thousand." He watched Parrish anxiously.

The lawyer's voice was cold. "You can write that off," he said callously. "They're going to sit on their wallets."

"They owe me!" Whittaker protested.

"How are you going to make them pay—bring suit?"

Whittaker swallowed. "They're reliable people. They owe, they'll pay." He gestured. "They've always paid before."

Parrish was the more seasoned adventurer, the more accustomed to the ways of man, the more cynical of the two. "They paid because they wanted to continue availing themselves of your services. Now they no longer can. So what new whip have you got to hold over them?"

"They have honor."

"Honor?" Parrish sneered. "They'll believe you killed your wife and any payments they made would be used by you to cheat the gallows. So much for honor."

"But I'm innocent."

"Until proven guilty. That's in the eyes of the law, not your neighbors." He waved an impatient hand. "Forget the bills. What kind of money can you actually lay your hands on?"

Whittaker wiped his mouth with the back of his hand and explored possibilities. There were stocks and bonds that his wife had— No, they weren't in his name.

Parrish was irked and impatient. "I'm talking about money you can lay *your* hands on: *your* assets. Do you understand? And if it's not any more than what you've said, forget it. You can't buy a defense with that kind of money. You might as well will it to your heirs and let the public defender handle your case."

There was silence. Parrish sat back, one bold hand on the table, his unblinking eyes fixed on the doctor. Whittaker shook his head numbly and tried to focus. Finally he managed a tentative glance at the fire-breathing man-eater opposing him. "What kind of money are you talking about?" he asked timidly.

"I'm talking about fifty thousand dollars for openers. That's just for a start—to get the defense rolling."

Whittaker winced. There was a longer silence this time. He broke it. "I thought you wanted to defend me. I thought—it wasn't—the money."

"I'd love to defend you," Parrish told him. "I believe in you. I believe you're trapped, and I want to get you out of that trap. There's nothing I'd rather do. But it costs money!"

Whittaker fumbled. "Well, I thought—I mean—it's a big case. It's getting a lot of attention. It would give you publicity. I thought that —you would be willing to waive your fee—some of your fee—for the opportunity—"

Parrish decided to end the writhing. "What opportunity?"

"The—ah—reputation you could make and—ah—the opportunity to defend an innocent man when the odds are stacked—"

Parrish laughed. It was a rich and caustic chuckle. "You're so transparent, Doctor." He hooked an arm over the back of his chair. "Was that Balin's idea? That you con me into taking your case for nothing by waving your innocence in my face?"

Whittaker flushed and looked away. "I didn't mean it like that," he mumbled. "Honest."

Parrish smote the table so hard he pulled Whittaker back. "I'm not going to take offense," he thundered. "I'm going to assume you're

71

under so much strain and are so ignorant of the law that you don't know what you're talking about. Do you think I might be right about that?"

Whittaker, compelled to nod, nodded.

Parrish's lip curled and his voice dropped to acid. "Just to disabuse your mind of these false notions, let's air these matters. First, this publicity you think your trial will produce. Let's see what we've got."

He held up his hand and folded down the first finger. "You're a small-town doctor. You may not think of yourself that way, but that's what you are. That's the first thing."

He folded down another finger. "Secondly, you're accused of murdering your wife. You're *not* accused of murdering Malcolm X, or Bobby Kennedy, or Martin Luther King, Jr. You're only accused of killing your wife, which is one of the most commonplace murders there are. True, your wife is from a fine old Philadelphia family and murder among the elite is more rare, and therefore more appealing than murder among us common folk. Reports of your trial might, therefore, extend a little beyond the boundaries of New Haven. I daresay you would make the Hartford papers, and your wife's hometown paper. And, possibly, you might even rate an occasional item in the back pages of the *Times*."

Parrish smote the table again. "What *would* give your trial the publicity you're talking about is not some public defender feebly attempting to counteract the case against you. It's your being defended by me. It's Cleveland Llewellyn Parrish coming to the aid of a man in hopeless jeopardy. What will create interest in the case is the question: Can Cleveland Parrish save this man?"

Whittaker started to speak, but Parrish waved him off. "Now we'll take up the next point, namely, my supposed willingness to volunteer my services in the interests of justice. I'll work for nothing to protect an innocent man. I believe that's what you were assuming?"

The attorney leaned forward and his voice took on an unexpected harshness. "I'm not a lawyer for fun, Doctor. I went into law to make a living. So you'd better understand, that I don't like not charging fees. And I mean, even to protect the innocent."

The voice softened again. "It's true, Doctor, that I have a passion for justice, that I'm like the surgeon who doesn't let an accident victim die because he can't pay the bill. I can't let an innocent man hang because he can't pay me. I don't know how you and Balin found my weakness but you have me at your mercy. You know I can't turn you down, fee or no fee."

Whittaker's eyes were hopeful, but Parrish stiffened dramatically and the hope was held in abeyance. "So understand," the lawyer said in measured tones, "when I said I would need fifty thousand dollars just to start the case, I wasn't talking fee. I'm forgoing my fee. I'm not going to charge you for my time, effort and experience. I'm taking this case to see what I can do to save an innocent man from a gross miscarriage of justice. That fifty thousand dollars I'm talking about is my minimum estimate of what it will cost to see that the miscarriage of justice does not take place."

He stopped and Whittaker was left to think it through. Finally, in a humbled tone, he said, "You mean it would take fifty thousand dollars just to cover expenses?"

The sun came out. The warmth of Parrish's smile flooded the room. "You understand! It's cost I'm talking about, not fee. And I'm sure you must realize that, much as I'm interested in your case, I'm in no position, nor of a mind to pay your costs out of my own pocket. Nor should you expect me to. Right?"

"Oh, no," Whittaker concurred vigorously. "You're absolutely right." Then he swallowed. "But fifty thousand dollars? Just for expenses? What expenses?"

The warmth was enveloping. "Do you know how I win cases, Doctor? By attention to detail. By looking into more corners than the prosecution does. Do you think it's my silver-tongued oratory?" Parrish laughed a little. "Oh, I can invoke a tear. In fact, I've made whole juries cry. I know all the tricks to win sympathy for my client. But that's grandstand. That's in the courtroom. That's show." Parrish waved it all away. "But those twelve jurors, when they get into that jury room together and start the cold, hard business of determining the future of a man's life, they leave their emotions outside—back in the courtroom—and they start paying close attention to the facts.

"And when that time comes, I'm going to have filled them with so many more facts in support of my client's position than the prosecution has been able to marshal against him that 'reasonable doubt' is going to be established without question."

The lawyer leaned forward and became more confidential. "Research, Jerry. Research. That's the key to victory. I win because I dig. I dig into everybody and everything. I dig ten times as deep as the prosecution—a hundred times as deep. My tactic is saturation.

73

Supersaturation. And it wins cases, Jerry. It wins cases. Do you know I've had as many as five different detective agencies working for me on one case?

"But it takes money. It takes a hell of a lot of money. But that's the way I work and that's the way I win. And I won't take a case unless I know I can do the job right. Because I don't take a case unless I know I can win. So I'm not worrying about my fee. I can stint myself on my fee. But I won't stint on the job. I won't let somebody go hang because I had to hold down expenses and couldn't investigate properly. I wouldn't take a case under those conditions. And you wouldn't want me to, would you, Jerry?"

Whittaker shook his head. He couldn't argue against such logic and a tear fell onto the tabletop. "But where can I get fifty thousand dollars?" he asked.

Parrish relaxed and sat back. "If that's what's worrying you," he said, "forget it. That shouldn't be any problem."

CHAPTER 17

They sorted through the possibilities, Parrish confident, Whittaker pessimistic. His parents? Absolutely not. His father had already offered help but Whittaker would not permit it. All they owned was a drugstore. It was their protection, their life.

"I'm not suggesting they sell it, just raise money on it."

"No, no. I couldn't ask them to shoulder that kind of a burden."

"It's only until you're set free. Then you can pay them back."

"With what?"

"You'd have your wife's money. You *do* inherit, don't you?"

"I don't know. She never made out a will."

"You inherit. Her insurance, her stocks and bonds and investments. It would be quite a nest egg, wouldn't it?"

"It must be a quarter of a million. Maybe much more. She never would tell me."

"There's nothing to it then."

"But if I've got that money, we can use that!"

Parrish shook his head. "You haven't got it. Not while you're accused of killing her. You have to be found not guilty first."

"What if I'm not?"

Parrish laughed. "If I couldn't get you off, I wouldn't waste my time with you."

The argument ebbed and flowed but it was an argument that Parrish, strangely and unexpectedly, could not win. Under no circumstances would Whittaker let his parents run risks for his defense.

Parrish, his eyes glinting, finally turned away. "All right, but it's your neck. You'd better think about that."

"I will, I will. But I couldn't ask it of them. And it wouldn't be enough anyway. We have to look somewhere else."

"What about your wife's folks? Would they go to bat for you?"

That brought forth an opposite response. Whittaker laughed a cold, bitter, explosive laugh. "Sally's folks? Ha ha ha. That's funny. That's the funniest story yet. They help me? They'd buy the gallows to see me hung." He fixed the lawyer with a baleful eye. "Those goddam creeps think I did it!"

Parrish watched the doctor clinically. "Why do they think you did it?"

"Because they hate my guts. Do they need a better reason?"

"Why do they hate your guts?"

"Because I'm uppity. Because I didn't come from their side of the tracks. I'm po' white trash and they're the First Family of Pennsylvania and they can't stand the thought of their darling daughter throwing herself away on dirt like me."

Parrish abandoned that line. He probed Whittaker for well-to-do friends, for contributors to a Whittaker Defense Pool. The doctor said he had none that wealthy or that willing.

"How about patients? Isn't there some rich old dame who thinks the sun rises and sets on you? A widow, maybe, with more money than she knows what to do with? Maybe one with marriage in her eye?"

Whittaker stared at him. "You really are a bastard, aren't you?"

Parrish remained unruffled. "I'm interested in winning cases, not popularity contests. I'm interested in finding money for your defense, something that ought to interest you too. Do you want to spend the next twenty years in jail because you can't raise the meager sum of fifty thousand dollars?"

"That's no meager sum."

"Against twenty years of your life it averages out to twenty-five hundred dollars a year. That's not only meager, it's downright measly."

"All right, but I don't know any rich widows. I wish to hell I did."

"You make it difficult." Parrish sighed painfully. "There isn't much else to do but scrape the bottom of the barrel."

Gerald Whittaker sat back and chewed his lip, his face dour. He believed there was no barrel to be scraped and he wasn't sure he wasn't glad. Because he had the strong feeling that one way or another the lawyer was going to be in his corner, money or no. "There's no barrel to be scraped," he said. "That's the trouble. I don't have anything."

Parrish contradicted that on the instant. "Of course you do. You've got an office full of equipment. How much do you think you can get for it?"

That one really hurt. Whittaker felt all the air go out of him. His office equipment? The X-ray machine, the electrocardiograph, the fluoroscope, the desks, the chairs, the microscopes, the billing machine, all those treasured items which measured his development as a doctor, which identified him, which marked his position on the path of life? Converting the complete contents of his office into cash for his defense was something that hadn't even occurred to him. It was like being asked to sacrifice his children.

He sat stunned and shaken. Parrish wanted a monetary estimate and all he could think was that they were beyond value.

"It doesn't matter," the lawyer said impatiently. "We'll call in an appraiser. Now, what about your house?"

The doctor's heart sank still further. All his office equipment gone, now the house. And, it quickly became evident, Parrish also meant its furnishings, the carpeting, the clothes, and everything that wasn't in Sally's estate. He meant the two automobiles and the boat.

"But I owe so much on everything—and—a forced sale—I'd get almost nothing—"

Parrish consoled him with a bit of good news. Things didn't have to be sold on the spot. Nor would Whittaker have to agonize over the selling. Parrish had experts to take care of such matters. "Just one of my services," he told the doctor. "When I take on a client, I take on his problems. Not only his defense, I mean all his problems." He shook his head at Whittaker sadly. "People in jail, especially sensitive people like yourself, get this unhealthy prison pallor. I don't want things any worse for you than they have to be, and that's for a selfish reason as well as an unselfish one. You are my exhibit when we go to trial. Part of my ploy, part of my defense is my defendant. I want you to go into court looking hale, hearty and confident. I want you to *look* innocent, not just *be* innocent."

Whittaker nodded. He had become conditioned to accept, now he could even be soothed. Now that he had made his sacrifices, all would be well.

Except, Parrish reminded him, they might not have enough money. Was there any source of income Whittaker had overlooked? Whittaker shook his head. "I've hit bottom," he said. "There's no way I can raise another cent."

"Maybe there is," Parrish countered. "You ever write anything besides prescriptions? You ever do any articles for medical journals, work for your college newspaper, go in for anything like that?"

"Look, Mr. Parrish—"

"Cleve," the lawyer corrected. "If we're going to work together, we're going to be as close as two people can get. I'm Cleve and you're Jerry."

"Yes—good. Uh—well—ah—Cleve—nobody's going to want to read anything I could write. I'm not a specialist in anything. I haven't made any discoveries. I don't have any views on medicine that count with anybody. And even if I did, the fact I'm under indictment for murder— Do you know the AMA?" He could even laugh. "Can you imagine them printing an article by an accused murderer? Think what that would do to their image."

"I'm not talking about articles for the AMA Journal. I'm talking about writing a book. I know an editor in a paperback house who will pay you five thousand dollars for a sixty-thousand-word book. Five thousand dollars will sweeten the defense kitty a lot. And that's only an advance against royalties. If you make the book really good, you could rake in a lot more than that."

The doctor shook his head in bewilderment. "But what on earth would I write a book about?"

"The title this editor suggests," Parrish said, sitting back in the chair, "is *My Life with Sally*."

CHAPTER 18

"*My Life with Sally?*" Whittaker came half to his feet. "You mean—"

"That's right," Parrish interrupted. "*My Life with Sally*, by Gerald Whittaker, M.D. First printing, two hundred and fifty thousands copies selling for sixty-five cents each, which means, on a royalty of six per cent, you've earned back the advance around the hundred-and-twenty-eight-thousand mark. For every copy they sell after that, the defense kitty will collect another three point nine cents."

"But that's, that's— I can't do that."

"If you can't, don't worry. I've got a writer who'll ghost the whole thing for a thousand dollars. All you have to do is provide the background material."

Whittaker pushed his fingers through his hair. "But—I couldn't. She was playing around. Everybody knows it. I couldn't have a book about our marriage. I'd look like a fool."

"You're right." Parrish was quick to soothe. "*My Life with Sally?* No. We'll have to change that." He looked into space for a moment and snapped his fingers, almost too quickly. "I know. We'll call it, *My Courtship of Sally*. You can tell how you won her. We'll play up the sex angle. A lay a day. That might be a slight exaggeration but it's all right. That's artistic license."

Whittaker stared with his mouth open. "My God," he said in awe. "I really believe you mean that."

"Of course I mean it," Parrish snapped. "How else do you think we're going to sell books?"

"You actually believe that I would write down—or allow to be

78

written down—for public consumption, a detailed exposé of myself and my wife in our most intimate moments? That's private."

"*Was* private. Your wife has been murdered and you've been fingered. Now you and she are public figures. Like Liz Taylor and Richard Burton. Like Jackie and Ari Onassis. You don't have a private life any more. The public wants to know what you eat for breakfast, what you gave your wife for Christmas, how you proposed to her. And the public will pay money for that information. And we need money!"

"All right, but I'm not going to talk about our sex life."

"The hell you aren't. Sex and your wife go together. The public knows it and expects it. She was an out-and-out shack-up job. She made a date to lay Walter Costaine right in front of your face. Everybody knows it. Sex is everything in this case. We may never find out who killed her, but the odds are a thousand to one sex was the motive. She wasn't giving it to the right guy or she'd stopped giving it, or something."

"Sally wasn't like that at all," Whittaker said protectively.

"She'd better have been," Parrish retorted. "And that's the way we're going to paint her. That's the way the public wants her and we're going to give the public what it wants. You're going to be courting and marrying the hottest broad this side of Hollywood."

Whittaker cringed. "No. I couldn't face our friends."

"Friends?" Parrish stood up. "What friends? Haven't you been listening to what you've been saying? I'm the only friend in the world you've got, the only one who'll lift a finger to help you. And if you want that help, you're going to do as I tell you. And what you're going to do is write me a three-page outline of your courting days, the parties, the dances, the movies you took her to. And if you can't give me the year, the month and the day, come as close as you can."

Parrish leaned and clapped the sunken man on the shoulder. "Don't fail me, Jerry, and I won't fail you!"

CHAPTER 19

Walter Costaine tramped slowly up the front steps of a Bronx tenement, entered the front hall and began to climb the stairs. His long face was slack and his thin chest, compressed between rounded shoulders and a little pot of stomach, was increasing its rhythm. Though he was short of forty, his dark hair was shot with gray and he looked a sad fifty. He had never been anything but an indoor athlete and four flights of stairs was more than his legs were geared for. He was a long time getting to the top and he was panting noticeably when he rapped at the door of the front apartment. Too much liquor, too much cigarette smoke, too much sitting. He coughed a smoker's hack and felt nervously of his tie.

He rang again and unbuttoned his overcoat. It was warm in the hall and the climb had made him perspire. The walls were a chocolate brown laced with crooked white repair lines. Noise from a rock record and the sour smell of garlic and garbage were with him. A baby carriage stood chained to the metal railing.

The door opened on his third ring. It was held by a well-formed twenty-year-old girl with dark, tossed hair, whose beauty was marred by a sullen, perpetual sneer. She was wearing a plaid flannel shirt and blue jeans; she held a half-smoked cigarette between stained fingers and her feet were bare. She looked at Walter Costaine and said, "Oh, Christ, it's you again."

Walter lifted his long chin a little. "That's not the way to talk to your father, Rita."

She lounged against the doorframe and sucked smoke from the cigarette. "You here to give me lessons?"

Walter let it pass. He was supposed to have a way with women, but it didn't work with Rita. His charm only made her claw. He said, "Where's your mother?"

"Looking for work."

"I thought she had a bad back."

"Not any more." Rita laughed with raucous contempt.

"What happened?"

"The crumb emptied the garbage in her kimona without her back brace on and an insurance company spy got pictures of her picking up scraps. So she settled for three hundred bucks and was damned lucky to get that. And now she's pounding the pavements, and it's about time. You want to find her, walk the streets."

Rita was ready to shut the door, but Walter persisted. "When will she get back?"

"Probably around four. She quits easy. Wait on the steps and you'll catch her."

"I'd like to wait for her here."

The girl paused and he felt his fate hanging in the balance. He was careful not to look pleading, not to look demanding, not to give her any kind of look that might antagonize her. He composed his face to be as nothing as possible. Finally she shrugged and turned her back. "Sure, come on in. You can wait in the bedroom. Ma's bedroom."

He stepped through into a small sitting room. A boy was on the couch with a guitar on his lap. His hair was to his shoulders, as long as Rita's. He wore granny glasses and a thin beard. He looked innocuous and stared unwinkingly as Walter passed through the room. Rita made no attempt at introductions and the boy never moved.

The bedroom of Morelle Costaine, Walter's first wife, was spare. It was a small room to begin with, but Morelle had introduced only a minimum of furnishings: a bed, dresser, and chair. The dresser top was bare of all but a hair-laden brush and a comb. The bedspread was white cotton to match the window curtains, and the only decorative touch was a large, faded Raggedy Ann doll. Walter remembered the doll. He had bought it for her at a fair. It had been a long-ago warm, sunny summer day and they had spent half an afternoon and the early evening there. Not that they were crazy about country fairs, but it was a way to kill time till it was dark enough to do what they really got together for.

As he looked at it now, he wondered if that was the night he had knocked her up. Maybe she'd kept it all these years in celebration, though getting herself pregnant wasn't really anything she should want to celebrate. She sure as hell hadn't been happy about it at the time. Neither had he. Jesus, there he was halfway through college and she was below the age of consent.

He'd wanted her to get an abortion. He knew a doctor; he'd used him with another girl. The doc was expensive: five hundred smackers! But he knew what he was doing and that was better than those kitchen table jobs and the high risk factor such economies entailed.

But Morelle was too scared. Or she pretended she was. Maybe she was in love instead. Maybe she wanted marriage. Maybe she only wanted to get her hooks into the son of a wealthy investment broker. Maybe she knew the abortion would not only be the end of the baby, it would be the end of the affair. In any case, she had balked, and when he tried to ditch her, she went to her parents. And that was that. It was marriage or jail.

So they had married and kept it a secret from his own folks until Morelle was in her seventh month. Then they revealed their "grand passion" to Papa and Mama Costaine, by which time they could hardly stand the sight of each other.

They gave the baby legitimacy. They even shared an apartment off campus through Walter's last year and a half of college, during which time he made out with half the female population of the town while Morelle stayed home with the baby.

They divorced the summer after graduation and Morelle Costaine got herself a handsome settlement. Her lawyer knew what the old man would pay to avoid a scandal.

The money was enough to make a tidy dowry should she marry again, but it wouldn't last a lifetime. Morelle had had to go to work. Unfortunately, she had very few skills and her efforts brought meager pay. She did get by, though, and Walter had, when he was flusher, given her sums from time to time. For the most part, though, he had had little to do with either Morelle or Rita through the nearly twenty years since their divorce. He visited occasionally and relations were cool but not unfriendly. At least such was his relationship with Morelle. Rita was less warm toward him. But Rita didn't act warm toward anybody. Walter could hear her now, bossing the kid with the guitar, telling him to stop inproving and play something decent. Ah well, Walter thought, Give a girl a pretty face and she'll think she doesn't need anything else.

Morelle didn't get home until half past five, at which time Rita told the guitar player to split. Then she said, "Your Ex is here. I stuck him in the bedroom."

"What's he want?" There was less than a welcoming note in Morelle's tone.

"Ask him."

Walter, waiting behind the closed door, chose not to go out. He let Morelle come in. She did, a graying, once-pretty woman in a cheap blue wool dress, with a shabby cloth coat hooked over her shoulder. The lines of her face had set, forming a hard, bitter mask that was reflected by the turn of her mouth and the cold blue of her eyes. "Well," she said, looking from Costaine to the mussed coverlet where he had been resting. "Making yourself at home?"

He smiled in greeting but didn't push. She was another who was not responsive to his charm. Not any more. "Just dropped by."

"We should be honored," she said, hanging her coat in the closet. "It's not often such a famous fornicator comes to call."

Walter wasn't sure how sarcastically she meant that. "Me and Casanova," he said noncommittally. He watched while she unzipped and stepped out of her dress. Her back was toward him and he noted, now that she was down to her slip, that her waist had thickened notably, even since last summer. She was going to fat the way they all did if they didn't watch. Nevertheless, she was far more feminine than when she'd been wearing the back brace and he could even contemplate the idea of going to bed with her. She wouldn't be hard to take. If she'd let him, that is. He had doubts about that. In fact, the possibility wouldn't even have occurred to him if she hadn't shed her dress in his presence. Was it a subtle invitation, or had her insurance loss so wiped him out of her mind she couldn't care less what he saw?

"You aren't wearing the brace," he said. "Rita said your back's better."

She muttered obscenities, hung the dress and slipped into a well-worn robe. Walter said, "You settled for three hundred dollars?"

She swung around, tying the sash. "What the hell else could I do?" she exclaimed bitterly. "Two years!" She cursed the long, drastic time and the brace she had worn through its entirety. Then she cursed the insurance company for stalling on the settlement. "Three hundred thousand dollars I could have had, and they kept stalling and they kept watching me. And I kept wearing that brace and going to doctors and saying how my back ached and how I couldn't bend. And the company kept spying on me and asking questions around the neighborhood." She went on petulantly, "I lived in that brace. I all but slept in it! As you goddam well know.

"And then I made one slip! Just one slip. I forget and empty the garbage without it, and they've got a spy watching with a camera. A movie camera. And he gets the whole thing. And then they show it to my lawyer and they offer him three hundred bucks to drop the suit, and he tells me to take it before they decide to sue me. And he got one third."

She went into the kitchenette and Walter followed. "That was a tough break," he said. "You could've been living pretty."

"Maybe that stupid, no-good lawyer asked for too much." She slapped a kettle on the stove. "Maybe two hundred grand they would have paid without keeping spies on me for two years. It wouldn't have been worth it for two hundred grand. They might've only watched me a year and said the hell with it." She got a coffee cup down from the cupboard over the stove and Walter noticed she didn't make it two. The welcome mat wasn't out. He uttered sympathetic noises and said he understood insurance companies were hard to convince when it came to undiagnosable back injuries.

"You can say that again," Morelle answered sourly. "Those were the worst two years of my life. I earned that three hundred thousand bucks. I earned it in blood."

Rita, thumbing through a magazine on the couch, said, "I earned half of it listening to you bitch."

"Don't you complain," Morelle flared. "If I could've got that little nest egg, you'd've been first in line to help me spend it." She got down instant coffee and the solitary cup on the counter made her aware of Walter again. "Say, what do you want here anyway?"

"I want to stay with you for a little while."

Morelle eyed him. "What for? You got hepatitis again?"

"No, no," Costaine assured her. "I just want to get away from all the reporters." He told her he'd been moving from motel to motel but the press kept finding him.

"I'll bet it broke your heart."

"It does. I'm not looking for publicity."

Morelle laughed. "After all your confessions to the press?" She went on. "So your wife threw you out? It took her long enough."

"Look, I don't need to be lectured to. I just want a place to stay."

"You're going to pay," she said. "In advance."

"Yeah, I know."

84

From the adjacent room Rita, still reading her magazine, said without looking up, "Where's he going to sleep?"

"On the daybed, of course. Where else?"

"Just wondering," Rita said. "Since he's healthy this time."

Morelle just managed not to throw the cup at her daughter. "Shut your goddam face." She fingered it and set it back down. "Those are the terms," she said to Walter. "You sleep on the daybed, just in case you got other ideas—like your daughter."

"Yeah, yeah. I understand."

"And you pay forty a week. In advance."

"Forty a week?" Costaine blinked. "Last time—"

"That's cheaper than a motel. You can afford motel rates, you can afford forty a week."

Rita said, "Is that with meals?"

Morelle said, "Fifty with meals thrown in."

Costaine was outraged. "Fifty a week? You're out of your mind."

"So go to a motel."

Rita said, "Don't forget, Ma's got to make up that three hundred thousand."

"One week then," Costaine said bitterly. He paid her the money and Morelle took down a second cup.

CHAPTER 20

Cleveland Parrish was granted permission to practice law in Connecticut as attorney for Gerald Whittaker by Judge McConnaughy in Superior Court on Wednesday, November 25. Such permission was an extreme rarity and the only precedent was the permission granted in the Black Panthers' trial due to its exceptional notoriety. Balin, coached by Parrish, made capital of that by pointing to the notoriety already given the Whittaker case and pleading that advantages given to black defendants should not be denied to defendants who were white. Judge McConnaughy acceded to the argument.

By this time Balin was having second thoughts about having lured the famous lawyer into the case. It would leave his friend Jerry penniless. Whittaker, however, was adamant. He had come under Parrish's sway and no one else would do. Balin was to get his papers ready for signing immediately, and that was that.

"Two things," Parrish said to Balin upon leaving the courthouse with McConnaughy's blessing. "The first is, what judges will be handling criminal cases between now and June? The second is, when can I have the wherewithal to get moving on this case?"

It was as fast as that.

Balin wasn't sure. He didn't think the papers would be quite ready today.

"How about tomorrow?"

"Tomorrow?" Balin blinked. "That's Thanksgiving."

"That would be fine. I want to see Jerry, I want to see the scene of the crime, and I want to pick up the papers. I don't want to waste a minute while Jerry sits in jail. Do you?"

Balin could do nothing but agree. "I guess I can work on them tonight."

"Good. I'll give you a call when I'm on my way." He clapped Balin on the shoulder. "That be O.K., Ed?"

Ed said it would be O.K.

The fact that it was Thanksgiving might have given Edward Balin pause, but not Cleve Parrish. Holidays were for families and Cleveland Parrish had no family. He didn't know what a family was. His mother had died giving him birth. It had been by Cesarean section, with peritonitis and the works. She was too slender, too frail for childbearing. Her bones were too small and delicate, the baby too big. Doctors had warned her, but love and passion and human nature had ways of ignoring doctors and a baby was spawned. Then she had been confidentially advised not to bring it to term. Arrangements could be made. Things could be done. It could be legal.

But Evita Parrish, petite, frail, blonde, young, almost angelic, only shook her head. God had let the baby be formed. She and Carlisle had taken all the precautions. But to no avail. She was with child. It was God's will. God understood the longing in her soul and He was telling her it was all right. Doctors, after all, did make mistakes.

Their warnings were well intentioned, but they didn't know everything. A greater power had taken over and she would have her child.

Bear it she did, but deliver it she could not. For fifteen hours she tried, before the doctors, belatedly, took it from her. They showed him to her just before she slipped into sleep, a lusty nine-and-a-half-pound screaming bundle of life. It was the only time she ever saw him, for her strength was gone and she had nothing with which to combat the onslaught of disease.

Carlisle Parrish took his baby home with him after the funeral. And a wet nurse as well. She was a stout and willing Irishwoman named Hannah who not only cared for the baby but for the house. She became its empress, its caretaker, its ménage. The only thing to do with the family that she did not take care of was the master. That was because Carlisle, after the death of his wife, used his home for little other than a stopover for a change of clothes or a look at the mail. Carlisle, who made his money in mining, was more than ever a roisterer, and for the boy, Cleveland, Hannah was the closest thing to family he had.

But Hannah, with the house as her domain and the master an inconvenience of small moment, put her big-boned body to the uses that had qualified her as a wet nurse in the first place. She figuratively hung up her shingle and the men came filing through.

Her interest was not in children; her own child she had put up for adoption without a moment's pang. Nor was the new baby, Cleveland, by any means a substitute. He was only a meal ticket and was allowed to interfere with Hannah's activities as little as possible.

He was kept in his playpen until he was big enough to climb out and stubborn enough not to. When spankings didn't work, Hannah, in a rage, struck him and knocked him down but, though he wailed and screamed, he still climbed. Hannah didn't dare strike him again and, in fact, lived for some days in fear he would report it when his father next appeared. He did not, which eased her mind if it did not enhance her liking for his irksome presence. She got around matters thereafter by sending him out to play and locking the doors so he couldn't disobey. Again she feared his father finding out, particularly in cold weather when little Cleveland would be frozen and in tears by the time Hannah's male friends finally departed and she could let him in.

87

In the end, however, she was the cause of her own undoing. Carlisle Parrish sent her packing when she was so far along with a new child that "buxomness" could no longer qualify as an explanation. The older Parrish spent an hour talking with his five-year-old son that time, learning about the hours he spent locked out in the fresh air, and all the "salesmen" who came to the door to sell Hannah things for the house. Parrish threw her out all but bodily, hopefully consigning her to starve in the streets. Hannah, however, wasn't making babies just for fun, and when she left the household after five years of employment, she had over twenty thousand dollars in the bank, the accumulation of nursemaid's salary, leftover household money, and the wages of sin.

Carlisle Parrish made the house his home again and, for a spell, tried being a father to his son. A boy needed a mother too and Carlisle supplied a number of such, their identity varying from day to day according to which of the bevy of ladies fair who adorned his life he wanted to make earn her keep.

They took the job seriously, for Carlisle was his own Fort Knox, a rare thing during the depression, and they felt that if Carlisle should choose to marry again, he might lean toward a maternal type who doted on his boy.

For Cleve it was an ambiguous experience. He liked having a father but the "mothers" were hard to understand. They came in different colored hairs but otherwise were hard to tell apart. They were all very beautiful, with very red lips and lovely clothes which they didn't want to get wrinkled, and they smelled gorgeous. They also had very long, red fingernails and smooth hands which they didn't want to get wet or dirty. He remembered their hands and their bodies mostly. They were very slender, their bodies, their arms, their hands and fingers. It wasn't at all like Hannah, who grew increasingly broad of beam, whose hands were thick and meaty, and whose nails were broken and dirty.

Hannah got her hands wet. And she did work with them. She cooked and scrubbed and cleaned. The ladies his father brought home did none of those things. All they did was hug and kiss him and ask him to call them "Mommy" and tell him what a sweet child he was and bring him presents. And when they got him alone, they'd ask him about the other "mommies" his father brought home and what they and his father talked about and what did his father say about them, and which one did he like the best?

It was not an arrangement that worked out well. Especially when he walked in on a couple of his "mommies" in the bedroom and they shrieked at him and called him names and told his father, couldn't he, for Chrissake, lock the goddam door or cane the kid so he'd stay the hell out?

Carlisle was soon persuaded he wasn't cut out to be a father and he booked Cleveland into boarding school the next fall. Then he sold the house and took an apartment. That way of life worked better all around. Cleveland was in more proper milieu, Carlisle didn't have to make mommas out of sweethearts, and he didn't have to worry about getting home sometime.

When his conscience bothered him—about every two months—he'd drive the limousine up to the school on a Saturday, bring Cleve a catcher's mask or football helmet, and ask how things were. Then he and the lady (there was always a lady) and Cleve would go into town for an ice cream soda. And, maybe, if there was a good matinee at the neighborhood theater, a Western perhaps, and a couple of serials, cartoons, and all that, why, they'd all three go and enjoy the show together. Except that his father and the lady never paid much attention to the screen. They were always kissing and doing things with their hands while he and the other kids were supposed to be watching the picture.

There was camp in the summer when he grew older. It was a good camp, an expensive camp. It had all the facilities: horseback riding, swimming, lifesaving, even such he-man sports as boxing. Cleve was big for his age, but he never did like it when the manly art of self-defense appeared on the agenda. He didn't like pain and suffering—when applied to him. He could claim he didn't like inflicting it either, but the view was hardly objective. In the boxing ring one had, in order to inflict, also to suffer, and Cleve discovered early that the kind of pain one experienced from a punch in the nose was a greater discomfort than the pleasure afforded by a similar depredation upon another. If he could have punched his opponent without return, he might have found it his forte.

In his childhood and early teens the only times he spent at home (meaning the male-oriented, female-slanted apartment of his father) were those hideously long Christmas and Easter holidays when the schools closed down and father and son had to change their life-styles accordingly and pretend it was what they were waiting for.

Through it all, interestingly enough, there was a bond between

89

father and son, even if it went no deeper than a realization that vacations were a sham, that each was putting up a pretense for the other and that, if, somehow, all the persiflage, the enforced togetherness, the constant presence of Carlisle's latest female could be removed, and if father and son could really come to know each other, a real affection might result. Certainly, they were both enough alike. They couldn't know it and they couldn't have explained it. There was thirty years between them and the one connecting link was unknown to the younger and but dimly remembered now by the older.

Their life-styles were not at all similar—even when ages was not a factor. Cleveland Parrish, at thirty, in no way resembled Carlisle at the same age. They were totally different human beings. And yet they were father and son. And there was more that they shared in common than that they knew apart.

Cleve's remembrance of vacations necessarily revolved around the different women who happened to be sharing the master bedroom when he came home. In time Carlisle stopped pretending they were new mothers for his only son, but he made no attempt to evacuate the female population for the duration of the Christmas or Easter recess. Carlisle's rationale was that Christmas and Easter were the happiest, most joyful times of the Christian calendar and to climb into an uninhabited bed was more closely akin to Hell. Certainly, to Carlisle's thinking, no man should be without a woman in times of joy. For, without them, where could joy be?

And Cleveland learned early not to ask who these women were or why the one who was there the last vacation wasn't there any more. Cleve had a father and there was no mistaking the ebullient, self-centered, self-assured, dominant, vividly living male for anything else. If God the Father walked the earth, there could be no question but that Carlisle Parrish was God the Father.

What was more nebulous was the kaleidoscope of women who passed through his father's life. Most of them, by adulthood, had totally left Cleve's memory or had had their images so overlaid by other, nearly identical images as to form a montage—of brunettes that answered to a harem of names, of blondes who combed long tresses with a variety of initialed brushes.

Almost none of the crop came across to him as individuals. There was one wan blonde, Cleve remembered. It was when he was twelve and, except for the straight sad way she wore her hair, she bore a remarkable resemblance to pictures Cleve had seen of his mother. She was slender also. She was nearly as frail. One might wonder about this girl too—whether she should bear a child.

There was a haunted look about her—as if she saw horrors that others were spared. He was at an age when he was more alert to nuances. At least he was more alert to her. She was not just like all the other blondes. She was special. She sensed the Cleve that lay inside. She knew about him what he did not know about himself. They even talked. Or he talked, while she listened. It was the only time in his life and the only person in his life to whom he did talk. Not that there was much he had to say. Only his stumbling incoherence about the world. He had no hates. He had no angers. He had no fears. At least there was none of this in him that he was aware of. Even baring his soul that one and only time he could point no fingers. He had no hidden problems, no secret torments. He had no soul to bare.

But she had understood. Whatever he was, she seemed to grasp it, and for her he had a special remembrance. He even started to write to her and she wrote back. But she was not the kind of woman his father generally attached himself to. She was a very forlorn person. She used to weep. And in front of Cleve, though she would never say why.

And she was sick. She was around for a longer time than most of the others. But the last time he was home she kept throwing up. She said it was indigestion and his father said it was nothing, but Cleve didn't hear from her that time after he returned to school and when he went home, she wasn't there any more and his dad had a new friend. Cleve didn't ask what happened to her, for he knew his father would only give him an answer he thought suitable (not to be confused with the truth). But he did get a letter from her once, a long time thereafter. It was very wan and very pathetic and very incoherent, and the address of a mental institution was on the envelope. Cleve never answered and she never wrote again.

Then, when Cleve was fourteen, when there was a war on in Europe but not in the United States, when America had finally turned the corner and depression and unemployment were becoming words of the past, when money was growing more plentiful and Europe's agony was pumping blood into America's economy, Carlisle Parrish dropped dead.

Though he died in bed, which is an admirable ambition, it was not his own bed, which made it something else again. It wasn't even the bed of one of his multitude of lady friends, but the bed of a common two-dollar whore who had never seen him before and who found it the shock of her life to have her charms prove so lethal.

She was a nimble-witted girl, however, and not so unnerved that she didn't empty his pockets and hire some help in removing him to an alley behind the building. When his body, clad in shirt and tie on top, shoes and socks on the bottom, and absolutely nothing in between, was discovered no more than half an hour thereafter, the site of his death was quickly determined. When, however, autopsy diagnosed the cause of death as cardiac arrest, there was nothing to do but bury the man and forget it.

So he was buried, attended—since his will did not include any of his girl friends and since his son had not yet been informed—only by his lawyer, who was the executor of his estate.

Since the circumstances which had found Carlisle rich while others were poor had been more the result of lucky strikes than good business, what was left of his fortune after taxes, lawyers' fees, burial expenses, debts, loans, liens, and a couple of lawsuits, was scarcely enough to keep a fourteen-year-old boy alive, let alone in school.

So Cleveland Parrish had to go to work for his education. He moved from the swank Gold Coast dormitory to a back room off the kitchen, He waited on table for his board, did janitorial service for his lodgings, sneaked out at night to set up pins in the local bowling alley till midnight, then cracked the books behind drawn shades till dawn.

It would have broken the back of a lesser youth but Cleveland Parrish, a C student at best, a known but unproven whorer, a plague to the administration, faculty, and school plant, turned suddenly sober, raised his marks to A, and graduated at seventeen, summa cum laude and top in his class.

He entered college in the middle of the war, too young to be drafted and too disinclined to volunteer. Soldiering was like boxing. One could experience physical suffering and this was something he would never willingly risk.

Although he became draft eligible while the war was still on, it was near enough its conclusion and his number was high enough so that the threat was no problem. He went through college with the same drive and energy he had lately exhibited in prep school and graduated with the same summa cum laude. Then it was law school and the same drive, and the law and the same drive. Cleveland Parrish never stopped. Or at least he never stopped if he could help it. To interviewers who were fascinated by his energy and apparent disregard of sleep, he had a ready explanation. "There is so much to do," he would say, "and so little time." It was a gallant explanation, full of nobility, conscience and a sense of responsibility. It was a diagnosis he was pleased to believe himself.

CHAPTER 21

So Cleveland Parrish came back to New Haven Thanksgiving morning to meet with Balin, consult with Jerry, and visit the scene of the crime. By now his requests had been carried out. Balin had, through yeoman effort, got Whittaker's papers in order, the moneys, the deeds, the transfers of ownership. There was a check for the sums in Whittaker's checking and savings accounts, there was his life insurance policy, the keys to his house, his two cars and his boat. Included also was a three-page résumé in Whittaker's handwriting of his courtship of Sally. In Balin's handwriting was the notation: "Harry Zogbaum, Dec. 1–Apr. 11; Willoughby Simms, Apr. 12–June 13." These were the judges who would follow McConnaughy in criminal court.

Parrish, sitting at Balin's desk, went over each paper carefully, was finally satisfied, and locked everything away in his brief case. He stood up to shake hands. "All right, Ed, we're in this together. Remember, I'm depending on you to give me the local scene, the local rules of the game. You're my right arm in this."

Balin swelled a little. "Yes, sir—ah—Cleve. Any orders?"

Parrish had several orders. Plea date was December second. He wanted to meet with the state's attorney before then, Monday the thirtieth, if possible. He wanted Balin to file a motion for disclosure and production right away. He wanted Balin to plead Whittaker not guilty on the second. Lastly, he wanted Balin to rack his brains for irregularities they could capitalize on. "You were there when the detectives arrived," he said. "Did they do anything illegal? Did they touch anything they shouldn't have? What about Jerry's arrest? Did they have a warrant? Do we have anything we can file a motion on to the effect that he's being illegally held, illegally charged, or was illegally arrested?"

"I don't know—I watched very closely, Cleve, and I think—"

"Don't think. If there's *anything* to hang a hat on, file a motion. Never mind if the judge denies it. Until he does, you can never be sure."

Balin made notes. He had to carry out so many orders. Law the way Parrish practiced it was new and strange to him. "Anything else?"

"Take care of our client. Talk to him. Cheer him up. Don't let him play the forgotten man. Jails stink and that one he's in stinks more than most. Who built it, Noah?"

They parted with warm assurances and Cleve got into the Cadillac. "Let's get some lunch and see Whittaker," he told Pete Tucker. "I'd rather be in jail than with that fathead, Balin."

Parrish and Whittaker met in the wire cage at half past two, after the prisoners had had their version of America's feast of thanks. The doctor was dull and lethargic and even the cigarette Parrish gave him didn't help. Parrish laid the paperback contract on the table along with a pen. "You've signed a lot of documents, Jerry. I've been looking them over. This is the last one."

Whittaker read the opening lines. "Oh yes," he said. "The pornographic story of Jerry and Sally."

Parrish shrugged. "You can write it yourself, you know. You can tell it any way you want, and put an extra thousand dollars in the kitty at the same time."

"You know I can't write." He picked up the pen, found the proper line, and signed the document. "Here." He chucked it across the small table.

Parrish didn't pick it up. He sat back and regarded the doctor. "Do you really want my help, Jerry?"

Whittaker's mouth tightened but he remained slumped and downcast. "I need somebody's help."

"I didn't ask if you needed *somebody's* help. I asked if you wanted *my* help. Do you want the services of one Cleveland Llewellyn Parrish?"

Whittaker said wryly, "I thought that was understood. I wouldn't have signed over everything I've got, plus that contract there for a book that's going to make Sally and me sound like a couple of sex maniacs. Which we weren't, I can tell you."

Parrish pushed the contract toward the doctor. "You can have it all back, the contract and everything else, if you don't think you're getting your money's worth."

"No, no." Whittaker shook his head. "I'm satisfied. I've got no complaints."

Parrish's voice sharpened. "Then if you haven't, sit up and act like a man. What do you think—that all you have to do is pay me money and lie down and wait for the doors of your cell to open? You may want me, but if you won't stand up and fight, I don't want you." He gave the contract another shove. "Make up your mind."

Whittaker showed emotion for the first time. He pitched the contract back. "That's not the way I want it. What do you think I am, a damned fool?"

Parrish warmed him with a smile. "That's more like it. Keep the fires burning. Nothing is as important as confidence. Confidence in yourself and confidence in me." He pocketed the papers and exuded a brisk, businesslike air. The time had come to get to the heart of things.

The lawyer started off with a ritualistic pitch. There was, he said, one requirement he made of every client. That was that the client be absolutely honest with him. "What my clients tell me must be the truth. I don't care what that truth is, so long as it's truth!" He fixed Whittaker with the standard hard-glowing eye. "Do you understand me?"

Whittaker responded as all clients did, with a sober and properly impressed nod.

"This is essential," Parrish continued. "I have enough problems defending my clients without building my fortresses on sand. If my own client betrays me, I cannot hope to battle successfully for his cause. Truth is what matters. Guilt or innocence is of no consequence." Parrish paused for a half beat, then said, "Except, perhaps, in your case."

It had the desired effect. Whittaker came instantly upright. "What does that mean?"

"From my position as your defense attorney, if I had my choice, I would prefer that you had killed your wife, rather than that you hadn't. I hope you understand no offense is intended."

Whittaker was wide-eyed. "What? You'd prefer—?"

Parrish was deliberately offhand. "I mean there are so many reasons why people commit murder. Very seldom is it for the cold-blooded, crass grounds that constitute premeditation with malice aforethought. There's accident, there's negligence, there's self-defense, defense of family and property. Those are some of the more overt causes. In addition there's temporary insanity, there are mental blackouts, there's the inability to tell right from wrong.

"You, Doctor, have been charged with first-degree murder. Now, really, the state doesn't have a prayer of convicting you on such a charge. Not if you really killed her. Of course, if you didn't, then it's another matter."

"Another matter?" Whittaker was almost out of his chair. "You mean I could get convicted of first-degree murder if I'm innocent, but not if I'm guilty?"

Parrish had his man properly set up and now he used a warning tone. "I only mean that juries are not God on High. They are bodies of twelve ordinary men who are motivated by, attracted to, and repelled by the very same things we are. I mean a jury would be sympathetic to a man who confessed that, indeed, he did kill his wife but he didn't mean to, and so forth and so forth. Particularly when we can show the jury the conditions that drove him to this regrettable act, conditions which the members of the jury—particularly the men—can understand and relate to. We can bring the jury to a realization of 'There, but for the grace of God, go I.' Under such circumstances, we can expect a most sympathetic verdict.

"But if the defendant pleads innocent, and the jury is persuaded that he is guilty, that jury will not be sympathetic. Because the jurors will view the defendant as, one, trying to put something over on them, which no man likes, and, two, trying to get away without making even a token payment for his crime. He wants the world, in other words, and is using the jury to try to get it. Jurors aren't going to take kindly to that kind of defendant."

Whittaker rubbed his chin for a long moment. "Are you saying an innocent man should plead guilty?"

"No, I'm saying that a guilty man should not plead innocent. Because he may not raise a reasonable doubt in the jury's mind. I'm saying it doesn't matter what you've told the police or the newspapers, whether it's fact or fiction. If you've lied to them, don't give it a thought. Just don't lie to me."

Parrish gave Whittaker another fraction of a pause, enough time for his words to sink in, but not enough time for Whittaker to get set. Then he said, as casually as if he were asking the time, "Did you kill your wife?"

CHAPTER 22

The question had an effect. Whittaker suffered a muscle spasm around one eye, a quiver and recoil. He blinked once and faced Parrish, his voice steady and even.

"No," he said. "I did not kill my wife."

Parrish smiled and said, "Good," but he didn't mean it. Plead "Guilty," the game was safe. "Innocent" was a plea Parrish could lose and he favored the sure thing. However, one had to play the cards that were dealt.

"I'm going to ask you to tell me what happened the day of the murder," Parrish said, lighting a cigarette. "I don't mean the night. Start with the day. Give me a picture. Talk, and if I stop you, stop." He gestured for the doctor to go ahead.

Whittaker lighted another cigarette himself. He puffed it jerkily and started slowly. There was this costume party thing at the Summer Club. It wasn't his dish, but Sally went for anything different and offbeat. She even designed and made her own costume—with the help of an expensive dressmaker.

The dance formed an excuse to get together with old friends Cindy and Bob Magnuson from Trumbull. Bob was a medical school classmate of Jerry's at Columbia and the foursome used to double-date when the girls were at Barnard. Sally had been Cindy's maid of honor.

It was arranged that the two couples would tailgate it at the Yale-Dartmouth game and go to the dance in the evening. Thus, when George and Henrietta Bakewell got up a pre-dance dinner party, the Whittakers' guests were included.

There were eight couples at the dinner: Bill and Nolene Shedd, Steve and Sandy Ferguson, Hank and Ruth Smith, Tim and Eunice Oliver, David and Alice Noyes, as well as the Bakewells, Whittakers and Magnusons, and Parrish duly recorded their names. The meal was a buffet with a busy bar beforehand and a steady stream of trick-or-treaters coming to the door.

The dance was from nine until one and the Bakewell contingent arrived at ten-thirty. Jerry danced once with Sally and spread himself around, trying to dance once with every woman in the group. Nor was Sally idle. She was constantly on the dance floor herself.

"Dancing with whom?" Parrish asked.

"I don't know."

"You weren't keeping tabs?"

"Of course not."

"If you can't name everyone who danced with her, name some."

"Damn it, I don't remember."

Parrish made note on his pad. "Think about it. The next time I see you I'm going to want to hear names."

Whittaker said, "All right," but it sounded like a sour, "Yes, sir."

"There was a contest, I believe. Your wife won a contest?"

The doctor nodded. Sally had received a bottle of champagne which they had immediately shared and which had added to the good spirits. Even Jerry got party-minded. "Usually these affairs bore me, but I was getting in the mood. Besides, we don't see the Magnusons often. So I invited everybody back to our place."

Parrish raised a hand. "Just a moment, Doctor—and I'm going to call you Doctor throughout this interview because that's what the state's attorney will call you. Your story is lacking in certain significant details. One that is germane here is that around this time Walter Costaine danced with your wife."

Whittaker passed it off. "So did a lot of other people. To me it's not worth mentioning."

"You cut in and took her away."

Whittaker's voice crackled suddenly. "Well, wouldn't you? If they were sleeping together there wasn't much I could do about it. But I'm goddamned if I'm going to have them dancing together. That's rubbing my nose in it."

"You took her away and she did what?"

"Came with me, of course. Back to the table."

"You were mad?"

"Naturally."

"What about her?"

"She thought the whole thing was funny."

"What did she say to Costaine when you broke in?"

"I don't know. I didn't pay attention."

"But the grand jury testimony has George Bakewell and Costaine both saying she said, 'See you later.'"

"Maybe she did. I couldn't have cared less. I didn't want her with him, that's all."

"And it was after that incident that you decided to invite the group back to the house to continue the party?"

Whittaker shrugged and said offhandedly, "I don't really know. I wasn't connecting the two events timewise."

Parrish smiled like a proud father. Gerald Whittaker would make a fine witness in his own behalf. He was poised, lucid, and sounded genuinely sincere. "Are you telling me," Parrish said, "that the idea for the party did not stem from the Costaine incident?"

"Of course not. I did it for the Magnusons. They were our guests."

He was slick. He had all the answers and he wasn't thrown off by the prosecution claims.

Parrish went after another of Jerry's oversights. "What about this fight you were having with Sally?"

"It was nothing. We were quarreling. All married couples quarrel."

"The grand jury took it more seriously than that."

Whittaker smiled dryly. "All right, so we weren't getting along. But if I was acting cold toward her, all I can say is, how would you act toward your wife if she was sleeping with some other guy?"

"Go on."

99

"We hadn't been having much to do with each other for some time. In the house we hardly spoke. Because when we did, we'd get into an argument."

"And you'd hit her?"

Whittaker responded angrily. "No! It was only that once. I called her a cheap whore. I shouldn't have, but I did. She slapped me, and I mean with everything she had. That got me mad and I slapped her back without thinking. Then she called me names and threw an ashtray and missed by a yard and that was it. That was the only time we ever came to blows. And Nellie had to be in the house somewhere!"

"The rest of the times she just called you 'impotent'?"

"That was only one of the things she called me. It was to cover her own guilt."

"How did you like what she was guilty of?"

"I didn't like it at all," Whittaker said angrily. "What the hell do you think?"

"But you didn't want to see her dead?"

"Hell, no." Whittaker relaxed with another cigarette and became philosophical. "I could even feel sorry for her, I suppose. She had to be alone a lot. I was working pretty hard. And she didn't have children to keep her busy. She didn't have hobbies and she didn't have friends. She always was a loner. Oh, she could be very charming in a social gathering. When she wanted to, she could make everybody's head turn. And back when she was single, believe me, that's what she wanted to do. She was a catch, I can tell you. I thought I was the luckiest guy in the world because I was the one who got her. You should have seen the swarm of guys I was competing against. But after marriage, well, I guess you'd say the need wasn't there any more. She had her man. When she was with people she would shine, but it turned out she was not an initiator. She didn't seek people. She waited to be sought. And you come to Madison and you can sit forever and wait to be sought.

"Most of our friendships developed through me—my practice, golf, the club. I'm more outgoing. Sally couldn't be bothered. She'd go sit on the beach somewhere. So I guess when some guy came along who had the time and inclination to attract her attention and give her something to get interested in, why, she was ready to go along with it."

Parrish smiled. "That's a nice, generous attitude. But the fact remains—"

"That I didn't like it, and I didn't like him. I'm frank to admit it."

The doctor leaned forward earnestly. "But if I was going to kill her, why wouldn't I have done it when I first found out?" He sat back again. "What the hell, it doesn't make sense."

Parrish smiled some more. "You'll do, Doctor. And I couldn't agree with you more."

"So why do they charge me? It's ridiculous."

"It may be, but you'll have to start looking at the matter from the prosecution standpoint. Masters may be an ambitious SOB but he made out a case against you that persuaded a grand jury. I think you'd better keep that in mind."

CHAPTER 23

They went on with the story and Jerry's voice was low as he described the events at the house following the dance. Three couples had returned with them and sipped highballs for an hour in the "wreck room": the Magnusons, the Shedds and the Bakewells.

Parrish dwelt on this part, questioning him exhaustively as to what was said, who sat where, what lights were on, what doors were locked, and who drank what. On one point Whittaker's memory was sure. The front door was unlocked throughout because he hadn't bothered to reset the catch. For the rest, he was appropriately vague, a normally unobservant man with enough to drink and a lack of interest in such details. All he could say with real assurance was that conversation was light and bantering, the atmosphere warm and friendly.

Parrish probed and poked in all the nooks and crannies of Whittaker's mind and the lack of detail left him dissatisfied. He told Whittaker to relive the party period in his waking hours and record whatever else might come to mind.

Continuing, Whittaker said the party broke up at half past two and the Bakewells were the last to leave. Sally and Henrietta got chatting in the doorway about fabrics and a shop in Cheshire where one could get discounts.

Parrish made him tell that part again and inwardly he smiled. Sally didn't sound like a girl eager to join her lover.

Whittaker chain-lit another cigarette and his hands were as steady as his eyes as he went on from there. While the girls were talking, he went up to bed. No, he hadn't cleaned up; he was too tired. No, he hadn't locked up; he'd left that for Sally. No, he couldn't be sure she had locked up.

"How long did Sally and Mrs. Bakewell talk?"

"Three or four minutes, I guess. Until George honked."

"Then what?"

"I heard the door close. I was getting into my pajamas. I heard the car start off when I was getting into bed. I left the light on for Sally and went to sleep."

"She didn't come upstairs?"

"Not before I dropped off."

"Did you wonder why?"

"I assumed she was cleaning up."

He went on and his words came faster. He slept. Then, slowly, he was aroused by the sound of frantic screaming. He thought it came from outside the house, far away, then woke enough to realize the light was still on, Sally's bed hadn't been touched, and the screams were from the living room below. That was when he knew the cries were from Sally.

He stumbled out of bed and into the hall. The only light came from the bedroom upstairs and the living room downstairs. The screaming had stopped and all he could hear was a thudding sound. He called Sally's name and the thudding stopped. He was just starting down the stairs when a man suddenly rushed to the front door, pulled it open and dashed out, slamming it behind him. Whittaker shouted at him, but the man looked neither left nor right as he fled.

Whittaker's story was so elemental, so basically simple, that despite the intensity of Parrish's questioning, it varied in no significant detail from the version Parrish had got from Balin. Thus far it was the same story Whittaker had told the police.

Parrish asked how the man was dressed.

"Slacks and a jacket," Whittaker answered without hesitation.

"They weren't matching. The jacket was lighter than the pants. And he was wearing a scarf wrapped around his ears."

Parrish asked about his hair and Whittaker said it was dark. The lawyer nodded. The picture still hadn't varied in any detail. "At no time did you see the man's face?"

"No."

"You can't be sure, then, that you know him?"

"Know him? I never saw—"

Parrish jumped in hard. "Answer the question! Just answer the question!"

Whittaker stopped and blinked. Color came to his face. "What do you think I'm trying to do?" he said testily.

"You were going to volunteer information that I haven't asked for."

"What of it? Don't you want everything I know? You've been pumping me hard enough!"

Parrish softened his attitude. The doctor didn't know and it was necessary for him to understand. "One day you are going to go on the witness stand and that is going to be the most important day of your life. You've got to be good and you've got to learn how to be good. And the first lesson you must learn is, do not volunteer any information that hasn't been asked for."

Whittaker protested. "But all I was going to say—"

"It's not all, it's nothing," Parrish interrupted. "Listen and understand! If the lawyer for your side is interrogating you, he's after certain bits of information and only those bits. He's after information that will help your side. He does not want information that won't help your side. He knows what you know and he knows what he's after. You don't. Anything you volunteer, therefore, can only be information he does not think will help your side. It might, instead, help the other side.

"When you're being interrogated by the opposition lawyer, he doesn't know what you know and he's trying to find out—in order to hurt you. Therefore, you do not want to tell him any more than you absolutely have to. Anything else won't help you and can do you real harm. Do you understand that?"

The doctor nodded. He said in a quieter voice, "But I'm not on the witness stand now."

"Pretend you are. From now on, regard yourself as living on the witness stand. Drill yourself. Act that way with everyone you talk to. Now, I asked you a question. I asked if you can be sure you know this man. Answer just that question."

Whittaker obeyed. "No, I can't be sure I know him," he said.

"But you do know people with dark hair?"

"Of course. Many of them."

"A simple 'yes' is sufficient. This man, you say, had a scarf up around his ears. Therefore you didn't get a look at more than the top part of his head, is that right?"

"That's right."

"How many people do you think you could identify—friends of yours—if they only showed you the top of their head?"

Whittaker reflected and shook his head. "I couldn't guess. I don't think very many."

"As a result, you have no idea in the world who it was?"

"That's right."

"He could be black or white, stranger or friend?"

"That's right, he could."

Parrish sat back a little and relaxed. He had undone the "unknown stranger" story Whittaker had given the police. A "stranger" left only a stray burglar, rapist or lunatic as an alternate murderer to Jerry himself, and that wouldn't wash. If Parrish were going to introduce reasonable doubt, he had to get Whittaker and the jury looking for more likely candidates.

In his relaxed manner, Parrish continued. "What did you do—what was your first reaction—when you found out Sally had a late date with Walter Costaine?"

Whittaker shook his head. "I don't know what you're talking about. I never knew she had any such plans."

It was a trap question and he hadn't been trapped. Parrish passed it off. "That's right, I forgot. But when you found her, she wasn't in the costume she'd worn to the dance?"

"That's right. She'd changed into a dress."

"What did you make of that?"

"I didn't think about it. What the hell, her head had been crushed. Who's going to worry about what she's got on?"

"All right, go on with it."

Whittaker finished the story. He ran down to the door and looked out, but the fleeing figure was nowhere to be seen. He closed the door and went to the living room, where he found Sally, smashed and dead on the floor. He hurried to her, turned her over and even tried to revive her before the fact she was dead seeped through. He laid her back as she was, rose, wiped his bloody hands on his already stained pajamas, went to the phone and called the one lawyer he knew, Edward Balin. Balin told him to call the police and came himself.

Parrish made a note. Those pajamas would make or break his story. If any of the blood on them was in spatters, he was lying. But if the spatters were there, surely Masters would have presented the fact to the grand jury!

"All right," he said, "we'll leave the subject of your wife's death for the time being and turn to something else. Tell me how you found out she was cheating on you."

Whittaker was silent for a moment and his face wore an unpleasant memory. When he spoke, it was bitterly and rapidly, as if swallowing a bad taste. Barbara Costaine had told him about it, he said. She phoned him at the office with the demand that he keep his wife away from her husband. In response to his shock, she said the pair were in the East River Motel at that moment.

Whittaker, incredulous, joined her there and was stunned to find Sally's car adjacent to Costaine's. When the couple emerged from their room, he was so livid he charged at Costaine but suffered the added indignity of stumbling into a punch and falling against another car. Before he was able to recover, Barbara was restraining him while Sally and Costaine fled.

The doctor began an alibi of his mishap, trying to get around the fact that Costaine had not only seduced his wife, he had knocked the irate husband down. Parrish, however, was not interested in fisticuffs. He wanted to know what happened between Jerry and Sally when he got home.

"We fought," was the way the doctor expressed it. "After the incident at the motel, I returned to my patients, and when I finally got home, she was upstairs in the bedroom in lounging pajamas watching television. It was half past six and there was no supper started, no nothing. So I come in and she gets off the bed and lights into me about what a lousy cheap trick it was for me to spy on her and how I degraded myself and if I wanted her followed, why didn't I hire a detective? I told her if she ever saw him again, I'd make it public and she said, 'Go ahead, it'll only show up your own impotence.'"

"Had you been having much sex?"

Whittaker looked away and shook his head. "Well, hell," he added defensively, "I'm not a young man any more. I don't have that much interest. And I am tired. People who lead active lives, who have many other interests and many other responsibilities, they just don't have the time for sex, or the inclination." He shrugged. "That was the trouble with us, I suppose. I didn't have the time and she did. I was too busy to think about it and she had nothing else to think about. I don't mean she was all that interested herself. I know in the early years she was the one who was begging off or saying, 'Not tonight,' or, 'I'm too tired.'"

Parrish watched the doctor's compulsive smoking. Whittaker was lighting still another cigarette. The lawyer said, "What other affairs did your wife have?"

The doctor started. "Other affairs?" The idea had never occurred to him.

"She had them, of course."

He blinked. "What are you saying?"

"I'm saying the man in your house who beat her to death with a poker was not a burglar."

"He wasn't?"

Whittaker sounded too naïve and Parrish's voice got snappy. "For Christ's sake, Doctor, don't you know why you got indicted? Listen to your story. You woke, heard your wife screaming, and rushed to her aid just in time to see an unidentifiable stranger flee the scene. Understand the grand jury's position. If a man beat his wife to death with a poker and wanted to pretend he hadn't done it, what kind of a story would he tell? He'd say he heard her screaming, ran to the rescue, and saw an unidentifiable stranger flee the scene. In short, Doctor, what happened to you unfortunately coincides exactly with the kind of story a murderer would make up. Can you blame the grand jury for not believing you?"

Parrish gestured contemptuously. "In fact, Doctor, if I took that story at face value I wouldn't believe it either. Don't be inane. Do you really think either I or a grand jury—or a jury of your peers— can be made to believe that a murdering rapist or burglar happened by at four o'clock in the morning and found your wife waiting up for him wearing nothing but a minidress?"

106

Whittaker slowly slumped in his seat and dropped his latest cigarette into the growing pile in the tin tray. "You mean I'm sunk?" he said.

"Did I say you were sunk?" Parrish hitched his chair closer.

"That's what it sounds like."

Parrish was still snappy. "You're not listening. What I'm saying is the state's built a pretty solid-sounding case against you. You're not going to knock it over with a bed slat. We don't win just by saying there's a doubt. We don't win by pointing out it's barely possible you didn't kill her. We win by showing that it's reasonably possible that you didn't kill her."

Parrish grew dismissive. "Now, the doubt doesn't have to be as strong as the probability. The jury doesn't judge that the odds favor you being the killer sixty per cent to someone else being the killer forty per cent and then find you guilty. If there's any kind of reasonable argument pointing toward someone else, the jury has to let you go."

He became stern again. "But a chance murderer dropping in? You won't get away with that one. Not when such a story would be the first refuge of a guilty man, not when it hasn't happened here before. Do you get what I'm talking about?"

Whittaker nodded unhappily. "It's a bad story and I'm stuck with it."

"It's a bad story, but that doesn't mean you have to be stuck with it."

"Why not? He didn't rape Sally, so it couldn't be a rapist. Nothing was stolen, so he couldn't be a burglar. And she wasn't even supposed to be in the house. She should have been in Costaine's motel room."

Parrish was impatient. "You're not thinking straight. It's only Costaine's say-so that she was supposed to be with him at the time she was killed. Not that he might not be sincere. She might actually have agreed to meet him. But it's very obvious that she did not go to his motel. It's also very obvious that she changed her clothes —after you were asleep. Later on, someone came to see her and they had a fight and he killed her." Parrish jabbed a finger at Whittaker. "Do you understand, Jerry? It was not a mysterious stranger who killed your wife. It was someone she knew!"

Whittaker's own brain was going now. "Hey, wait a minute. Costaine! He's waiting for her and she doesn't come, so he drives to the house to see why. She's changed her mind. She's decided to give him the gate—"

"Forget it."

"No, wait. Costaine's hair is pretty dark. And in the dark hall—Now that I think of it—"

"Forget it, I said."

Whittaker stopped. "Why?"

"We don't know what Costaine was doing. We don't know who he was with." Parrish shook his head in rebuke. "I want you to give this matter thought, Jerry, but don't let your imagination run wild. Don't try tailoring this mysterious figure to fit whomever you'd like to get in trouble."

Whittaker flushed. "I didn't say I recognized him. I just said he had the same color hair as the man I saw."

"So do seven men out of ten." The lawyer rose. "All I want you to do over the next few weeks is think about it. Get used to the idea that Costaine wasn't Sally's only lover. See if you have any ideas on who the others might be."

Whittaker came to his feet and promised faithfully. He shook hands and it was hard for him not to cling, not to sit up and beg. He was the helpless puppy and Parrish was his master, his sunshine, his world. "What are you going to do now?" he asked.

Parrish freed himself. "Right now I'm going to take a look at your house."

CHAPTER 24

The house bore an oppressive smell that was more than mustiness. If death had a smell, that was the odor that hit Cleve Parrish when he fitted Whittaker's key in the front door lock and entered the hall. He stood for a moment, adjusting himself, then tried the light switches. The great chandelier blazed into incandescence, chasing the gloom of the gathering November darkness.

He examined the lock on the door. A push of the button on the inside knob and the outside knob wouldn't turn without a key. A twist of the inside knob or the use of the key popped the button out again and the door was unlocked.

Parrish lifted the hall telephone and got a dial tone. The house had been unoccupied for nearly a month but everything still functioned: water, power, phone.

He went into the living room slowly, carefully. He approached the large bloodstain on the apricot rug. That would never come out. The rug would have to be cut up for smaller rooms. There might be a market for the leftover square containing the stain. There were museums. There were aficionados who might want to say, "See, under this glass, that blood belonged to Sally Whittaker." It would depend, of course, upon how notorious the case became.

He went around the death room then, like a cat exploring a new environment. He noted the brownish spatters, the damaged lamp, the disturbed furniture, the fingerprint powder stains. Nothing had been touched since the police had left. The evidences of the violent struggle were as they had been, depicting for the trained eye the sequence of her attempts at escape. The hideousness of the crime had been pent up in the room so long it cried out to be told.

Parrish could almost see the desperate girl's frantic dodgings and turnings. He could all but hear her screams.

But he studied the scene with two sets of eyes. One assessed the crime and the other assessed the quality of the furnishings. And the quality of the articles in this room was very grand indeed. They were far dearer than Whittaker's purse could afford. This was Sally's room, her showcase. Her own money, or her family's money, had produced its substance. Her taste had chosen the pieces and put them together. That bronze sculpture, those large paintings. They were good. The artists were unfamiliar but they would become known. Sally had chosen wisely and these works would increase in value.

Cleve left the living room, shutting off the lights, and went to the opposite side of the house through a short hallway beyond the stairs. That brought him to the "wreck room," the entertainment room, the place to which the couple's friends would repair after they had passed the show room.

Strange that Sally should have died in the room she didn't use, the room where nothing had grown worn, where the heavy glass of the coffee table glistened with polish under its collection of dust.

The wreck room had been tidied and, from its pool table in the corner through the booths and tables, chairs and built-in bar, it had no stories to tell. Fingerprint powder lay on much of the wood surfaces but little had been learned from it and nothing from anything else.

He went back past the downstairs bath and into the kitchen. Jerry Whittaker had sat at the breakfast table when the detectives questioned him. Balin had been there, making him coffee, warning him against answering questions, trying to advise a friend who hadn't asked him to come and hadn't asked his advice. "Sally's dead," Whittaker kept saying. "I've got to answer questions." Ultimately Balin had offered to make the necessary phone calls and managed his escape.

Parrish opened the dishwasher. The glasses used by the post-dance guests were still there, cold, clean, sterile and lifeless. He unlocked the sliding glass doors in the breakfast nook and stepped onto the darkening patio. He could see the back lawn out there, forty feet of it, and the taller grass of the slope beyond that dipped gently down to the marsh. To the left was the nearest house, a hundred feet away, behind a thin screening of trees. Between that house and the marsh lay thicker woods, through which the lights of Neck Road could be seen a quarter of a mile distant. On the other side, the nearest neighbor was farther off and the screening trees were denser.

Parrish spent five minutes on the patio, pacing its length, studying the surroundings, getting the lay of the land. Then he relocked the doors, looked through the dining room and opened the drawers in the buffet. He examined the hallmark of the china and counted the silver. Whittaker had underestimated his own worth. There was much more value here than he had realized. Parrish wasn't surprised. This was Sally's bailiwick; Jerry's joy was his medical machines.

Parrish would have it all assessed, of course. He had a dealer in New York whose major source of revenue was appraising the endless array of goodies Cleveland Parrish picked up in lieu of cash. Parrish had another man whose sole job was managing what Parrish called his "collection"; the real estate, the property, the *objets d'art*, the jewelry, and the rest. His business was to unload each item at the moment of maximum profit. When he took on the Whittaker house, for example, he wouldn't hold a local auction to sell off the contents. He would try the New York markets first. He would contact dealers, he would exploit the fact of the crime and gain what mileage that would allow. Only at the end, to get rid of the leftovers, would he probe the Madison market.

Parrish moved through the upstairs rooms, opening drawers, poking, probing, acquainting himself with his new estate. The clothes were something. Sally had a huge wardrobe. He found her prizewinning Hallowe'en costume on a hanger in the dressing room closets. He took it out and held it up, but it was a dead, careless nothing with no Sally to give it life. He looked through the rest of her things and knew most were too rich for Whittaker's wallet.

The bathroom produced more of the smell and taste and essence of the dead woman: the bath oils, the soaps, the powders, the deep thick towels. All was as she had last left them. In the bedroom, on her vanity, were her creams, ointments, and perfumes, the hair tints, combs, brushes, curlers. The room below, tinged with the odor of its bloodstained carpet, had the feel of the dead Sally. It's pictures, its furnishings were her memorial. But here in the upper bedroom Parrish could feel a living Sally. He could almost expect to turn and find her saying, "What are you doing with my things?"

Parrish tested the bed table lamp, the one Jerry said he had left burning. It worked. He emptied the laundry hamper into a pile on the bathroom floor. He wasn't looking for a pair of blood-spattered pajamas, for if such a pair existed, the police had it by now. Instead, he examined the container and the other items of clothing for blood that might have rubbed off.

There was nothing.

On a closet shelf was a photograph album. There were honeymoon pictures, a score or more; beach pictures of Sally in a bikini; tennis pictures of Sally in shorts; close-ups of tossed blonde hair and a saucy young face. There were even two semi-nude shots of a sleeping Sally, eyes closed, breasts exposed. The young bridegroom had wanted to freeze her as she was forever.

There were pictures of Jerry, and a few of them together, but most were of Sally and showed her at her alluring best. It was how young Jerry saw her and it was how he photographed her.

The post-honeymoon pictures were fewer and less personal. There were group pictures; there were shots of the house, their first and last home; a picture of Jerry's first office with the sign outside. There were a few snaps of Sally being "domestic," of Jerry mowing grass, of their first boat.

The album ended less than two years after their marriage and later events were recorded in a stack of loose pictures in an accompanying box. Parrish sorted through those but none meant anything and none had been taken in the last two years. The whole story of the deterioration of a marriage could be told from the pictures on that closet shelf. It could even be told by their hiding place.

Parrish put the box back and tucked the album under his arm. That was a little gold mine. Jake Settler, editor of the paperback house Whittaker had signed with, would give the fillings in his teeth for a chance to include those nude and bikini-clad pictures of Sally in the book. And Parrish would demand every last filling.

CHAPTER 25

Parrish's involvement in the Whittaker murder case was made public by him on Friday, November 27, in his Empire State Building office. Not for Parrish were press conferences on courthouse steps, or press releases distributed in conjunction with the likes of Edward Balin. When Cleveland Parrish had a story, he broke it in the proper manner; which meant inviting all the communications media to his spacious New York office, serving drinks and *hors d'oeuvres*, jollying up the boys with chitchat, letting them ask questions about everything except the statement he had prepared. Then, after the libations had been removed and the guests' attention gained, he would read his piece and Melody would distribute copies. Then the questions would come from all hands and he could dwell on them at length—"How is Dr. Whittaker going to plead, Mr. Parrish?"

"Not guilty, of course."

"He's persuaded you that he's innocent?"

"He IS innocent. Persuasion doesn't enter into it."

"Do you think you can get permission to try a case in Connecticut? Will an effort be made to keep you out?"

"I was given permission the day before yesterday."

"Have you talked with the DA or whatever they call them in Connecticut?"

"Edward Balin, Whittaker's attorney of record, phoned me less than an hour ago. We're meeting with the state's attorney Monday at nine o'clock."

"You think he'll drop the charges, knowing what he's up against?"

"I hope he'll drop them no matter who's defending Jerry. It's not right for an innocent man to stay in jail."

There was a half hour of questions and the reporters went away happy. Cleveland Parrish was superior copy and he served superior liquor. And when he called a press conference in his seventy-fifth-floor office in the Empire State Building, you could guess it was going to be something big.

So he was going to defend Jerry Whittaker? How come we didn't get a tip on that earlier? He said he was in New Haven on Monday? And Wednesday, and Thursday? What the hell do they do in New Haven? That should have been picked up. Did anybody else know about it? Apparently not. There hasn't been a word in any paper. Well, trust Parrish. The news isn't going to get out until he wants it out.

Anyway, that prosecutor—what did Parrish say his name was—Masters? He's got his work cut out for him. When that Costaine guy, who was having the affair with the wife, gets on the stand, Parrish will slice and dice him into mouse dung.

Hey, do you suppose *he* could be the murderer? You know, he's waiting for the dame and she doesn't show, so he gets sore and drives over to see what's up? And she answers the door and tells him she's through with him; he doesn't use the right underarm deodorant or something? And he blows his cool and bashes her? You think that's what Parrish is keeping up his sleeve? Well, it's too early to tell, but that's a trial I'd like to get sent up to New Haven to cover!

After the press conference, Parrish had a meeting with a man named Herbert Lancer. Lancer was a short, seedy writer who was facile with words, dirty of mind, and short of ideas. To him was given the task of converting Jerry Whittaker's three-page résumé into a salacious, full-length Jerry and Sally novel. The choice was a good one because Lancer, for all his faults, was even in quality, fast and dependable. If Herb Lancer undertook to write a fifty-thousand-word novel in ten days, he would deliver it in ten days.

Lancer was followed by the lanky redhead, Dan Price, of the Webster-Smith Detective Agency. He gave Melody a kiss on the forehead and a pat on the fanny and wondered if she was as cool in bed as she was in the office. In the inner sanctum he was given a shot of rye and a chance to forget about Melody. Cleveland Parrish was putting him and the rest of the organization to work.

Price departed and Melody—who did not wonder what Dan

was like in bed—came in for dictation and the satisfaction of her curiosity. Parrish had sounded confident in his public appearances but she wanted it confirmed. "Do you think it's going to be hard getting him off, Cleve?"

Cleve shrugged. "Not if he's really innocent."

"You mean you have doubts?"

"My dear girl," Parrish said patiently, "I urged him to tell the truth. I threatened to abandon him if he ever lied. I even told him he'd be easier to defend if he were guilty. That does not necessarily mean, however, that when he still claims he's innocent, he must therefore be telling the truth."

"But, for heaven's sake, Cleve, under those circumstances, why on earth would he lie?"

Parrish tilted back his chair. "Because his wife was worth a quarter of a million dollars and the only way he can ever hope to touch that money is by being found innocent."

CHAPTER 26

At five o'clock on Saturday, Walter Costaine walked out of a Forty-second Street movie house into the cold, neon-lighted darkness of a November afternoon. He had been watching a triple feature, a trilogy of seventy-minute films featuring a lot of nudity and very little else. The voyeurism of nudie flicks wasn't really Walter's dish. He preferred his nudes in three-dimensional living color and he liked to be a participant. He was a doer rather than a spectator. However, his fortunes were at low ebb and his forms of entertainment limited, all of which rather restricted his choices. And Walter Costaine had to concede that a black and white, two-dimensional nude, performing out of reach, was still better than no nude at all.

It was the first day he had truly ventured forth from Morelle's flat and he was desperate. He had moved in to avoid the press, but almost instantly regretted it. Should he be recognized, all he would have accomplished would be to point the finger to his first wife. To be connected in the eyes of the world to his present wife, Barbara, was all right. And to his children. He could be proud of them all. To have his relationship with Sally bandied about was glorious. To have his reputation flaunted was an equally agreeable circumstance. Had not the term "Casanova" been applied to him sixteen times, by his own count, over the last weeks? He was revitalizing the sobriquet. Perhaps it would become permanently affixed to him and he known as the great lover's twentieth-century reincarnation.

But not his first wife, and not his first child. He did not want that dreary aspect of his past dredged up and publicized. That first round mistake would not enhance his image.

So he had hidden in the small apartment, wishing the time away and fighting the battle of the fidgets. Rita and Morelle were out during the day, Rita at her small job, Morelle trying to find one. Now that her gamble for a gigantic insurance settlement had evaporated, she had to find work. Rita had been the mainstay of the pair's support while the gamble was in progress, but not any more. Now she blamed her mother for the bungling that had erased their hopes. Now when they were together the air was blue with recrimination in the "Battle of the Bitches."

When it came Saturday and the pair of them were home all day as well as evening, it was unbearable and Walter fled. He camped in the darkness of a cheap theater and there began to unwind.

Originally, in the back of his mind had lain the thought that possibly, just possibly, Morelle might welcome him into her bed. It had happened before. Though their marriage had been a farce, there was no real bitterness between them. If there was no love lost, there was no hatred either and since Morelle had no other ties, when their paths did cross she had, upon occasion, allowed herself to be charmed into bed.

But there had been none of that this week. Morelle was in a haggish mood and turned as quickly on Walter as on her daughter. And Rita was even quicker. They were a pair of harridans and Walter couldn't even think of them as women.

Now, coming from the theater, he felt more like a male. Those girls on the screen, feeble actresses as they were, and of modest charm, were still feminine. They sought to appeal and, with Walter, they succeeded.

He looked around as he buttoned up his coat. There was a raw wind that cut. It teared his eyes and made him fumble for his gloves. Traffic inched and a bus spewed gray exhaust.

Walter turned his back to the wind and started to walk toward Fifth, appraising all the girls. That one there. She was a pross. She was slender and young and not bad looking—statuesque, in fact —but a little too eager. She couldn't wait to get inside somewhere. He could have a good time with her, but there was one hitch. She'd want twenty dollars. At least twenty. And she'd want to go to a room as well. She'd know some quick, nearby fleabag joint that wouldn't cost an arm, but it didn't matter. He couldn't afford the first twenty. Not with what Morelle took out of him for rent.

What he had to look for were the amateurs, maybe some of those young (but not underaged) disillusioned girls—ex-hippies, or would-be actresses—somebody who might settle for a reasonably priced meal, who might have a walk-up somewhere and the kind of room-mate who wouldn't be home or who didn't mind going out for a long walk.

Costaine strolled slowly, keeping a welcoming eye out. A squad car turned west from Fifth and its green lights made him think. If he kept patrolling a stretch of Forty-second Street, he'd be noticed by more than just willing girls. Shopkeepers would look out at him. That same squad car would come back.

Walter crossed to the public library side of the street. It was darker there, with fewer people. The wind felt colder but he was less likely to be noticed. He stopped at a newsstand and picked up a paper. The thing to do was go to a lunch counter and dawdle over a cup of coffee. Keep one eye on the paper and the other on what-ever else there was to see. Hopefully a woman. He could sure use a woman.

As he waited for change, his eye was caught by a front page picture which looked very much like—it was—Jerry Whittaker. He'd seen it often. It was the standard portrait photo all of the papers had been using. Next to it was an equally large photo of another man and above them both was the big headline, "WHITTAKER WELCOMES PARRISH."

Costaine, pocketing his change, anxiously turned to the inside pages and read. The announcement had been made yesterday morning. Cleveland Parrish was going to handle Jerry's defense. Cleveland Parrish! Walter Costaine knew that name. Anybody who read anything about anything knew that name!

And Parrish had announced it yesterday? It must have been in all the late papers, and the early Saturday *Times*. Now the evening editions had a follow-up story. Somebody had got (or made up) a quote from Jerry that he was "delighted."

Never mind Jerry. What mattered was Parrish and his investigative techniques. There it was in the article: that the Parrish method was to sic detectives on everybody. His style was to get to the bottom of everything.

Walter Costaine shuddered. Was he already under investigation? Were detectives trying to find out where he'd gone? He hadn't told anyone. He was keeping it a secret—let the police worry, let the papers ask questions if they wanted. He was on vacation. But now there would be detectives tracking him down. Maybe they were already at it. And if they should find out about Morelle—Oh, Christ, damn! He should have stayed in the East River Motel. He should get the hell back there as fast as he could.

He stuffed the folded paper in his pocket and headed for the subway.

CHAPTER 27

The courthouse in New Haven stood on the corner of Church and Elm streets facing the green. Its marble exterior was shaped like a Greek temple with long low steps rising to an entrance set behind great Doric columns supporting a pediment.

Inside the entrance hall, past the elevators, the building opened into what was known as "the corridor," a spacious well that looked up three floors to the glass roof above. To the left, under balconies, were courtrooms, to the right were the state's attorney's offices and judges' chambers. At the rear was the largest courtroom, floored in red tile, equipped with a marble bench and dark, heavy furnishings.

Cleveland Parrish arrived early for his meeting with Vincent Masters. He got out of the mauve Cadillac in front of the courthouse, walked up the broad steps, paused to study the flanking statues of seated thinkers, and turned for a view of his surroundings. The green was in two rectangles, with the memorial flagpole and the newly erected Christmas tree on the half in front of him. On the other half, facing the Temple Street divider, stood the well-known three churches. Around the green were shops and banks, New Haven's City Hall, the post office and, on the far Temple Street corner, the Plaza Hotel. On the right, beyond the churches, stood the Old Campus of Yale University.

Parrish surveyed the scene at length, getting the feel of the place. All courthouses were the same, but different. In common they all smelled of law and legalese. They all were hangouts for lawyers. The shoes that wore out their carpets, their tiles, their marble floors and granite steps were lawyers' shoes. Oh yes, there were others— the public, the clients, the defendants, the families and friends, the prisoners; but they left no real imprint. They were background. They were shadows against a screen. Courthouses belonged only to those with legal training. The sheriffs, clerks, bailiffs, the court recorders and the rest, they were the furniture, the trappings, the milieu. It was the judges and the lawyers who owned the citadel, who made it work, who made the rest necessary.

That was their sameness, and to the man in the street, that sameness would have painted all courts an identical color, would have made the decor of one undifferent from another. To a lawyer, however, every such scene has its own characteristics. Just as no two judges are alike, and a lawyer has to consider the nature of the man on the bench, so no two courthouses are alike, though they be in the same building.

Parrish was a connoisseur in this field and a first step in his defense was to get the taste and feel and smell of the trial town's atmosphere. His jury would come from there. That city would be their backdrop, their honing strop. If he could get the feel of the city, he could get the feel of the jury.

When he turned and entered the building, he looked as closely at the interior as he had studied the exterior. It wasn't his first visit but it was his first appraisal. Close by the elevators was a list of the judges presently serving the Superior Court, their names in gold on polished wood plaques. Judge William McConnaughy's name was still among them but it would be replaced next day and Judge Harry Zogbaum would preside over the criminal court. If Jerry Whittaker came to trial within the next four months, Zogbaum would be sitting on the bench.

But Jerry Whittaker would not come to trial in four months. Cleveland Parrish would make sure of that. Webster-Smith had already produced an in-depth analysis of Judge Zogbaum, and Judge Simms, who would follow him. Zogbaum was a stickler for the letter of the law. He was didactic. He ran a tight ship. He would ride close herd on Cleveland Parrish and Parrish liked to roam.

Judge Willoughby Simms was more like it. He was a former law professor, filled with the philosophy of the subject. He viewed law in its overall application to the condition of man. He saw it as the one integrating force that enabled men to live together in a society. Now that he was out of the groves of academe and into the world of reality, he was determined to spread his doctrine to the unanointed. His fatal flaw was that his sense of mission left him fearful of making a wrong move and betraying that mission. Simms, therefore, was the slowest, most reluctant decision-maker on the bench. He would be a soft touch for Parrish.

"Ah, here you are."

Parrish turned, and it was Edward Balin with one minute to go. Parrish wasn't surprised. He would have bet that Balin had loitered around the corner, timing it to enter Masters' office on the stroke of nine.

They crossed the corridor and Balin couldn't help remarking that he'd drafted an outline of his chapter. Parrish had to think to realize what he was talking about. Then he said, fine, excellent, and he hoped a contract would ultimately be signed so it wouldn't be for naught.

"I don't mind," Balin said. "It's good practice trying to write. The thing I notice, though, is that it's hard not to talk in legal terminology—I mean, to make myself talk in language the layman could understand. I've had to write an article or two," he confided, trying not to preen himself, "and it's hard not to make it sound like a brief."

Parrish muttered agreement and walked a little faster. No one in the world was a bigger bore than Balin.

A dark-haired receptionist welcomed them and rose to open the door to the state's attorney's private office. Parrish went through first, making Balin give way, and there, standing behind the facing desk, was his tall, quiet, youthful, dark-haired opponent, Vincent Masters.

"I'm Parrish," the lawyer said with a disarming grin and advanced to shake hands warmly. "I guess you know Ed Balin here."

From Masters there was polite New England reserve. "I know Mr. Balin," he allowed.

The greetings subsided, chairs were taken, the front one by Parrish, a side and deferential one by Balin.

Masters, behind the desk, sat back, pressing his fingertips together. So this was the great Cleveland Parrish, he thought. He's not as tall, not as strong, not as straight as I. And he doesn't look as honest. What will this mean in the contest? If endurance were a factor, I would win. Parrish has been living too well. But if he's soft in the stomach, he's not soft in the head. He didn't make his money and his reputation soft-soaping old ladies. He knows more tricks than I, and he'll be using them all.

Masters knew he would do well not to be deceived by the heartiness of the New York lawyer, his friendly "let's lay all our cards on the table" air. Cleveland Parrish was dynamite and the real trouble was you never knew where or when the explosion would come. Vincent Masters decided his ploy would be to play it cool, act easily led, readily agreeable, a little like a country boy who didn't know what city slickers were all about. That would be the best response to Parrish's palsy-walsy-all-the-while-stealing-the-gold-out-of-your-teeth approach.

Cleveland Parrish, meanwhile, was doing his own analysis. He noted Masters' appearance and the good image he presented. Careful, reserved, humorless. Sunday School, moralistic son of a bitch, no doubt. Too young for the job, too. He hasn't made his pile yet. That meant Masters was one of those dedicated bastards. He was going after Whittaker not because he thought he had a case, but because he truly believed the guy was guilty.

That was a bad piece of luck. Those dedicated SOBs didn't know the meaning of the word compromise. They wouldn't sacrifice one iota of righteousness to solve a problem. They were the ones who would be gung ho on Unconditional Surrender all the way. They were hell to do business with.

Conversation started with pleasantries but Masters moved it immediately to the matter at hand. He smelled danger in Parrish's comradely, leisurely, oblique approach, so he took the offensive. How did the defendant, Gerald Whittaker, intend to plead? Masters, knowing Balin was the lawyer of record, but that Parrish would run the show, carefully addressed the question to both men.

Balin didn't even pretend to be in charge. He turned and waited for the great man to speak.

Parrish smiled. Was Masters trying to steal a tempo? How gauche. He said laconically, but with eyes that were alert, "Let me first ask you a question, sir. Do you have, among your items of evidence, a pair of blood-spattered pajamas?"

Masters was the epitome of guileless innocence. "Do we have, in our possession, a pair of bloody pajamas?"

Parrish raised an admonishing finger. "I didn't say 'bloody' pajamas, sir. I didn't say the pajamas Dr. Whittaker was wearing when he knelt in his wife's blood, or when he wiped his smeared hands. I mean pajamas that are spattered with blood—the way the rug and furniture are spattered—the way everything within range was spattered when the killer beat poor Mrs. Whittaker to death."

Masters managed to keep his eyes steady. He parried. "Is it your contention, then, that Mrs. Whittaker's killer was wearing pajamas?"

Parrish pressed his advantage. "Stop stalling, sir. Do you have any clothing worn by the killer during the commission of the crime?"

"Are you waiting for my answer to decide how your client will plead?"

Parrish had guessed that the answer was no. Now he was growing certain. "Damn your answer," he said. "I only wonder at your arrogance in bringing charges against my client without evidence at least *that* substantial to go on. As for his plea, you've heard his story. Could you be in doubt as to his plea?"

Masters, acting less like the country hick, said dryly, "I thought perhaps he might have changed that story by now."

Parrish grinned wolfishly. "It's interesting how things go, isn't it? Now here we are, come to talk to you, fully expecting that you've been having second thoughts about *your* story." He sat back. "Come now, Masters, you don't have any case and you know it."

The state's attorney abandoned the guileless role as a bad job. Parrish was making him play it his way. He met the New York lawyer look for look. "We have a case against him, Mr. Parrish, that is going to put him behind bars for the rest of his life."

"Like what?"

"We are prepared to prove to the satisfaction of the jury that Sally Whittaker was having an affair with one Walter Costaine, that Jerry Whittaker knew about it, that he tried in vain to stop it, that his wife not only refused to stop, she taunted him with the fact. She drove him until he couldn't stand it any more. The final straw was when she dressed to go see her lover with Whittaker's full knowledge that that was her intention. He seized the nearest weapon, the fireplace poker, and ended her life."

Parrish knew now there was no blood-spattered clothing. The hard, sure evidence that would convict was missing. His laugh was almost gloating. "That's a good story," he said. "It ought to sell a lot of newspapers. But telling that story and making a jury believe it are two different things. What are you going to use for evidence, the fact that Sally's parents don't like Jerry?"

"We've got a little better evidence than that. Good enough to make it stick."

Parrish deliberately scoffed. "Yes, I've heard about your evidence. Jerry told me what you fed the grand jury. It might have teased the grand jury into wanting to look further, but it's going to be different when you try to eliminate reasonable doubt."

"We didn't present everything we've got to the grand jury, Mr. Parrish. There's a lot more."

"Such as?"

"A number of things." Masters refused to be drawn out, but he was well aware that Parrish knew the reason was he had no clincher.

Parrish wouldn't leave it. "You don't have to be secretive, Mr. Masters. Ed, here, has already filed a motion for disclosure and production."

Masters essayed coolness. "When it's granted we'll make all the evidence available to you. Then, perhaps, you might reconsider."

The state's attorney was trying his best to worry his adversary, but Parrish knew it was bluff. He gave his rich, resounding laugh. "It doesn't matter," he said. "The plea is 'not guilty,' no matter what you think you've got. So don't try to whip us with it. You're going to have to produce it in open court. You're going to have to show it to the world. And then we'll all see how good it looks."

Masters could only say he expected to do so, and conceded that this was a case which would obviously come to trial. He moved from that lost ground to the issue of when the trial should take place. How much time did Mr. Balin and Mr. Parrish think they needed to prepare their client's defense?

Parrish was casual. He didn't think it would take too long once they were in possession of *all* the prosecution evidence against the doctor that their motion would produce. "Once we have that information, I think we could be ready to proceed in about six months."

"Six months!" Masters sputtered. Parrish might as well have said ten years. Even Balin blinked.

"Yes," Parrish said, as if it were tomorrow. "I'd guess somewhere in June."

"What the hell do you—?" Masters controlled himself. He'd lost the first round. Did he want to lose the second? He relaxed and put on a smile. "What do you think it'll take you six months to do?"

Parrish didn't deign to use the excuse he was involved with other cases. Judges can sometimes compel a rearrangement of priorities and, besides, he wanted to rub Masters' nose in it. "Why, get the case ready," he said. "Complete our investigation, get our witnesses together, iron out technicalities. You know."

Masters switched his attention to Balin. "I don't see why that should take more than a couple of weeks. We ought to be able to start as soon as the Panther trial is over—around the beginning of February."

Balin mumbled something about that being rather soon and Masters said, "Whittaker's no friend of mine, God knows, but I certainly wouldn't want to see him cooped up in that jail there for six months while you put a defense together. Out of consideration for the defendant I would expect you to prepare your case with as little delay as possible."

Parrish thought: Masters wants Zogbaum to try the case, not Simms. He wants to keep my wings clipped as short as he can. Aloud, he said, "I couldn't agree with you more, Mr. Masters. If I had my choice, I'd let him go right now. In fact, I can't understand why he was ever arrested."

"Perhaps you can't," Masters said, "but the grand jury could."

Well! Masters could be arch.

"That's what I mean," Parrish retorted. "The investigation was slipshod and incomplete. The evidence uncovered gives an entirely false picture. That's why the grand jury indicted him. They didn't know any better. But you, Mr. Masters! You were aware!"

Balin shrank and Masters colored. "Are you suggesting," he said tensely, "that my office did not do—?"

"That's exactly what I'm suggesting," Parrish broke in. "What was your star witness doing during that period he claims he was in his motel room waiting for the deceased to come to their rendezvous? Do you really know what he was doing?"

Masters, red with fury, said, "You're God damned right—" and then he caught himself. Parrish was baiting him, goading him, fishing for information. He sat back and the color left his face. "Why, yes," he said ingenuously. "Walter Costaine was in his room, waiting."

But Parrish had learned what he was after. Costaine wasn't one of those murderers who couldn't keep from implicating himself. He had a solid alibi and Masters had checked it thoroughly.

Parrish switched subjects. "What about the other lovers in Mrs. Whittaker's life?" he continued, without missing a beat. "Did you check them out before bringing charges against Jerry?"

Masters was on guard now. He didn't say, "What other lovers?"

He said, "If you can produce any lovers who don't have alibis, I certainly hope you will do so—at the trial."

It was a standoff thereafter, with Parrish staying with the June trial date and Masters urging that they set it earlier and ask for postponements if more time were needed. At the end, Parrish made a great concession. He said he'd meet the state's attorney halfway, and checked his wallet calendar carefully. He'd settle for an April twentieth trial date and, just possibly, he might be able to meet it without postponement.

Masters gained solace from winning even that small a victory, but it was no victory at all. Simms would be on the bench, which was what Parrish wanted. And, despite what he had told Masters, he should be ready with his defense a good two months before that.

CHAPTER 28

Charles Zacharias Whittaker fluffed the pillow and put it behind his wife's head. Janet was sixty years old, some eight years younger than he, but she looked ten years more ancient. The russet of her hair was gone and the gorgeous mane that had once bedazzled him was a scraggly, fading gray. She had been plump but her face was thinning, her skin turning to wrinkles. He would have to take her to the hospital for more tests. The pills, the injections, the treatments weren't working. There was more wrong with her than they knew.

He set the small folding table beside her and tied back the curtains to improve her view. If she leaned forward, she could see black children frolic on the sidewalk. "Leslie's little sister's out there," he said. "She's climbing all over the porch with no coat on."

Janet Whittaker smiled but she didn't try to look. It was too comfortable resting against the pillow. "You get back," she said. "You might have a customer."

"Leslie's there."

"It might be a prescription customer. Don't worry about me. I'm all right."

She patted his hand and he patted hers. She was reading his anxiety and he knew it. He never could hide anything from her. The business was so very bad he couldn't afford the time away. But Janet was very bad too. And now Jerry wasn't around to get her into the hospital quickly for tests, or to enlist the favors of top specialists. Jerry was in jail and that was another worry.

"Let me get the tea," he said. "And a book?"

She permitted that and he hurried to the kitchen. A television would be good. It would help Janet pass the time. But they had no television. Zacharias had regarded it as a corrupting influence. One could, he felt, put one's time to better uses. A book would be good. Janet could lose herself in reading, could forget the pain. Except her eyes were giving her trouble now. She was getting those headaches.

Zacharias poured water over the tea bag and carried it in to her.

"I wish I weren't such a bother," she apologized.

"No bother, dear. Where's the book you were reading?"

"By the bed. But don't you worry about that. You get on downstairs and wait on the customers."

"I'm sure there aren't any." Zacharias hurried to the bedroom and found the book. He felt a little frantic and frustration was gnawing at him. What else did she need? What was he going to do about her? He didn't have Jerry to lean on now. He could ask Arnold, but Arnold was a pill. He could never come around without telling Zack how to run the store. How can you ask help from someone who keeps telling you if you'd only follow his advice you wouldn't need help?

He gave Janet the book and looked out the window. Good heavens, a huge car was parked in front of the store. It was a wealthy customer. It must be.

"Wait," Zacharias said to Janet. "Wait right here. I'll have to go down." He hurried away to the back stairs beyond the kitchen and down to the storeroom behind the store. He caught his white jacket off the tree by the prescription room door and came through to the small, white-shelved, glass-paned space where he performed the magic of his office.

Through the glass he could see the customer. She was up front at the cash register talking with Leslie, and Zacharias had never seen such an elegant woman. With her pert face, her blonde hair and her rich furs, she looked as if she had stepped in from another planet. In fact, Leslie, whom Zacharias regarded as smart and pretty, looked childish, gross and dowdy in contrast.

Zacharias made his presence known, coming out of the prescription room and past the rear counter. The fur-clad creature floated toward him and introduced herself. She was Melody Stevens, she said, and gave him a card bearing the name Cleveland Parrish, Attorney-at-Law. Mr. Parrish was in the car outside and wished to speak to him about Jerry.

Zacharias Whittaker shivered with a sudden, nameless fear. He had heard of Cleveland Parrish. He had read that the great lawyer would defend his son. He knew that was supposed to make everything all right. Yet he shivered. It was as if a heavy foot had stepped upon his grave.

He nodded numbly and followed the fur-clad girl outside. What was there now that made her seem unholy? Were those well-shaped, well-cared-for features pinched? Was there something heartless in the cool, brown eyes? If they had come to help Jerry, why did he feel trepidation?

An icy wind cut across the sidewalk, reminding Zacharias that he wore only his white work jacket. The remains of snow around the curb was brown with dirt. The concrete of the walk was cracked and even the trees looked shabby and ill. The contrast between the surroundings and that shiny, sparkling, waiting mauve Cadillac seemed to tell stories. The Bible said the meek shall inherit the earth but it was the strong man in the car who was the inheritor. The meek did his bidding. The meek had to pray to him for help. Zacharias Whittaker, for all his careful life, his attention to virtue, was unable to save his own flesh and blood. This rich outsider was the one who held the power to save. Young Jerry's fate was in Parrish's hands, not Zacharias', and as Zacharias approached the car, doubt seized his mind as it never had before. Was his world the true world after all? Was there a compensating salvation to make his sacrifices worthwhile? Or did the race go only to the swift and the battle to the strong?

He climbed into the Cadillac, smelling its newness and its carness, and settled into the jump seat the big man had pulled out for him. The fur-coated girl got in behind him, closed the door and sat in the opposite corner. From the car pocket she produced a notebook and pencil and made ready, but Zacharias Whittaker didn't notice. All he saw was the large, competent man in the expensive coat lounging like a king, puffing on an aromatic cigar.

"I'm Parrish," the king said. "I've been retained to represent your son. I'd like to ask you some questions."

To Zacharias it was obvious that if anyone could save Jerry, this man was the one. The mark of the winner was all over him. His confidence bordered on the arrogant and he oozed command. Zacharias would co-operate with him, not because it would help Jerry, but because he could do nothing else.

He held out a hand for the lawyer to shake and said he'd answer everything he could. Parrish made the handshake a hearty one and said he was sure Mr. Whittaker wanted to co-operate in every way possible. They both wanted Jerry freed.

The lawyer then asked the questions and Zacharias, had he wanted to lie, could not have succeeded. No sooner did he answer one, than another followed, totally unrelated, forcing a reorientation of his thinking. They were rapid-fire and he found himself not daring to hesitate longer than he could manage. It was rhythmic, systematic and compelling, forcing confession out of Zacharias, his feelings for his son, his son's upbringing and former life, the whys and wherefores of it all, the complete background picture.

Jerry, Zacharias admitted, was not an athlete. Zack himself had dissuaded him from violent physical contact. Not only was there danger of injury, but there was the threat of heated emotions. War was wrong. Boys should be taught not to fight. Children should be given to understand the beauty of life and the glory of God, not the ugliness of the devil. This was what Zacharias and his wife had sought to instill in their three children, and in no one did it take hold more firmly than in Jerry.

As for parenthood, Zacharias didn't know why Jerry and Sally had never had children. It wasn't a subject one talked about.

Not even with one's own son? Did Zacharias Whittaker really believe that a taboo subject?

Well, yes. His son was an adult and it was his own private matter—his and Sally's.

Could Zacharias venture a guess?

Well, much as he wouldn't want to say anything about his daughter-in-law, he did have the feeling she wasn't child-oriented.

As for the Costaine sequence, Zacharias had to admit he was

shocked. He was simply stunned. That Sally might cheat on Jerry had never entered his mind.

Given the fact, what did Zacharias think Jerry might do about it?

Zacharias shook his head, and noticed for the first time that the lovely blonde girl was taking notes. "I just don't know," he said. "I can't imagine."

"What would *you* do about it if such a thing had happened to you?"

Zacharias thought about the question for a long moment and slowly answered, "I think I would turn to the Good Book. I think I would do a lot more praying than I had been. I think I would try to lead a better life."

"In hopes it would cure your wife?"

"In hopes it might make her more content with me."

Parrish left that area of questioning. It would have been a good point to plant in a jury's mind if Jerry Whittaker had shown any kind of religious feeling. As things were, the suggestion that Jerry might go to his Bible was ludicrous.

At the end, Zacharias Whittaker was left feeling inept and unsuccessful. He had given the lawyer everything he could, but the lawyer had a way of making it seem not enough. Zacharias was sure it wasn't. Zacharias feared nothing would be enough until the gates of the jail were opened and his son walked forth, free and clean. Even his expressed conviction of his son's innocence was dismissed all too casually.

A silence fell and Zacharias felt the impact. The interview was over, but nothing had happened. Jerry's fate was as uncertain as ever. Zacharias didn't know what to say and he couldn't leave on such a note. "If there's anything I can do," he said. "Any way I can help—"

Parrish, lounging against the cushions, looking upon the man with a show of benevolence, allowed as how there might be a way the elderly druggist could help.

"Just name it," Zacharias said passionately.

"Has Jerry talked to you about money?"

Zacharias stopped. "Money?"

"He needs it."

Zacharias swallowed. Janet was sick and he didn't know how bad. There would be hospitalization and tests and then there would be treatment. He had no idea how much that would cost. There was seven thousand in the savings account, the retirement fund. He would have to cut into that for Janet. He didn't know what that would leave for anything else.

"Jerry," he said, beginning to perspire, "wouldn't talk about money. I asked him, after he got indicted, if he would need financial assistance, but he assured me he had plenty of money. And Jerry wouldn't lie."

"Of course he wouldn't," Parrish answered. "He just didn't know how much a defense would cost—the kind of defense that would win Jerry his freedom, which is the only kind of defense to have."

"I was just going to say that," Zacharias replied. "I would be glad to help any way I can. I might be able to spare fifteen hun—maybe two thousand dollars."

"I'm talking about MONEY," Parrish said. "Thousands, not hundreds."

Whittaker trembled. Did Parrish need everything they had in savings? But what about Janet? He stammered as he said he didn't have much money, only a little bit of a nest egg to tide him and his wife over when he could no longer work.

"What are you going to do about that store? You going to *will* it to Jerry—if he's still alive?"

Zacharias felt himself sinking. The face of Martin Wraxler floated into view. Wraxler was licking his lips.

He knew he was going to lose the store. He was going to lose the only security he had, the only hedge against the future. Where would he go? What would he do? What of Janet?

He spoke very slowly. "Does Jerry want me to sell the store?"

"No, he doesn't, Mr. Whittaker." Parrish was admirably gentle. "Jerry doesn't want you to help him at all. He's a noble boy, your son. He's generous to a fault. Even when his own life is at stake, his thoughts are of others."

"You mean he needs my help but doesn't want to ask for it?"

"He wouldn't take it if you offered it to him." Parrish shook his head. "Of course, in all fairness, I think it should be said that he doesn't fully understand the seriousness of his predicament."

Zacharias didn't fully understand it either, but Parrish was willing to explain: Jerry was obviously innocent of any wrongdoing, but the case against him was very strong. The absence of an alternate suspect was damning. If the jury had nowhere else to turn for a killer, it would have to find him guilty. The essense of the defense, therefore, wasn't merely pointing out what an impossible choice Jerry was, it was establishing other possibilities. But this would require investigation and did Mr. Whittaker have any idea what able investigators received for their services?

Mr. Whittaker conceded that he did not, and Parrish said, "And neither does your son. He's given me what money he can and I'll use it judiciously, but it's not a great amount and I have explained that to him and urged him to seek more." Parrish hitched his shoulders. "I'll be frank, Mr. Whittaker. I've asked Jerry if he couldn't get help from you and he has flatly refused. He thinks—or perhaps the proper word to use is 'hopes'—that what he's been able to raise will be enough. For his sake, I hope it will be too, but I don't like taking chances with another man's life. Even if the man himself is willing."

Zacharias Whittaker's body sagged with his spirit. His voice trembled. "How much would you need?" he whispered.

"How much can you get?"

Zacharias closed his eyes against the image of Martin Wraxler licking his lips. "I could ask for a mortgage," he said. "I don't know how much they'll give me."

Parrish leaned forward to assess the shabby store through the car window and Whittaker winced against his cold-blooded stare. Maybe Martin Wraxler was right. Maybe it was only worth twenty thousand. And maybe, if Martin Wraxler knew Zacharias wanted to sell, he might cut the offer even lower. "I've been offered twenty to sell," he said, trying to soften the lawyer's expression.

"Twenty?" Parrish opened the door on his side. "Let me take a look inside. I might be able to get you more than that."

He went around the car and Zacharias Whittaker, his heart pounding with hope, climbed out and followed.

Melody sat in her corner, small and silent. In the driver's seat, Pete Tucker ran down his window and spit in the street.

CHAPTER 29

"Sally wasn't really one of us," her father said to Parrish. "She wasn't a Demarest. There was nothing of her in my side of the family."

Howard Demarest, a lean, gray, six feet two, was sitting in a ramrod posture beside his wife in the family living room, trying to explain his daughter. Though normally reticent, the couple was no match for Parrish's interrogation technique and the first admission that Sally was "unusual" was followed by the definition "high spirited," which gave way in turn to "willful" and, ultimately, "obdurate" and "recalcitrant."

"She wasn't a Robertson either," Martha Demarest replied. "I don't really know where she got her traits, particularly her unwillingness to conform."

They discussed it as if it were important, deciding that maybe Uncle Ben, who was Demarest's great-uncle, but on his mother's side, exhibited many of Sally's characteristics. He had run away to sea and had never come back to settle down to the family responsibilities. He had never really amounted to anything; married some Polynesian girl and ended his days in Hong Kong.

Or perhaps it was William Austin, a first cousin of Martha's mother. He had gotten a girl in trouble in college around the turn of the century, he had been thrown out of three Ivy League schools, quit a less prestigious place, and gone to Europe for three years on money that came to him at twenty-one. When he returned, he chose to live in New York, joined the Army as a colonel in 1917, and got himself killed at the Marne.

Parrish let them talk. He had worked to get them loose. Jerry had told him the Demarests would pay for his gallows and that made a trip to Villanova important. He needed verification of the hostility and a chance to size up the enemy.

Mrs. Demarest was taller than average for a woman, but she looked petite beside her husband. Like him she was lean, but in her case the leanness bordered on the gaunt. She was too Spartan in her diet, too self-denying in her tastes. Like her husband she had the finely chiseled features and the iron self-control. With her, however, the loss of a daughter appeared to require more strength of discipline. Her thin lips did not tremble, but it was an effort of will and her jaws were tight.

Their quiet modesty was evident in their surroundings. The living room was so low-key it almost bordered upon gentile poverty, except that when one stopped to note the quality of the upholstery, the rugs, the paintings, the antiques, the everything, one realized he was dealing not only with money beyond counting, but beyond thinking there was a need to count it. Cleveland Parrish was seldom impressed, and never out of his depth, but the Demarest home came close to making him feel inadequate.

When they paused, Parrish guided them back. Sally had had a mind of her own? How had it manifested itself?

They gave college as an example, and Mrs. Demarest was relaxing her guard. She and her family had attended Bryn Mawr for simply centuries. So had her elder daughter, Charlotte. But not Sally. She would have none of it, not because she didn't think well of Bryn Mawr, but purely and simply because everybody else had accepted it. She went off to Barnard instead. "That was Sally," Mrs. Demarest sighed. "She had to be different, no matter what the cost."

"Of course Barnard is a fine school," her husband added. "It's just that we couldn't keep in close contact with her there."

"She always rejected contact with us," Mrs. Demarest said, and in back of her eyes were times untold. "In those days they didn't call it a generation gap, but I suppose that's what it was."

Parrish turned to a routine area. He asked about enemies.

The couple shook their heads. They had no knowledge of such things. "Sally wasn't one to confide in her parents, Mr. Parrish."

"How about back when she was growing up?"

Demarest decided this was a foreign area and he left the answers to his wife, listening with the same intentness as the lawyer, as if to learn, too late, who his daughter was.

"Oh, she had her fights," Mrs. Demarest admitted. "But enemies?

People who would bear the kind of malice that would—?" She shook her head. "No."

Parrish pressed her about the fights. Mrs. Demarest was reluctant, she was distressed, but she was as incapable of resisting the lawyer's questioning as she was of dissembling.

Yes, it turned out, Sally had got into a number of fights in her growing-up years. She was a bully. She was the torment of her sister, Charlotte, who, though two years older, was frequently reduced to tears.

Young Sally Demarest was very much a discipline problem and no denying it. She was not above attacking those who aroused her ire with more than just her teeth and nails. She could throw a stone like a boy and once gave another girl a scalp wound it took three stitches to close. There had been complaints before but no more thereafter. Whether Sally realized she had gone too far, or whether she was out-growing that method of attack, she never did it again.

"How about her husband?" Parrish asked. "Did she ever hit him?"

The two parents looked at each other as if the thought had never occurred to them. Finally Mrs. Demarest said, "Why, I wouldn't think so."

"Would he hit her?"

"She never talked to us about her personal life," was the answer. "We, ah, didn't communicate on a very intimate level."

"Do you think Dr. Whittaker is capable of striking a woman?"

It was Howard Demarest who answered. "I really couldn't say," he replied, but his tone said it was likely.

"What kind of a temper did he have?"

Again the couple were of no help. Whittaker had always behaved with great propriety around them, always dutiful, always polite, al-ways proper.

"But you don't like him. Why?"

Demarest became defensive. "I don't know that you can say that."

"It's obvious. Your every word and gesture reveals it. Both of you. I'm wondering why."

The two looked at each other again before Demarest conceded the point. "It's personality differences, I suppose. If we didn't warm up to him as much as you think we should, it would be due to that."

"Do you think he killed her?"

Again the two turned to each other for agreement, and Demarest

said slowly, "We have to confess we do not regard the possibility as unlikely. I'm sorry to have to say that."

"Don't apologize. That's your opinion and that's what I'm after. Now I want to know why you have that opinion."

Demarest took his cue from his wife and went into those aspects of Whittaker's personality that created the differences he had mentioned. Gerald's background was extremely modest. He was the son of a New Haven druggist, and while the drugstore provided a living, it was a far cry from the kind of life the Demarests enjoyed in Villanova.

"The amount of money a person makes doesn't really matter to us," Demarest said, and then in the next breath admitted that it did matter. "Naturally we would like to see our children marry in their own social class, marry people from families who are accustomed to the same style of living, know the same people, share the same religion. It's more conducive to harmony in their married lives, not just between them, but between their families. Gerald's family came to the wedding, but we never laid eyes on them after that until the—funeral."

Having contradicted his claim, Demarest now sought to back and fill. "But this doesn't mean that people from without one's own class can't enter it. We know of many cases where our young men and women have married someone outside and the newcomer has fitted right in."

"But Dr. Whittaker didn't?"

Demarest shook his head. "I got a feeling about him. We both did —Mrs. Demarest and I. The first weekend Sally brought him home you couldn't get away from the impression he was mentally putting a price tag on everything we had. If he poured cream from the creamer, you could almost see him thinking to himself, 'That's real silver and very old. I'll bet it's worth thus and such amount of money.'" The elderly man shrugged and said wryly, "One could hardly fail to get the impression that he looked at Sally and thought, 'That Barnard girl is a Philadelphia Demarest. I'll bet she's worth thus and such amount of money.' It made us wonder just what his interest in Sally was."

Parrish sat back. His face was expressionless but his thoughts were sour. Howard Demarest could do Jerry a lot of harm upon that witness stand. You put an impression across to a jury that a guy marries

136

a girl for money and that jury is not going to be the least bit sympathetic to his protestations of love and grief.

But Parrish had to know the worst and he wanted it unadulterated. He crossed his legs and asked casually, "Did you ever find out—about his interest in Sally?"

Demarest, fortunately, could produce no more bad news. He coughed delicately into a snowy handkerchief. "Hard to tell," he said. "We've seen very little of them after the marriage."

"Did he come into money?"

Demarest blinked. "He? I don't think his family had any."

"I mean, through Sally. You say he looked as if he wanted to acquire money through marriage. Did he acquire any?"

This they couldn't answer. Sally had money. She inherited a good deal from her grandparents, as did her sister and her cousins. But while her holdings were substantial, the income wouldn't be more than ten to twenty thousand a year. Whether Whittaker had the use of that or not, they couldn't say. Whether, in fact, Sally had signed over everything to Jerry they couldn't say. But they strongly doubted it. Sally was too shrewd.

Parrish relaxed a little. That supported Jerry's own claim he never got a sniff of Sally's money. That would help discount the idea that money was his motive for marrying. He said, "You think he didn't *get* her money, but you think he was *interested* in her money. Is that your view?"

The couple exchanged looks again. This time Mrs. Demarest spoke. It was still in that soft, almost beseeching voice. "We don't want to be unfair, Mr. Parrish. He was going to medical school and doing very well when he started courting Sally. He did not need to marry money. It was quite apparent he could make plenty on his own." She was apologetic about it now. "I wouldn't want to say he didn't love her. I'm sure he did. And certainly, at the wedding, they did look to be very much in love."

Parrish nodded. He was deciding the Demarests were harmless. Money would be no factor in the case.

Then Howard Demarest scowled and spoke with a sure voice. "They may have looked in love and they may have been in love, but that man likes money!" He coughed again, covering it with his handkerchief, but there was nothing apologetic about the action. "You will note," he went on, "that he set himself up in practice in a very wealthy town. He went to medical school not because he wanted to heal the sick, but because he knew once you get that M.D. behind your name, you can live in comfort for life. You don't even have to be good. Because the AMA will protect you.

"You want my opinion? Gerald Whittaker is a very shrewd man. Gerald Whittaker knows exactly what he's doing."

CHAPTER 30

Melody opened the slim velvet box and lifted out the ruby and diamond bracelet inside. There had been undergarments before, the black, sexy kind she didn't fancy but which Cleve liked to see her in. And there had been a very handsome wristwatch. But this bracelet, this was really something. This must have cost the lawyer at least two thousand dollars. "Oh, Cleve," she said, holding it against her wrist, "it's beautiful."

She was sitting on the floor at his feet in front of the Christmas tree, wearing a peach lounging robe—one of last year's gifts, with the wrappings of opened presents around her. It was a childlike situation, one she enjoyed as much as Cleve who, in bathrobe and slippers, sat back paternally in a large lounging chair, a cup of coffee at his elbow and his own gifts beside him. His own gifts, meaning the gifts from her, included an inscribed leather cigarette case and matching lighter, a leather-cased set of the most expensive after-shave lotion and bath powder she could find, a set of monogrammed hair brushes, and a bottle of twenty-four-year-old scotch.

These were not the only gifts Cleveland Parrish had received for Christmas. The gifts from other sources came early and often, presents from clients, from former clients, from would-be clients, from the investigators he hired, from the suppliers of his needs, which included anything from office equipment to planes to cars. His tree, large as it was, could not have begun to encompass all the loot that had come to his apartment and office throughout the month. But the tree was not for them. It was for him and Melody and their own private party. They spent Christmas Eve and Christmas day together as a tradition, for she was the closest thing to family Cleve had and he didn't want to be alone on that day of all days.

Later the tree would serve as decoration for a post-Christmas bash when he repaid his social obligations. Some of the guests would be donors of his gifts but it was not to pay them back. Cleve did not believe in repaying gift for gift. Melody would dispense thank-you notes and that would be it. Melody herself was the only one to whom Cleve Parrish gave presents, the only one for whom Cleve shopped.

If Cleve needed Melody to serve as family, Melody did not need Cleve. Her parents, her brothers and sister were within easy reach, all of them very family-minded on Christmas. Now, while her brothers' and sister's offspring were still small, they gathered at the Stevens homestead Christmas day for a great family get-to-gether. "Almost like when the children were growing up," was the way Melody's mother expressed it.

Except for Melody. If only Melody could attend the Christmas gatherings, everything would be perfect. But Melody had her big important job. It made her glamorous, it made her rich, it made the whole family proud, it made them all glad. Except that Melody can't come home for Christmas. She is never free on the big holidays.

She must work awfully hard. But such clothes! Do you see how stylish she is? Why, you don't see clothes like hers on anybody. You have to look in fashion magazines to see her kind of clothes. They must cost an awful lot, but she says she has to have them for her work, that Mr. Parrish wants to impress his clients. So the clothes are a business expense and they don't cost her anything. She picks them out because she has an eye for style and Mr. Parrish trusts her judgment. And the bills come under the heading of office expense. But I guess he can pay for it. He's got offices in the Empire State Building, and he's got an apartment that costs over seven hundred dollars a month, so he must be very rich.

But it would be nice if Melody could come home for Christmas.

Melody leaned back against Cleve's legs and held up her arm with the bracelet against it. "It's just gorgeous, Cleve. You shouldn't have."

He laughed his deep-throated laugh and fastened it in place. "When I saw it, I thought, 'No, it's too lavish. It'll spoil you.' But I couldn't leave it alone. It kept whispering to me, 'I was made for Melody's wrist.'"

She sighed and rested her head against his knee, admiring the bracelet and the way the stones gleamed. "I'm glad you can whisper," she said to it.

Parrish drained his coffee cup and fondled Melody's hair. He did enjoy giving her things. Or, really, watching her receive things. He felt a warm glow at having her with him right then, affectionate, impressed, beholden. It was the closest kin to love he knew. And as he stroked her hair, the thought crossed his mind, Would you like it like this all the time? Have her here all the time? But the answering response was rudely sharp. No, he would not. As an interlude, yes. What could be more pleasant than Christmas Eve and Christmas day together? Or Christmas morn—a whole day would be rather much. A whole day of doing nothing? Already, in fact, he had had his fill.

Melody said, twisting her wrist to make the bracelet sparkle, "I wonder what the poor people are doing," and he laughed. "Eating better than I am. I thought you were going to make some breakfast."

She got up and said, "Of course," kissed him and went to the kitchen, letting him go shave.

It was a cozy time, she reflected, and they'd have a nice breakfast, the traditional crepe suzettes. And the bracelet was really scrumptious.

The kitchen clock said almost eleven. Joe and Peggy and their three youngsters would be on their way to Ma and Pa's right then. In fifteen minutes they'd be arriving, the kids screaming with glee. (How old were they now? She couldn't keep track. In fact, she wasn't even certain of their names.) Then they'd unload all the presents and put them under the tree. She could imagine that when the whole family had gathered, the presents must cover half the living room.

It wouldn't be as good as other Christmases, of course. Not with Gary out of work. The others, including Melody, were chipping in to keep him going, but it wasn't a good arrangement. Gary hated it. He saw debts piling up and he never was good when things came at him faster than he could dispose of them. Let the pressures build and he'd lose some of that charm he had. He'd be really hard to get along with. In fact, Lottie, in her most recent phone call, had said Gary and Priscilla were at each other's throats half the time. Shep had told Gary to forget about paying anything back, but that didn't answer Gary's need. He didn't want to grub through life like Shep Junior, Joe, or Lisa's husband. He wanted to make it big like Melody and he thought he was on his way when disaster struck. Now he was accepting handouts from his inferiors and it made him bitter.

Except that his first unemployment check had finally come through just in time for Christmas and that was good news. He was even able to joke over the phone, so everything would be fine for Christmas. There'd be the big turkey dinner and everyone would say, "Too bad Melody couldn't be here to make the day perfect."

Melody made a face. "Melody's got hers," she said sourly and looked at the bracelet. If only Cleve didn't need her so goddam much. If only she could have Christmas off. She'd give up the bracelet for one Christmas at home. She didn't need the goddam thing. Where was she going to wear it? Rubies weren't really for someone with her coloring. Not that she'd knock it. It really was a lovely piece of jewelry. But where else would it end but in the safe-deposit box with the other pieces—not as grand as this one, she had to admit—that she'd collected over the years. Insurance against old age, perhaps. Insurance against the wolf at the door, a hedge against the time when Cleve might opt for a younger, prettier secretary. She lived in an insecure world. She had to keep and save. She couldn't be too wasteful. A Christmas at home would be nice, but it probably looked better from a distance. She loved her family, but they really were a boring crew. After a few hours there was nothing to say. And the noisy children began getting on her nerves. And she and her father would start bickering. But of course, Christmas would be special. Everyone would be in his best spirits and it wouldn't last long enough for the bickering and the boredom to start. Christmas was that special day when she could fully enjoy her family. But it couldn't be and there was no point in fretting or complaining. The grass on her side of the fence was pretty green too, even if she couldn't have everything.

By the time she had breakfast ready, Cleve was dressed and they ate in the breakfast nook. He mentioned the food, how good it was, and he repeated what a fine Christmas it was, but all it told Melody was that he had already lost interest. She would have liked to play some of Cleve's records (he had a fabulous collection though he had no interest in music himself) or perhaps walk with him through Central Park. They might take in a show. But no. Cleve was getting bored, as he always did if he were away from his work for more than a few hours.

"Say, I wonder," he said, stuffing a large forkful of crepe suzettes into his mouth, "what Jerry Whittaker's getting for Christmas dinner."

Melody's thoughts strayed for a moment to the turkey (maybe there'd be two) cooking in her mother's oven. "I don't know," she said wistfully. "Turkey, I suppose."

"Poor, innocent bastard, spending Christmas in jail."

Parrish hadn't given a thought to Whittaker in three weeks and Melody knew it. Not since he'd talked to both sets of parents. A few investigative reports had arrived from the agency, but Cleve was involved with more pressing cases. Then, two days ago, transcripts of the prosecution witnesses' statements had come in. Cleve had devoured them and turned them over to Melody to study. That had been the trigger and Jerry's plight was again in the forefront of his mind. Melody knew what was coming and she steeled herself.

"Say, you know what we ought to do, Melody?" he continued, following a well-worn script. "We ought to go up and see that poor son of a bitch. We ought to bring him a little Christmas cheer. Nobody ought to be all alone on Christmas."

Melody said, "His folks live in New Haven. I'm sure they've gone to see him."

"Yeah, but what can they offer him?" He was enthusing now. "What can they do but pat his hand? What would really cheer him up would be a visit from his lawyer. Not only can I bring him hope, I can show him I care."

"I don't know whether—"

"You know, I got a report from the agency. They've turned up two broads in Madison that son of a bitch Walter Costaine's been fooling around with. Now, those are two females I'm going to want to talk to just as soon as I can. It wouldn't be a wasted trip."

"You wouldn't call them on Christmas!"

"Hell, no. There wouldn't be time. What I'm thinking is we can go up today and see Whittaker, stay overnight in New Haven, and see those women tomorrow. And Costaine's wife. And Walter himself. He's a man I want to meet. And I want to see if there are any more pictures of Sally around. Jake Settler will buy every one I can lay my hands on."

Melody said, "The book is done? How is it?"

"I didn't read it, for Christ's sake. Lancer gave it to Jake. Reading is Jake's job."

"I mean, he likes it?"

"Of course he likes it. Herb knows how to write for Jake. And he likes the pictures of Sally. He wants all he can get. Make a note, will you, so I don't forget while I'm there."

Melody got up obediently for a note pad. She said, "Why don't we drive up first thing tomorrow?"

"Because I want to say hello to Jerry on Christmas day, that's why."

"Pete's celebrating, you know, with his family. It's his day off."

"It isn't his day off. He doesn't have days off. He gets paid to do what I want where I want when I want. Get on the phone and tell him to have the car in front of the door at one o'clock."

Melody went to the phone without a word, but she went to the bedroom one, where Cleve wouldn't hear. Though she didn't care for Pete Tucker, she got no perverse delight in seeing him put out. She knew what she was missing at her own home and she really felt like a heel pulling Pete away from his.

He was the one who answered and he returned a cool and waiting, "Yeah?" when she identified herself.

"Listen, Pete, Cleve wants to go riding."

"It figures."

She felt called upon to make him understand she wasn't a party to it. "I'm sorry, Pete. I really am. I tried to talk him out of it—"

"Don't apologize. I expected the call. Like Thanksgiving. Like last Christmas. And the Christmas before. He hasn't missed yet."

"I didn't realize."

"The pay is great. The holidays are lousy. What time does he want me and where are we going?"

She told him one o'clock and New Haven and to pack a bag. She didn't know when they'd be coming back.

Pete said, "Tell old Grapes of Wrath it shall be done. Even to the seventh son of the seventh son."

CHAPTER 31

The lethargy Gerald Whittaker had exhibited on Thanksgiving had turned to stupor by Christmas. He was somnambulant, unshaven, and pasty. His weight had shifted: he was thicker in the belly, thinner in the chest, and gaunt in the face. Since he got enough food and exercise, it was obvious that jail took a toll of the Gerald Whittakers of the world.

His thinking was slow and torpid too. Though he'd had a month to ponder, he couldn't produce any potential lover for Sally. He'd tried, he said. He'd gone over all their friends, their acquaintances, everybody in the club.

"What about caretakers?" Parrish asked impatiently. "What about the milkman, the clerks in the supermarket, waiters, the rubbish collector, all those other people whose paths crossed hers?"

"Oh, she wouldn't have anything to do with people like that."

Parrish wanted to slap the man. "What the hell's the matter with you? Sally wasn't husband hunting! Lonely wives aren't shacking up with some man because he's rich or handsome or her family will say, 'What a wonderful catch you made.' She does it because he can fulfill a need. All she wants out of the guy is sex and that makes anybody over fourteen a candidate. Do you get the idea?"

Whittaker was sluggish about it, but he said yes.

Parrish went after the other side of the lover coin. What had been Sally's interest in sex over the preceding year? Had it waned, and if so, when?

Again Whittaker was no help. He had been so drained by work, he said, that he had little interest in sex, and Sally, tiring of being the aggressor, became bitchy instead. Ultimately, she ceased even being bitchy, which he took to mean she had become adjusted to the role of wife to a busy doctor. But when that had happened, he didn't remember.

"Come on, Jerry. Was it before last May? Was it before Costaine?"

There was no spark in Jerry's eye, no ray of hope. Still he said, "Yes, I suppose so. Yes, I'm almost certain."

Parrish couldn't be sure whether he was telling the truth or being agreeable. "Think about that," he ordered. "I want specifics and I want dates. 'Yes,' or 'I think so,' won't do."

Whittaker said he'd try.

"What about this past summer? Did Sally get horny while Costaine was away?"

"No."

"Didn't you wonder who was taking care of her love life during that time?"

Whittaker shook his head. "I didn't know he was away. Besides, she wouldn't have come to me for sex if her life depended on it. We never had any more sex after I caught her in the motel."

The damned fool wasn't lifting a finger to help his own cause. And if he kept going downhill at his present rate, he'd be a total disaster on the witness stand come trial time. Parrish was counting on his testimony and his personality in front of the jury.

Parrish was an hour with his client, a short hour to him, but a bitterly long one to Melody, waiting with Pete Tucker outside. Pete was readily adjustable and no sooner had the lawyer disappeared than he had switched on the radio and leaned against the seat cushions of the mauve Cadillac seeming to listen to "The Nutcracker Suite."

It was not for Melody to stay cooped up with Pete Tucker and she went for a walk. The trouble was the jail was situated in an unprepossessing part of New Haven. Along Whalley Avenue were shops and car lots. Down the side streets were frame houses, bleak and cheerless in the cold December air. The snow along the curbs was rimy and dirty. All the stores were closed, all the people were inside, warm and snug, sharing their Christmas pleasures.

Melody stayed away as long as she could but, ultimately, frozen feet, numbed hands, and the raw cold of the day drove her once more into the warmth of the Cadillac's rear seat, cursing Cleve and wishing him back. She was thankful for the warmth but uncomfortable otherwise. It was always awkward to be left alone with

Pete Tucker. He never said anything. He never looked at her. Like now. She knew he blamed her for this trip. He believed she talked Parrish into it just to wreck his Christmas.

She smoked two cigarettes in uncomfortable silence. Pete lighted one of his own, so he wasn't asleep. She wished he were. She mashed out the second cigarette and couldn't stomach a third. That left her with nothing to do. The silence grew oppressive but Pete wasn't disposed to break it. He was only listening to the radio, or maybe just staring out at the cloudy sky. He didn't have nerves. But Melody did. "I'm really sorry about this trip," she finally said.

"So'm I."

There was more silence. She said, "We're staying at the Plaza. It's real name is the Park Plaza."

"That's great," he said, running down his window and flicking out his cigarette. "Ever since I was a kid I've dreamed of staying at the Park Plaza."

"You don't have to be nasty. I couldn't help it. Coming here wasn't my idea."

He laughed. "You sound like it hurts you more than it does me."

She looked around at the bare, snowy, unfamiliar surroundings. "Merry Christmas," she muttered to herself, then thought guiltily of the bracelet. Pete didn't get a bracelet. "I don't know why we can't be friends," she said aloud.

"Come on, Melody. You don't want to be friends with me. What would your elegant friends think of you mixing with the hoi polloi?"

"You don't think very much of me, do you?"

"Relax, sweetheart. I don't think about you at all."

God, he could be cutting. What was she bothering for? She had that third cigarette after all. "The hell you don't think about me," she finally said. "You hate my guts."

"I don't hate your guts. Why should I?"

Why should he? She couldn't see why. Except that she was more important than he. She made more money. Cleve could buy a dozen pilots, chauffeurs, mechanics, whatever Pete's particular position was called, but he'd be a long time replacing a Melody Stevens. She wanted to say so to Pete, but that was just the kind of thing that would make him sneer.

She put more sweetness into her voice. "All right, Pete. If you don't hate my guts, what is your opinion of me?"

146

"Why don't we drop it?" he said irritably. "What do you care for? Let's listen to the radio."

"I'm curious. You've got some kind of view of me. What is it?"

"If you want my opinion," he said, "I put you down as a cool, and beautiful—bitch."

Tears stung her eyes. It wasn't what she wanted to be. It wasn't the view she wanted anyone to hold of her—not anyone who knew her. Well, she'd asked for it and she got it. "I see," she said.

Pete said, being bitchy himself, "And now that you have that bit of priceless information, what are you going to do with it, take it to our Great White Father?"

"No," she murmured. "Of course not."

"I didn't want to tell you," he said defensively. "You're the one who had to know."

"I'm not blaming you. I'm just a little surprised, that's all. I'm sorry you feel that way."

"Don't lose any sleep over it. It's not important."

Melody bit back tears. "No, it's not important," she murmured. She mashed out her cigarette and sat back to wait for Cleve.

The lawyer came out grim-faced, down the steps and into the car, unaware of Pete and Melody, concerned only with his client. "It's a crime to make an innocent man suffer in jail while his lawyers build up a defense," he said bitterly. "We're going to have to shoot some adrenaline into our boy if we're going to replace his prison pallor with the pink cheeks of hope. Pete, we're going to the Plaza Hotel."

They went to the Plaza, where Parrish had the presidential suite and Melody had a connecting room. Pete had a room too, on another floor. Parrish's suite looked out on the New Haven green, its three churches and giant Christmas tree. There was a view of the court-house, diagonally opposite, where, at a future date, Gerald Whittaker would go on trial for his life.

Parrish pointed it out to Melody before they went up to the cocktail lounge on the top floor. It was dark by then and they watched the lights of the city over drinks and celebrated Christmas dinner with roast beef in the Napoleon Room on the second floor. It was plush and comfortable there. For the Gerald Whittakers of the world it was a dismal holiday, but for the Melody Stevenses it wasn't a bad Christmas after all.

CHAPTER 32

Sitting on his bed in the motel room, Walter Costaine puffed nervously on a cigarette and watched the confident, well-dressed man get out of the mauve Cadillac in front. It had to be Cleveland Parrish.

Costaine licked his lips, reached for the bottle on the table, and poured another two fingers of rye into his tumbler. His bed was unmade, his face unshaven, his eyes bloodshot, and his head hung over.

Barbara had been decent. She had let him share a little Christmas with the children. He had bought a few things for them, more than he could afford, but he wanted it to be memorable. It was bad enough that he was no longer around.

The Christmas, for all that, had been strange; very uncheery, very unnatural, very wrong. Nine-year-old Nellise had wept because Daddy wouldn't stay, and seven-year-old Briggs had asked why not. Walter had mumbled something about business and Barbara had reminded the children that they had been told not to ask questions.

There had been the exchange of gifts. Nellise gave him socks and a tie selected by Barbara, and Briggs gave him an ashtray he had made in school. Walter had given the children transistors and a wristwatch each. In addition, he had given Nellise five changes of wardrobe for her teen doll, and Briggs an electric train set. The two were properly overwhelmed, but their glee was restrained, as if they read something in the presents that Walter didn't see. Barbara was restrained too. He and she refrained from exchanging gifts, but she did not approve of his extravagance with the children. She always felt today's youth was being given too much.

There had been a light Christmas supper in place of the traditional roast beef. Times were tight and motivation weak. All in all it had been a strained event, but better for Walter than spending the day in his motel room. Anything was better than that.

And there had been that phone call to Barbara from Cleveland Parrish's secretary to arrange an interview. The secretary got Walter on the line as well. She had such a pleasant, attractive voice that it made him wonder what she looked like. The message, however, was disturbing. Parrish wanted to talk to him; how about noon on the twenty-sixth, at his room? What could he say? He would have to face the lawyer sometime.

So he had gone back to the motel in the evening and had phoned what girls he knew, but all were out or busy. The one time he really needed companionship nobody was around. He knew a cathouse but he didn't have the fee. Nor could he afford a pickup. Besides, who the hell would be out, around and available on Christmas night? He ended up drinking too much and sleeping too little.

Walter picked up the tumbler and tossed off the rye. Cleveland Parrish seemed in no hurry to come to the door. He was looking around instead, going down the row of rooms and out of sight. He was early anyway. It was only eleven forty-five. Probably wants to get the lay of the land, Costaine thought. He wants to decide whether someone like Sally would be caught dead in a dump like this. Well, she was here all right. And not just once.

Costaine rose and threw the bed together, pulling the spread over careless covers. Might as well look halfway presentable. He moved closer to the window. There was a chauffeur behind the wheel of the huge Cadillac. Someone else was in the back seat. Could it be the secretary? He'd like to get a look at *her*.

Where was Parrish now? Oh, there, where the feeble fight had occurred. Walter snorted at the thought of it. He and Sally coming out of the room—the same room he had now—and Jerry and Barbara waiting. It was something of a shock finding them staked out like that, but there was something stupid about it too. Walter had felt more rage than dismay. Barbara had spied on him, found whom he was with, and gone for the woman's husband. She had forced a totally unnecessary confrontation. Then Jerry had come charging at him with all the traditional bombast of a cuckolded male. It was banal. And Walter had no choice but to hit or be hit. Walter was no fighter. He'd rather make love than war, but Jerry was equally inept, and wide open as well. Walter had landed a wild swing on

149

Jerry's left eye and Jerry fell down beside the car. By the time he got up the girls had come between them and it was over before it started. They left in the cars they had come in, Walter in his, Sally in hers, Barbara and Jerry in theirs. It was silliness, but it was the start of all that came after.

The wait was growing interminable for Walter before the clock reached twelve and the man outside rapped on the door. He finished another finger of rye in a gulp, braced himself, and turned the knob. He had to be smiling and friendly. He had to be his charming best, make the charm the women found so enticing work on the men. "Yeah, Mr. Parrish," he said. "Come right in."

He gestured at the little room as he closed the door, at the twin beds, the minimal furniture, the drafting table and stool in the corner. "It's not much, but it's home," he essayed, watching the lawyer for his response, judging its effect. "If you'd come this afternoon, I'd be in better shape. A little too much Christmas cheer."

The lawyer didn't answer. He took off his overcoat and appropriated the easy chair. He looked around. "How long have you lived here?"

"Since early July, when my wife threw me out. Except that I was over in Italy half the summer buying marble."

"Buying marble?"

Costaine sat down on the near bed and rubbed the stubble on his face self-consciously. "Yeah. I'm a consultant for architectural firms and one of them sent me to Italy to choose marble for a hotel they're doing. I got home the middle of October and came back here."

"Same room?"

"Same room. Sally would have known where to come that night." He saw the lawyer's eye go to the whiskey bottle on the bed table. "You like a drink?"

"No, but help yourself."

Costaine was tempted but thought better of it. "I've had enough for a while. I've been drinking a lot since it happened. She was going to come here, you know. She told me so the night of the dance. I hadn't seen her since I got back. Two weeks it was. But she hadn't changed the way she was feeling. We were going to make up for those two months. I waited for her but she never came." He shifted in the following silence. "I guess that's what you want to hear about. Everything that happened that night?"

"Later," Parrish said. "Later I'm going to want to hear it all. First, though, I want to know how you met."

That was all right with Costaine too. He didn't mind talking about Sally. He enjoyed it.

He relived it in the telling; the day three summers ago when he had encountered Sally sunning herself in a bikini on an empty part of the beach. That was the thing about the Summer Club. It was right on Long Island Sound, with miles of sand, but it also had an outdoor pool and hardly anyone but children went near the sea. For loners like Sally, the beach was the place. So Costaine, walking along the water's edge in bathing trunks, picking up shells and feeling the ripples about his feet, had come up to her, had said, "What's a beautiful girl like you doing all by yourself like this?" She had asked what was wrong with where she was and he'd said beautiful girls, by rights, should be surrounded by eager men and she had no business trying to escape her fate. She had laughed; he had responded, "Take off your sunglasses so I can see if I know you." She had taken them off; he had decided he didn't know her and that if the situation wasn't remedied immediately, he would throw himself beneath the waves and drown.

Parrish said, "Did you know she was there when you went down onto the beach?"

Walter giggled a little and decided the lawyer was a very savvy man. "Sure I knew she was there," he said. "What the hell do you think I'd be wandering along the beach for otherwise? I hate the water."

The lawyer laughed and Costaine realized they spoke the same language. He allowed as how the meeting was a calculated maneuver because he'd seen Sally a number of times, found her attractive, and noted her inclination to solitude. To him this meant she was available and he moved in.

They met a number of times on the beach that summer, sitting together, discussing life, men, women, religion, politics. With the passage of time they even included the more intimate subjects of marriage and sex.

In the fall the Whittakers invited the Costaines to a dinner party. In the winter the Costaines reciprocated. They encountered each

151

other at social gatherings and the chances for Walter and Sally to converse together grew more frequent.

Parrish, nodding, said, "Did you have seduction on your mind throughout all this?"

Costaine shrugged and laughed. "How do I know? I cast bread upon the waters and see what happens."

"Meaning it's a behavior pattern? You have your antennae out for women and if they're interested, you're available?"

"Something like that. I like women. Women like being liked and therefore they like me. Most men flock together at a party. They hang around the bar and talk golf or politics. I go where the women are and I talk about them. You'd be surprised how effective it is. So when they need a shoulder to cry on or if they're hungry for the affection they're not getting at home, they think of me."

Parrish smiled and Costaine decided he might take just another finger of rye. Parrish was a good sort who wouldn't read anything debauched in it. He helped himself and sat back again. "You see," he continued, trying to explain his philosophy, "I love women—the whole gender. To me, nothing on God's earth is more beautiful than a woman. Any woman. They can be old and fat and they're still beautiful to me. Just to be female is to be beautiful." He leaned his elbows on his knees, sipping the rye and cradling the glass. "Now, you take Sally Whittaker. Physically, she was a luscious specimen, especially in a bikini. Now, you were asking if I was trying to seduce her the whole time. I wasn't. Not really. I just got a pleasurable sensation sitting beside her on the beach, being able to look at her, talk with her and listen to her. She was a warm person really. She and Jerry didn't get on, but it was his fault. He took her for granted. He left her alone. It wasn't just that he was busy. Even when he was free he left her alone. He should have been sitting beside her on the beach. He didn't, so I did."

As for the details of the first seduction, Costaine remembered them vividly. "It was back on May fourteenth, a wet Thursday. Since I'm a consulting architect I do most of my work at home. So I'm around a lot. I ran into her shopping and we had a cup of coffee. She was in a state. She'd been squabbling with Jerry. She was frustrated and irritated by his lack of interest, his being too tired to go to bed with her, his having no time." Costaine finished his rye and smiled. "As you can see, we'd reached a rather intimate stage of conversation."

He put the glass on the table beside the bottle and sat back. "I took her for a drive in the country. I sympathized with her. I told her she had never been made love to properly, the way a girl of her beauty and appeal deserved. So we went out in the woods and I showed her how it should be done."

"And after that?"

"After that we started meeting regularly. Doing it in the car was awkward. So we came to this motel and used it from then on. Even after Jerry and Barbara caught us."

"And Barbara threw you out?"

"Not right then. She said she would if I didn't stop seeing Sally. I pretended I did, but she wouldn't be fooled. All the times before she made out she believed me, but not now." He shook his head, bewildered. "I thought she understood. I thought she was a modern, clear-thinking woman. I thought she knew I loved her, that it didn't have anything to do with her. It's just my way." He spread his hands. "Hell, I kept her happy. I gave her plenty of sex too. It wasn't like she was being deprived."

After that, Costaine said, he moved into the motel and Sally came there for their liaisons. Such was the arrangement until he went to Italy on the marble-buying trip near the end of August.

Parrish made notes and asked a casual question. What about the other lovers in Sally's life?

Costaine grinned. "Other lovers? You got to be kidding."

"Why?"

"There weren't any."

"You mean she *told* you there weren't any."

Costaine shook his head. "I don't mean that's how I know. How dumb do you think I am? I mean it's the way she was. You can tell when a woman's been around. They know the ropes. They have a certain ease about them. You take them into a motel and they don't blush like a bride when you sign the register, or try to keep the proprietors from getting a good look at them. And when you make love to them, they don't have the inhibitions of a girl taking her first false step. A woman getting laid by someone other than her husband for the first time is a lot like a virgin. She's got guilt feelings. She has trouble letting herself go. She's extremely conscious of what it is she's doing.

"And that was Sally that first time."

CHAPTER 33

"That lying son of a bitch Costaine! Everything he says is a lie. He's lying all the way down the line!"

Cleveland Parrish threw the latest Dan Price report across Melody's desk with such vehemence it skipped and fluttered to the floor. He recovered, hid his disgust behind a laugh, and bent to retrieve the clipped sheets himself.

Melody accepted them with a poker face but she was concerned. When Cleveland Parrish insisted that a prosecution witness had to be a liar, it meant Cleveland Parrish lacked a rebuttal for the witness's testimony. And when he threw papers like that, or got argumentative with a business associate, as he'd just done with Jake Settler, it meant the witness's testimony was vital to the case.

She skimmed through the detective's report and it revealed that Walter Costaine was very much a liar. For one thing, whatever Walter Costaine had done for six weeks that past summer, he hadn't gone to Italy to buy marble. Nor was he, as he had claimed, a consultant for architectural firms. He was a free-lancer who picked up farmed-out drafting jobs when architectural staffs got overloaded. It was the most elementary sort of work, the starting point in the business.

"He's a liar, all right," Melody agreed. "You weren't worrying about proving it, were you?"

Parrish turned his back and stared at the window. "Hell, no. A philanderer is a liar by definition. The trouble is, there's a difference in a jury's mind about lying to fool your wife and lying to put a man in the electric chair. Our job is to prove he's the electric chair kind of liar."

Melody indicated the report. "Doesn't this help? Here he's lying about things he doesn't have to lie about."

"Those are lies a man tells to make himself look big. It's still a long way from lying to kill a man." He stalked back to the office, lost

ine report, watched him go to the
d seen him worried before but she'd
There was no cause for alarm, except
imes did get lost.
that she didn't hear the click of
re that she had company until a

job were in separate compart-
Yet there was Gary Stevens,
ome, the most spoiled of the
ence.
a smile. She was glad to see
ished he hadn't come to the
lly in such a mood), that he
e hadn't walked in in such—
nd—let's face it—inexpensive

dn't sprung full-grown from
a family, and he knew the
a couple of pictures in her
wanted their separate worlds
n the suavest young blade in
w York cocktail party one

ce but to welcome him and
of course, when she turned,
exchange, knowing this was
ice or a counter clerk taking
was nothing to do but in-

hich she was thankful. He
his coloring was dark rather
nblance. And he didn't em-
t secretary he thought she

And Gary, bless him, didn't say he was out of a job and ask if Mr. Parrish could inquire among his friends about opportunities for an ambitious young engineer.

Then Cleve was all business again and Gary became part of the furniture. "Melody, we're not going to let this son of a bitch Costaine show us up. Get Jerry Whittaker's old man on the phone. This is going to cost a lot more money!" He went back to his office and closed the door.

Melody winced as she sank into her chair. Two unbidden pictures came forcibly to mind: of that poor, desperate little pharmacist with his run-down shop and sinking wife, and of Pete Tucker, in the front seat of the Cadillac, spitting contemptuously into the street.

Gary edged through the gate. "Hey, Melody."

"In a minute," she said impatiently, flicking open her number box and picking up the phone. Cleve had done a quick assessment of the little shop and upstairs apartment on that November visit but he had only shrugged at the end and said nothing.

The faded druggist hoped he could keep the place, but the fall of the ax had not been canceled, it had merely been postponed.

She got the old man on the line and his voice sounded haunted. For a moment he didn't understand who wanted to speak to him. Then the message got through and the unsteady voice slipped a little deeper into despair. He knew what he did not want to know. She put Parrish on the line, hung up her own phone, and tried to erase memory with the act.

Gary was on her in an instant. The baby had come a week late, a girl, Rh-negative. He had lost out on Blue Cross, bills were piling up, and there was a limit to what the family could do for him. He absolutely had to have a job! What the hell, he deserved one. Hadn't he studied hard, kept his nose clean, met his responsibilities? And where was the payoff? What was in it for him? What was the advantage of being a good citizen?

"I don't know," Melody said. The yellow light of Parrish's call beaming on her button phone distracted her. "Goodness knows I've done everything I could for you here. If you need more money—"

"It's not money, God damn it, it's work! I've got to feel useful. I've got to support my own family. I've got to advance my career. I'm in my middle twenties. That's the time a man has got to be productive." He beat on the fence. "That's why I'm here. Melody, you've got to help me."

Melody indicated the report. "Doesn't this help? Here he's lying about things he doesn't have to lie about."

"Those are lies a man tells to make himself look big. It's still a long way from lying to kill a man." He stalked back to the office, lost in thought.

Melody, holding the Costaine report, watched him go to the window behind his desk. She had seen him worried before but she'd seen him pull rabbits from hats. There was no cause for alarm, except that you never knew. Cases sometimes did get lost.

She was so immersed in thought that she didn't hear the click of the outer door and she was unaware that she had company until a familiar voice said, "Hi, Sis."

She wheeled in shock. Family and job were in separate compartments. Never the twain were to meet. Yet there was Gary Stevens, the youngest, most dashing and handsome, the most spoiled of the clan, standing grinning by the visitors' fence.

"For heaven's sake!" She gave him a smile. She was glad to see him. She really was. Except that she wished he hadn't come to the office when Cleve was around (especially in such a mood), that he hadn't walked in without a job, that he hadn't walked in in such—well—non-New York, non-lawyerish, and—let's face it—inexpensive clothes.

To be sure, Cleve did know she hadn't sprung full-grown from the head of Zeus, that she did have a family, and he knew the number of its members. He'd even seen a couple of pictures in her bedroom, but that was as close as she wanted their separate worlds to come. Like Gary. He might have been the suavest young blade in Ebbs Falls in his teens, but at a New York cocktail party one would only wonder who had let him in.

But there he was and she had no choice but to welcome him and let him kiss her cheek at the gate. And, of course, when she turned, Cleve was in his doorway, observing the exchange, knowing this was not a messenger boy from the postal service or a counter clerk taking food orders from the delicatessen. There was nothing to do but introduce him.

Cleve was as nice as could be, for which she was thankful. He shook Gary's hand warmly and told him his coloring was dark rather than fair, but otherwise he saw the resemblance. And he didn't embarrass her by telling Gary what a great secretary he thought she was.

And Gary, bless him, didn't say he was out of a job and ask if Mr. Parrish could inquire among his friends about opportunities for an ambitious young engineer.

Then Cleve was all business again and Gary became part of the furniture. "Melody, we're not going to let this son of a bitch Costaine show us up. Get Jerry Whittaker's old man on the phone. This is going to cost a lot more money!" He went back to his office and closed the door.

Melody winced as she sank into her chair. Two unbidden pictures came forcibly to mind: of that poor, desperate little pharmacist with his run-down shop and sinking wife, and of Pete Tucker, in the front seat of the Cadillac, spitting contemptuously into the street.

Gary edged through the gate. "Hey, Melody."

"In a minute," she said impatiently, flicking open her number box and picking up the phone. Cleve had done a quick assessment of the little shop and upstairs apartment on that November visit but he had only shrugged at the end and said nothing.

The faded druggist hoped he could keep the place, but the fall of the ax had not been canceled, it had merely been postponed.

She got the old man on the line and his voice sounded haunted. For a moment he didn't understand who wanted to speak to him. Then the message got through and the unsteady voice slipped a little deeper into despair. He knew what he did not want to know. She put Parrish on the line, hung up her own phone, and tried to erase memory with the act.

Gary was on her in an instant. The baby had come a week late, a girl, Rh-negative. He had lost out on Blue Cross, bills were piling up, and there was a limit to what the family could do for him. He absolutely had to have a job! What the hell, he deserved one. Hadn't he studied hard, kept his nose clean, met his responsibilities? And where was the payoff? What was in it for him? What was the advantage of being a good citizen?

"I don't know," Melody said. The yellow light of Parrish's call beaming on her button phone distracted her. "Goodness knows I've done everything I could for you here. If you need more money—"

"It's not money, God damn it, it's work! I've got to feel useful. I've got to support my own family. I've got to advance my career. I'm in my middle twenties. That's the time a man has got to be productive." He beat on the fence. "That's why I'm here. Melody, you've got to help me."

"Gary, I keep telling you there's nothing in New York. I've looked. I've looked everywhere."

She meant it too, according to her standards. Hadn't she gone as far as was politic in venturing questions on the matter? (One only tactfully explores the need for unemployed engineers. One doesn't, of course, fall on one's knees.)

Gary would not be put off. "There's got to be. There's nothing anywhere else. And this is where all the people are, all the jobs are."

"Not engineering jobs."

"I'll take anything. I'm not proud."

"Have you looked in the want ads?"

"Yes, but I don't mean that kind of stuff. You've got contacts, Melody! Damn it, you know everybody who matters! You're friends with famous people. We've heard about them for years. And one of them, somewhere, has got to have a spot for someone like me. You can't make me believe there aren't any jobs at all."

Melody swallowed. "But I have looked."

"Look harder! God damn it, I'm your brother!"

She said desperately, "Don't you think I want to help? But I know New York and you don't." She got an idea and went on. "Look, Gary, do you have a place to stay? Never mind. You can have my apartment. Mr. Parrish is moving to New Haven at the end of this week and I'm going up there with him. He's got to work on a case there. Jerry Whittaker. You know the one? Well, we're going to be very busy. He's got to interview all kinds of people and I'll have to be on hand. So I'll be moving out of my apartment and you can move in. You can use that as a headquarters until you find a job."

He was less grateful than she had hoped. He accepted it but he still thought she could wave a wand and produce employment. She couldn't make him understand.

"Yeah, yeah." He jerked a thumb at the inner office. "But what about him? He ought to have something a guy like me could do."

"He doesn't. You don't know what you're talking about. You don't know this city. Here." She fished in her bag for the duplicate key, gave it to him and promised she'd call the doorman. Eddie would be on that afternoon. There'd be no trouble.

The other phone line rang and it was Dan Price. He sounded pleased with himself, called her "sweetheart," and asked if the great man was on hand.

"He's on the other line. Do you want to wait?"

"No, I'm in a hurry. Just tell him we've picked up a hot piece of news for his Walter Costaine file. Barbara isn't Costaine's first wife and Nellise and Briggs aren't his only children. He's got a twenty-year-old daughter by the original Mrs. C."

Melody brightened. Perhaps that was the information Cleve needed to shatter Costaine's testimony. Perhaps Jerry's father wouldn't have to sell his store. "Another wife? Where does she live?"

"Up in the Bronx. I'm going to see her now."

"That's great," Melody said, surprised at her excitement. She never got involved.

Gary was still waiting when she put down the phone, looking as if he needed some good news too.

"I'll tell you what," she said. "I'll take you to lunch and show you the apartment and introduce you to Leopold. He's the super. You can make yourself right at home."

She picked up her purse and coat. The apartment would be good for Gary's morale, and the sooner she got him out of the office, the better her own morale would be. She scribbled a message to Cleve and picked up the want ad section of the morning's *Times* on her way to the door.

CHAPTER 34

Parrish looked up darkly. "What do you mean, I don't need the store?"

"I was thinking about Dan." Melody gathered up the letters Cleve had finished signing.

"Dan Price? What about him?"

"His discovery. About Costaine's other wife."

Cleve tilted his chair and stared at her. "Make sense, will you?"

Melody knew she wasn't putting it well, that she was flushed and nervous. She tried to be lucid. "Costaine's got another wife and another daughter he's been hiding all these years."

"So?"

"This may be the break you've been waiting for, the thing that can destroy him—his credibility."

"So?"

"I was just thinking, this would cut down the amount of investigation you have to do. You wouldn't need as much money in the defense fund."

"And I wouldn't need old man Whittaker's store? Is that it?"

She tried to be offhand. "Something like that."

Parrish snorted. "Come on, Melody, I thought you had a better head than that. Would you please explain to me exactly what leverage the fact that Costaine has an earlier wife is going to give me in court?"

She looked away. "I don't know. I thought his trying to lie about it—"

Parrish sat up in the chair. "Leave the decisions to me, my pet. Understand this. If we are going to save Jerry Whittaker's neck, we're going to need a hell of a lot of research. Because we have got to turn up either of two things. One, a second lover for Sally; or, two, a reason for Costaine lying about Sally's proposed visit to his motel. And I fail to see how an earlier wife and daughter in Costaine's life is going to satisfy either need. So don't tell me I don't need old Zacharias' store. It's an essential."

Melody accepted that, but couldn't help remarking, "Jerry will explode when he finds out."

"Jerry isn't going to hear about it. I told old Zack to keep it a deep dark secret."

Melody chewed her lip at the information. "Then he's going to—does he want to sell?"

"I've got him persuaded. It's not hard. Jerry's his favorite son."

Melody thought hopefully of Art Canaris, who handled Cleve's real estate deals. At least he might make it worthwhile. "Do you think Art can get a good price for his store?"

"That crumby joint? I wouldn't embarrass Art by asking him to handle it. Let Whittaker sell it himself. He's got a ready-made buyer."

"But that buyer is only offering twenty thousand."

Cleve shrugged. "I told him I needed fifteen. Anything over that he can keep."

She thought of the old man and his invalid wife and she thought of

Pete Tucker, who called her a bitch, a cold and beautiful bitch. She wasn't a bitch really. People blamed her for what Cleve did. Just because she was his secretary. It wasn't her fault. She only did her job. The decisions were his.

She returned to the outer office as Dan Price entered from outside. He was laughing and called her "sweetheart" again, only this time he didn't just pat her fanny in passing, he gave it a little squeeze. She looked after him as he went through Cleve's door, more aware of him than usual, but all she thought was, "What the hell's got into him?" She was not in the mood to have her fanny admired.

Cleve called her into the office. "Dan's been to see Costaine's ex-wife," he said. "This you ought to hear."

Melody took a seat and Dan related that the ex-wife, while claiming she had scarcely seen Walter Costaine over twenty years, nevertheless had enough "dirt" on him to destroy him completely if he ever dared get up on a witness stand.

Cleve laughed. "Now, what do you think about that, Melody?" He added to Price, "Tell her the punch line."

Dan grinned and sipped rye from the shot glass Cleve had poured for him. "She says I can have this destructive information for a price."

Melody, uncertain, said, "How much?"

"Ten thousand dollars."

Both men roared. Parrish said to Melody, "Now do you see why I need the store?"

She sat, small and tight, not joining in the merriment. She wanted to leave, but she wasn't sure Parrish was through with her.

Cleve let her sit. He said to the detective, "Is she for real?"

"She's a money-hungry broad. Her antennae have dollar signs all over them."

"What'd you tell her?"

"I said I'd give her five bucks for everything she knew." Price shrugged. "She wouldn't budge. She really thinks you'll meet her terms."

Parrish paid often for information, but he wouldn't buy pigs in pokes, even though it was the client's money. "What kind of guarantee does she have that her information is worth that kind of money?"

"None."

"I presume you demanded some?"

Price nodded and killed the rye. He leaned to pour a little more. "Sure I did, but she doesn't know the rules. She only told me she wasn't opening her mouth until her palm was crossed with the whole ten gees. The only other word I could get out of her was that what she had would shoot him down like a pigeon. One word from her and he'd move into a cave."

Parrish turned to the unmoving girl. "You think that's worth Zack Whittaker's store, Melody? Or do you think we ought to spend the money in other areas?"

She did not answer.

Parrish drummed on the desk top and Melody was no longer in his mind. He said to the detective, "You think she's got anything worth pushing her for?"

"I think *she* thinks she has."

"Can you wear her down?"

"I can try, but where a buck is concerned, I think she'll outwear glass."

"She's got a child?"

"A daughter, Rita. Twenty. I'd sooner tackle a tarantula, but if you want me to pressure her—"

"You think she knows whatever it is her mother—"

"I doubt it. And I doubt she'll wear any easier than the mother but, as I say, if you want me to bear down on the two of them, I'll work at it."

Parrish shook his head. "I know the type. They won't give away anything they think they can sell. Offer them a hundred. If they don't buy it, forget it. If they won't sell for that, it's a safe bet what they've got isn't worth anything." He turned to Melody. "Don't you agree?"

CHAPTER 35

Melody poured herself a good slug of scotch from the living room cabinet. Gary was in the guest bedroom with the door nearly closed and she looked around guiltily when the neck of the bottle clinked against the glass. It wasn't that he thought she didn't drink; it wasn't that she didn't want to drink in front of him. It was, really, that she'd just come home and hadn't even taken off her hat and coat.

Gary did not materialize, waving an accusing finger, and she carried the glass with her into her own bedroom. She took a swallow of the liquid, then stationed it on the dresser while she put her things away. She wasn't usually like that. In fact, she almost never drank alone.

She came back for the glass, took another swallow, a little larger than she intended, and it made her shiver. What was she doing with scotch anyway? It was not a drink she cared for. Rye was her choice. True, rye was a pedestrian drink, but it didn't have the unpleasant medicinal flavor of scotch. Scotch was what she drank in public. Scotch was what she ordered with Cleve, what she had on hand for him in the apartment, what he gave her when he brought her gifts. Now she had poured it by habit rather than design. Oh well, she was using it for medicine so it might as well taste like it.

She sat down on her bed, one of the twins, and set the glass on the intervening table. She took the phone in her lap and dialed nervously. She was going to do something she had never before done in her life.

A woman answered on the fifth ring. It would be her luck to catch the wife. "Is Mr. Whittaker there, please? This is Mr. Parrish's secretary calling from New York."

Fortunately old Zacharias wasn't down in the shop. He would be there in a minute. Melody could hear the squeaky voice of the woman calling. It was frail and thin, the reedlike tone of the dying.

"Mr. Whittaker speaking."

That was a firmer voice, but with a dead weight in it. She remembered him getting out of the car to show Cleve his store. The weight lay under his hope even then.

She told him who she was, speaking rapidly. She paused for one more gulp of scotch and went on with it. Mr. Parrish had talked to him about selling his store, had he not? And there was a buyer for it? There was someone who would pay twenty thousand dollars? Mr. Whittaker was then to turn fifteen of that sum over to Mr. Parrish for trial expenses? Was that the understanding?"

Mr. Whittaker, in the same heavy voice, said it was.

"Have you done it yet, Mr. Whittaker?"

No, he hadn't. The old man sounded stricken with panic. He hadn't had time. The buyer hadn't come in since he'd had the call. He didn't realize Mr. Parrish needed it done so soon. How could he make amends—?

Melody felt shaken by his fright. It was wrong for her—for anyone to have such effect. Grown men shouldn't quaver. "No, no, it's all right," she interrupted hastily. "That's what I'm calling about. It won't be necessary."

There was stark silence at the other end for such long seconds she feared he might have collapsed.

"Mr. Whittaker?"

At last he responded, uncertainly. "It won't be necessary to sell?"

"That's right," she said gently. "You can keep the store."

"I don't understand."

"Mr. Parrish does not need your money."

"But this morning—to save Jerry—I don't mind selling, Miss. I'll do anything to save Jerry. He didn't kill that woman."

"I know that. I know he didn't, Mr. Whittaker. And Mr. Parrish will convince the jury of that, rest assured. But you don't need to sell your store any more. Things have changed."

He couldn't believe it. It was too big a concept. "But if Mr. Parrish had the money, he could do a better job. He told me so."

"Mr. Parrish will do the best job that can be done, Mr. Whittaker. Your money won't make any difference. He's got enough money." She had to get it through to him. "Do you understand me, Mr. Whittaker? Mr. Parrish has enough money."

163

Whittaker still couldn't grasp the realization and she had to go over it with him two more times before the reality began to dawn: He could keep his store and Jerry would still have all the defense he needed. Selling the store was no longer the difference between life and death.

"Well, I'll be," the pharmacist finally exclaimed. He was almost chipper now. "You know, Miss Stevens, I prayed to God and He's spoken to me. I asked His forgiveness and I asked His guidance. And He has rewarded me. To think I can keep the store!"

"Yes," Melody interrupted, "but there's one thing."

He became frightened again. "What's that?"

"You must not let Mr. Parrish know I talked to you. Just sit tight and do nothing. Pretty soon he'll call you and ask where the money is. When he does, you tell him you've changed your mind. Tell him you've decided not to sell. Don't tell him why. Do you understand? Don't answer any questions. And don't let him talk you into anything. He'll try. He'll work on you to sell so he can get your money. He'll tell you he can't defend Jerry without it. But don't listen to him. Because it's not true. And even if it were true, he'd still get Jerry off without your money. Because he'll do anything to win a case including spend his own money."

"I see," the man said uncertainly, and she had to hope he spoke the truth. She had to hope he'd have the guts to stand up against the high-powered Parrish.

"Remember, you've got to think of your wife," she added, to reinforce his determination. "Don't mention me, pretend it was your own decision, and stand by it. Have you got that?"

He said he had, and the call was concluded. Melody drained her glass and set it back on the bed table, holding onto it almost as if it were a support. She had never gone behind Parrish's back before. It was almost sacrilege. But Cleve was making a mint on Jerry's belongings. He didn't need the old man's too.

She sat there, brooding and worrying. Cleve would worm it out of old Zack. She was as sure of it as she was afraid. What would she say when he faced her with it? Would she say, "I did it because he has a sick wife"? Or, "It would have killed him"? Or, "I did it because Pete Tucker spit in the street"?

"Please, God," she prayed under her breath, "don't let him hear about it. Give the old man strength."

She rose at last and went to the kitchen. There wasn't much in the refrigerator. She should have shopped. She forgot she had a boarder. Well, there were plenty of eggs. She could make a Spanish omelet.

Gary came by the doorway, stopped, and entered with a grin. He was wearing bedroom slippers and was settled in already. The place became him. He should live in high-class surroundings. She and he. The others in the family were geared for lesser stations, but Melody and Gary, the eldest and the youngest, this, she thought to herself, was where they belonged.

"I don't have much," she said. "I'll be going to New Haven. Would you like a Spanish omelet?"

Gary said that would be fine.

"Did you go through the want ads?"

He nodded. "There's nothing there."

"Of course there is."

He grinned and leaned against the refrigerator door as she started breaking eggs at the adjacent stove. "You're really something, Sis," he said.

"What's that mean?"

"Do you make a practice of double-crossing your boss?"

Her heart missed a full beat. She turned slowly, scowling. "I don't know what you're talking about. I wouldn't double-cross anybody."

"That business about not selling the store? That's not a double-cross?"

He'd been on the extension. There was no point in pretending she didn't know what he was talking about, no point in berating him for his meanness. "You were listening," she said, and he grinned.

It was so long ago she'd forgotten. She'd been gone from home too many years. He'd been like that. When the boys came to call, Gary was the brat behind the couch. He was the eavesdropper, listening in on her phone conversations, her dates. And the time he surprised her and Tim Mulcahey in his car in front of the house, her with her blouse unbuttoned and her bra around her neck. She never could be sure how much he saw that time.

But she went away to college and she forgot, or she assumed Gary had outgrown that pesky quality. Or she thought it was only directed against her and her boyfriends. But he hadn't. And now he had caught her again, only worse than with Tim. He couldn't be sure then just what they were doing, but he damned well knew what she was up to now. "I was just giving a client some advice," she said.

His grin broadened. That grin of his, she noted, wasn't so beguiling

165

after all. Nor was he as handsome as she had assumed. Didn't he look sneaky around the eyes? "Do you think your boss would approve of the advice?" he asked her.

"He trusts my judgment."

"That's not answering my question."

She faced him. "Gary, you don't know anything about the legal business. You don't understand all the elements of my role as Mr. Parrish's secretary. I'm not just a stenographer. I am deeply involved in everything Mr. Parrish handles. I am, you might say, a semi-partner. I carry a good share of the decision-making responsibility. You wouldn't understand."

His smile was mocking. "All I understand, Sis, is that you're making a unilateral decision that's going to cost your boss fifteen thousand dollars. And it occurs to me that he might like to hire someone like me to report on the decisions that are being made behind his back."

"I don't like the way you're talking," she said, feigning anger, but knowing terror.

"I wasn't particularly impressed with the way you were just now talking, either. You know, Sis, I don't think Mr. Parrish would have been impressed either."

She sighed and essayed a new tack. "What are you trying to do, Gary? Are you trying to get *me* in trouble? What do you think that's going to prove?"

Gary shook his head. "Me?" he said innocently. "I'm not trying to give anybody trouble. All I want to point out is that I've got a wife and three children, one of them a newborn baby, and I don't have a job. I don't have any money."

"And you think you can blackmail me?"

He lounged more comfortably against the icebox door. "No, dear sister. I'm not trying to blackmail you. I don't want your money. I want a job. And it occurs to me that this big, rich lawyer you work for could find some employment for me if he put his mind to it. All I need is someone to make him see how important it is." He gave her that boyish, beguiling grin again, the one she was starting to detest. "Seeing as how you have so much to do with the decision making, how about throwing a decision my way?" He turned serious. "I'm good. You know I am. I'll do a job. And I'm loyal, which is more than you can say. If he buys me, I'll stay bought." He was sincere now. "Come on, Sis. I'm not trying to throw my weight around, but I've got to have a job. And he's the kind of man I'd like to work for."

Him and her both working for Parrish? Anything but that. Her glamor would wear off, and she had to guard her family status jealously. But her options were narrow. Gary had the power to destroy. "Cleve's going to New Haven tonight," she said. "I don't know when I'll get a chance—"

"Cleve? You call him Cleve?"

God, he'd be finding out about their relationship next. "Of course I call him Cleve. Didn't I say I'm a semi-partner?"

"Well, when you go to New Haven to see your semi-partner, why don't I go too?"

CHAPTER 36

Cleve Parrish, breakfasting late in the presidential suite of the Park Plaza in New Haven, stopped poring over background data on Gerald Whittaker's Madison patients to answer the phone. It was Edward Balin again, which was enough to make a suit of armor puke. Balin was on the goddam phone twice a day seeking orders, *mon capitaine*. And if that wasn't bad enough, he was nearly through the first draft of his damned chapter on corporation law, which chapter was running better than seventy pages. Parrish was going to have a time keeping from getting it crammed down his throat.

"Yes, Ed," Parrish said, finding it daily more difficult to exude charm. He grunted and read background reports and cut Balin short with assurances that everything was under control and he'd be glad to go over the essential elements of the defense as soon as he had them worked out. The essential elements of his defense had long since been worked out, but Balin wasn't going to learn about them until the jury did.

Parrish grunted to more reports about *THE CHAPTER*, got rid of the lawyer and went back to his studies. His defense would be in two parts. All Parrish defenses were in two parts: Attack and Parry. The hell with neutralizing prosecution blows. Go for the jugular. Get those prosecution witnesses up on that stand and don't just destroy their testimony, destroy THEM! Tear out their secret hearts and hold them up for ridicule. Pull the skeletons out of their closets. Hurt, damage, ruin. Terrify the next witness with the fate of his predecessor.

The door opened and Melody came through from her connecting room.

"Where the hell have you been?" Parrish demanded. "It's almost noon."

She latched the door and paused by the dining table. "I could have taken an earlier train," she said. "You didn't say what time you wanted me."

"You ought to know I've got a lot for you to do. I've been interviewing patients for a week. Almost forty of them." He poured more coffee and asked about the affairs in New York she had been handling. She opened her notebook and gave him a rundown while he sipped. He did not offer her coffee, nor did she help herself.

She finished and he approved. He leaned forward and gave her some of the Webster-Smith reports on Whittaker patients. "Go through the ones that aren't checked and arrange appointments. Now that you're here, maybe we can start to move on this thing."

She flipped through the sheets with a practiced eye. "By the way," she said, "I, ah, brought my brother up—from New York."

"Yeah?" Parrish couldn't care less. He sorted through the other sheets on the breakfast table.

"He's not going to stay."

Cleve sensed the strain in her manner. He hadn't known her six years for nothing. "What'd he come up here for?" he asked, still sorting.

"He's out of work. Did I tell you he was out of work?"

Now it's coming out. Now we're beginning to see the light. "No, I didn't know he was out of work."

Melody rushed ahead. Gary had such a bright future as an engineer, but recession set in and lots of engineers got fired. Gary was one of those unlucky ones. It was so unfair. He was such a talent. And so personable and popular. Everybody liked him. Why, before he got married, there wasn't a girl in their hometown who didn't have her cap set for him.

Parrish watched her. She was dog-earing her notebook. "Yeah, it's tough," he said. What was she after, a recommendation or subsidy?

It was neither. She wanted an outright job for the boy. Gary was desperate. He'd take any kind of work. Anything at all. Didn't Cleve have something he could do: clean the apartment, be a valet, run errands? Or did Cleve know of anyone who could use an able, willing, and so personable a young man? He had to have something right away!

Parrish didn't know how desperate the young man might be, but Melody was desperate. He wondered why. If he could find something for the kid to do, he might find out. But what was available? He'd seen the youth. The imbecile couldn't interview, he couldn't research, he couldn't bookkeep, file, sort, type, or know how to find out information. —Except? All the girls in the old hometown had their caps out for him, had they?

Parrish smiled. "Where is he?"

"Down in the lobby."

"It's just possible," he said, and watched Melody's eyes light up. Very interesting response. Something was going on. "I might have a little job he can do. Call him up."

She did, eagerly, and Gary was at the door in less than five minutes, brushed, scrubbed, bright-eyed and hat in hand. "Yes, sir, Mr. Parrish."

The lawyer, seated at the table, said, "I understand you're good at making friends and influencing people."

Gary shifted his feet and twisted his hat. "I guess I do all right."

Melody broke in. "He's too modest, Cleve. He does better than all right. Don't be so modest, Gary. You know how popular you are."

Gary grinned like a country bumpkin. "Well, I guess I do O.K. I haven't heard any complaints."

Parrish tore out a piece of notepaper and wrote on it. He folded it and showed it to the boy. "This is the name and address of the first wife of a man named Walter Costaine. He's involved in a case we're handling and this wife claims she has some information about him that would be very damaging. Do you understand me?"

Gary nodded. "Yeah. She's got something on him she could blackmail him with."

"That's right, Gary. That's just right. Now, what I want to know is what that piece of information is. If you would like to go after that information and if you can bring that information back to me, I will

169

pay you a thousand dollars." Parrish offered the slip. "Are you interested?"

"Are you kidding?" Gary Stevens waited only long enough to read the name and address, shake Parrish's hand, and get directions back to the railroad station before he was on his way. Melody watched him go, and Parrish watched Melody.

CHAPTER 37

Zacharias Whittaker started to tremble. The phone in his hand wobbled against his ear. Melody Stevens had just asked him to hold the line, that Mr. Parrish wanted to talk to him. His wife was looking toward him from her chair by the window but her expression was curious, not solicitous. Was her vision so far gone that she could not read his panic? He covered the mouthpiece and told her it was Mr. Parrish.

That did it. Her own anxious fingers plucked instantly at the afghan over her lap and her bleary, magnified eyes widened behind their lenses. "Zacharias," she said. "Hold fast."

He would. He nodded that he would. He would lash himself to the mast against the siren song of the lawyer. He had promised. And he reminded himself that he mustn't mention Miss Stevens' name.

"Hello there, Mr. Whittaker, how are things?" The lawyer's voice boomed with heartiness, camaraderie and concern. Mr. Parrish was such a kind and helpful man. Hadn't he taken the time to appraise the store, and hadn't he, when the need to sell arrived, recommended acceptance of Martin Wraxler's terms? Zacharias would be lucky to get twenty thousand, Parrish had claimed, and one could tell from his analytical, calculating eye that he knew value.

"I'm all right," Zacharias answered in subdued tones.

"That's fine. How are things progressing?"

Zacharias swallowed. Mr. Parrish had a way of getting right to business that was discomfiting. Zacharias would have liked to discuss the weather or Jerry's condition first, to fortify himself. "Progressing?"

"The store. Martin Wraxler. You've got the sale arranged, haven't you?"

Zacharias wished he could say that Martin Wraxler hadn't been in but it wasn't quite true. Wraxler had dropped by just two days before, the fifteenth of January, to be exact, the day Zacharias had taken his wife to the clinic. Wraxler had made his customary offer, but Zacharias, his heart pounding, had put his trust in Melody and turned him down. "I haven't had a chance yet, Mr. Parrish," he said and convinced himself that it was the truth. He did have that doctor's appointment on the fifteenth. Even if he had accepted Wraxler's offer, he wouldn't have had a chance to do anything more. That was Friday and today was Sunday.

"You haven't had a chance?" The accusatory tone that could come into the lawyer's voice was frightening. "What have you been doing?"

Whittaker looked to his wife for strength. "He—you see, he hasn't come in. As of Friday, when I had to take my wife to the doctor's, he hadn't come in."

"Come in? What does he have to come in for? Why don't you phone him?"

Whittaker's voice was very small. "I don't know where he lives."

"You don't know where he lives? What's the matter with you? Don't you have a phone book? Can't you call information?"

Melody had told him to say he'd changed his mind. He hadn't been able to make himself do that.

Janet was bolstering him. "Tell him we won't sell," she said. "Tell him."

He nodded. "I, ah, I—"

"I say, why can't you call him?"

"Well, I suppose—ah—I could. I guess I didn't think of that."

Parrish was angry now. "Well you'd damned well better! The kitty is very low and as I made it clear to you, I won't do a job if I can't do it right and I can't do it right if I don't have the budget."

"Yes, I remember."

"You love your son, don't you? You don't want to see him lose this case, do you?"

Whittaker shook his head and leaned against the wall. Janet could see him all right now. She was scared to death. Maybe her eyes weren't as bad as he feared. "No, I don't," he said, and his voice quavered. What was he going to do? Had Miss Stevens lied to him? Was she wrong in believing money was no problem? Mr. Parrish certainly wouldn't be belaboring him for money if he didn't need it. Mr. Parrish sounded almost frantic about it. If only Miss Stevens had kept out of it. Selling the store would be better than this agony.

"Then get with it, man! If we don't get this money soon, it's going to be all over. Don't come to me with the money when we've already lost. I'm not going to want it then. It's got to be now or not at all. Don't sit on your fat ass. Move! You can't wait till tomorrow. It's got to be today. Do you hear me? Now you get on the phone to that Martin Wraxler and make whatever kind of a deal you can." The line went dead, leaving Zacharias Whittaker white with terror.

He was not alone. Melody, in Cleve Parrish's bedroom, was also cowering. It had been her retreat ever since she had put the phone call through, for she knew Cleve Parrish too well. If she were in his sight, he would read her fear. He saw to the depths of the soul and he was devilishly clever. He could add two and two five times as fast as his nearest competitor. She had seen his knowing eyes when he hired her brother and she still lived in dread of how much he understood.

Now Zack Whittaker had brought her new terror. He was supposed to be stern but he couldn't be stern. And she knew he couldn't. He crumbled under Parrish just like everyone else. Why had she done this thing? Why had she elected to walk a tightrope? Zack had managed to hold up but he was a thin reed if not quite a broken one.

"Melody!"

It was a bellowing Parrish and she put her head through the bedroom door.

"I've got to ride herd on that son of a bitch," he roared. "He's turning chicken. On his own son, for Christ's sake!"

She mumbled something about not understanding why and fled to the kitchenette for more coffee. The phone rang as she poured with a shaky hand and when she reappeared, Parrish had the receiver at his ear at the breakfast table and was trying to brush off the caller. No, he was busy; no, she couldn't have an appointment with him. He wasn't seeing visitors.

He frowned all at once. "Lord? I don't recall any such name." He listened again, then snapped his fingers at Melody and covered the phone. "Do we have a Katherine Lord on the list of Jerry's patients?"

172

She put down the coffee and sorted quickly through the long list with the checks and crosses and question marks and blanks that showed Cleve's progress in drumming up character witnesses. She went through it a second time more slowly. "No, Cleve. No Katherine Lord."

Cleve said into the phone, "I'm sorry, Miss Lord, we have no record of you being a patient of Doctor Whittaker's at any time." He listened further and his brow clouded. Finally he said, "All right, if you insist you were a patient, I'll take your word for it. You may come up." He put the phone down slowly and turned to Melody. "She claims she's an unrecorded patient of our client's and she's got a story to tell."

That was ominous. Melody said, "Where is she, in the lobby?"

He nodded and a corner of his mouth twisted. "Christ," he said, "don't tell me he does abortions!"

It was Melody who let her in. The girl was in her middle twenties, like Melody in height, but dark of hair, with a face that was rounder and prettier, though less beautiful than Melody's. Her lips were fuller, her eyes larger, and far less knowing. Wonderment could still be seen there.

Her clothes were attractive but not expensive, black cloth coat, black wool dress, gold clip, and scarlet scarf at her throat. She was from Madison, like most of Whittaker's patients, but she was Madison hick, not Madison swank. She didn't have the background. High school; secretarial school maybe. That would be it.

Parrish rose from the breakfast table to greet her and she could have been a princess. He introduced his secretary and helped the young lady out of her coat as the secretary, with notebook, moved to an unobtrusive seat in a corner. Don't stay alone with a strange woman behind closed doors was a Parrish motto.

In this case it was a sound idea, for this girl had a figure that would race a mummy's pulse. The only flaw was that the dress wasn't made for it. That was the trouble with off-the-rack clothes, Cleve noted. Melody had spoiled him. She paid a lot for what she wore, and looked elegant in everything. But then, she herself was elegant.

Not this girl. Despite her admirable assets, she was unsure of herself, nervous, a little overwhelmed at the luxury of the presidential suite.

Parrish was kind. He ushered her onto the soft cream cushions of the sofa, offered her cigarettes, withdrew them at her refusal, assured her she could speak freely in front of Miss Stevens, and sat down upon one of the large adjacent sitting cushions. He smiled at her and gathered his papers. "So you were a patient of Dr. Whittaker's?"

She nodded and flushed. To face him she had to keep her back to Melody. It helped her forget the third party. "I heard you were interviewing his patients," she said. "I kept thinking you'd call me."

"I would have, but somehow your name isn't on the list."

She said, "Maybe it's because I only saw him once."

Parrish eyed her sumptuous figure and prepared himself for the worst. Whittaker wouldn't look much like a saint on the witness stand if he gave abortions to young girls. He helped her along. "You saw him once—and?"

"After that I stopped being his patient."

It was like playing a game with a child. "And why, Miss Lord, did you stop being his patient?"

She said, very softly, "Because I became his mistress."

CHAPTER 38

Cleveland Parrish hated surprises. Surprises, to lawyers, were bad news. But this surprise hadn't been engineered by the opposition. This came from his own side.

He was quiet for a moment, digesting this new plum and feeling he wasn't going to like it. He studied the girl's lowered eyes and prettily flushed face. "You are a mistress of Jerry Whittaker?"

"The mistress." She stressed the "The." He had only one mistress. Or so she believed.

Parrish shook his head in self-rebuke. He must be losing his touch. All that crap from Whittaker about being too tired for sex because he was working so hard. Whittaker stayed away from Sally for totally different reasons. Why hadn't he suspected something like this? Why had he let Whittaker deceive him so readily?

And why the hell hadn't Whittaker told him about this girl? Lying, stinking clients! If it weren't for the money, the publicity, and the challenge of the case, it'd be a pleasure to throw it back into Balin's lap.

But that wouldn't do. Never let the emotions rule the intellect. Parrish let his pulses subside and said to the girl, "Why are you here? What is this all about?"

She related the story haltingly. She was twenty-six years old, born and raised in New Haven, went through high school and junior college, got a job as a bank teller, was engaged to a boy who was killed in Vietnam five years before, married another boy the following year on the rebound and divorced him within ten months.

She transferred to the bank's new Madison branch the following summer, renting a room and establishing a new milieu. She dated and made friends and met Jerry Whittaker when she suffered a scalp wound water-skiing.

With them both it was one of those incredible love-at-first-sight things. Jerry told her later that while he was putting the three stitches in her scalp, it was all he could do to keep his hands off her. And she told him that all the time he told her not to be frightened, she wasn't trembling from fear but from proximity.

They tried to hide it but their senses knew. She made two visits to his office to have the dressing changed and then he claimed a busy day when it came time to remove the stitches. He had her come at six, after the nurse and receptionist were gone. As he said later, he wanted to see what would happen. And she waited outside until the nurse and receptionist were well down the street, for the same reason.

That time he no sooner removed the dressing than they were in each other's arms. As the dressing went, so went the dress, and from that moment, they were a pair possessed.

Her rented room in Madison wasn't suitable for visitors so she took a bungalow in the woods of Clinton, where he could come in secret. Thereafter, that was the way of their world and they met as often as possible until his wife's murder.

After his arrest he wrote her a letter, treating her like a patient in case it were read. He thanked her for her solicitude and said she couldn't visit him in jail because only his lawyer and relatives would be permitted in. He also hinted obliquely that it would not be wise to write him until the mess was over, which he hoped would be soon. And he hoped she wouldn't "need to find some other doctor" in the meantime. As if she could!

She sat still then and waited, her eyes anxiously searching the lawyer's face.

He regarded her at length, solemnly and without pleasure. Finally he said, "Miss Lord, again I ask, why are you here?"

She clasped her hands tightly in her lap. Her fingers were not long and tapered like Melody's. They were delicate, but stubby, the nails square and short. "I want to help."

"You want to help? Why did you wait so long?"

She started to say, "I thought you'd come to me," but realized that was no answer. She hunched her shoulders and looked away. "His letter. It was—he was trying to make it plain that I should keep out. And I *have* tried." Her voice broke a little. "But you don't know what it's like, Mr. Parrish. Day after day, week after week. Knowing he's there. Worrying about him. Wishing there was something you could do. Trying to obey him. But you love him and it's terrible not even being able to exchange letters. I thought—I thought you'd know better than him what I should do. I thought maybe you could be our go-between. I thought maybe I could testify or do something to get him out of this mess." She looked at Parrish earnestly. "Do you need a character witness for him? He didn't kill Sally. I know it just as surely as I sit here. I could swear to it on a stack of Bibles with just as much certainty as he could."

Parrish smiled dryly. "Is that what you want to do, tell everybody he didn't kill his wife? That's what you're here for? Or is it to have me play Western Union?"

"I'm here to do anything. Anything!" She leaned forward again. "Could I see him, Mr. Parrish? Could you get me in to see him? I wouldn't even have to talk to him. He wouldn't even have to know I was there, if I could just see him?"

He parried that question. "Does he know you're here?"

She shook her head violently. "Oh, no. I think he wouldn't be pleased. He as much as told me to pretend he'd left on a trip and I'd have to wait for him to come home. Like the wives of sailors."

"He's quite a romantic," Parrish allowed sourly. He sat up. "My dear Miss Lord, quite apart from your willingness to protest Jerry's innocence, which, I can assure you, will not move the prosecution one inch, do you have any knowledge or testimony that can help him?"

She nodded. "He loves me. That ought to prove he didn't kill his wife."

"How does it prove that?"

"Why does he care if she sleeps with another man? Why would he care what she does?"

Parrish's mouth curled. "Husbands have a habit of caring what their wives do even if they *don't* like them any more. There are other motives for murder besides love. Pride, for instance. Anger. Jealousy."

"Jealousy? He wouldn't be jealous of her."

"I'm not saying that's an applicable motive in this case, but it might be made to serve. There happens to be a double standard in the world as far as men are concerned. Just because he thinks it's all right for him to play around with you doesn't mean he thinks it's equally all right for his wife to play around with Walter Costaine."

She drew herself up. "We do not play around. We are in love."

"*You* are in love."

"And so is he. I *know*."

"Just as you *know* he didn't kill his wife."

Her eyes widened. "Why—you, you—don't believe him! You think he's guilty!" Her voice came up. "You're supposed to defend him and you don't believe him. You're going to betray him!"

She started from the couch with the threat of violence and hysteria.

"Sit down," he bellowed so sharply that she fell back unnerved and forgetful of what she was about. "Sit down and listen," he went on, dropping his voice. "You don't listen."

He waited until she was quiet, then he said, "I don't think he killed his wife. I believe him. I believe he's innocent. But I don't *know* he's innocent. I don't know anything of the kind at all. There's a difference between believing and knowing and I want you to appreciate it. Now, if you want to help him, don't go feminine on me again. He's in bad enough trouble without that."

She bowed her head and fumbled in her purse for a handkerchief. "You don't know what it's been like," she whispered into it. "Sometimes I think I'll lose my mind."

"I'm going to ask you some questions," Parrish said. "I want straight answers. Have you and he ever talked about marriage?"

She nodded and blew her nose.

177

"But it wouldn't work out?"

She inclined her head again in agreement.

"What was his excuse?"

She sniffed and put the handkerchief away. "I know what you're thinking, but it's not like that at all. You think he's the one who makes all the excuses, but that's not true. I have excuses too."

"What are *his* excuses?"

"It's not an excuse, exactly. It's just a reason. I mean, if he divorced his wife and married me, it would hurt his career in Madison. We really shouldn't do that unless we were going to start all over again in a new town. He doesn't like that idea, and you can't blame him."

"I don't blame him one bit," Parrish said caustically. "I'd use the same kind of excuse if I were in his shoes."

"It's not like that!" she objected. "I *agree* with him. I wouldn't *want* him to jeopardize his career on my account."

"You buy it too!" Parrish laughed harshly. "He's really got the best of both worlds."

This time the girl did stand up. "I should have known better," she told him bitterly. "You don't care about Jerry. You don't believe him. You don't believe me. All right I'm going to write him. I'm going to tell him about you."

Parrish came to his feet too. "Now, sit down," he said more gently. "I'm only testing you. You come in here and pull a complete surprise on me. What do you think I'm going to do, take your story at face value? What kind of a lawyer do you think I am?"

"You don't have to make it sound so dirty," she complained. "He's not that kind of a man."

Parrish warmed her with his smile. "I know he isn't. Don't you think I know that? If Jerry didn't really care for you he wouldn't have kept you a secret from me. He's trying to keep you from being touched by any of this."

The lawyer didn't believe such claptrap but it did have a mollifying effect on the young lady and that was what counted. He had to manage the girl and keep her down. A love affair didn't sound, off-hand, like a good thing for the doctor's image. The honest, if unhappy husband, was the picture Cleve wanted to sell to the jury.

He got Miss Lord seated again by holding her hand and soothing her ruffled feelings. The best thing was to persuade her to go back into hiding. "I can't let you in to see him," he told her, "but I can be the go-between you wanted. If you write him letters, I'll deliver them, and bring out his letters to you. That way nothing will go through the jail censors and nobody will find out you exist. That's the thing that's important. Jerry wants me to keep you out of it, and so do I."

She was eagerly grateful. If she could just have word from him her lot would be much easier to bear. With him incommunicado it wasn't like having a lover off at war, it was like having him dead. "Thank you, Mr. Parrish. Thank you." She was almost kissing his hands.

"Just call me Cleve, Katherine," he urged. He liked holding her and patting her shoulder. He liked the warmth of her emotion toward him. He could understand that part of her story which had Jerry fighting her magnetism while he sutured her scalp. She had magnetism to burn.

He broke away finally and had Melody give her writing materials. Katherine's face shone like the sun as she sat down to communicate with her beloved, and she penned like the wind, covering three pages in firm small script before Cleve could finish a cigarette. She gave them to him with a shy smile and he folded them in thirds and tucked them into a large envelope. "Jerry will be surprised and happy," he told her, slipping the envelope in his pocket and helping her with her coat.

"You'll call me?"

"I'll be in touch as soon as I can."

She said good-by to Melody, but not by name; she didn't remember her name. Then she was gone and Parrish was latching the door behind her. "That son of a bitch, Jerry," he said. "I was going over to twist his old man's arm, but I've changed my mind. I'm going to twist his. Tell Pete I want the car."

He gave Melody a wry grin and jerked a thumb at the door. "So what did you think of her?"

And Melody, acid-eyed, said, "She's got big tits."

CHAPTER 39

Most of Cleveland Parrish's clients were pathological liars, but he had expected better of Jerry, especially after his lecture on truth telling. Thus he was in the sour mood of a woman betrayed when he met the doctor in the conference cage that afternoon. He tossed the thick envelope at him and said, "You're a hell of a client."

"Why? What?" Whittaker withdrew the close-written pages and flushed in recognition.

"I warned you not to lie to me."

Whittaker tucked the papers back into the envelope but held it hungrily. He licked his lips and turned innocent eyes on the lawyer. "But I didn't lie, Cleve."

Parrish, leaning on the table, was a towering figure. "You didn't tell me about her."

"I know that," Jerry answered, pressing the papers against his chest, "but I didn't lie. Everything I've ever told you is the honest-to-God truth. I don't know how to lie. I mean it." He nodded to reinforce his claim. "All I did was I didn't tell you about her. I never said there was no other woman. I just didn't say there was."

Slick. Very slick. Parrish had to concede the point. He sat down and eased up. "Why didn't you tell me about her?"

"I don't want her dragged into this mess. How did you find out about her?"

"She came to me."

Whittaker shook his head morosely. "That's Katherine. She would. But she shouldn't have. I told her."

"Whether she should or shouldn't is neither here nor there. I should have been told! If I'm going to conduct a proper defense, I've got to know everything that's for or against you."

Whittaker protested, "But she's neither one or the other. She's something totally apart from the rest of things."

"You're not the judge. I am!" Parrish smote the table. "Dammit, if you're going to help me beat this charge there'll be no more secrets. Understand?"

The doctor nodded and subsided at last. It had taken a little time to cow him. The letter from Katherine seemed to have stirred new life in his listless manner. Well, there might be some side benefits at that.

Parrish, with the upper hand, moved in on Whittaker again. "Now then, how many other women have you got stashed away?"

The doctor looked genuinely startled at the idea of a harem. "But there aren't any other women. I don't philander."

"What do you call this business with Katherine?"

That wasn't philandering, he insisted. That was a once-in-a-lifetime love. Until Katherine, he had never looked at another woman.

Not even attractive young girls he gave physical exams to?

No, not ever.

"Except for Katherine Lord."

To that, Whittaker shrugged. "What can I say? There is, for every man, the perfect woman. Some very few men are fortunate enough to be married to the perfect woman. Some others, like myself, find her after they have married someone else. When that happens, then you have problems—the kind that go down in history or that authors write novels about. Most men, I suspect, never do meet the perfect woman and don't even know or believe such a person can exist. But they do exist and I know it because I've found mine."

God, Parrish thought, the dumb jerk really means it. What's worse, he could make a jury believe he means it. He would have the jurors believing there was nothing in the world he wouldn't do for that woman. And if—just suppose—Sally had found out about Miss Katherine Lord? Suppose that was what the fight was about at the party?

Whittaker flatly denied the suggestion. Sally did not know. Nobody knew. And there was no reason anyone should need to know.

"Except," Parrish reminded him, "I need to know." He leaned on an elbow. "Does she have any money?"

"Money? No, of course not. Just what she makes at her job, plus what I've given her. Why?"

"You're in jail for murder. You need money for your defense. If she really loved you—"

181

Whittaker came out of his chair. "Why you greedy, goddam blood-sucker! If you try to squeeze a cent—"

Parrish laughed disarmingly. "I'm not after more money, Jerry. We've got enough to get by on. I was only asking why she didn't make the offer."

"It's because she didn't know I needed it. It's because I've purposely kept her out of things. I don't want her suffering through this nightmare with me. I want it to be a hiatus with her. Then, when it's over, we can be together again."

Parrish told him to spill out the whole history of the affair, but Whittaker balked. Katherine had to be protected. He yielded, reluctantly, when Parrish pointed out there was no guarantee the prosecution wouldn't find and subpoena her. Parrish had to know everything in order to fight back.

Satisfyingly enough, the story he told was the same as Katherine's in every particular: the scalp wound, the suturing, the instant, death-less love. Once they had found each other, they could no more have stayed apart than they could have stopped breathing.

Had they talked marriage?

Of course, but they were powerless.

"Why?"

"I already had a wife."

"There's something called 'divorce.'"

"From Sally? Fat chance."

"What's that mean?"

"She wouldn't give me a divorce. Sally's not the type."

"You discussed it with her?"

"We didn't 'discuss' it, but it was made plain when things began to turn sour that she had no intention of letting me go. Why do you think she took up with Costaine? Because we had stopped having sex, but she didn't want to stop being a doctor's wife. She liked the prestige. She liked—"

"Prestige? Are you kidding? She had that to burn. She didn't need you for prestige."

"She didn't like Main Line prestige, if that's what you're talking about. It was too isolated for her, too insular. She didn't think living on the Main Line was living in the real world."

"Madison, Connecticut, is the real world?"

"It's closer to reality. You're closer to where it's at if you're only upper middle class than if you're upper upper."

"That's a lot of crap."

"Maybe it is. Maybe it isn't. All I know is that's the way she looked at life. You can take my word for it."

Parrish shoved the philosophy aside. "All right, if she wouldn't divorce you, why didn't you divorce her?"

"I couldn't."

"What do you mean, you couldn't? I don't know Connecticut's divorce laws, but I do know adultery is good anywhere. You could make her run to Reno in a minute just by threatening to name Costaine corespondent."

Whittaker chewed his lip and said nothing. That was bad news. Parrish leaned forward and hit him with it. "Why didn't you do it, Jerry? It's because you didn't really want to marry Katherine, isn't it?"

He shook his head and reached for a cigarette. "No."

"It's because Sally gave you prestige. She had the family, the education, the background you wanted in a wife, while Katherine, charming and lovely as she might be in your arms or in your bed, wouldn't be the kind of girl who would enchant your friends. She hasn't the education, the worldliness, the experience, the ease with people, the poise that Sally had. That's it, isn't it, Jerry?"

"No it isn't," Whittaker said doggedly.

"Well, I can tell you any goddam jury in the world will believe it is. Either you come up with a better answer or that's the one you're stuck with."

Whittaker sighed. "I don't like to say things about the dead, but all right. You want to know what kind of a girl I married? Why do you think she was so blatant about Costaine? Do you think she didn't know the ammunition she was giving me? But she didn't care. That's the real thing about her. She was always a maverick. You think she'd run to Reno if I threatened to file suit in Connecticut? Like hell. She as much as dared me to. She'd make it just as dirty and messy as she could. If it'd make her look bad cheating on her husband, she figured it'd make me look worse: the cuckolded male, the lousy lover, the impotent fake who drove her to it. She knew I didn't have the stomach for that kind of mudslinging. I preferred to slip over to Katherine's and get enough peace and quiet and love and affection to keep me going."

Parrish sat in silence. It was a story that would do. The question was, what would it do? He shook his head. "No matter how you cut it, Katherine sure as hell doesn't help your cause."

"I told you that. That's why I wanted to keep her out of it."

"I mean, she serves as motivation for divorce, but you don't get a divorce. And all the reasons you give me can, looked at in a different light, serve as motivation for getting rid of Sally with a poker."

"Which I didn't do."

"Which you didn't do, but which the prosecutor is going to try his damndest to make the jury think you did."

Whittaker said sourly, "I don't know why it doesn't occur to that prosecutor that if I wanted to get rid of Sally it would be far easier to go through the mud bath of divorcing her than a murder trial for killing her."

"Because he knows something you keep forgetting—or maybe you only pretend to forget. She's worth money and you're living on the narrow edge: a house to pay off, office equipment, two cars and a boat, and less than two thousand dollars in the bank. If she should die—so long as you didn't kill her—you get that money. If you divorce her, you don't. You can marry Katherine, but she can't bail you out."

Whittaker laid the envelope on the table in front of him, smoothing it. "Sally wouldn't bail me out either," he said. "Do you think I got a smell of her money? Not a whiff, let me tell you. Not a whiff. Not that I would have touched her filthy lucre," he added, perhaps not hastily enough. "I'm no gigolo. Even if I'd needed it—and I didn't!"

"I know you didn't. I've had my accountants go over—"

"You mean you even did that?"

"I do everything, Jerry. Now I'm ready if Masters tries to suggest you had an interest in your wife's money. I'll put my accountants on the stand and make him look sick. So be thankful I pay attention to such things."

Whittaker mumbled an affirmative, but more audibly he said, "I feel like I've got no privacy."

Parrish got up. "That's right, you haven't." He told him good-by, he could read the letter from Katherine now and write one in reply that he'd pick up on the morrow.

Whittaker, still thinking of his lost privacy, looked at the bulging envelope and up at the hovering lawyer. "You read this too?"

"Of course not," Parrish said. "Even prisoners have some rights."

But of course he had.

CHAPTER 40

Melody, in her hotel room, was in the midst of a letter home when she heard a knock. It was one of those newsy, chatty letters that was easier than a phone call, all about New Haven and the excitement of the case, about Gary and the fine job he was doing. Actually she was a near prisoner in the goddam suite, and, as for Gary, she had to guess how he was making out. Over two weeks had gone by and he hadn't been in touch. And he had apparently moved out of her apartment. She'd rung the number at all hours and got no answer.

Those weren't things you put in a letter, however. Keep it light, cheery and pleasant. Start talking realities and the family would draw a blank. They lived on the other side of the world. Right now she wasn't going to tell them why she was writing—because it was dark and nearly six and she was lonely waiting for Parrish, cocktails and dinner.

She got up to answer the door and found Pete Tucker in the hall. That was a surprise.

Pete nodded at the adjacent door to the presidential suite and said, "Where's Kubla Khan?"

"I don't know. Getting a haircut or something." She wondered why he was there. She didn't know Cleve was going anywhere. "Where're you taking him?"

Pete grinned. "Uh-uh. He's taking himself." He grasped her hand and put the Cadillac keys in it. "I'm going home. First train out."

For two weeks Pete had been billeted in the hotel at the ready for chauffeuring duty, tolling up the miles as Cleve made call after call to interview the promising names his investigators had dug up. For two weeks Pete Tucker had not seen his wife and children. It was part of the game, of course, the occupational hazard Melody knew so well.

She looked at the keys and at Pete. It was not the Parrish touch. "He's letting you go home? Is someone sick?"

Pete continued to grin. "Hell, no. And he isn't letting me go, he's sending me. Maybe he wants to try the power steering, or maybe he's developing a heart. Personally, I suspect it's the former."

"He's not that bad," Melody said loyally. "He can be very thoughtful and considerate."

"Like a boa constrictor. Well, ta-ta." He gave her a snappy salute. "I'll give your regards to Broadway." He was gone.

She returned enviously to her letter writing. She wished she could be going back to New York, living again in her own place. Hotel life was not her bowl of cherries. Once it had worn a glamorous air but the appeal had long since eroded through custom and overuse. She had to admit, though, that it was worse for Pete. He was away from his family while she, at least, was with the man in her life.

The man himself knocked on the connecting door an hour later, when she was wondering if he'd ever show up. She was hungry, thirsty, and impatient. She let him in and gave him the keys crossly. "Pete says you sent him home."

Parrish glanced around the tidy room diffidently. "He needs the break." He smiled. "If I want to keep my staff at top efficiency, I have to keep them happy."

She felt like reminding him her own efficiency level was slipping but he wasn't through talking. "Has he gone yet?"

She nodded. "He said he was taking the first train."

"Rats," Parrish said irritably. "I let him go too soon." Then he told her. Something had come up and he had to make a call. She should go have dinner by herself or order something sent up. No point in waiting for him. He didn't know when he'd be back.

"What'll you do about supper?"

"I'll get a sandwich somewhere along the line." He closed the door, leaving her to the bitter emptiness of the room and the loneliness of the letter to her family. She could feel one of those pangs coming on.

In his own suite, Cleveland Parrish phoned for the car, changed his shirt and tie, put his overcoat back on and went out to the elevator. The car was waiting in the curve of drive outside the lobby doors with the attendant standing by. Cleve climbed in, drove it up Temple to the Oak Street Connector, threaded his way between the Hartford and New York forks onto I-95 where the signs said New London. He hadn't paid attention while Pete was chauffeuring him, but a little care, attention to signs, and reliance on his subconscious, and it wasn't hard.

He drove out the black, sometimes lighted turnpike for half an hour to the Clinton exit labeled 63. He bridged the turnpike, turned right onto Glenwood Road, and took out the notebook in which he had jotted the rest of the directions. There was another right and a left onto winding Ironworks Road into the woods, then left up a steep driveway beside a large mailbox, to a tiny green ranch bungalow buried in the woods beside a one-car garage.

There wasn't room for the great Cadillac to turn around so he left it facing the garage and went to the front door. Katherine Lord was waiting expectantly. "You're so good, Mr. Parrish," she cried. "I don't know how to thank you."

"Tut, tut," he answered, patting her on the shoulder and following her inside. "It's nothing at all." She not only had big tits, she had a swinging, shapely rear. "And please don't call me Mr. Parrish," he reminded her. "It makes me think there's a generation gap between us. The name is Cleve."

"All right, Cleve." She laughed self-consciously at the familiarity with a man so much older and so famous. In the living room she controlled herself. She wanted Jerry's letter on the instant, but there were amenities. Her guest had to take off his coat and be made welcome.

But the great Cleveland Parrish understood and when she turned he already had the envelope out and was smiling at the glow in her eyes. "You might as well read it now," he chuckled. "Otherwise you won't hear a word I say or know a thing you eat."

She flushed and laughed and tried not to accept the envelope too eagerly. "Do you mind?" she asked as she ripped it open. "I wish I could offer you a drink, but I don't have anything in the house."

"That's all right. We'll have a cocktail when we have dinner. Sit down and relax and enjoy yourself. I don't mind."

He watched her as she sank onto the sagging couch in the cluttered little room to devour the letter. What she could do for herself and her figure if she could afford the kind of clothes that Melody had! Given the wardrobe and the poise to go with it, Katherine Lord would be a sensation. She was pretty good already, but Cleve couldn't help thinking what he could do with her in the right New York shops. Melody had always had the poise but she had similar clothing lacks when she first started to work for him, back before she became his mistress. Once he started spending money on her, though, all that changed. He really shaped her into something. Cleveland Pygmalion Parrish.

Katherine was a long time with Jerry's two foolscap pages and she wept over them. Parrish wasn't surprised. Jerry had been so overwhelmed by her letter that his loneliness, his emptiness, the horrors of his environment all burst through. Her tears fell on the pages and she made no move to stop them. When Cleve offered her a handkerchief she shook her head and didn't look up. She was living in Jerry's world and she didn't want to leave him yet. And when she finished, she still sat, head bowed, weeping on the pages in her lap, and it was a time before she regained enough control to swallow and look up and say, "Oh, Cleve, what are we going to do?"

"Do?" He joined her on the couch and put a comforting hand on her knee. "You're going to keep writing him. You're going to be his contact with the outside world, his support. You and I together. You'll give him moral support while I give him legal support."

"You ought to read what he says," she cried, pushing the pages into Parrish's lap. "It's so terrible for him."

"No, no," Parrish said, pushing them back. He'd already read them and he didn't want to do it again. Nothing was duller than love letters to someone else. "It's your letter. I don't want to intrude. But I know what he's going through, believe me, my dear. Remember, I see and talk to him myself."

"Oh, I wish I could too!" She turned to Cleve hopefully. "Do you suppose it's possible? I mean, if I stood outside his window? Could I stand outside his window and see him?"

Though he did not know Jerry's location, Cleve shook his head. "He's in an inside cell," he told her, then patted her knee reassuringly. "But it won't be long, Katherine. You'll see him when we go to trial." He helped her to her feet. "Now powder your nose and get your coat and we'll have a cocktail and a big lobster dinner in that place you named in—what is it, Killingworth?"

She nodded. "You don't really have to take me out to dinner, Cleve."

"Of course I don't. But I'm hungry and I'm sure you are. And I know you want to talk about Jerry."

She even smiled. "You understand a lot about women."

"Oh, not I," he declaimed. "But I do know you haven't eaten out or gone out in a long long time. You've been living in as big an isolation booth as Jerry. Maybe bigger. And I'm not going to let you go stir crazy."

CHAPTER 41

Katherine Lord did not mention dinner with Cleve Parrish in her next letter to Jerry, not because she didn't want to praise her benefactor's largesse, but because he specifically told her not to. And who should know better what to do than a great lawyer like Cleveland Parrish, who was helping them both and was going to save Jerry? The only course for a girl like Katherine Lord was to obey him blindly.

Cleve did not deliver her letter the following day. Let's not let this sudden correspondence get out of hand. Also, there was other business: like what the hell was holding up that drugstore sale? Already he had told Melody to set up an appointment for that afternoon and she had reported back that Mrs. Whittaker was going into the hospital for tests and old Zacharias would be tied up for the whole week. God damn it, if that wasn't a stall, Cleve Parrish would like to know what was. All right, he'd give him till next Monday, but, by God, if that old fart tried another dodge, Cleve Parrish would get on that phone personally. And he was only giving the mealymouthed fraud that long because he still had a week's worth of important other interviews to make.

The phone rang while he was still steaming about the druggist, and the excited caller identified himself as Gary Stevens. Cleve couldn't remember who the hell Gary Stevens was until he mentioned Morelle Costaine. "I've got it, Mr. Parrish!" he exclaimed. "I found out what Morelle has on Mr. Costaine!"

Then it all came back, including the thousand-dollar fee Parrish

189

had promised for just such information. What had made him do it? Something about Melody, the way she was acting. Christ, he must have been out of his mind. There was nothing wrong with Melody's behavior. And now this crumb was coming to collect his filthy grand. Well, Cleve Parrish, you really blew a gasket on this one.

"That's very interesting," he said to Gary and wondered if he could get off on a technicality.

"You'll never guess what it is."

"That's right. I never guess. So spare me the suspense, please. What is it?"

"It's two things and I guess they ought to be just what the doctor ordered. Here's the first one. You know what it is? Mr. Costaine was arrested when he was nineteen for kiting a check. You know what kiting a check means?"

Parrish assured Gary, dryly, that he knew what it meant. "And what happened? Did he go to jail?"

"No, but that's because of influence. His father was rich and he squashed it."

"He actually squashed it?"

"Well, maybe not squashed it. What he did was pay the difference to make the check good and the other man, who was an acquaintance, didn't press charges."

"That's not the same as squashing it. Not by a damned sight."

"Well, even so, that's a pretty hot item, don't you think? I mean, no wonder Morelle wanted to be paid. I think—"

"What's the name of the man who didn't press charges?"

Gary didn't know.

"That information is no good without a name. There's no way of verifying it."

"Yes, I can see that, Mr. Parrish. But don't you worry. I'll find it out. You can bet your life on it."

Parrish was unhappily sure that he could. "What's the other story?"

Gary chuckled with glee. "This one is really good. Did you know that Mr. Costaine claims he went to Europe last summer on business? He tells that to everyone, even the papers. Well, I've found out that that's not true. All that time he was supposed to be away, he was staying with Morelle and Rita. He was renting from them."

"What for?"

Gary's laughter grew richer. "You'll never believe this, Mr. Parrish. He told them he was having special treatments for non-infectious hepatitis. That's what he told them, you see? So I went to the clinic where he told them he was having the treatments to check it out. This wasn't easy, Mr. Parrish. It wasn't easy at all. The hospital didn't want to give out information about patients. But I was able to get to, shall we say, 'special sources' to get the lowdown. This cost an extra thirty-five dollars, Mr. Parrish, but I think you'll agree with me that it's money well spent." He laughed. "Wait till you hear what I found out. Walter Costaine was at the clinic all right, but it wasn't for non-infectious hepatitis. He was being treated for venereal disease. He had a case of clap—that's gonorrhea."

Gary Stevens laughed again. He was waiting for the plaudits to rain. Parrish said, "Who gave you the information?"

"About the gonorrhea? A nurse at the clinic, a Miss Rhodes."

"I mean the alleged secrets. Who told you them, Morelle?"

"No, Rita. But Morelle confirmed it." There was a moment of hesitation, then, "Uh, Mr. Parrish, when can I get my money?"

"As soon as I check out your stories. I want the name of the doctor who treated Costaine—"

Gary already had it and gave it.

"And the names of the check-kiting victim."

"I'll get that."

Parrish told him that was fine and tried to hang up. Gary persisted. If Mr. Parrish found the evidence was true, that ought to prove he was a pretty good worker, wouldn't it?

"If it's true, you don't have to worry. You'll get your thousand dollars right away. And the extra thirty-five."

"Oh, I trust you, Mr. Parrish. I'm not worrying about the thousand. What I mean is, I'd be good for other jobs. You could give me other assignments."

Parrish let a little coldness into his voice. "Sorry, I don't have any other assignments. But I'll keep you in mind."

Gary pleaded a little and the lawyer's voice grew still colder. Gary caught the hint. "Yes, sir, Mr. Parrish," he said, trying to re-establish manliness. "I understand, sir. I'll appreciate your doing whatever you can."

He was on the phone again that afternoon with the rest of his assignment completed, but this time it was Melody he reached, for it was her room he phoned. She wrote down the identity of the check-kiting victim dutifully and acknowledged what a fine job Gary had done. Ma and Pa and Priscilla ought to be proud. And how was the baby?

Gary cut off the family chitchat. "Now listen, Sis, you got to do something for me."

Some of the pleasure went out of Melody's voice. "Oh?"

"Parrish is going to pay me after he verifies what I told him. And it'll be verified all right. But then he tells me that's the end. He says I'm out of a job again. I want something done about that."

That was the trouble with blackmail, Melody thought. It never ended. She plucked a cigarette from the pack beside the phone. "Listen, Gary, I got you that job. I can't get you any more. I can't manufacture jobs for you. He just happened to have one assignment—"

"He had an assignment because you asked him for one. So ask him for another."

She lighted the cigarette, took a drag, and tried to be calm, cool and reasonable. "Gary, you don't understand. I don't run Cleveland Parrish. I work for him. Nobody makes him do anything he doesn't want to do, least of all me. Pestering him wouldn't get you a new job, it would only jeopardize mine."

"Yours is already jeopardized, Sis. You've got nothing to lose."

Her heart was pounding and she felt that empty tug in her stomach. "I'm sorry, Gary. There's nothing I can do."

"Are you forgetting, Sis, what I can tell your boss about the drugstore?"

"No," she said, keeping her voice steady. "I know what you can tell him. I'm only saying, go ahead. Tell him anything you like."

She hung up on him and went to the hotel window to finish her cigarette. The snow-crusted green, long stripped of its Christmas tree, stretched out below. She'd suggested the hospital excuse to Zack Whittaker that morning to help him keep his store. As soon as she collected herself now, however, she'd call him back, tell him a crisis had come up and he'd have to sell.

In Melody's apartment in New York, Gary listened to the click of the disconnection. He said angry hellos into the mouthpiece and slammed the receiver into the cradle. It looked like Melody wouldn't be bluffed any more. He swore at the phone. For two cents he'd really call Cleveland Parrish and tell him what kind of a secretary he had. Deep down, though, he trembled at the thought. He could see himself stammering against Parrish's icy distaste, ending up without even his thousand.

He turned away and went into Melody's bedroom. Rita Costaine, in one of Melody's elegant negligees, was combing her hair at the dressing table. "So she wouldn't heel," she said. "I had a hunch." She went on to describe Melody in four-lettered terms.

Gary knew the words, but he still couldn't get used to the way they poured effortlessly forth from the mouth of such an attractive girl. In his part of the world, only roughneck men used such words, and sparingly at that.

In his part of the world, he would have fought such men had they used such epithets against his sister. Now he only sat down on the bed and said, "Well, at least we're getting a thousand for the information. That's ten times as much as that detective offered."

CHAPTER 42

Melody Stevens ate dinner alone in her room again Wednesday night. Parrish had another "business" appointment, another dinner engagement with Katherine Lord.

It was much like the first except Jerry's letter didn't make her weep and they didn't spend quite so much of the meal talking about him. Instead, Katherine was more interested in the trial. As for Parrish, he probed her fruitlessly for anything she might sense or suspect regarding Sally.

Parrish didn't deliver her letter to Whittaker until Friday, but the prisoner didn't languish. Ed Balin had been pressed into service to take up the slack. That was pretty much Balin's role now. Parrish had conditioned him to a "Don't call us, we'll call you" status. He even had him trained not to talk about his chapter on corporation law.

Before making his Friday visit, Cleve sent Melody to New York for the weekend. The detective agency had verified Gary's claims and Melody could take him a big fat check for one thousand and thirty-five dollars.

To Melody the vacation was an added delight for her cup was already running over. Old Zack Whittaker had more spirit than she'd dared hope, and when she had done her turnabout and told him to sell, he got his back up. Too much funny business was going on and he determined he would not let the store go unless Jerry himself asked him to. That left Cleve with his hands tied, and Melody free from Gary's threats. Nobody would believe Gary now that Zacharias was making his own decisions.

She could even relent a little in her harsh views of her brother. He was frightened for his future, that was all. Perhaps she and he could talk it out once she made him see he couldn't threaten her any more.

Cleve Parrish was in a less happy frame of mind over loss of the store. He didn't take setbacks well, especially when he didn't know where he'd gone wrong. He'd thought the fish was already landed when, in reality, it was wriggling off the hook. He couldn't remember having made a mistake like that before.

Nor was he happy about the thousand dollars he had to pay Gary Stevens. That was another bit of poor tactics. The dirt Gary uncovered was maybe worth a hundred, which was all Cleve could have expected. He was hard put now to remember what induced him to offer a thousand. He was turning into a goddam Santa Claus.

However, there was a bright side. The check did let him get rid of Melody for a few days. He could have his next dinner with Katherine without having to explain to Melody about still another "business" appointment. Too many of those in the standard Parrish-Stevens routine would alert a savvy girl like Melody and there was no point in courting trouble when one isn't being paid to court it.

He took messages to Katherine and entertained her at dinner both Friday and Saturday evenings. Each time the restaurant was different, to keep the girl under wraps.

His attentions were having their effect. Katherine had been pretty when she first walked into Cleveland Parrish's life, but there was a drawn quality to her face, a pinched expression. She had been agonizing too long over Jerry's fate, but more than suffering marked her. She was a hermit, living a hermit's existence. Outside of the compatriots and customers she saw during banking hours and the shoppers she rubbed against when she got her food, she had no contact with human beings. She returned nightly to her isolated bungalow, prepared a small meal, and used television to make the evening pass. The rest of the night she blacked out with a sleeping pill, lest she lie till dawn weeping over her beloved.

Cleveland Parrish had brought her out of this. He had re-established contact between her and Jerry and between her and the world. Jerry's letters were only part of it. Credit had to go to Parrish himself. Man was not an island, least of all Katherine Lord. She needed people. She responded to them. And it was this need, this awareness of others, particularly those of the opposite sex, that gave her her magnetism. Now that Cleve was drawing her out of herself, her awareness and her magnetism were increasing. She was more alert and open, more ready to have fun. Now that Jerry's conditions and his spirits were known, her despair was gone. She could think of other things, of other people.

Parrish noted the change, not just because he was observant by training, but because he was expecting it. He intended it to happen. He was making it happen. He was a manipulator outside the courtroom as well as in.

He saw her again on Monday with another missive from Jerry, but this time there was a variation in the customary theme. They would eat *in* instead of out. She had been wined and dined so much and was so grateful that she did not wish to impose further. Now it was her turn to treat. Wasn't Cleve tired of restaurant food? Wouldn't he like a home-cooked meal? Cleve said he would be honored and that he would bring the wine—and something to make the cocktails with. (A meal at home should be prefaced just as in a restaurant.)

She went through Jerry's letter briefly while tending the stove and before the cocktails. Cleveland Parrish was making so many trips back and forth that correspondence was no longer a novelty. Jail routine permitted little variation and Jerry wasn't the kind of man who could fill pages with "I love yous."

Nor did Katherine need that kind of assurance. They were, after all, beyond the romantic notions of youth. Both knew the other side of the bridal veil and both were aware that there was more to marriage than love, and more to love than physical attraction. That Jerry might sleep with Sally didn't fleck Katherine's mind with jealous thoughts. As long as she had exclusive possession of his love, she didn't need exclusive possession of his body.

Cleve made drinks with a practiced hand, pouring a more liberal portion into the glasses than bartenders were accustomed to do. If you're going to make a drink, make a drink, was Cleve's motto. Don't cut the booze, use good booze and use it generously.

He told her of his day, the visit to Jerry, the fact that Jerry was willing to swear that Sally was too contented while Costaine was away to make it believable she wasn't getting sexual satisfaction somewhere else.

"That's good, isn't it?" she asked, sipping her drink and taking another cracker.

"It's good from the standpoint of telling us we're on the right track," Parrish answered. "I wouldn't want to vouch for the effect it'll have on the jury. It's the kind of thing one would expect Jerry to say whether it's true or not."

"But it would be true. Jerry wouldn't lie. He wouldn't ever lie."

"Well, we hope so."

"I know so," Katherine said emphatically. "Has he ever lied to you?"

Cleve had to confess he hadn't and Katherine nodded knowingly. "You see? You rely on woman's intuition, Cleve, and you'll be surprised how right you'll be. It's something that just doesn't fail."

He smiled. "What does your woman's intuition tell you about me?"

She smiled back. "You have a noble heart."

Cleve laughed heartily. "I'm sure."

She leaned forward earnestly. "Don't do yourself an injustice. I know you're worldly wise—far more so than I—and you fancy yourself a cynic. And I know that you make lots of money and I know that you don't care whether a man is guilty or innocent, you just care about setting him free." She waved her glass. "You see, I read you very well. I'm not a dummy, even if I haven't been around as much as you. But underneath all that, your heart is still noble. Look at what you've been doing for Jerry and me. Look at all the trips you've made back and forth, just for us. That's not your job. You're not getting paid for that. Yet you'll take the time because you know what it means. And taking me out to dinner all those times. You have an instinctive way of knowing what a person in trouble needs. I didn't know it myself. I didn't know how much

196

being with somebody, especially being with a man, being escorted someplace, really meant to me. You know, I never had that with Jerry. We always had to sneak everywhere we went. In fact, most of the time we didn't go anywhere. We just stayed here. But we had each other and I thought that was enough. Then there was all that time without him and I just kept on living the kind of life I'd been living with him—hardly ever seeing another person, hardly even speaking to another person. You're so wrapped up in that one man you love you take the attitude the rest of the world can go hang. And I was letting it go hang and I never realized what it was doing to me until you took me out. I didn't realize how withered I was getting."

"Doctor Parrish is the name."

"Oh, you won't be serious."

"Sure I will. Finish your drink because we've got some more and then I want to see what your cooking is like. Because if it's good enough, maybe I'll leave Jerry in jail and keep you for myself."

She sobered instantly. "I don't even want to joke about a thing like that. I'm so afraid he might really have to stay in jail."

Cleve was immediately soothing. "That's your trouble," he said, patting her knee. "You don't have faith. Because you can rest assured the only reason I joke about something like that is because that's all it is: a joke. I'm going to get Jerry out of jail. You can bet your life on that one. But you aren't quite as sure of that as I am and that's why you get upset."

She accepted that and she accepted another drink. They had a third as she served the dinner and Cleve was liberal with the wine as they supped by candlelight. It was an intimate, cozy meal, the bereft young girl with the savior, and its impact upon her, along with the alcohol, found her weeping quietly before they got to the dessert.

Cleve put a hand on hers. "It's all right, my sweet."

The tears came faster. She buried her face in her napkin. "I can't help it," she sobbed. "I'm so sad."

"I know." He was out of his chair, helping her from hers, guiding her to the couch.

"Poor Jerry," she cried. "I miss him so. I ache for him so much, living in that terrible jail."

The savior sat with her and pulled her head against his shoulder, murmuring soothing words, supporting her with his strong, saving

197

arm, stroking her hair and her cheek with a gentle, saving hand. She wept in self-pity and for her beloved, while Cleve encouraged her and held her close. She was docile and unaware, but the magnetism was there and Cleve's pulses were pounding with the passions of youth. He hadn't felt the same breathless quality, the same tingle of anticipation since before college. He hadn't felt it back in law school when he was screwing every broad he could con, persuade or cajole.

He kissed her hair, still crooning sympathy, and let his hand slide over her breast. She seemed not to notice and he returned his hand more boldly while the other unzipped the back of her dress.

She raised a tear-stained face and said thickly, "Cleve, you mustn't."

Their lips were close and he kissed her, his fingers deftly undoing her bra strap. For a moment she abandoned herself, then pulled away and turned her head. "Please, Cleve, we can't."

She pushed at his hands and he didn't fight her. "We can," he murmured against her hair. "You knew when you invited me here." He stroked her bare back.

"No, no," she sobbed, paying obeisance to her guilt. "It wouldn't be fair to Jerry."

"Of course it's fair," the savior told her. "We're not touching your love for him. It's to help us save him."

"But I've got to be faithful."

"No, Katherine. You're not a child. You're a grown woman who's been married. It'll be months and months. Think how withered you were becoming. Jerry wouldn't want that."

She was weakening. He was able to get his hand onto her breast again. "But he has to wait," she said, trying feebly to resist.

Cleve kissed her ear. "Why should two have to suffer because one does? If he were away at war, instead of jail, you know he'd have women. And you know it wouldn't affect his love for you. And you know you'd want him to have them. Because you love him too and you wouldn't want him to suffer."

She nodded against Cleve's cheek and the tears came faster. Cleve tilted her chin. It was Jerry, Jerry, Jerry, and he had to make her forget him. He kissed her and could feel her melt. The liquor, the loneliness, the need, and Cleve's own magnetism were wearing away her guilt. She began to respond and her growing eagerness was awesome. For once in his life, Cleve felt his control slipping. It would be almost impossible for him to stop now, even if he tried.

He didn't have to try. Her inhibitions were forgotten or hopelessly muddled and the dams were letting go. Her clothing was flung to all corners of the room and she was wrestling him for his.

Katherine's tits were not only big, they were luscious. Everything about her was luscious.

CHAPTER 43

Cleve spent the night. It had not been his intent, but much of what went on had not been his intent. Katherine affected him more than he would have believed possible and before the evening was half over, he knew he wanted this to be more than a one-night stand.

It wasn't love, of course. It was that primary appeal known as physical attraction. He had the hots for her.

No wonder Jerry was so infatuated. And a weak person like Jerry might well let his emotions rule his head, might risk his career and even his wife's money for a girl like Katherine. Cleve felt the same tuggings. In fact, for the first time since his fortieth birthday, when he felt he had to prove himself, he came twice in one night. To his even greater surprise, it wasn't difficult.

So he stayed the night, but it wasn't all fireworks and rockets. In the heat of their first emotion, Katherine displayed a passion for males and for sex that was even a little frightening. But when it was over and she was temporarily sated, when he brought her back woozily to the dinner table, she choked on her food and had to rush to the bathroom.

She was sick for a while and then, plagued by cold sweats and weakness, she lay down and that was when Cleve, ruefully deciding he had given her too much liquor, sought to comfort her by bathing her moist, pale body with warm washcloths as she lay on the bed. It soothed her but it aroused him and his second mounting was in the nature of an unbridled emotion on one side and passive non-resistance on the other. She wasn't stirred. She didn't even want him. But she was too weak and ill and—it might be added—too polite to deny him.

She slept finally, nude and under the covers, but not until Cleve had made her tea, given her aspirin, and constantly felt her forehead for fever. Then Cleve, equally nude, climbed in beside her. If this were to be more than a one-time affair, he didn't want her awaking in the morning to an empty bed and a departed lover. That might do for old wives like Melody, but not for new brides.

When she did awake, however, it was not for soothing assurances from Cleve or another bout on the bed. She had forgotten the alarm clock, had overslept, and was suffering a hangover. Her resultant activities were a rush for her clothes, calls to Cleve to put the water on, a swallow of aspirin, and three gulps of coffee. Last night wasn't even in her mind.

It was over the coffee, with a half-dressed Cleve, that she clapped a hand to her head and said, "Oh, my God. I haven't got anything for you to take back to Jerry."

Cleve gazed sourly into his cup. If it wasn't bad enough that he couldn't try screwing her a third time, she didn't even remember the first two. One would think his lovemaking should take precedence over a headache, getting to the bank on time and writing her damned letters to that incarcerated jerk. The broad was positively insulting. But, God, she was beautiful.

"Why didn't I do it first thing last night?" she berated herself. "Cleve, you can't see him today. Please. Don't go see him."

"I won't go see him," he assured her; then, because his mind was on that third screwing, he added, "I should see him tomorrow, though. Can you get something written that I can pick up tonight?"

She said she could and added, matter-of-factly, "If you come for dinner, don't bring any liquor. I'm not going to drink for a week."

"We'll go out for dinner."

"I can make something if you want."

"We'll go out," he replied and then, so she wouldn't mistake his intentions, added, "but we'll come back here for coffee."

She thought that would be nice, and promised to have the letter ready. Then she ran for her coat.

CHAPTER 44

Gerald Whittaker dreamed he was standing on a muddy plain. It was a smooth, dark gray ooze. The landscape was flat and even and empty, the sky sullen, with fast rushing clouds. The clouds were gray too, a dirty gray, with ragged fingers, and they ran so close overhead he wanted to duck. And they came from behind, sweeping off to the far horizon, running away.

Gerald Whittaker was all alone in his landscape. There was not so much as a broken sapling, not so much as a dried leaf. And a cold wind was wailing. He could hear it now, the hollow moaning that from time to time rose to a keening shrill of anger.

The wind came from his rear too, and it drove the clouds like whip-lashed horses. Jerry could hear it howl but he could not feel its force. Around him the air was still.

Behind, the sky darkened and the clouds went faster, fleeing as Jerry wanted to flee. The darkness wasn't the night, or the blackness of storm. It was a looming presence, blotting out the sky, shutting out the light.

Jerry couldn't turn his head. He couldn't see what it was, but he didn't want to see it. He only wanted to escape. But his feet were anchored in the muck and all he could do was cringe.

It was coming closer. He could feel its nearness, could measure the unseen, shortening distance. The clouds skimmed his head, hostile clouds that nipped at him and made him cower. They were the pursuit hounds of the black horror that was coming for him. The clutching darkness rose over him. It would seize him now. He screamed and woke up.

He was lying on his bunk, the black shape of the overhead bunk above him, the dim glow of night lights visible through the bars of his door. He was bathed in sweat and his body shook. All except his feet. They were taut and motionless and he wondered in the first moments of wakefulness if they were still fastened in the mud.

Had he really screamed? He listened anxiously for angry cries. When there were none, his trembling eased. The terror of the dream did not have to be replaced by the terror of the inmates. He was in the maximum security section and kept apart from the others. It was for his safety, for while the crime of which he was accused did not outrage the others, he was so distant from them in all respects he would have been an irresistible scapegoat for their aggressions. Even apart he could feel their contempt and the hungry eye they cast upon him. It was like living in a pit of alligators, clinging to a post only inches beyond the snap of their jaws.

But that was a terror he could contend with. He could judge his protection, hover near the guards, make sure the locks were secure. That was not like the terror of the night and the horror that had just seized him.

He shivered violently and tried to regain control. It wasn't that bad a dream, was it? Already the details were fading. He moved his feet gingerly. Ah yes. They weren't paralyzed or caught in the mud. There was nothing to be afraid of. The hideous, approaching shape-lessness was a figment of the imagination. Stop trembling, Jerry Whittaker. Be a man for once.

He lay still, gazing at the dimly lighted corridor beyond the bars. It was stark and barren, but it was solid and visible and gave him comfort. It was making him feel more like an adult and less of a child. There was nothing so terrible about the dream, now that he thought of it. The real world did not contain grasping shadows. The real world contained horrors, but not terrors. Terror was the milieu of the child. Terror lurked only in the abysses of the un-known, and man now knew so much that even the nature of the un-known had been reduced to the quality of expectation. The unknown offered nothing greater than horror to a modern man. The age of terror faded as the age of knowledge grew.

But it was the second time he had had that dream. It had shaken him two nights before: the same dream, the same impact, the same moment of awakening. Was this the start of a recurring sequence? Would he, night after night, find himself calf deep in mud while the black, threatening unknown crept closer? That was a thought as disturbing as the dream. Then he would dread approaching night, lie on his bunk afraid to sleep, succumbing at last to fatigue and then, in his weakness, suffering the awfulness of the dream.

What had brought it on? It was Cleveland Parrish, of course, and the visit he had made two days ago. Wednesday the third of February it was.

Interesting how easy it was to be good at dates in jail. He'd always had to consult a calendar for even the simplest gaps of time. But he'd had a secretary who minded appointments for him, freeing him for more important things. Now there was nothing more important than watching the days go by, marking each in his mind, checking off the fact that there was now one less day until he would say good-by to this unbearable world of stone and steel, a world where the greatest comfort at night was a dim bulb that let him see the stone and the steel.

He thought of Katherine and freedom. He thought of the jury saying he was not guilty. The sun would start shining and the sky would turn blue. And he would never again in his life pass within a statute mile of the accursed jail.

But such thoughts were brief and almost guiltily thumbed through. They were stolen thoughts that he had no right to and he would shut down hard on them as soon as he could muster the strength, lest indulging in them jeopardize the very future he prayed for.

When he was free, there would be no more nightmares.

That's when they started, on Wednesday the third. It was the day Cleveland Parrish said he was going away. He had to interview and investigate in Pennsylvania.

It was necessary, of course. Sally's background and friends would be important to the trial. So why had Jerry felt like crying at the news? Had he become so needful of the lawyer, so dependent upon him for hope that the whole world crumbled in the great man's absence? Or was it that, for the duration, there would be no more word from Katherine? She was the anchor of his life, her messages his sustenance.

Tears of pity filled Jerry's eyes. He wasn't a fighter and he didn't know what to do. How could he help himself? He needed Cleve to tell him. Yet all Cleve ever wanted was to find a second lover for Sally. It didn't matter who it was, it only mattered that he be revealed.

But Jerry didn't know of any other lovers. He wouldn't have known about Walter if Barbara hadn't dragged him to the scene.

Jerry had been so wrapped up in Katherine he hadn't noticed what Sally was up to. But Jerry would be glad to pretend he had noticed. He could say that Sally had told him—not the name, but the fact. That would be like Sally!

Yet he didn't dare present such a story to Cleve. A couple of times he'd tried to suggest he'd noticed something, but Cleve had smelled the falsehood instantly and would have none of it. "Only the truth, Jerry," Cleve kept saying.

But the truth wasn't doing the job. Sometimes one had to garnish the truth a little to get at the real truth. With Cleve's help there was no reason why they couldn't work out a testimony that would absolutely convince a jury that Sally had at least one more lover.

Only Cleve wouldn't help. And why? Was he afraid Jerry would confess to collusion under stress? He should know Jerry would die before he'd tell. Was Cleve too honest? That was doubtful. Didn't he have the reputation of trying any trick, any ruse, any tactic to get his clients off? Besides, wasn't a lawyer supposed to go to bat for a client? Wasn't he supposed to give his all? Cleveland Parrish was carefully keeping his own skirts lily white. All Cleve was doing was throwing Jerry a rope to pull him out of the mud. He wasn't wading into it himself to pick him up and save him bodily. Was that right? Shouldn't a lawyer get personally involved? Parrish acted as if he cared, as if he were involved, but he wasn't, really. He could go off to Pennsylvania for as long as he pleased and Jerry could rot in his cell. Jerry couldn't go anywhere. Jerry couldn't help himself. Jerry couldn't even hold up his head without help. Jerry was a blob, totally dependent upon others. He couldn't even tell a lie in his own behalf. Cleveland Parrish wouldn't let him.

And what about Ed Balin? Ed made his duty calls like visiting a patient in the hospital. Ed never knew what to talk about. Ed wasn't in on the trial preparation. He didn't know as much about the case as Jerry did. All he could do was sympathize and ask how he could help. But he wouldn't break any rules, so what kind of help could he give?

Then, when the visit was over, Ed could go home in his fine automobile to his elegant home and his elegant wife and he could forget all about Jerry Whittaker and the ugly, hideous jail he lived in until the next time.

Jerry began to weep in earnest. He was sure it would never end.

CHAPTER 45

Cleveland Parrish did not take Melody with him to Pennsylvania. While there was much she could help him with and while he had a distaste for loneliness, he didn't want to go to bed with her and he didn't want her wondering why.

It was all because of Katherine Lord. She was such a demanding and ambitious partner he had scheduled the Pennsylvania trip to get away. She really drained him in their sessions and he sensed that if he didn't space his visits, his manhood would be in jeopardy. He wondered how Jerry had been able to cope with her. No surprise Sally had called him impotent. Katherine Lord left a man too weak for anyone else.

If this was a flaw, the flaw was in the man. Her real flaw was her ingenuous disregard of the Cleveland Parrish ego. Her distress when she learned he'd be leaving town was not because he'd be away. It was not even because there'd be no sex. It was because there'd be no communication with Jerry. In bed she was as worldly as Eve and as guiltless as she was worldly. Out of bed, she was as true to Jerry as if she had totally absorbed Cleve's argument that sex had nothing to do with love. What was worse, Cleve was left with the intolerable suspicion that when they were making love, she was pretending he was Jerry. Something would have to be done about that, for Cleve would play second fiddle to no one. Meanwhile, a vacation from women would be a good thing.

For Melody the separation was equally welcome. He'd been driving her hard these past weeks, keeping her busy with so much minutiae that she seldom could dine with him or do more than fall into bed exhausted at night.

Now she was free of him and back in New York, where she

could pace herself and tend to a family matter that was labeled "urgent." Gary Stevens and his thousand dollars had not come home. He had not called, he had not written, and the family was frantic. What was worse, her father had a way of making her feel to blame. No matter how many times she told him she had given Gary the check, that he had packed and left her apartment to get a Boston train, he kept poking at her as if she were holding him captive. God damn it, just because she hadn't actually put him on the train. In addition to suggesting she was at fault, he thought she ought to do something about it. Gary had come to see her, hadn't he? Gary hadn't come home. Find him.

She would have liked to remind her father that Gary was twenty-five years old and more than able to look after himself—witness the blackmail attempt, if you please. But one didn't talk that way to Shep Stevens. And, of course, there was always the possibility that something actually had happened to him.

So she promised she'd see what she could do, and when she moved back to New York, she asked Dan Price to find the boy. It was, she told him, a personal job, one she would pay for herself, and she'd just as soon Cleve not be told. Dan grinned and reminded her a client's business was automatically confidential and saw her out of the agency office without giving her a pat on the fanny. Now she was a customer, not a customer's secretary; but he rather liked keeping a secret with her from Cleve. Now he wondered more than ever if she were a private preserve. With Cleve away, it might be the time to find out.

That was on a Friday and the following Monday morning, he stopped by her office to report. He could have phoned, but the office wasn't that far away and there might be a chance to socialize. And you never could tell what might develop.

He was breezy and casual. Had she been worried? She need fear no longer. Gary was alive and well and not at all hard to find. He was bunking in with Morelle and Rita Costaine.

What happened to Melody amazed him. Revulsion and horror crossed her face and a white red colored her cheeks. He had thought her more worldly than that, but it had been a real sledgehammer. He dropped his bantering manner and said gently, "You going to see him?"

She hadn't thought, but she guessed she'd have to. She nodded numbly.

"You want company?" He kept it light, but it was an offer to help. "There's no charge."

She shook her head. It was bad enough that he had to know, that anybody had to know. She thought belatedly that she could have checked that possibility for herself without hiring a detective. Now it was too late. Dan knew and Dan's office. But he didn't have to be privy to whatever scene might develop when she went to get him. And she'd have to go. She said, "Is he there now?"

"He went to bed there last night. I don't know if he's on the premises this morning. He might have a job. I can find out if you want."

"No, no. It's all right." She made herself smile. "Thanks, Dan."

He grinned at her reassuringly. "You change your mind, you know my number."

It was thanks, but no thanks, and there was nothing for him to do but leave. Too many bad omens. So much for socializing.

Melody wasted no time after Dan's departure. She got into her coat, locked up the office, and took a taxi to the Costaine address in the Bronx.

There were four tedious flights in the old tenement and Melody paused frequently for breath. Part of it was her excessive smoking, the result of nervous tension—"occupational hazard" was the way she rationalized it. Part was uneasiness and fear. Melody Stevens was supposed to be forever "cool," forever in command. Good old, reliable Melody; the shoulder to cry on, the haven for the afflicted. If you have troubles, particularly if the family has troubles, Melody has the answers.

If Melody has troubles, where, then, are the answers? What a question to ask! Melody has no troubles. Melody, like God, is just there.

So part of it was uncertainty, and part was the need to preserve the image, to be in command in front of Gary. She couldn't let him report back home that Melody was at a loss. She could see the sneer on her father's face.

At the top to the right of the stairs, where it said Costaine, she knocked. It was almost noon. The stairwell was warm and smelled of cooked cabbage. She was perspiring under her coat. A sound could be heard on the other side of the door. Someone was coming. She uttered a momentary prayer without wondering when was the last time she had prayed.

Bolts shot back and the door was pulled inward. The girl was young and dark, with a bold, contemptuous face and a sneer on the mouth. She was wearing toreador pants tight enough to pass for a layer of skin, and a buttonless man's shirt with rolled-up sleeves and a knot around the midriff to expose a strip of stomach. Behind her the curtains were drawn and the room was dim and unclean. "Yeah?" the girl said, giving her a cool appraisal.

Melody hadn't planned her approach. She said, "I want to see Gary."

The girl was neither taken aback nor upset. Her appraisal grew more calculating and she said, "Who the hell are you?"

"His sister."

The girl snorted. "Oh, Christ, you must be out of a book." Then she turned and shouted, "Hey, Gary, your sister wants you." She left the door wide and dropped into a nearby overstuffed chair. "What are you going to do?" she asked. "Spank him?"

Melody stepped inside and fought the flush that stung her cheeks. The girl was settling down to watch a show. The sneering mouth was twisted into a grin. It was going to be fun.

They stayed like that, Melody straight, in a pose of command, Rita slouched and amused. From the interior of the apartment there came no sound. Rita raised her voice and hollered again. Then she got out of the chair and disappeared into the bedroom. Her raucous tones said, "Get your ass out there, you clown," and Gary came stumbling into the hallway, barefoot, in pants and undershirt, while Rita gave him a boot from behind. "That's right," she said, returning to the chair. "Say hello to your sister."

"Listen, Sis," Gary said, coming to a halt beyond striking range, "I can explain. It's not what you think."

Melody was operating by instinct. She neither plotted nor planned what she would say. "Get your things," was her peremptory command.

"Well, yes." He half turned.

That was when Rita sat upright in the chair. "You stay where you are!"

Gary froze in midstream. Then Rita was on her feet, coming to Melody. "Out!" she said, jabbing a finger at the open door behind. "Out, out, out!"

Melody stood her ground, her eyes on Gary. "Priscilla needs you."

"Out!" Rita threw herself at Melody with filed talons.

Melody raised her arms in shocked defense and the quiet part of her mind said in wonder, "This can't be happening. It's not real."

A nail gouged her cheek and she thought of her looks. She grabbed at the girl's wrists and tried to hold her off. Her young opponent was fiercely strong and tore loose. Clawed fingers went for Melody's eyes and animal sounds came out of the girl's throat. A nail caught the flesh just off the corner of her brow and Melody screamed. It *was* happening, and the consequences could be terrible.

She flailed like a wild woman but the dark-haired Rita was relentless. Melody was frantic. She screamed again and Gary, suddenly aware that this was more than two squabbling women, grabbed Rita and pulled her away. She struggled and kicked and the animal sounds became cries of rage.

Gary thrust her away, but she came on again. He grabbed her and flung her against the couch. She seized and threw a heavy glass ashtray at his head. It smashed through a window and went down the side of the building to the street, a miss, but so close Gary turned white. "Get out!" she screamed at him and hurled the table lighter. He twisted to get out of the way but it struck him heavily in the back.

He pushed Melody toward the door and she pulled him with her. Rita snatched up the guitar on a nearby chair and swung it against him like a bat. "Look out," he cried and attempted to fend it off with an arm. It cracked and she swung it again. It started to splinter. Gary escaped into the hall with Melody before she could wield it a third time. She was screaming obscenities at him now, interspersing them with cries of "Out!" and when the two were in the hall, she slammed the door so hard it resounded and echoed down to the first floor.

Melody and Gary stood stunned and shaken in the tiled corridor. Two of the other doors were open and tenants stared. There was much to stare at. Melody had blood trickling down one cheek. Gary, disheveled and half dressed, had a cut on his left temple. They stood together at the stairwell, staring at the metal door, and a woman in the nearest doorway said, "Are you all right?"

Melody nodded. She didn't want help. She didn't want the curious people to become real. Gary said, "Sis, you're bleeding." He took a handkerchief from his trousers pocket and dabbed at her cheek. Melody said it was all right, but she didn't resist. Someone was showing concern and such moments were to be cherished.

The door opened again with a suddenness that brought Gary around with his guard up. Melody had the wild, momentary fear that Rita had a gun and would open fire. It wasn't a gun, it was a shoe, Gary's shoe, and Rita hurled it at his head. "And take your goddam things with you," she shouted. She followed the first shoe with the second and then his open suitcase filled with his clothes.

"And don't you ever come back," she said in violent parting and flung the door shut with as much impact as she had before.

Melody, Gary, and Gary's belongings were left alone with the staring neighbors in the hall.

CHAPTER 46

Melody, her face crimson, stooped to pack her brother's suitcase. That way she didn't have to look at the staring neighbors and read the stories in their minds. Gary drew on socks, resting his rear against the wall. He called Rita vile names under his breath but Melody ignored them. He put on a shirt and buttoned it and stuffed it inside his trousers. Melody was crouched below him, doing unnecessary folding and arranging, and all she showed him was the back of her head. It was enough. He could read the distaste and disgust as clearly as if she were turned around. He crouched beside her to put on shoes. "It's not what you think," he whispered.

She ignored that, but turned when he slipped into his jacket.

"Where's your overcoat?"

"I lost it," he muttered back.

Doors were closing. The neighbors were shutting themselves back inside their three-room worlds.

"What do you mean, you lost it?" Melody stood up and put her hands on her hips. Her voice was normal and cutting. She was as Gary always remembered her when she was disapproving. It was that icy, condemning, big-sister, parental kind of scourging that she never learned from Ma and Pa. Ma was soft on all the kids and Pa thought Gary was the greatest thing since Santa Claus. But Melody could freeze the younger kids and make them cringe. Gary could feel it now. It squeezed answers out of a person. "I left it in a bar," he said.

"You left it?"

She knew that wasn't quite it. She knew everything. That's what that look said: "I know the truth so don't try to fool me with lies. Don't add lying to your sins."

"Somebody stole it. I had it hung up in a bar and—"

"Pick up your bag."

He obeyed, bending to shut and latch it. When he rose he saw the drying blood on her cheek. "She scratched you bad. I should've grabbed her sooner."

"Come on." Melody was impatient. She led the way down the stairs.

They rode a taxi in stony silence and Melody didn't break it until they entered her living room. "Take your things in there," she said, indicating the guest room. "You can stay here tonight and go home in the morning."

Gary nodded and set the bag down. "Yeah, well, Sis—" He swallowed.

She gave him the ice treatment. "Yeah, well, Sis, what?"

"I want to explain."

"You can explain to Priscilla."

He flinched. "This is what I want to talk about. I want you to understand. I was looking for a job."

"In Rita Costaine's apartment?"

"Her mother lives there too, you know. I was just renting a room."

"Stop it, Gary, before I vomit."

Gary reddened and stopped. "What I really mean is," he went on lamely, "I really was trying to find work."

She went at him then, berating him for not communicating with Priscilla, for leaving his parents worried and frightened. Nor would she accept his apologetic claims of forgetfulness. Did he have no sense of responsibility for his family? Did he intend to abandon his wife and children? Would he have ever left Rita—and her mother, it was the both of them, wasn't it?—if she hadn't come for him?

Gary protested innocence. He didn't know what Melody meant. He wasn't that kind of a person.

"How much of the thousand dollars have you got left?"

Gary whitened. He finally managed to say, "Not very much."

"How much?"

"I haven't counted."

She held out her hand. "I'll count it."

"Part of it was Rita's."

"What are you talking about?"

"I had to pay her for the information. We split."

Melody raised a hand at him and Gary cringed. He was the little boy of seven again, afraid of his bold and confident fourteen-year-old sister.

She didn't strike him. "You stink," she said.

He was starting to blubber. "I know. I'm no good. I couldn't help it."

"Do you have any money at all?"

He shook his head.

"Give me your wallet."

He produced it without a murmur and she went through it. There was a YMCA membership card, a grocery list, a few worn papers and a driver's license. Not so much as a dollar bill was in the money compartment. Even the pictures of Priscilla and the children were missing.

"I was afraid to tell you," he whimpered.

"Shut your face." She thrust it back at him. "How do you think you're going to get home? What are you going to buy a ticket with?"

"If you could lend me the money, Sis, I'd pay it back as soon as I get a job. Just enough money to get home on."

"And then what are you going to do, beg?"

"Ma 'n' Pa can help me out. Pa wouldn't let anything happen to me and Pris. I can borrow it from Pa and pay you back. He'll make it good."

"You're into him for a hell of a lot already."

"He's good for it, Sis. He don't need much to live on these days. It's only him and Ma. The house is all paid for and he's sold off the best of the land. What pleasure's he gonna get out of what he's got except doing things for his kids? He'll make it good."

"I'll give you the fare," Melody told him. "I don't want you prying it out of Pa. But I'm not giving you cash. I'm buying you a ticket. I'm not paying you to go back to that bitch."

"Honest, I swear to God." He held up his right hand. "I want to see Pris and the kids. And the baby. You know I've hardly seen the baby since she was born?"

"I don't notice you remembering the fact."

"I wouldn't go back to that bitch. You saw what happened. You saw how she threw me out. Honest, Sis."

"You'll get a ticket home. No cash. You'd lose it before you got to the station."

She went into her own bedroom and looked around. That bitch, Rita, had been there, she was sure. She had noticed some of her clothes were rearranged after Gary had lived there. Now she could guess why. She looked in the mirror at the dried blood on her cheek. She went into her bathroom and gently soaked it off with a warm washcloth. Rita's nails were long and sharp, and it was a nasty scratch, but it wouldn't leave a scar.

When she came out, Gary was in the doorway looking hangdog. "I meant to ask you, Sis. You won't say anything to Pris about where I've been, will you? Or Ma and Pa? I mean, nothing happened. I was just boarding there. But you know, they might not understand."

"What you mean is, they *would* understand. What got into you with that girl and her mother, anyway?"

"I was just trying to find out some information, was all. And I did find it out."

"Yeah," Melody conceded. "You did find it out. That's some technique you've got."

Gary flushed. "Anyway, promise me you won't say nothing to nobody?"

Melody shrugged. "It's none of my business. Tell it any way you want."

He was relieved. "Thanks, Sis. Pris might leave me otherwise. I swear to God she might."

"When you show up without that thousand dollars, she damned well ought to."

That was the other point he was trying to work around to. Could Melody possibly advance him that much money? He'd pay her back. He'd make it good. With interest even. Maybe she could let him have nine hundred dollars and he could say he'd spent a hundred on living expenses while he tried to find more work?

Melody's mouth twisted. If she wouldn't give him train fare in cash, he was naïve to think she'd lend him nine hundred dollars. She told him what she'd do. She'd write him out a check for one thousand dollars, for deposit only, and he could show it to Priscilla and to Ma and Pa and tell them Melody had the power to sign checks for Cleveland Parrish and pay his bills.

Gary was more than willing, and when she made it out, he was profuse with his assurances that he'd pay it back just as soon as he could get work.

Melody was not that much of a fool. She knew she'd never see the money again. Normally she was parsimonious, but today she could even write out the check with a grim smile. That should put an end to Gary's blackmail game.

CHAPTER 47

Cleveland Parrish got up from the bed and plucked a cigarette from the pack on his Louis XIV bureau, the gift of a client. He turned and Melody was still stretched out on the sheets, flat and bare and spent. She was well formed and he noted the fact, but it was different now. Formerly he had accepted that bit of data with a certain satisfaction. Now he couldn't avoid comparisons. Katherine Lord's body was bigger and more buxom and—let's face it—he preferred his women that way. It wasn't that Melody was any worse than she'd been, although, now that he noticed it, her face was starting to age. She was, after all, a good six years older than Katherine and her beauty wasn't as fresh.

Cleve lighted the cigarette and wondered what was the matter with him. Sex with Melody had been as good as it always was and certainly he had done right by her. She was half asleep and if he didn't get her up, she'd drop off entirely. The act had been as successful as it always was, but he felt a strange dissatisfaction. It was better with Katherine. Melody didn't let herself go the way Katherine did. Melody was not as demonstrative, she was not as eager. Melody was cool, the precision girl, the capable one. It made her a super secretary, but Katherine was the hot, passionate one in bed.

He had stayed away from Melody throughout his Pennsylvania sojourn and he hadn't missed her. It wasn't like that with Katherine, though. He thought of her during the working days and his heart beat faster. He relived their intimate moments in fancy and it was an effort to concentrate on business. It got so bad that twice he made sneak trips to New Haven to reassure Jerry, deliver messages, and sleep with Katherine.

Though Pete Tucker drove him both times, Cleve took the car upon arrival in town and it was obvious to Pete that the Ultra Sonic Potentate of Law had secret appointments mere chauffeurs weren't to know about. It wasn't the first time private trips had left Pete sitting in hotel rooms (or lobbies or bars) for hours on end while Cleve went his secret ways in his very unsecret mauve Cadillac.

Nor would Pete have been surprised to learn the secret was a woman. He would have bet everything he owned that Melody was sleeping with Parrish, and he would have bet nearly an equal amount that Cleve would snatch whatever else he could get on the side. Pete had an assessment of his boss which was probably closer to reality than anyone else's.

Now Parrish was back in New York for two weeks of research in the Columbia Med-Barnard College complex to see who remembered what about Sally Demarest and Jerry Whittaker. And while he was at it, he was doing his duty by his secretary. He didn't want Melody to wonder, like Sally, about impotence.

He aroused her to dress and poured himself a drink at the living room bar. He hadn't brought her to his apartment just to screw. He had planned a work session, putting together what they had for Jerry's defense, studying what they would still need. But now he was dissatisfied and disturbed and he wanted her home.

It wasn't just the sex problem that was bothering him. There were lots of things. Like Jerry's goddam father and his strange turnabout regarding the store. Most parents would sell their souls for their children (even if guilty) and a Bible-reading, moralistic son of a bitch like Whittaker was made to be one of them. When Cleve returned to New Haven, he'd really twist screws into the old man. Fifteen thousand bucks was worth working for.

Then there was the problem with the defense. The detective agency still had no smell of a second lover and the very fruitlessness of the search diminished the likelihood of his existence. Let the likelihood fade to such unlikelihood that it slipped below reasonable doubt and Jerry would be in deep trouble. No matter what character references could be established for the noble doctor, no matter how circumstantial the prosecution evidence could be made to appear, if there was no alternative to exclusive opportunity, there could be no alternative to a "guilty" verdict.

Of course matters weren't all that bleak. A second lover might not have to be produced if Sally could be shown as willing to take one on. And if she'd go with the likes of Walter Costaine, she must have been an easy mark. In the couple of weeks remaining in February, Cleve expected to uncover Barnard witnesses who would say so.

He went back to the bedroom. Melody was nearly dressed. He said, "You want a drink before I call down for a cab?"

Melody knew the proper answer to that question. She said no, she wanted to get along. She had to wash her hair. Then she said, "By the way, have you got today's paper?" Cleve had and she told him to look at the murder story on page one.

The paper was on the buffet with the mail and the story was prominent. Two hippie hitchhikers, a boy and a girl, were being sought in the murder of a family of four in Arizona, whose bodies were found in a gully, their car missing. Not only had the family been killed, but the bodies of the adults and elder child had been defiled and parts of the baby's body had been eaten.

Melody came out of the bedroom adjusting the bow of her blouse. Cleve nodded at the story. "What about it?"

"The two hippies were picked up in California this morning."

"In the car?"

"I don't know. I didn't ask."

"Where'd you hear this?"

"The boy's father called up. His name is Claude Decker. He's big in L.A. real estate. He wants you to defend his boy."

Parrish's worries about the present case receded and a light came into his eye. What a case! Not just murder, but cannibalism! His

216

mouth took on a wolfish look. "California real estate?" he said. "What's he offering?"

"A quarter of a million dollars if the boy gets off—not guilty. He'll pay a hundred and fifty thousand for anything less than life, and he'll pay you fifty thousand dollars if you'll take the case, no matter how it comes out."

"Two hundred and fifty, one hundred and fifty, or fifty—and expenses, Melody. Tell him, 'and expenses.'"

"As soon as we're through here?"

"That's right. Next on the agenda. Never mind. I'll tell him."

"You'll tell him?" Melody arched an eyebrow.

"You're damned right. I want a complete briefing."

She said, "I thought you never mixed cases."

Parrish laughed gloatingly and rubbed his hands together. "When it comes to cannibalism I make an exception."

Melody nodded. Did he mean cannibalism, or did he mean two hundred and fifty thousand dollars?

CHAPTER 48

At one o'clock on the first of March, Cleve decided to play cat and mouse and put a call through to State's Attorney Vincent Masters. His bags were unpacked, he was back in the Park Plaza presidential suite for the long haul, with Melody due the next day, and he was loaded for bear.

Vincent Masters was in a hurry to get the trial going, was he? Well, Cleve was feeling in a generous mood. His preparations were coming along so well he could advance the trial date one week. Would Mr. Masters like that? Of course there would be pretrial motions, the usual things: throw the case out of court, request a change of venue, and the like. And, by the way, did Vincent really plan to go through with it? Couldn't he see that there was insufficient evidence to eliminate reasonable doubt?

(Later he'd go meet that bastard druggist face to face and make him buckle. And there was a distant relative of Claude Decker in the area it might be worthwhile talking to for a slant on that cannibal case.)

Vincent Masters got on the line in good humor. Judy's birthday was on the morrow and a spanking new blue bicycle was standing in a corner of his office winking at him. The case looked good to him too, and Cleve Parrish looked correspondingly toothless. He listened to Cleve's proposal and said that, naturally, he'd be pleased to advance the trial date a week. In fact, he'd like to advance it a month. "I can't understand why it's taking you so long," he said. "Are you having trouble finding character witnesses for the doctor?"

(Cleve would have liked to advance it a month too and get it over with. But he'd draw the wrong judge.) "Oh, I've got thirty or forty of them. All patients. I'm surprised you didn't explore that area more. Or did you find their universal love of the doctor too damaging to your prejudiced view?"

Masters only laughed. "Oh, I wouldn't call my view prejudiced, Parrish. In the beginning I was only too willing to assume his innocence. It was only as the mountain of evidence piled up that I was reluctantly forced to change my mind. By the way, are you still going to plead him innocent? You aren't even going to try for manslaughter?"

"Sorry, the plea is innocent. I never allow my clients to confess to crimes they didn't commit."

Masters laughed again and Cleve, lighting a cigarette, frowned. He didn't like the way the conversation was going. Masters was the one playing cat and mouse. He had something, or he knew something, and he was feeling particularly confident. He thought he had the case in the bag, Cleve or no Cleve.

"That's too bad," Masters said, answering Cleve. "Because I was going to be very generous. I don't usually do this sort of thing, but since it's you, I was going to say the state would be willing to accept a plea to murder in the second degree. That way we could save all this trial business."

He really did have something, the son of a bitch!

Parrish said, "Thanks, but I always believe that prosecuting attorneys ought to be given the chance to show their stuff. I mean,

218

you've been working hard, there's the publicity and all. No lawyer would want to miss the chance to wow 'em in a spot like that. I mean, everybody ought to have his day in court, don't you think?"

"I suppose," Masters said with mock sadness. "Well, if you won't change your mind, I guess I'll just have to go through with it." He took his leave and was about to hang up when he suddenly said in an offhand tone, "Oh, by the way, I meant to tell you. We've added another witness to our roster. You'll be getting notification in a day or so, but I might as well tell you now. A friend of yours, I believe. Girl by the name of Katherine Lord."

Cleveland Parrish finished the conversation on a light note but when he hung up, he mashed out his cigarette and swore a stream of blue obscenities. So that was it! They'd got to Katherine! How the hell had they found her out? It didn't matter, they'd done it. No wonder Little Boy Blue was being so cutsy-cute. God damn Vince Masters' soul.

He thought of Katherine on the witness stand and it made him shudder. She was so guileless, so innocent, so hopelessly honest she'd be a disaster. One could never guess what she might reveal under examination. She would tell ALL in the conviction that the truth would set men free. God damn. This was real bad news.

He lighted another cigarette, picked up the phone, thumbed through his pocket notebook, and gave the operator the number for the branch bank in Madison. It was the first time he had called Katherine at work, but this was a special situation. Very special.

There was a wait that went on and on. Where the hell was she? He lighted a third cigarette from the second. What were they doing, setting up a wiretap?

Then there came the soft, gentle tones of his—or was she Jerry's —paramour.

"Oh, Cleve," she said excitedly when she heard his voice. "I've been waiting for you to call. Something's happened!"

Something had happened all right. The sky had fallen. He asked her when.

"Friday. Right here in the bank. This detective by the name of Coyne came in—"

Parrish wasn't interested in the details. That it was Friday was enough. "Look," he said, "I want to see you. I'm seeing Jerry this afternoon. I'll bring you a message from him and we'll have dinner—"

"Oh," she said, "I don't need messages any more. I've been seeing him!"

"Seeing him? Jerry?"

"Yes!" She was alive with joy. "Mr. Masters arranged it. Isn't it wonderful?"

That bastard! That lousy, stinking, upstaging bastard! Parrish said, "You've seen Jerry, then?"

"Saturday and yesterday, and I'm coming in today as soon as I get through work. You've been wonderful, Cleve, but you don't need to deliver messages ever again. Isn't that good?"

"That may be," Parrish said, "but I'm going to want to see you."

"Maybe we can meet at the jail."

Was he being given the brush? Was she now so beholden to Vincent Masters she had lost track of where her and Jerry's best interest lay?

"I don't mean see you-and-Jerry," he snapped. "I mean see *you!*"

"Well, I know—" She was definitely diffident. "But under the circumstances—"

"I've got to talk to you!" He stressed the word talk. "I've got to find out some things from you. I want to know how this happened and what you've said, and I don't want to do it over the phone or in front of Jerry."

She could understand. That was all right. But where to meet? She brightened. How about the lobby of the hotel, say, around six?

Not in a million years. Parrish didn't hang around hotel lobbies. "Call my room," he told her. "We'll have cocktails and dinner."

"Oh, you don't have to do that. We could just talk in the lobby."

Who the hell did she think was running the case? "Cocktails and dinner, I said. I don't play show and tell in lobbies." He put a smile into his voice. "After all, if we're planning Jerry's coming-out party, we ought to make the occasion festive."

"Coming-out party" was all she had to hear. It would be as he wished.

CHAPTER 49

They sipped cocktails in the rooftop bar and she told him about it, how she had been called away from her window and there, with the bank manager, was this great big redheaded man who was introduced as Detective Coyne and who wanted to ask her some questions. They used the manager's office and the detective asked if she knew Dr. Whittaker. She said she'd gone to him once. He asked if she'd seen him since his arrest. She told him no. He asked when she had last seen him before his arrest. She was very nervous. She said she wasn't sure, she couldn't remember. He asked if it was at her house or somewhere else, and she couldn't remember that either. Then he asked her how long they'd been going together and in no time the whole story came out.

He let her go back to work but when the day ended, he drove her to the courthouse in New Haven, where Mr. Masters talked to her for a long time and then drafted a statement for her to sign outlining the arrangement she had with Jerry, and he told her she would have to appear in court to testify at his trial.

"You should have refused to answer any questions Coyne put to you," Parrish growled. "You should have called me."

"But I didn't know where you were. Besides, he knew everything anyway."

"He didn't know anything. He was fishing. He connected you with Jerry somehow. He suspected something. So he moves in on you with all this 'right in the middle of work' routine, catches you off guard, has you all shook up, and, presto, you spill the whole thing. He must have thought you were too good to be true."

Katherine looked shriveled. She felt shriveled. "I'm sorry, Cleve.

Honest to God. But I've never been questioned by a detective before."

Parrish forgave her. She was so stupidly honest, so untutored in her legal rights, what else could he expect? Besides, he was starting to get the hots for her just brushing knees under the tiny table.

"All right," he said, "the harm has been done, what there is of it."

"Is it very bad?" she asked him, round-eyed and troubled. "Mr. Masters is such a nice man, so considerate and kind."

"Yeah. He's good to his mother, I hear."

"I mean it, Cleve. When he found out how Jerry and I feel about each other and how you'd been carrying our messages back and forth—"

"So you told him that too?"

"Well, yes."

"Did you tell him we'd been to bed together?"

She flushed and dropped her eyes. "No," she whispered. "After all, I'm not going to tell him everything. Besides, he didn't ask me."

"If he had, you would have told him?"

"No. I would have said I don't remember or something like that." She looked up. "But I don't suppose he'd believe me. I'm not a very good liar."

That was the understatement of the decade. Parrish hailed the waitress but Katherine wouldn't accept a second cocktail. "I have to drive home," she alibied.

"Yes, but not for a while."

"No, but after dinner."

Parrish didn't push. They finished the drink and moved down to the second-floor restaurant. There, she tried to order the least expensive meal and Parrish had to be stern to get her to have the roast beef. She said she really wasn't that hungry, but Parrish told her he did not take people to dinner to have them spare his pocketbook. It was an insult to his work.

They had the roast beef and Katherine told him how Mr. Masters, after he found out about the messages Cleve carried, explained to her that while prisoners were only supposed to be visited by their attorneys and their families, the rules weren't intended to keep apart people who truly loved each other, so he arranged visiting privileges for her.

She spent the rest of the meal expressing concern over Jerry, how much jail had changed his appearance, how wan he had become and how much grayer. Parrish found himself heartily sick of the subject by the time dessert was served. In the first place, he didn't share Katherine's passion for the man, and in the second, he was jealous. He wanted the women in his company to be very much aware of his presence, especially when he was with a woman who made him so very conscious of her presence. It was a definite put-down to share a meal with this luscious girl and hear nothing out of her mouth but Jerry, see nothing out of her eyes but Jerry. She wasn't in the Napoleon Room with Cleveland Parrish, she was in the damned visitors' cage with Jerry Whittaker.

"You're worried about him," he finally said, to shift her attention. "You're worrying about what's happened to him. I think you ought to worry about what's *going* to happen to him."

She looked at Parrish innocently. "He's going to come to trial," she said, "and you're going to set him free."

"Thanks for the vote of confidence," he replied, "but it's not that easy."

"You mean he might not—?" She put a fist to her mouth and stared with such panic that Cleve had to rush to reassure her. He didn't mean it wouldn't be done, he meant there were certain difficulties that they ought to discuss.

Her alarm eased, to be replaced by bewilderment. "But what's it got to do with me? I mean, you defending him and all?"

"That's what you and I are going to talk about—after dinner."

"Oh, but I can't," she said. "It's almost eight o'clock. I have to get home."

It wasn't just a put-down, it really was a brush-off! Cleve masked his fury. "You don't have to go home at eight o'clock," he said with an iron smile. "It's not the witching hour. And it's important that we work a few things out together. You've given Vincent Masters a whole new angle to the case, a lot of new ammunition to use against Jerry. Just because he sweet-talks you and gets you visiting privileges doesn't change the fact that he's out to lock Jerry up for life."

"But Mr. Masters—he was very sympathetic when I told him Jerry couldn't have done it. He said it was quite possible that Jerry hadn't done it and that was exactly what the trial was for. To find out whether he had or hadn't. You know, Cleve, he doesn't want to see an innocent man punished."

"And neither do I, and neither do you, which is why we're going up to the suite and take a close look at where this new development leaves us, and what we're going to do about it. That's the least you can do for Jerry, don't you think?"

And she said, as she had to say, "Of course."

The curtains were open in the suite and Katherine went to the windows, drawn by the sparkling lights and nighttime traffic below. Cleve wasn't interested in the view. His lust had been growing since the knee touching over cocktails. He could hardly sit through dinner and now he wanted her so bad, he didn't even hang up her coat. He threw it over a chair and went after her.

"Isn't it beautiful?" Katherine exclaimed, staring out at the scene and he, coming up behind her, said, "It's probably the outstanding view in the city." He looked at it over her shoulder, put his hands under her arms and slid them over her full, rounded breasts. Their texture, the combination of softness and firmness, and the size of them was almost more than he could stand.

She pulled away before he could get hold. "Cleve! For heaven's sake!"

It was difficult for him to control his anger. "What's the matter?"

She went around the front of the couch. "What's the matter with you? We came up here to talk."

"We'll talk. We've got plenty of time." He moved around the couch too. She backed off past the seat cushions into the dining area. Christ, what was it degenerating into, one of those goddam scenes where the amorous executive is chasing the pretty secretary around the office? He wasn't going to chase her. He couldn't have that happen.

"No," she said, keeping her distance. "We'll talk now. I've got to get home."

He stayed where he was, by the side of the couch. "What's the big rush to get home? What's supposed to happen home?"

"I've got some clothes to rinse out and I want to wash my hair—"

"The washing can wait. The hair can wait. We've got things to do here."

"I know. We're going to talk."

"And we're going to do some other things too." He took a small step forward and put a gentler note into his tone. A girl likes to be wooed. "I've missed you, Katherine," he said. "I've missed you very much."

She swallowed. "I'm sorry, Cleve. I really am. But we've got to stop that sort of thing."

His heart skipped. She was saying no to him and it hit him—not just in his ego either. He really did go for the girl and he needed the response to be mutual. Let her dream of Jerry so long as she was embracing him! "What are you talking about?" he said, sharpening his voice to hide his fear.

"Us." She gestured. "What we've been doing together. Sex. We've got to stop."

"Why?"

"I'm not lonely any more." She tried eagerly to explain. "Now I can see Jerry and it's all different. I don't need anything any more at all. Just being with him a few minutes every day is like food and drink and sex and everything rolled into one."

"That's just fine for you," Cleve said coldly, "but that doesn't do anything for me. You may have undergone some great transformation, but I haven't."

"I know," she said gently, "and I'm very sorry."

Damned if she wasn't being patronizing. She was going to give him sympathy and he wanted sex. "Being sorry doesn't help. You're letting me down, Katherine."

"Oh, not really, Cleve. There are lots of other women. There must be hundreds who'd be thrilled to death to be made love to by you. You're so good at it. You really are."

She wasn't only being patronizing, she was soft-soaping him as well. Who the hell did she think she was talking to, some half-brained pre-humanoid just down from the trees?

"Listen, Katherine," he said, keeping his voice steady, "it's not as simple as you're trying to make it. You and Jerry and I are in this together. We're a team. And we've got to remain a team for the duration. Do you understand that?"

"Yes, but that—"

"You and I are working to free Jerry. Nothing else matters. We've got to set Jerry free."

"I know that, but—"

"You recognize, don't you, that when you weren't seeing Jerry you turned inward. You shut yourself off. You became crippled. You remember that? You admitted it yourself."

She nodded. "I know—"

"And we went to bed together and you got better. It did you good.

And I'm glad it did you good. But you led me on, Katherine. You made me need you and now, when my need is the greatest and I'm looking forward to seeing you again, you give me the back of your hand. You invite me in and when you've got what you want, you kick me out."

Katherine bit her lip. "I didn't mean to lead you on, Cleve. I swear I didn't." She was nervous. She wasn't good at scenes.

"What you meant to do isn't what matters. What you did do is what counts. And you led me on. You made me think you enjoyed my visits."

"I did. I honestly did. You're a very good lover. I told you that. But I never meant for you to think—I mean, I always made it perfectly clear that Jerry is the only one who matters to me. I like you, Cleve, you know that, but I never intended you to think I might come to love you. You couldn't possibly have believed that."

"No, I wasn't believing that. But that's not what I'm talking about. What I'm saying is you've got Jerry now and you don't need me any more. That's all right. I can understand that. My feelings aren't hurt. But I don't have any Jerry to turn to for inspiration. I only have you."

"You'll find someone else," she said gently, hopefully. "You'll see."

"Some other time, perhaps," Cleve persisted. "But right now we're a team. You and I. We're working together to set Jerry free. You're my inspiration in this case, Katherine. Not someone else. You. You're the one who helps make it worthwhile. Don't talk about other women. It's you I need."

Katherine was white, her expression stony cold. "What you're saying is that you want me to take care of your sex needs until Jerry gets out of jail."

She was not the brightest girl in the world but she did have an animal instinct that led her to the heart of the matter—as well as a pithy way of expressing it.

He didn't try to deny it, he only tried to make it sound better. "We want Jerry free. We both agree that's all that matters. If we're going to set him free, I've got to be at my very best. I've got to be at the top of my form. I don't want to alarm you, Katherine, but the evidence against Jerry is very strong. We *can* lose. That is what we have to do our damndest to avoid. You're my inspiration in this case, Katherine. You're the one who lifts me out of myself. You get me to do my best. And that's what we want, isn't it? You wouldn't want me not to be at my best, would you, when Jerry's life hangs in the balance?"

He knew she could read the threat but he no longer cared. He wanted this girl and he meant to have her and he didn't give a damn what it took to bring her to heel.

"Put that way," she answered in tones as cold as a dead man's heart, "what can I say?" She reached behind her head for the zipper of her dress, then behind her back to pull it down. She stripped off the dress and laid it over her coat. She faced him and said bitterly, "Do you want me to undress here or in the bedroom?"

The bedroom suited him and she went in, turned between the beds and proceeded to take off the rest of her things, laconically, with no shame, no heat, no feeling.

He stripped too, sensing the flush on his face, glad the only light came from the hall. It was better than being thwarted, but it wasn't what he wanted.

He brought her down with him on the bed and she gave way like mosquito netting. She was docile, inert, as responsive as cotton batting. It spoiled things and it angered him. It was a slap at his ego, his manliness, at the Casanova quality that he prized so highly.

He strove to arouse her, to make her his in more than a technical sense. He kissed her, but she kept her teeth clenched. He plucked her nipples but they did not respond. He sucked them but she only stared at the ceiling.

What angered him most was that he himself was aroused. It was the rottenest, most miserable, most ineffective lovemaking session he had ever experienced. Everything about it damped desire, yet he had to work to keep himself contained. That was the worst of it, that she had this power over him, that he lacked a greater power over her. He wished he could have scorned her, that he could throw her out naked into the hall and tell her, begone, but she awakened desire in him as no other girl ever had.

He worked harder on her breasts but she never so much as closed her eyes. He felt between her legs and she was as dry as the desert.

"Hurry up," she said with scathing impatience. "Get it over with."

He worked at entering her and it was difficult. Though she gave no sign, he felt he must be hurting her, for it was hurting him. He hoped he was hurting her. He wanted to do something to her that would elicit a response—a shudder, a moan, a cry of pain, anything.

When he was fully within her, he sought to kiss her, to be tender, to woo her some way or another, but she turned her face away. She didn't say it again but her manner was telling him to hurry up and finish.

"Don't be like that," he whispered in her ear. "Get with it, kid. You're supposed to inspire me."

Then she screamed—one piercing, keening shriek.

Cleve could feel her clamp on him. He raised up quickly and looked around.

Melody Stevens was standing in the doorway, silhouetted against the light.

"You filthy bastard," she said to him in a hissing whisper. She turned and was gone.

CHAPTER 50

Parrish let himself go even as Katherine struggled to get out from under him. It was the last chance.

Then he was out of her and on his feet while she rolled away from him, sobbing bitterly—at what, he couldn't imagine.

Goddam broads. He'd like to belt this weepy one and give her something to cry about.

Now that he was sated and could view her with less passion, he could see her as a stupid, unfeeling, ignorant, and callous animal. Take away that goddam body and he wouldn't give her the box top off his breakfast cereal. Jerry couldn't really want to marry her. He couldn't possibly be that dumb. (That's a point to remember if Masters tries to paint Jerry as serious. She's to sleep with, not live with.)

And that other broad, that goddam, disobedient secretary—that cool, ash-blonde witch who so arrogantly comes to town a day ahead of schedule and so arrogantly stalks into Cleveland Parrish's bedroom! Does she think Cleveland Parrish has no life beyond her? Are we going to have to post "keep out" signs to keep her in her place?

"It's all right," he said impatiently to the sobbing girl as he got back into his clothes. "There's nothing to get upset about."

"What is she going to think of me?" Katherine moaned. "What if she tells Jerry?"

"She's not going to think anything about it," Parrish answered. "And nobody's going to tell Jerry." He zipped up his trousers and looked at Katherine's backside with displeasure. He didn't want to be stuck with this bawling girl. He wanted her out of there and off for home. "Everything's going to be all right," he said in more soothing tones. "Miss Stevens won't do anything. Now, you get your clothes on and don't *you* say anything to Jerry, and I'll call you in a couple of days. Come on. I want to talk to Miss Stevens and you ought to get on home."

Katherine rolled over and sat up, wiping her eyes and sniffing. "I feel just terrible," she moaned.

Cleve looked at her breasts, so large, so well shaped, so exciting, and knew with regret that it was for the last time. There would have been other occasions. He would have reawakened her responses. He would have made her like it—if that bitch of a secretary hadn't killed it.

Katherine started getting into her underpants and Cleve watched the operation, remaining until she, ignoring him and still sniffling, slipped into her bra and hooked it in place. Then he gave her more reassurance that all would be well, told her good night, and walked out to the dining room and the connecting door to Melody's room.

It was unlocked and he opened it. Melody, her back to him, her suitcase open on the sofa bed, was packing. She heard him but ignored his entrance, folded a slip and put it in place.

He closed the door and stood with feet planted. "I will overlook just once your walking into my quarters unannounced, but you'd better understand, my fine miss, don't you ever do it again." He lightened the sternness a little. "You're getting too cavalier, my pet."

"Don't worry," she said in an iced voice, folding away a pair of black lace panties, "I won't walk into any room you're in again, ever."

Black lace. That was Melody. White cotton pants was Katherine. "And what," he said acidly, "are you supposed to mean by that?"

"It means I'm leaving," she said, still without turning around. "I'm handing in my notice. I'm through. I quit."

Cleve snorted. "Because you find me in bed with another woman? For Christ's sake, Melody, stop acting like a midwestern housewife."

She wheeled on him. "It's not that I find you in bed. It's who I find you in bed with." Her tone became scathing in its contempt. "The great Cleveland Parrish! He's defending a man charged with murder. And how does this champion of the downtrodden, of the victimized innocent, handle this responsibility? By seducing their women! You've done some low things in my association with you. You've made my stomach crawl. But this is a new low, even for you. Making that poor kid go to bed with you—"

"Making her?" Cleve was outraged. "Do you really think I make—"

"You made her do it," Melody said savagely. "I saw the look on her face—hating it, enduring it. I've gone with you. I've suffered with you. I've felt the hate that's directed at you. It's rubbed off on me too. But I've borne it all because somewhere, deep down, I thought you had some kind of integrity, that when the chips were down you would do right by your clients—"

"And right by you too, I daresay," Parrish retorted. "The trouble with you is, you're jealous."

"Yes, I'm jealous. Among other things I'm jealous. But don't try to con yourself with the idea that's all it is. I don't hate you because I'm jealous. I hate you because you're despicable. I hate you because you have no honor and no conscience. You wouldn't sell your soul because you've already sold it. You and your big reputation. You're such a goddamn shining knight to everybody in trouble who's rich enough to pay your price. Well, you're not going to fool people any more because I'm going to show you up for what you really are."

Parrish spoke firmly, as to a balky child. "Like hell you are. You're going to take a tranquilizer and get some sleep. And next time I want you someplace, you're going to arrive the day I tell you to arrive, not the night before."

She shook her head. "You don't get it, do you? I'm leaving you. L-E-A-V-I-N-G. It's a word you don't know very well. Because nobody's ever left you before. You've always thrown them out. But if you want to throw me out, you'd better fire me fast because I'm taking the next train back to New York."

The dumb blonde really was upset. Maybe she shouldn't be pushed too far. She might just go ahead and do something that stupid. Cleve said quietly, "You mean, leave without the customary notice?"

"Without any notice at all. That's right, Mr. Cleveland Parrish. Without notice. Bang." She snapped her fingers. "Just like that."

He tried the subtle threat. "Without even waiting for me to write you out a recommendation?"

"Don't worry. I'll live without a recommendation from you. You're the one who's going to be stuck. Because you can't hurt me, but I can ruin you."

"Ruin me?"

"That's right. I can hurt you where you hurt the most. In court. I can make you lose this case. Because I know all the angles you're going to pull. I know all the tricks you have up your sleeve. Because you've tested your whole defense on me. I can tell Vincent Masters everything you've got. I can lay you open so he can crucify you."

Cleve shrugged and said in a beaten tone, "You don't have to go to Masters to beat me, you know. You can crucify me just by doing what you're doing—just by leaving me right now, deserting me when I need you most."

"And that couldn't give me greater pleasure. I hope I do crucify you. I hope I ruin you. I hope you never win another goddam case."

"Oh," he said softly, "I suppose I'll win some more cases—in time. When I've found another secretary who can help me half as much as you have. But that won't be right away. I won't win any more cases for a while."

"Good and good-by." She turned to her suitcase and threw in a shoe.

Parrish said musingly, "I hope they don't give Jerry the chair. I hope it's only life imprisonment."

She stopped for a second, then went on packing. "Don't try that one on me," she snapped. "You'll get him off."

"Not without you."

"Forget it," she said. "I'm not going to give Masters your battle plan. One betrayer in this family is enough."

"I know you wouldn't do that, Melody. You wouldn't deliberately sink Jerry to get at me. You wouldn't hurt an innocent man. But you don't have to go to Masters to make me lose the case. You can guarantee my losing just by walking out this door."

She folded a nightgown and packed it. "That's a lot of crap and you know it."

Cleve took her arm and turned her around. "Now, I want you to

231

listen long and hard," he told her. "Because when Jerry goes to prison, I don't want you telling yourself it wasn't your fault. You can't walk out on me without making waves and you know it. In fact, that's why you're doing it. Because you know I can't win without you."

He was giving her the same I-can't-win-without-you argument he'd given Katherine half an hour before, only this time he could almost believe it himself. "But I'm not the only one who can't win without you. Jerry can't win either. And that's what's going to lie on your conscience when this is over. You can only hurt me, but you can *kill* Jerry. And remember, Jerry isn't some criminal I'm trying to get a light sentence for. He's an innocent man who'll spend the next twenty years of his life behind bars if we can't establish his innocence."

"I'm not going to do anything to hurt him," she said defensively. "But you don't need me. You've mapped out your defense."

"I've got to map out a whole new defense. That one's no good any more."

She was startled. "Why? What's happened?"

"The fat's in the fire, kid. Masters knows about Katherine."

Her eyes widened. "How?"

"I don't know how."

"He's going to use her against Jerry?"

"You're damned right he is. The grand passion and the wife who was in the way, or maybe the wife who threatened to put an end to it. It's a whole new ball game, Melody, and a whole new set of problems."

The gleam was coming into her eyes. She caught herself. "You son of a bitch. You think you're going to supersales me—"

"It's the truth, Melody. Masters is going to use the woman who loves him to railroad Jerry into the chair. And we've got to stop him. And I mean 'we.' I can't do it alone and you know that just as certainly as I do."

She turned and picked a cigarette from the pack. "I knew I wasn't going to get out of here," she sighed. "I knew you'd find a way to keep me. I didn't know what kind of a line you'd use, but I knew you'd find one. So Jerry's life is in my hands. That's a pretty good appeal. Who can say no to that one?"

"But it's also true."

"Which is why I can't say no." She lighted her cigarette and took a deep drag. It had the air of resignation about it.

But Cleve wasn't fooled and he had to let her know that he wasn't. "And," he said, "aren't you a little glad you can't say no?"

She gave him a level look. "Only for Jerry's sake. I'm only staying till this is over. Anything after that is up for grabs."

He took her arm in comradely fashion. "All right, unpack, and tomorrow we'll take a fresh look at things."

She removed his hand. "And meanwhile, keep the hell out of my room."

He left her and heard her bolt the door behind him. Well, he'd leave her alone for now. He didn't want her anyway. At least she'd stay with him through the trial. And after she felt she'd saved sufficient face, they would resume their former ways. Or else he'd throw her out.

He toured his own suite but Katherine had vanished. Her clothes, her bag, even the smell of her was gone.

CHAPTER 51

Judge Willoughby Simms slipped into his black robes in chambers and checked his image in the mirror. He smoothed his gray hair, adjusted his glasses and wished he had an Alka-Seltzer or Pepto-Bismol to soothe a queasy stomach. It was the fourth of May at ten o'clock in the morning, the pretrial motions and selection of a jury had finally been completed, and this was the day he was to go forth and preside over the actual murder trial of the State versus Gerald Whittaker.

Though he'd been a judge three years and had handled two prior murder trials, he felt as nervous and ill at ease as that first day on the bench when he'd come out of the ivory tower of law school to enter the real world of real crime and real law and the real use of law—not theory, but practice. What made him nervous was the fact a very famous and skillful attorney was representing the defendant, a man who had mastered all the tricks of a lawyer's trade and invented a dozen others besides. He would try tactics that would test Simms's mettle. He would seek to evoke error from Simms. He would seek to evoke bias from Simms. He would seek to evoke emotion from Simms. He would be doing this in order to claim a mistrial if things went ill for his client.

Never mind that he had been docile through the defeat of his pretrial motions and the long two-week period of jury selection. This was only another Parrish trick and Simms would have to be extremely careful. After all his noble lectures on the theory of law and the beauty of law and the glory of law, how fallen he would be if he were incapable of upholding the very essence of law he espoused.

He had accepted this judgeship as his chance to put into practice his theories about the law. And it would be safe. He would not be descending into the arena, he would be on the bench above. Nobody could fight him there. And from that bench he could leave his legacy: his interpretation of law, his ideas of its uses and meanings and purposes.

He had therefore enjoyed being a judge. But now he was nervous. Cleveland Parrish regarded the bench as part of the arena. He involved his judges in his fights, seeking to provoke error without committing error. Simms would have to be particularly astute to keep himself above this fray.

He took a deep breath, left his chambers and crossed to the courtroom. The bailiff cried, "All rise, please," and the crowd that was eagerly waiting, stood. What a crowd it was, Simms noted as he mounted the bench. Extra chairs filled every space and still more spectators pressed around the public entrance against the ropes and the guards.

Simms gave the order to open court and tried to look in command as the bailiff sing-songed the ritual. Photographers were banned but Simms felt himself indelibly etched on a hundred minds before the bailiff said, "Be seated," and he could lower his profile.

Now he could take final stock. Jerry Whittaker was at the defense table, flanked by Parrish and Balin. It was a customary seating, but didn't Parrish sit straighter this morning and look more like a tiger?

At the table in front of the jury box sat Vincent Masters and his assistant, Jeff Kelly. If Parrish were tigerish, they looked unperturbed. Purchell, the court stenographer, was at the same table. He was one of the last to use pen and ink; good old solid-as-a-rock Purchell. Simms had never paid attention to him before.

Beyond the rail were the people. All those people. It was only the first day but the line had begun forming at dawn. It was an enormous audience, which didn't help Simms's nervousness. If only Cleveland Parrish would behave himself. Simms hoped he would, but he felt an ulcer growing. Parrish, without breaking a single rule, could make a shambles of a courtroom. The air was electric with waiting. "Make it good, Willoughby, make it good," he murmured to himself and knocked wood secretly before asking that the jury be brought in.

He found the roll call soothing. The acts of tradition had a way of easing tension. He listened carefully to the reading of the indictment and observed its sobering effect upon the intent faces of the jurors. A man's future, even his life, hung on the deliberations of those dozen men and women and every one of them knew it.

Then the reading was over, the clerk sat down and changed glasses, and the eyes in the room looked up at Simms. He rose to the occasion. His manner became regal, his elocution perfect. There was the slightest gesture of a hand as he said to Vincent Masters, "The State may proceed."

CHAPTER 52

The State's first witness was Grace Felton, the Madison dispatcher who had received Whittaker's distress call at four twenty-five on the morning of November first. She was quickly replaced by Jack Falmouth, who described his findings at the scene and his phoning the Madison detectives.

At quarter of five, he continued, Edward Balin, an attorney, arrived. Mr. Balin explained his presence by saying that Whittaker, a good friend, had called him at four-twenty that his wife had been killed and what should he do? Balin advised him to notify the police, dressed, and came to see what assistance he could render.

QUESTION: Based upon your experience as a police officer, would you say that a man who called his lawyer before he called the police had something to hide?

PARRISH: Objection, Your Honor. The question calls for a conclusion by the witness. It is irrelevant and immaterial.

SIMMS: Sustained. The witness is instructed not to answer.

So, thought Simms, Masters is trying to sneak one through. But he wouldn't have let it go, even if Parrish hadn't objected. If he could keep his poise and detachment, what with the notoriety the case was receiving, this could be his showpiece case. It could stand as his tribute to jurisprudence, a monument for future lawyers. ("If you young gentlemen who aspire to the practice of law want to see law in its purest form, used as it was meant to be used, doing what it was meant to do, then I recommend to you, *Connecticut* versus *Whittaker*. Observe Judge Simms's handling of that case, and particularly his handling of Cleveland Parrish. This is the law at its best!")

Masters had no further questions, but Parrish did. He was coming right back at the state's attorney. "You did not touch the body, Mr. Falmouth?"

"No, sir."

"Did you observe the bleeding?"

"Yes, I did."

"Was the blood wet?"

"Yes, it was."

"Would this not indicate that death had occurred only shortly before your arrival?"

Masters jumped to object as if he'd been shot. Parrish was pulling the same trick, but his was deadlier. The wetter the blood, the later the death and the more innocent the doctor. Masters had tried a pin-prick but Parrish was aiming for the jugular.

Simms sustained the objection, but his pulse was racing. They had only begun the routine business of establishing that a crime had been committed, but Parrish was already going after everything that wasn't nailed to the floor.

Dr. Elizabeth Allen, the local medical examiner, came next. She testified that she had declared Sally Whittaker dead, that she had called the coroner and recommended an autopsy.

On cross-examination, Cleveland Parrish again worked on the time-of-death angle. Had Dr. Allen touched the body? She had. Was the body warm? It was.

"Was it nearly as warm as a living body?"

"It was."

"And was the blood dry—or wet?"

"It was still reasonably wet."

"And you examined the body at what time?"

"About quarter after five in the morning."

"Just about an hour, then, after the police had first been notified of the tragedy?"

He left it at that and it was up to Masters to undo the skein he had woven. Masters rose to re-examine. "Doctor, how slowly do bodies cool?"

Dr. Allen laughed. "Well, sir, that depends on many factors; obesity, the temperature of the surroundings, how much clothing is worn."

Masters had an open book in his hand. "I read from *Modern Criminal Investigation*, by Soderman and O'Connell, page two seventy-seven, regarding the rate of cooling of dead bodies. I quote:

'Normally, however, the temperature becomes gradually lower until it approaches the temperature of the surroundings within six to eight hours.' And I quote: 'The temperature is said to drop one degree Centigrade for each hour after death.' Would you regard that as a fair rule of thumb—one degree an hour?"

She assented.

"So if the victim had been dead since, say, quarter of three, her body temperature would only have dropped two and a half degrees in that time. She would then still be very warm, wouldn't you say? Almost as warm as a living person?"

Dr. Allen agreed and Parrish's thrust was blunted.

The hospital attendant who had undressed the body for autopsy was next to testify, his message being that under the minidress the body was completely nude. Then came the state's chief medical examiner, Dr. Elliot Grove, to describe the findings of his autopsy. In layman's terms, the deceased had died of multiple skull fractures and massive brain damage, the result of repeated blows with a blunt instrument.

Yes, a poker could have inflicted the injuries.

Yes, there was other damage besides that to the head. The right forearm was fractured in two places, the right collarbone was broken, there were contusions on the right side of the face and fractures of the right cheek and jawbone. Two molars had been broken and several vertebrae had been chipped. Medical conclusion was that the victim had tried to defend herself and escape from her attacker, that he had rained blows upon her repeatedly, hitting her all around the area of the head, frequently missing the mark while she could still move, then, while she lay unconscious or dead, striking blow after blow with deadly precision upon her skull.

Masters had now established the cause of death but he refrained from questioning the ME as to the time of death. He knew the answer would be imprecise and he was saving testimony on the subject till it would have maximum effect.

Parrish also knew Dr. Grove could not be precise, but he wanted to prepare the jury for lack of precision. Could Dr. Grove give an estimate as to when death had occurred?

Yes. He would put it between two-thirty and four-fifteen of the morning preceding his examination.

"Can you explain why you place time of death in that particular time interval?"

"Yes. Because I understand she was last seen alive at two-thirty and found dead at four-fifteen."

"In other words, nothing about the body itself would enable you to pinpoint death as occurring within that period?"

"No."

Parrish then questioned the doctor about the ways of estimating time of death. What about rigor mortis? What about body temperature? What about post-mortem lividity? What about analysis of stomach contents?

Grove explained that rigor mortis customarily started from two to six hours after death and was usually complete in ten to twelve hours. It could, however, take as little as eight or as long as twenty. It usually disappeared again in two to three days, but might take five. The time for its appearance and disappearance varied so much because it depended upon so many factors, most notably temperature and the strength of the muscles. Though rigor was complete when he did the autopsy, this only proved that death took place before seven-thirty that morning and after October twenty-eighth.

The post-mortem lividity indicated the body had been lying on its back, which was its position from the time it had been removed from the scene. That meant the body had been moved not too long after the slaying. This would be consistent with a four-fifteen time of death, but he wouldn't concede it was inconsistent with a two-thirty death.

Regarding stomach contents, of which there were none, he explained to the jurors that digestion was usually complete in two to six hours. Thus the victim had eaten her last meal two to six hours before death. He could be no more precise than that.

After Grove, the prosecution devoted the rest of the morning to the introduction of physical evidence. There were scale diagrams of the Whittaker house, there were photographs of the house, the neighborhood, and the swamp in back, taken from both ground and air.

These were properly identified, labeled and studied by the jury, after which a lunch break was called.

CHAPTER 53

The afternoon session was given over to the testimony and exhibits of Madison detective Edward DuBois. He had been busy with his camera and there were photographs of the body, the murder room, the bloodstained furniture, the fireplace stand with its missing poker. There was DuBois's sketch of the scene, exterior photos of the house, then one of the bloodstained poker lying in deep grass, whose handle, despite the blood and hair, was identifiable as belonging in the stand.

Masters asked DuBois how the poker had come to be found.

"The murder weapon wasn't with the body or in the house. The poker was not in its rack and the injuries to the deceased were consistent with the type the poker would inflict. So it became of interest to us to endeavor to find the poker. Or to find whatever weapon had been used to effect the homicide.

"Inasmuch as it seemed unlikely the perpetrator would want to keep the weapon in his possession any longer than necessary, we felt he would probably dispose of it in the area. Accordingly, Detective Sergeant Hallock and I organized a search of the surrounding terrain. It was during this search that Mr. Durkin, a member of our auxiliary police force, discovered the poker in the deep grass behind the house near the swamp."

Masters said, "Is that deep grass visible from the road in front?"

"No, sir."

"Then anyone using the grass as a hiding place for the poker, would have to be familiar with the area, would he not?"

Parrish said, "Objection. The question calls for a conclusion by the witness."

Judge Simms sustained and Masters smiled. "I daresay," he announced, "that that would not only be a conclusion by the witness, but a conclusion by everyone in this courtroom."

That got him a laugh, and even Parrish smiled. Masters plunged on, exploring the ways in which the poker could have got there. DuBois said, "You could take it from the living room to the breakfast nook, out the glass door to the patio and either fling it or walk with it to the point where it was found. Or you could go out the front door, left around the garage and house, or right around the house to the back and from there again either throw or carry it to that location."

Masters said, "I call your attention to exhibit A, the ground floor plan of the Whittaker house. Will you step down and trace for the jury the three paths?"

DuBois did so, indicating the routes with his finger while Masters looked on approvingly. Masters fancied the visual approach. Let the jury see how much longer it would take to go around the house, how much more exposed the way, how much poorer a route it was if one wanted to cast the poker into the grass. At the defense table, Whittaker swallowed uneasily.

DuBois resumed his seat and Masters established that all doors and windows in the house, except for the front door, were locked, and there were no signs of breaking and entering.

"You say you dusted for fingerprints? What luck did you have?"

DuBois said that in the murder room he found nothing identifiable, only a few smudges. He found two partials of Mrs. Whittaker in the kitchen, and one by Nellie, the maid. He found one of Dr. Whittaker's on his bathroom mirror and a couple on bottles in the "wreck room" bar.

"You found just Dr. Whittaker's prints and Mrs. Whittaker's and one lone print by the maid?"

"That's all."

"No strange prints? No unexplained prints? No mysterious prints of unknown people?"

"No, sir."

"Your witness."

Parrish rose, picked up a photograph from the table and approached the detective. "I show you exhibit C, an aerial photograph of Whittaker's house and surrounding area, including a section of Neck Road. Will you show the jury the shortest distance from Neck Road to the Whittaker house?"

DuBois obliged, drawing a line with his finger through a spot of thin woods, across a neighboring yard to the left rear corner of the house.

"How long a distance would you say that is?"

"About two hundred yards."

"So if someone wanted to sneak up to the Whittaker house unobserved, he wouldn't come in by River Edge Farms Road, he'd go farther up Neck Road and come through the woods and into Whittaker's yard near the tall grass where the poker was found?"

"That's one way of approaching the house," DuBois conceded.

"Is it the darkest, as well as the shortest way?"

"Yes."

"If you wanted to pay a secret visit to Mrs. Whittaker, that would be a good way to come, would it not? Park the car on Neck Road, sneak through the woods into Whittaker's back yard and circle around to the front door?"

"Yes."

"And if you left the house in a panic, having slain Mrs. Whittaker, it would be natural to return to the car the same way you came, wouldn't it?"

Masters objected and was upheld.

Parrish went on. "Do you know if a car was or was not standing on that empty section of Neck Road up until around four-twenty in the morning on the day in question?"

"No, I don't."

"Was any attempt made to find out?"

"Yes. We talked to everyone in the area looking for stray cars."

It was a survey that Parrish's forces had also carried out. No car had been seen, but no car hadn't been seen either. It could have been there.

He turned to the matter of fingerprints. None at all were found in the murder room? Not the doctor's, not Sally's, not the maid's?

"No, sir."

"Nor any prints by some mysterious stranger?"

"No. No prints."

"So it can be stated unconditionally that the murderer, whoever it might have been, did not leave any prints at the scene?"

"That's right."

Parrish left it at that.

242

CHAPTER 54

Melody laid the jury data sheets down on the rest of the clutter when the phone rang. The dining table in Cleve's presidential suite was really a mess. Normally she was neat. Her office desk never looked like that.

She got up and rubbed her eyes. They felt bleary and tired and she wondered if she needed glasses. Maybe it was worry. The second day of the trial had just ended and she was back in the hotel, pawing over papers and fretting. Not that anything damaging had happened that second day—anything that hadn't been expected. The poker was identified as the murder weapon, but that was no surprise. Then there'd been testimony about the lack of crime in Whittaker's area— Masters' attempt to rule out "strange intruders." There was that little bit about Sally's finances, including the $300,000 insurance policy Jerry had taken out on her life. But Cleve had killed that one fast by forcing the insurance agent to admit Jerry had a similar policy on himself and paid the premiums on both.

It was the same with the fight they'd been having at the party that night. Masters tried to make something out of it, but Parrish got Nolene Shedd to concede that the Whittakers usually fought, Jerry usually drank a lot, and nothing about their behavior was out of the ordinary.

What really worried Melody was the jury. It'd taken two weeks to pick that jury and she didn't like the result. Cleve had thirty challenges and he had used them all, judiciously to be sure, but she wished he'd had one left to bump that black factory worker at the end. He was out for whitey, no doubt about it.

Cleve, of course, had a background report on every member of the array, so he wasn't working in the dark. The jury was probably as

243

good as he could make it, but what did he have to pick from? There were the usual middle-aged women and retired men, but this array had a lot more blacks. The recent Panther trial had made everybody color conscious. Not that she or Cleve minded blacks on juries. In fact, it was good for Cleve's image. But the four who were on this jury couldn't be good for Jerry. He was Madison, which was posh and white, and they were New Haven, which was getting blacker and poorer. Jerry would be judged, not by his peers, but by aliens.

Of course there were some hopeful people on it, like Ellsworth Deming, a retired history professor from Yale, and the Guilford farmer whose son's leg had been saved by a team of doctors. And the woman whose uncle and grandfather were doctors, and the romantic spinster who would visualize herself on a desert island with handsome Jerry.

The rest Melody viewed as either neutral or hostile, especially that factory worker. The two black women weren't so bad and there was a twenty-nine-year-old black embalmer named Edgar Milford who appeared intelligent and responsible and seemed to bear no malice toward white people.

Nevertheless, she was worried, and it didn't help knowing that Walter Costaine, the State's star witness, would be next on the stand. Usually, she had little to do with Cleve's cases, but this time she had gone to court every day, she had sat on the edge of her chair and chewed her nails over every move of Parrish and Masters. And all because Jerry Whittaker was the defendant. Because Jerry Whittaker wasn't the usual run of Parrish client—crooks, thieves and murderers trying to escape their due. Jerry was clearly a true and innocent victim of extraordinary circumstance, and that gave her a personal stake in his exoneration.

The phone gave a second ring. It wasn't Parrish's phone, it was in her own suite and she thought heavily of her mother as she picked it up. She wasn't in the mood for a tedious blow-by-blow of family problems, related at her expense.

The voice was male. It was Gary direct, and Melody suddenly wished it was her mother collect. She said, "Where are you?"

"In the lobby. I thought I'd see if you were in."

She'd believed she was rid of him. But blackmailers have a way of returning. There was an unwelcome note in her voice. "Why aren't you home?"

"Because all hell's broke loose. I quit home and with good reason."

She knew he wanted her to express curiosity. She didn't give a good goddam, but she made the proper response. "What's happened?"

His voice was curdling. "You know that sweet, dear little wife of mine, the one who just had a baby, who was working for that florist while I was in New York trying to get a decent job?"

He was delaying, pausing, making her reply. She said, "Yes, I know Priscilla."

"You know what she was doing behind my back?"

"What?"

His voice came up in outrage. "She was playing around. She wasn't just playing around either, she was sleeping around. You know how I know?"

"No. How?"

"The worst way possible. Because she contracted VD. That's how. And now I've got it!" He was almost frothing. "So you know what I did? I told her to go to hell and packed my bag and got outta there. She can beg on her knees, I'm not going back!"

Melody threw her head back and laughed, first a tinkle, then, as she lost control, wildly. Oh, God, it was beautiful.

"What the hell's the matter with you?" he exploded. "Didn't you hear what I said?"

"I heard," she said, panting with exertion. "Sure I heard. But you didn't tell it straight."

He was yelling. "Tell it straight? Ask Ma 'n' Pa if you don't believe me!"

She sat down on the bed. Her face ached from laughing. "Come on, Gary," she said, laughing again, "what you really mean is *you* gave it to her and when she found out what she had, she threw *you* out! That's what really happened, isn't it?"

"I told you," he screamed. "Ask Ma. Ask Pa. Call Pa right now and ask him."

"I won't ask Pa. I'll ask Priscilla."

He swore at her—words he'd learned from Rita, words he'd never used in her presence before, let alone at her. "I'm not calling you up to argue! I'm not even calling you up to tell you what Pris's been doing behind my back. I'm calling you up because I'm through with her and with Massachusetts and all the rest of it. I'm calling you up because I want to go to work for your boss and I want you to fix it for me."

She felt nothing but contempt. "That's a big fat laugh."

245

"You won't think it's so goddam funny if I told him what I know about you. You'd laugh out the other side of your face if I was to tell him you cheated him out of fifteen thousand dollars."

This time there was no pang. What could Cleve do? Fire her? But he'd begged her not to quit.

"Hey," she said, enjoying her power. "I'll tell you what. You tell Cleve that, and I'll tell Ma 'n' Pa where I found you in New York, and where the gonorrhea really came from. Come on up. I'll let you into Cleve's apartment and you can wait for him."

"You bet I will!" He slammed down the phone.

"All right, let him," she said to herself, hanging up. It wasn't with conviction, though. Now she could feel the nag of worry. Had she misread her brother's desperation and outsmarted herself?

She locked the connecting door to Parrish's suite and opened the one to the hall. She'd have to see it through.

There were bureau top articles to rearrange and a cigarette to smoke. Through it all, she kept returning to the doorway to look down the empty corridor. How long would it take him? Shouldn't he be here by now?

She got out her bottle of scotch, poured an inch into a tumbler, looked at her watch and lighted a cigarette. She made the scotch and the cigarette last a full ten minutes. He wasn't coming. He couldn't be coming now. He was as chicken as she knew he was.

Her spirits soared and her grin broadened. It wasn't the tight amusement that had made her face ache before. This time it was the relaxed, good kind that made her dance a couple of turns around the little room.

She pulled the door wide for a last look down the hall. The man approaching wasn't Gary, it was Cleve, and he was grim and scowling.

She ducked back and sat down on the bed. Good God, had Gary collared Cleve in the lobby? She wanted to hide, but she couldn't even close the door. Parrish had seen her.

He stopped and pushed her door wider. She didn't look up. He said, "I need some of that," and came in, going straight to the open scotch bottle on the bureau.

She watched him then, eying his broad back as he put down his brief case, pulled the wrapper off the other glass and filled it a quarter full. He turned to her and said, "I put in a call to Dan Price." He gulped half his whiskey, set down the glass and unbuttoned his top-coat. "You know, I think he's slipping as a detective."

It wasn't Gary. It wasn't Gary. She wanted another drink herself, but she was too weak to get up. Her heart kept pounding. "You mean," she said mechanically, "because he can't find a second lover?"

Parrish nodded and gulped the rest of his drink. "Two days into the trial. He's had five and a half months and he can't produce. Look at the spot that leaves me in."

Melody felt light-headed and wished she could forget about Gary. "Maybe there isn't another lover."

"Use your brain, for Christ's sake," Parrish said with unaccustomed sharpness. "If there isn't another lover, then who killed her—if it wasn't Whittaker himself?"

She wasn't being very bright and she pulled herself together. "But they have to prove he did, Cleve, and what have they got? Where are the clothes he wore, for example? They can't find them. That seems to me worse than not being able to find another lover."

Parrish picked up his brief case. "You sound just like Dan Price. He tries to sell me the idea that my position is good because Masters' position is no better. I don't give a damn about Masters' position. It's my position that counts and I can't find an alternative killer that any jury would accept. That's a crippling weakness, goddam it, and Price's alibis don't cure it."

He tried to open the door to his suite, swore when he had to unlock it, and went inside, slamming it behind him.

CHAPTER 55

Vincent Masters rose and said, "I call Walter Costaine to the stand." He was the first witness on Friday morning and a buzz swept over the sardine-packed courtroom like a gale-force warning. The press people scribbled and looked around. Katherine Lord's and Melody Stevens' eyes met. Walter Costaine was Jerry's accuser. As Costaine went, so went the trial. The bailiff rapped with his gavel and rapped again, but the buzz would not still. It kept pace with the steps of the man who advanced.

Walter Costaine, looking seedy in a two-hundred-dollar suit, came forward, pale and lean, a shamble in his walk. His graying hair was even grayer and the hangdog look of a loser afflicted his face.

His name had made headlines since his shattering story of a date on the murder night with the murder victim, but until this moment, nobody beyond the confines of the case knew what he looked like. If there was not an actual gasp of surprise when he stepped into view, the sudden silence that greeted his appearance created that effect.

Who could call him good-looking? He was not even attractive, and members of the jury let their gaze move from him to the handsome doctor at the defense table.

At the prosecution table, Masters kept his poker face but had to bury his hands in his lap to hide their trembling. He knew his witness looked like anything in the world but a Casanova, and he knew that the task he had to accomplish was to get this witness to persuade a hard-nosed, skeptical jury, as he had persuaded Masters himself, that he was the catalyst that had provoked a crime. Another night, another circumstance, and it wouldn't have happened.

The circumstance was the kind from which insanity pleas are born, and Masters would have accepted insanity if Whittaker had been willing to plead it. But no. The doctor chose to plead innocent instead. There was the rub that forced the issue. Now it was all or nothing. Now the doctor either got life (possibly even death) or he would walk out a free man with his wife's inheritance and insurance money in his pockets and his mistress on his arm. And who then could say crime doesn't pay?

Masters had to keep that from happening. Jerry Whittaker was a cool and calculating villain, gambling all or nothing, counting on Cleveland Parrish to bail him out. And he, Vincent Masters, had to head him off with the likes of Walter Costaine. It was a large order. It was a petrifyingly large order. It would make the hands of a superman shake.

Vincent Masters took a large handkerchief from his pocket and brushed it over his brow as he rose. Costaine had been sworn and seated and looked as nervous as Masters felt. It gave the state's attorney some calm. He had to be the strong one, the guide, the artist. Whatever Costaine had in him, Masters had to draw out. He tucked the handkerchief away as he approached the stand and his voice was gentle, his manner sympathetic.

Carefully he went into his game plan and led Costaine through the details of his background. Costaine's shabbiness of nature could not be hidden and Masters' scheme was to pull Parrish's teeth by bringing out all the ugliness of Costaine's past himself. His approach was to have Costaine confess all in hopes that, sordid as his confessions might be, his frankness might win him favor.

Thus there was the bit about the kited check, about the monied, pampered, undisciplined background that induced the attempt. There was a recounting of his whoring days in college, before, during and after his shotgun marriage, his emphasis on sexual, rather than intellectual achievements, the resulting difficulty of getting into a worthwhile architectural school, the effect that such proclivities had upon his marks. Upon the witness stand, Walter Costaine acknowledged he had become an architect not because he had talent, not because he had desire, not even because his father had desire. The old man was a partner in an investment firm and originally hoped to see young Walter take up the reins. But Walter was without talent in the field of finance or, so far as his father could determine, in any other field. He would have been a disaster in law, he couldn't begin to get through medical school, and architecture became his specialty only because it was about the only area in the professions he might conceivably pass courses in and do some kind of a job in.

His parents were now dead and his father's money was his, but its buying power dwindled year by year and his own earnings were too scanty to matter. The suit he was wearing was the one he saved for the club and party occasions. The rest of his clothes were thrift shop or bargain basement.

Up to this point his voice was as shallow as his character. Now Masters led him into the story of his relationship with Sally and a change came over Walter Costaine. The voice deepened perceptibly, he sat straighter in the chair. If he didn't have respect for himself, he had respect for her. He grew more animated, more self-assured, more willing to volunteer information.

The jurors felt the change. They sat forward more intently. He was starting to grip them. They were with him now, hanging on his every word, believing his every word.

They were believing! Walter Costaine was an acknowledged liar, but he was talking about Sally and the jury believed him. It was Masters' ploy of letting him hide nothing. Confession was good for the soul. It purged it. It wiped out the evil and let in the good! At least, as Parrish sourly conceded, that was what the religions of Western civilization taught. That's what Western man believed. That's what these jurors were believing right now. Walter Costaine had confessed all his sins and now his statements would have to be true statements. He wouldn't confess sins and then lie!

Cleve Parrish stared at his pad, making occasional notes, watching Costaine and Masters and the jury out of the corner of his eye. Costaine was coming through as a far more effective witness than anyone would have imagined, far more than Masters could have hoped.

If he would only trip himself up somewhere, make one little slip, tell one little lie! Parrish knew everything about his background and was just waiting.

Costaine reached the point where he arrived back from his "European" trip. He had told Sally he went on business. He had told everybody that. But the truth of the matter, he now told the jury, was that he had contracted a social disease from a girl in New York and had to drop out of circulation until he had been cured.

(God damn it, that was the thing we were going to hang him on. But the son of a bitch confessed even to that!)

After the cure he came back to town but he hadn't seen Sally. He wasn't sure of her response. Unlike his other girls, she was entitled to certain expectations, certain treatment. Other girls you did with as you chose because they didn't know how not to let you. They had no power over you because you could always go to someone else if they withheld their favors. And their favors were all they had to offer.

Sally, however, was special. Not compelled to yield to him, she merited courting and consideration; and after such an absence he wasn't sure of her reaction. Might she not say, "You could have at least sent a postcard from Rome? Nobody could make a case out of one postcard!"

The dance offered him what he wanted, the chance for a casual encounter. He could test her reaction, see if things were still on or not, and respond accordingly.

What he learned, to his pleasure and amazement, was that things were very much still on. She was delighted to see him. She was not offended over his failure to keep in touch. Thus he was emboldened to ask when they might get together again and she indicated any time would be fine with her. He could sense, he said, she was having husband trouble, but he had missed her and wanted her and wasn't fussy as to the reasons why he got her.

Therefore, when she indicated she was available "any time," he said, "How about tonight?" And she indicated she was all in favor of making it that night, as soon as she could get away after the dance. There it was left, and only just in time, for Jerry came stalking over to tear Sally away. And he muttered to Costaine, "Keep your filthy paws off my wife."

As for Sally, she looked daggers at Jerry and said meaningfully to Walter, "See you later."

Walter returned to his motel, very much uncertain whether he would see Sally or not. He knew she would come if she could, but it was likely Jerry would restrain her—by force if necessary. The look in Jerry's eye told him that.

Costaine said he waited in the motel room until four o'clock before giving up and going to sleep. He was not surprised that she hadn't come. What he was surprised to learn about was the reason she hadn't come. She was dead.

Later, as he thought about it, he wasn't so surprised and, after a couple of days debating with his conscience, he felt it was his duty to report these matters to the police and let them take it from there.

CHAPTER 56

Vincent Masters' timing was impeccable. Costaine's testimony took the whole of the fourth day of the trial. When he was finished, it was too late for cross-examination and Costaine's story had a whole weekend to soak into the jury. Thus far Masters had been calling all the shots and he knew exactly what he was doing.

Balin tagged along at Parrish's side leaving the court, but was thoroughly ignored by the bigger man, who worked his way through the departing throng like a bull. As always, reporters intercepted him with questions, but today Parrish did not give out statements. He smiled and looked relaxed, but the trial was on, he said. They were getting to the core of the case and he didn't want to comment.

What did he think of Walter Costaine's testimony?

"No comment."

"Do you think what he said today hurts your chances?"

"Sorry"—with a smile. "You tempt me. But no comment."

Melody had escaped the crowd and gone ahead, but not Balin, worse luck. Who needed a goddam leech at this point? To add to the grief, the gray sky had opened up and rain was falling in a deluge. It rattled and pounded, gushed and spattered. Parrish stopped under the portico and surveyed the dismal scene.

Balin said, "Costaine sounded pretty damaging today, Cleve. We got any weapons against him?"

"He's a goddam liar. That ought to be a good weapon."

"You mean, you don't believe his story?"

Parrish wanted to tell him "no comment" as he had told the reporters, but he forced himself. "Six weeks away from that sleazy scab ought to make her think twice about shacking up with him again."

"You mean, you think Sally gave him the air at the dance?"

Parrish moved aside to let a woman with an umbrella venture forth.

"That's what I would have done."

Balin was getting excited. "You think he did it?"

"No, but the jury might."

"Except, I suppose Masters would have checked him out pretty thoroughly."

"He tried." Parrish glowered at the torrents again. "Say, how the hell can I get across the green in this damned rain?"

Balin was quick with an answer. "My car's in the office parking lot around the corner. Want me to take you over to the hotel?"

"I'd appreciate it. I don't even have a raincoat."

Neither did Balin, but the parking lot wasn't far and he did welcome the chance for a few minutes alone with the great man. Balin hadn't felt so much a co-lawyer as a flunkie, a messenger, or even a useless appendage. He had thought he would learn volumes but Parrish was not a sharer. He kept his own counsel, made his own plans, conducted his own defenses. Not that Balin blamed him, but it would be nice to have a little inside information on what that defense would be. Now he might have a chance to find out. And he might also (forgive me, Jerry) ask Cleve if there was anything new on that law book he was supposed to put together. Edward Balin had worked long and hard on his chapter and he was proud of it. It deserved to see the light of print.

Because of one-way streets, Balin had to go around several blocks, wait for lights, and come down Elm toward his own office to pull up in front of the courthouse steps. He didn't mind, for he'd have to deliver Cleve via a similarly circuitous route. It would take longer to drive to the hotel than to walk. They could have a fifteen-minute conversation.

"Jerry looked despondent today, didn't you think?" Balin said for openers as Parrish settled in beside him.

"Well, you hear all the crap Costaine was throwing out, I'm not surprised. Costaine would depress a manic."

"The jury seemed to believe him. That's the trouble. Watching the way the jury hung on his every word made *me* nervous, and I'm not on trial. I don't blame Jerry for being down."

Parrish glowered at the rain in silence.

"Say, Cleve, you indicated—I mean—I wonder if it'd be smart to point a finger at Costaine. I mean, his alibi would be pretty ironclad."

"It might not be smart, but it might be necessary."

"But why?"

"If Jerry didn't kill Sally, who do you think did?"

Balin bit his lip. "We're in trouble, huh?"

"We're not taking candy from babies."

They were in front of the Plaza before Balin could get around to the law book. He opened his mouth, but Parrish was out of the car with a quick "thank you" and through the glass doors of the hotel.

Parrish entered his suite scowling, threw his brief case on the nearest chair and went to the bar. Melody was there, staring through the windows at the rain-drenched green. "I didn't see you come across," she said.

"I rode with Balin. How do they make people so dumb?" He poured some brandy.

She turned with concern in her eyes. "How're you feeling?"

"You were there. How do you think I feel?" He gulped the brandy and poured some more.

"Was the jury as convinced as I think they were, or is it my imagination?"

"They believe Sally was going to his motel after the dance. And you won't blast that belief out of them with dynamite."

"So what are we going to do about it?"

She'd said "we." That's what he liked to hear. She was still on the team. "We kill him," he said, swirling the brandy idly in the snifter, feeling the glow of the "we." Actually, Costaine's testimony had left Parrish toothless and he was bitter. "That goddam Masters made Costaine look good by showing off how bad he was. I think that son of a bitch confessed to every lie he ever told, every woman he didn't help across the street, every whore he ever laid. Even the VD treatment. That was going to be my ace in the hole. They left me with nothing to cross-examine him on except what he was doing at four o'clock that morning."

"You *know* what he was doing. He was in his room. Masters has two witnesses to say so."

"Masters has two boozy witnesses to say they left a party at the motel at four o'clock and one of them put a paper cup on the trunk of Costaine's car. And the manager will say the cup was still on Cos-

254

taine's car four hours later when he went out at eight in the morning. That might sell Masters, but it doesn't sell me."

"It might not sell you, but what about the jury?"

"That depends on how it's handled. Like what I do to Costaine on Tuesday."

"Suppose you can't shake his credibility. How bad off are we?"

"I'll shake it. He's their goddam star witness and he's not going to get out of there untouched. I'm going to kill him. I'm going to kill him and I'm going to kill his story. Don't ask me how, because I haven't worked it out yet. But I will."

CHAPTER 57

Cleveland Parrish rose slowly from the defense table. On the witness stand, waiting for cross-examination, sat Walter Costaine, calm but not overconfident, careful but not afraid. It was Tuesday, the eleventh of May, a fresh, new sunshiny day in a fresh, new sunshiny week, and a whole morning and afternoon stretched before the court. Cleveland Parrish could conduct however lengthy a cross-examination he chose, with large chunks of it uninterrupted.

"Mr. Costaine," he began, "are you aware of the Supreme Court's view on the death penalty?"

Costaine said that he wasn't, really.

"Are you aware of the speculation that the Supreme Court may soon strike down capital punishment?"

"No."

"It's been in the papers a lot of late."

"Well, I don't read the papers that much. Once in a while I see a headline. I don't buy papers very often. It's a needless expense."

"Yes, we all know how poor you are. We listened to that Friday." He turned from the witness for a moment, and back again. "To acquaint you with the facts, sir, while it is uncertain what the Supreme Court may decide next month or next year, as of this present moment, in Connecticut, the electric chair still exists as a punishment for capital crimes. That means that if Dr. Whittaker were to be declared guilty of the charge he is being tried for, the jury would then deliberate upon the kind of sentence that should be meted out to him —life imprisonment or—death. Do you understand that?"

"Yes, I do."

Masters interrupted. "Your Honor, I fail to see how this is germane to the issue before this court."

Parrish said, "I believe it is perfectly germane, Your Honor. The testimony of this witness could conceivably result in the death of a fellow human being. I want to make sure that he understands that, that he is fully prepared to take the responsibility for whatever may come to pass, including the death of another man."

Simms decided that was all right and Parrish said to Costaine, "Do you understand that?"

Costaine nodded. "I understand all that."

"Do you like Dr. Whittaker, Mr. Costaine?"

Costaine paused a moment to ponder his answer. "There are people I like better."

"You're not being responsive, Mr. Costaine. I asked you if you liked Dr. Whittaker."

"Not particularly."

"Yes or no. It's a simple enough question. Either you like him or you don't."

"All right, no."

"You do not like Dr. Whittaker?"

"No, I said I didn't."

"I just wanted to make sure I understood you." Parrish walked back to the table for a newspaper. He asked Costaine if he'd seen the front page that morning. If he hadn't, Parrish had a copy. He showed it to the witness and to the jury. Walter Costaine's name was upper right in a prominent headline.

His name, though in smaller type, was on the front page of the Bridgeport paper. Parrish displayed both front pages briefly and, laying them back on the table, remarked. "I'm reminded of the politician who said, 'I don't care what they print about me so long as they spell my name right.'" He made a point of looking once again at the headlines and added, "I see that they spelled Mr. Costaine's name right."

Then he started in on the matter of the kited check. Why had he kited it?

Because he needed more money than he could get from his parents.

What for?

A big New York weekend with college friends.

Why hadn't he canceled the weekend?

It was all planned. There were going to be girls. He couldn't disappoint them.

Couldn't he have budgeted?

What fun would that be? Girls expect to be shown a good time and you aren't going to get far with them if you aren't a big spender.

It was important to make it with the chicks?

It sure was.

Even if it meant spending more than you could afford, even if it meant kidding them into believing you had more money than you did?

Of course. Girls warm up to you better if they think you've got money. It's the way they're made.

"And is showing off the way men are made?"

"That's what I believe."

Parrish queried him about posing as a better architect than he was, getting him to admit he did it to impress people, men as well as women. And the story of going to Europe to buy marble? That wasn't just to hide the real problem, it was also to impress.

And, of course, the tale that Costaine had recounted on the stand of his seduction of Sally Whittaker. That was a pretty impressive story. She was quite a feather in Costaine's cap, wasn't she? She wasn't just another easy mark.

"You really thought she was something, didn't you?"

"Yes." Costaine was wary despite Parrish's encouraging tone. He didn't know what the lawyer was up to.

"How did your wife find out about her, by the way?"

"I believe she followed me. She got suspicious and followed me."

"Did she ever follow you before?"

"Not to my knowledge."

"Something about your behavior told her this was a special girl?"

"I don't know."

257

"Did you, subconsciously perhaps, want her to find out what a prize you'd won?"

"No."

"Did you, subconsciously perhaps, also want Jerry Whittaker to find out?"

"No."

"But when he did find you out, you didn't act guilty or apologetic, did you? You gave him a black eye and kept right on seeing Sally. Your wife threw you out of the house but you still kept on seeing Sally, isn't that right?"

Costaine nodded. "That's right."

"When she died, if you hadn't gone to the police, nobody would have known about you and Sally, would they—except for your wife and Sally's husband?"

"I guess not."

"Your name would not now be on the front pages of newspapers all over the country? Nobody would know what a great lover you are?"

Masters objected and Parrish innocently explained he was only seeking information. He was curious as to whether there was any way the police could have found out about the affair other than by Costaine telling them. He felt that Costaine was very likely equipped to answer that question.

The judge directed the witness to answer and Costaine conceded he didn't believe the police could have found out any other way.

Parrish was homing in now. "When you met Sally at the dance, if, instead of throwing herself into your arms, as you claim, she had told you she didn't want to see you again, what would you have done?"

"Nothing."

"I mean, in what way would your behavior that evening have differed from what you actually did? Would you have gone back to your motel, for example, and gotten plastered?"

"No."

"You would have gone back to your motel and not gotten plastered?"

"That's right."

"But that's exactly what you claim you did do, isn't it?"

"Yes, but that's not what Sally did."

"I didn't ask you what Sally did. I'm saying that your behavior, by your own admission, would have been the same regardless of whether Sally threw herself at your head or told you to go to hell. I'm saying that, therefore, it's only your word that Sally threw herself at you."

"It happens to be true," Costaine said testily.

"If she had told you to go to hell that night and then she was killed, nobody would know, would they—the world would not know—of the great achievement in your life, your finest accomplishment, your one proud feat: the seduction of Sally Whittaker?"

Costaine squirmed uncomfortably at the acid question.

"Jerry and Barbara wouldn't tell, so no one would ever know, would they?"

"No."

"Unless you could find a way of broadcasting it yourself. Unless you went to the police and bragged about how she threw herself at you?"

Costaine yelped. "No, no. It's true what she did. It's true what I said."

"And if Sally Whittaker had told you to go to hell that night, do you really think we believe you'd take it lying down? Of course this is what you would have told the police—that you returned to your motel room and didn't even get plastered. But if she had turned you down, you would have wanted an explanation or a chance to talk her out of it. You would have gone to see her, wouldn't you?"

"No," he said nervously. "Of course not."

"It's only your word that she welcomed you back, and it's only your word that you stayed in your room, isn't that so?"

"No. No. Other people know I stayed in my room. A guy left a paper drink cup on my car and the manager saw it there the next morning. That proves I was in my room! That proves she said what I said she did." He leaned half out of his chair with triumphant desperation in his voice.

Parrish knew he was following a risky course but he had to open the door. "And," he continued, ignoring Costaine's response, "if I were going to see Sally Whittaker, and if any man on the jury were going to see Sally Whittaker to find out why she'd broken off with me, and I found that paper cup on my car, do you know what I'd do? I'd put it on the car beside mine. I'd put it there and forget about it, because my thoughts would be on Sally Whittaker.

"But now, let's suppose that I had a fight with Sally Whittaker because she wouldn't come back to me, that she had taken off her costume and got into something comfortable to clean up in, and we fought and I killed her. What would I do then? I'd flee back to the motel and put my car into the same slot I'd taken it from. I wouldn't even need to think about it. My instincts would tell me to. And when I got out of that car, I'd see the drinking cup on the next car. Would I leave it there? Not for one minute. Those same instincts would make me put it back on my car in the exact same spot it'd been before. That's what I'd do and that's what anyone would do if they sneaked out and committed a murder. And that's what you'd do too, isn't it?"

Masters came to his feet to object: Costaine wasn't on trial for murder, Gerald Whittaker was.

Simms, however, upheld Parrish on grounds that he was proposing a hypothetical situation, that Costaine had testified that he had stayed in his room and this testimony was open to cross-examination.

The judge turned to Costaine and a stricken Costaine turned to Parrish. "It's a lie," he shrieked. "You can't accuse me. We've got proof! I never went near their house. I never left the motel. She promised to come, I tell you. She promised to come!"

Parrish turned his back, fiddled with papers, and returned to the witness, speaking in a quiet voice. "Mr. Costaine, when was the last time you told a lie?"

Costaine, recovering from the last blow, wasn't prepared for the new one and his jaw sagged. Masters wasn't prepared either and objected. This was irrelevant and immaterial.

"Just a moment," Parrish retorted. "This witness testified Friday that, among other less than honorable activities he had engaged in during his life, was the business of lying. He is a confessed liar. Therefore, it is perfectly proper for me to explore this subject. His testimony, as I have pointed out, may have much to do with the future of a man he has admitted he doesn't like."

Simms ruled for Parrish but, for what it was worth, Masters had bought the witness time. The defense attorney repeated the question. "When did you last tell a lie?"

Costaine chewed a lip and, with everyone in the room hanging on his words, confessed he didn't know.

"Then you can't tell me what your last lie was about?"

"No."

"Then tell us about a recent lie. What did you recently lie about?"

Costaine swallowed and cast a helpless look at the judge. He was starting to perspire.

Parrish didn't ease the man's distress. He waited. He stood, staring with piercing eyes at the agonizing Costaine, and waited. Still Costaine didn't answer. Still Parrish held his own silence. He didn't complain to the judge, he kept the pressure to break silence on the unhappy man.

On the bench, Simms began to wriggle. Should he direct the witness to reply or would that break whatever spell Parrish was trying to create? Should he try to rescue this miserable man from his acute embarrassment, or should he refrain from interjecting himself into the proceedings? It was his court to run and he was the man so sensitive to the essence of justice. This was the case to serve as inspiration for others. But what was the proper path to follow? If he stepped in, would he not be helping the witness for the prosecution? If he did not, wouldn't he be helping the defense? Where was his neutral role to be played?

Finally, a craven Walter Costaine got him off the hook. "I don't remember a—any—recent—"

"Recent what?" Parrish asked, remorselessly making him say the word.

"Recent—lies."

"You don't remember any of your recent lies?" Parrish was incredulous.

"No," Costaine mumbled.

"Why can't you remember them?"

"I—I don't know."

Parrish thundered his reply. "Isn't it true that that's a lie right now? You don't remember any recent lies? You don't know why you don't remember? Those are lies right there, aren't they? Those are recent lies, aren't they?"

"No, no. I'm telling the truth."

"Sure you are. Just the way you told your wife the truth. Just the way you told every girl you seduced the truth. Just the way you told Sally Whittaker the truth. Just the way you told the police the truth. Just the way you told this court the truth."

Costaine pleaded that he was telling the truth and Masters objected that Parrish was badgering the witness. Parrish denied the charge and protested that the witness was an avowed liar, and the state's attorney had made a great point of that on direct examination. Now when the defense seeks to question him about his lies, he fails to divulge information by saying he doesn't remember. In view of his confessed reputation as a liar, is not the defense entitled to suspect him of telling still another lie? Is not the defense entitled to take strong measures to try to get the truth out of the witness?

The witness pleaded, "Listen, I've told lies. I've admitted it. I've lied to my wife and I've lied to other women. But I never lied to Sally. And I never lied to the police. I swear I never lied to the police. And I swear I'm not lying to the court."

Parrish turned to him with wide eyes. "You never lied to Sally? Is that what you said?"

Costaine swallowed. He wished he hadn't committed himself quite so definitely. Was he all that certain? But he had to answer. "I was honest with her," he said. "I didn't try to fool with her."

"Is that right, Mr. Costaine?" Parrish was properly sardonic. "But did you not tell her you were going to Europe for six weeks to buy marble when, in reality—or so you told this court—you underwent treatment for venereal disease for six weeks? Who were you lying to, Sally or this court?"

"Well, I didn't want to tell her—I think that's understandable."

"So you lied to her. And you just now told this court that you had never lied to her."

"Well, I meant—I never misled her."

"You *were* misleading her."

"I mean, in other ways."

"That may be what you mean but what you said under oath was that you never lied to her. You never told her a falsehood at all. But it turns out you did tell her a falsehood after all. You did lie to her after all, didn't you?"

"Yes, but it's not import—"

"Not 'yes, but.' You did lie to her, didn't you?"

"Yes."

"But you told this court that you didn't lie to her, just as you told this court you never lied to the police and never lied to the court."

Costaine was pasty and trembling. "But I didn't lie to the police. I swear it. I wouldn't ever lie to the police. And I wouldn't lie under oath."

"You wouldn't ever lie to the police?" Parrish queried. "Do you recall being arrested when you were nineteen for kiting a check? I believe you testified to that yesterday."

Costaine blanched. His "yes" was barely audible.

"Do you remember what you told the police when they questioned you?"

Costaine bowed his head. "I meant now," he mumbled.

"When they questioned you, did you or did you not tell them you hadn't done it?"

Costaine looked up at the lawyer. "I thought you meant this time," he said desperately.

"Did you or did you not tell the police that you had not kited that check?"

Costaine's mouth twitched. "I did."

"So you *did* lie to the police. But a minute ago you told this court, under oath, that you had *never* lied to the police."

Masters said, "I object, Your Honor. The witness obviously misunderstood the question and counsel is trying to twist a legitimate mistake around to look like perjury."

"Your Honor," Parrish pleaded, "I must protest. I remarked in passing that the witness had lied to the police. And the witness took the opportunity to swear, under oath, that he had never lied to the police. He didn't say yesterday or today, or the last time he talked to them. He said he *never* lied to them. What, then, am I to do? He is accusing me of a falsehood in claiming he has lied. Am I not entitled to point out to the jury which of us is the liar and which tells the truth?"

Simms had to concede that Parrish was justified. An unhappy Masters sat down and Parrish returned to the attack. "Now then, Mr. Costaine, I suppose if I quote your most recent remarks in that witness chair as evidences that you have lied to the court—under oath—you and the prosecutor will plead again that you misunderstood the question, that when I said you lied to the police you thought I only meant this policeman or that policeman. Just as, when I said you lied to Sally, you misunderstood me to mean only about certain things. I suppose it's therefore going to be your claim that anything you say on this witness stand that doesn't coincide with the truth isn't really a lie, it's a misunderstanding. Am I right in that?"

Costaine nodded. "Believe me, I wouldn't lie on the witness stand. Not on purpose."

"But you have given us answers that aren't true."

"Yes, but they're mistakes."

"They're mistakes." Parrish nodded and faced the jury. "Fortunately for these jurors we were able to catch two of those mistakes. If we hadn't picked you up on those two occasions, the members of the jury would have gotten a wrong idea about you, wouldn't they? They'd really believe you never lied to Sally and they'd believe you never lied to the police. It's very lucky they found out differently, isn't it?"

Costaine was trapped. There was nothing he could do but mumble, "Yes."

Now Parrish wheeled on him and his voice became a roar. "All right, Mr. Costaine, how many other questions have you misunderstood on that witness stand and given false answers to?"

Costaine swallowed and shook his head. "No others, sir."

Parrish snorted. "Oh come now, my question was really rhetorical. If I hadn't called it to your attention, you wouldn't be aware of the two false answers I've charged you with, would you? You wouldn't suddenly say, 'Oh, I forgot. I have lied to Sally after all. I have lied to the police after all.' If I hadn't caught you, the jury would still be misled, wouldn't it?"

Costaine was slow in answering. He didn't want to concede the point but he feared what trap he might walk into if he didn't. Parrish prodded him with a sharp, "Come, come, yes or no!" And he had to say yes. He knew he was supposed to and for that reason he wanted not to, wanted to upset the lawyer, catch him and hurt him with his answers as the lawyer was hurting him with his questions. But he was not equipped and he backed off from defiance.

"So, Mr. Costaine," Parrish continued, the contempt dripping from his voice, "you would be the last person in the world we should turn to to find out what mistakes you've made in your testimony, or how many you've made. Except that we may note that you misunderstand and therefore misanswer the simplest of questions. In fact, you mislead us on two simple questions in a row. It makes me wonder, Mr. Costaine, what, if any, of your testimony might be free from false answers." He turned away. "No further questions."

It was now left to Masters to rise on redirect and seek to repair the damage. He did it carefully, working with Costaine to make the point that he was only guilty of two harmless slips. What he did when he was nineteen was all but forgotten and it was natural, when asked about the police, that he think in terms of his present-day relationship with them. With regard to Sally, he interpreted lying as harmfully deceiving her, misleading her as to his intentions. Quite obviously no man would tell a girl he was absenting himself to be cured of VD. He couldn't be called a liar for not owning up to that.

As for the defense's suggestion that Costaine might have committed the murder, that was an obvious attempt to throw suspicion away from the defendant. In the first place, what murderer would voluntarily inject himself into the murder case? Secondly, such a suggestion contradicted the defense's other claim—which was equally ridiculous—that Costaine made up the story of his date with Sally in order to get headlines. Costaine's desire to impress people was only normal. All men did that. But no man in his right mind would brand an innocent man a murderer to make an impression.

On recross, Parrish only asked one question. Had Costaine undergone psychiatric examination? The answer was "no," and Parrish said, "In the absence of supportive testimony, I question whether a man who seduces every girl he can, who gives their husbands black eyes, and who would suffer ostracism from his wife and family to take up life in a mangy motel rather than give up one of those women can be regarded as in his right mind; or that there is any act too 'ridiculous' for him to perform."

It was early afternoon when at last a shattered Walter Costaine stepped from the stand and into oblivion. His testimony would be dutifully assessed, repeated, and commented upon by the columnists in attendance. A sketch of his woeful face and hangdog posture would grace a syndicated feature, leaving readers to wonder what Sally Whittaker could have seen in the likes of him, especially married to such a handsome, dashing-looking husband.

Except the husband was looking pretty hangdog too these days and sketches of him that were done in the courtroom showed him old and failing. Courtrooms and sin and crime and the corruptions of the soul wrought a vengeance on their merchants. Jail at the least, and God knew what else, was destroying the handsome doctor. At the same time, another set of fatal flaws had made the architect a parody of the one-time charmer who had seduced the star-crossed maiden who was the key of the piece. Barbara Costaine, sitting in the courtroom and shivering at the sight, could hardly recognize the

265

faded replica of her husband. Motel living, with nothing but the dingy company of his soul, had done him in, and part of what made her cringe was the uncertain question, Have I wrought this?

She suffered watching him, but not for him. He evoked no feeling in her at all. Now and again she would try for some emotion. She would remind herself that that man in that chair was the father of her children. They had had a life together, such as it was. She had forgiven him a thousand infidelities trying to keep an ill-fed marriage from flying to pieces. But, as she thought about it, she realized she didn't do it to keep him. She did it for the children. She had ceased to feel anything for him years before she threw him out, though it was only now that the truth came home to her. She took him back, she brushed him off and straightened him up and presented him to their children over again as a symbol of parent. But he was no parent. She knew that now. The children were ripening more healthily under her lone tutelage than when they had a disinterested father as a supplement.

Then it was Barbara's turn on the stand. Masters called her as soon as Walter stepped down, but she waited till he was clear of the area before she rose and came forward. Costaine looked at her, unbidden, but she did not look at him.

CHAPTER 58

Masters may have suffered a setback with Costaine but he had his secret weapon ready for unveiling. Thursday afternoon was the time he picked and it came after a day and a half of legal sparring over details of the post-dance party and the time the maid overheard Whittaker strike his wife. Both lawyers had worked over the witnesses and it had been pretty much of a standoff.

Well, those were small and unimportant points. Now Masters

would put a witness on the stand who would have a major impact on the jury. This was the backup to Walter Costaine, the other one on whom Masters depended to give motive for murder.

He called the name of Katherine Lord and noted the total disinterest of the press and spectators. She was a woman who was completely unknown to all but the prosecution, the defendant and Parrish. He smiled a little. In five minutes the room would be buzzing. In five minutes Katherine would be a name and a person nobody would forget.

She came forward to be sworn with shy reserve and took the stand for her two days of drama flushed of face, red of lip, nervous of manner, modest in appearance. She was wearing a black dress, high cut in front, with a white collar and a skirt that, while mini, reached nearly to her knees. The white-cuffed sleeves came below the elbow and she wore white gloves.

Again the cut of her clothes failed to emphasize her physical attributes, the large bosom and narrow waist, but now it was not the accident of poor design but the purpose of Vincent Masters. He was presenting this girl as the love life of a prominent doctor. He wanted the jury to believe in a grand passion, a love that transcended all. Whittaker's fights with Sally were to appear the result of his frustration because she stood in his way. The jury was to believe that Katherine was the woman Whittaker would marry if he went free, that only Sally's existence had kept him from marrying sooner. She had, therefore, to appear as much a woman of his class and background as Masters could make her seem.

Parrish smiled wryly. He had not set eyes on her since that night in the bedroom and he had only spoken to her once. That was over the weekend. He had phoned to ask if she still would do anything to save Jerry and she had said a passionate yes.

"No matter what happens to you?"

"No matter," she had breathed. "I don't care anything for myself. I'll lie if you want—"

"Don't lie," he had told her. "Above all, don't lie." Then he had warned her he might have to play rough; would she mind? She wouldn't mind a bit, so long as it helped Jerry.

"I wouldn't be rough unless it would help him," he had said. "Remember. All that matters is that he win his freedom. That's the way it is with me. Is it like that with you?"

"Yes. Oh, yes."

"Good, then just answer my questions when I ask them. Answer them truthfully, but don't volunteer anything. Don't volunteer anything to anybody, to Mr. Masters or to me. Answer only what you're asked. Answer yes or no wherever you can. Nothing more. Can you remember that?"

She had said she could and now she was in the witness chair, hopefully with that uppermost in her mind, as she answered the basic questions of name and address before Masters let the bombs fall. She glanced once at Jerry. It was supposed to be a quick look, but it hung. She hadn't meant to act as if she knew Jerry at all, but he made her heart ache. Yet he did look better than in prison. He was wearing a coat and tie, not the khaki shirt and pants that identified the untried prisoners.

So she looked, but she had no right. Mr. Masters was making her testify and he was against her beloved. She didn't want to answer his questions and she wished there were things she could say that would spoil his plans, that would prove to him that Jerry was innocent. She would have sworn anything to accomplish that result, but Cleve Parrish had warned her to tell only the truth. He was a great believer in the power of truth, and that was a fine thing in a great lawyer like Cleve. It spoke well of the law and Cleve and mankind in general. What was it the Bible said, or somebody said, "The truth shall set you free." Maybe that's what Cleve had in mind. All she had to do was tell the truth and Jerry would go free. Just the same, she felt guilty looking at him. She felt as if she were on the other side.

Parrish, watching, could read her mind. She was so transparent. It was enough to keep his heart in his throat. She would do anything to save Jerry, but all she did was play into Masters' hands. She was wearing the kind of dress he wanted her to wear, had probably suggested she wear, and she doubtless was taking his advice on grounds it was respectable courtroom attire. She wouldn't read his ulterior motives. She wouldn't know that he was getting more out of her than the answers to questions. She was too guileless, too innately trusting. Masters was a gentleman, a family man, a good citizen. Even though he was prosecuting her lover, he was nevertheless chivalrous. He would be eager to see him found innocent. And what a goddam con game that was! Parrish knew the type. Those sons of bitches with their saintly faces and impeccable credentials, they were the worst of all. You weren't on guard against that kind. Parrish had to outsmart and outsnarl and outmaneuver people to get what he wanted. Lucky bastards like Masters only had to smile and the apples fell into their laps. What a sitting duck for him Katherine was!

Masters started out gently, asking if Miss Lord were acquainted with the defendant, then how long she had known him, and then he asked what her relationship was to the defendant. She replied, in that quiet, even voice of hers, totally free of shame, malice, or regret, "I'm his mistress."

The courtroom rocked. There was a gasp of disbelief, a moment of awe-struck silence, and an excited, astonished buzz. Reporters, with their mouths open, grabbed pencils and scribbled furiously. Columnists and sob sisters put down exclamation points and pondered how to reorient themselves and their readers. The doctor had a mistress!? He was playing the same game? What could this mean? Here we all thought he was jealous of Sally! But it's the prosecution, not the defense, who's introducing this new wrinkle! They're going to use the mistress to help prove he murdered his wife! Would it be for her? Well, she's pretty enough!

The bailiff rapped for order and had to rap harder. Voices trailed away and Simms looked around with what he hoped was an authoritative air. He indicated that Masters proceed.

"You say that you and the defendant are lovers? For how long have you been lovers?"

She told him and he said, "Then your relationship with Dr. Whittaker antedated Mrs. Whittaker's relationship with Mr. Costaine—by that I mean you and the doctor became lovers before last May?"

"That's right."

He led her, then, through the story of their romance, through the business about the stitches Whittaker took in her head while both of them were aquiver with sexual heat (she called it "love"), through her return to have them removed, her arranging to catch him alone, and what happened when she did. Her tale of love, as she recited it, was as romantic as anything in *Idylls of the King,* as pure and clean in her own eyes as a Walter Scott novel, pure not in the sense that their behavior was above reproach but because their love was eternal, like *Romeo and Juliet.* It transcended all things.

But, of course, the picture the jurors got was a little more tarnished.

They saw a grubby Dr. Whittaker sewing up the scalp of an innocent young girl, knowing she was palpitating over him, and encouraging it. A doctor ought to know better. And the return engagement—! She went to his office looking to get laid and he, a married man, a pillar of the community, a trustworthy (supposedly) physician, took full advantage of her eagerness. He should have given her a pill, or taken one himself. Instead, he leaped to betray his wife—before she ever betrayed him, mind—and then compounded the sin by continuing his relationship with this young girl. It might have been love on her part, but it was obviously passion on his. Setting her up in a house in Clinton, sneaking over there when his wife thought he had night office hours, deceiving, scheming, chasing this innocent—no, not innocent, *deluded*—young thing? He should have done better. He should have cooled it.

Now we see Sally's fall from grace in a different light. She was frustrated and unhappy for her husband was expending his energies across the border in the next town while she lay in a lonely bed. Of course she was ripe for someone like Costaine. How readily we can see that now. Whittaker is to blame for everything that happened. And for him to storm at Costaine and fight with him? How could he have the presumption? Bully for Costaine for beating up the lecherous old goat. But wait. There's more—

"Did you and the doctor ever talk marriage?"

"Yes."

"To what effect?"

"We didn't think it was feasible. It would hurt his career."

"What would hurt his career?"

"Getting a divorce. He'd have to get it, you see, because Sally wouldn't. She refused."

Parrish raised an objection and Masters clarified the matter. "What you mean, don't you, is that Dr. Whittaker *told* you she refused?"

"Yes. That's what he said."

"You never talked with Mrs. Whittaker yourself?"

Katherine shook her head. "No. She didn't know I existed."

Parrish started to object again and Masters quickly said, "You mean, don't you, that Whittaker *told* you she didn't know you existed?"

"Yes."

"So the situation was that you wanted to marry Dr. Whittaker but he said he couldn't marry you, is that it?"

"No. He wanted to marry me, but I didn't want to marry him."

"Why didn't you?"

"I told you. He'd have to divorce Sally because she wouldn't—"

"You mean," Masters interrupted before Parrish could object again, "that's what you believe."

"Yes."

"What else did you believe about their getting a divorce?"

"He'd have to go to Reno to get it and wait six weeks and he couldn't take the time. Or he'd have to get it in Connecticut, but then he'd have to have a good reason, which would mean he'd have to publicize Sally's affair—"

"Objection," said Parrish. "What affair is she talking about?"

Katherine turned to Parrish. "I mean the affair he told me she was having. I mean, that man testified to it right here in court, didn't he? I heard him. That ought to prove Jerry doesn't lie."

Parrish subsided. He should have known better. You can't get a woman to keep her goddamned mouth closed. Hadn't he told her how to act? Why didn't she listen? She was supposed to be saving Jerry, not putting him away.

As for Masters, he, of course, wanted the jury to believe that Jerry wouldn't lie—about Sally's refusal to grant a divorce. Let the jurors believe he'd have to resort to severer measures to rid himself of an unwanted wife. Masters was trying to give them not one motive for murder, but three. Profit, jealousy and love. Give them their pick. Let them put the motives together in any combination or degree of desirability, just so long as they all arrived at the same conclusion: It was Jerry Whittaker who had wielded the poker.

The first two motives he had gone to some length to establish and now he worked carefully on Katherine Lord, an unwilling but co-operative witness who, earnestly seeking to help her love, was being used to tie the knot around his neck. He delved further into Whittaker's professed eagerness to marry her and her persistent refusal to let him damage his career.

When he got the jury's orientation well established, he said, "Now, Miss Lord, did Dr. Whittaker ever indicate that there might be a solution to the problem? Did he ever indicate that something might happen that would change your mind?"

"Yes."

(At least that was a concise answer. Maybe she was finally remembering not to volunteer information.)

"Would you tell the jury about it?"

She obliged. "He told me there was a way around the problem, that she wouldn't be able to block us much longer."

"'Block us,' you said? Doesn't that sound as if she *did* know about you?"

Masters was trying to bring in still another motive. He wanted the jury to believe Sally knew about Katherine and was threatening their relationship. Parrish said, "Objection. Conclusion by the witness."

"Sustained."

But Masters had insinuated the thought and that was what he wanted. He went on. "Miss Lord, did Dr. Whittaker tell you what idea he had that would get around the problem?"

"No."

"Did you ask him?"

"No."

"When he told you he had an answer, you didn't ask him what that answer was?"

"No. He said she wasn't going to be a problem much longer and I told him he was dreaming. He said he had a way out. I think that was the way he put it, and I said something like, 'I'll believe it when I see it,' or, 'I've heard that one before.'"

"How long did that take place before she died?"

For the first time Katherine glimpsed the horrors that Masters was tryng to promote. In her own mind the connection had never occurred. She blinked and recoiled. "Now, wait a minute. If you think that's—Listen, that's not what he meant. He had other ways. He was full of schemes—"

Masters didn't want to bother the jury with Jerry's schemes. He cut her off sharply. "Miss Lord, I asked you a question. How long before Mrs. Whittaker died did Dr. Whittaker tell you this?"

She was flustered and upset, almost in tears. "About two weeks," she said helplessly. "But he didn't do anything to her."

"Your witness." Masters turned and sat down.

CHAPTER 59

Cleveland Parrish came forward, the soul of sympathy. His eyes were melting and his voice was velvet. "You've had a bit of a shock, Miss Lord?"

She nodded and dabbed at her eyes with the corner of a handkerchief.

"The prosecution's suggestion that when Jerry said he had a way out he meant murder never occurred to you, did it?"

She shook her head and said, "No."

"Nor would it ever occur to me. There are so many other, better ways. And even if he were the type to think such thoughts, I can hardly imagine him hinting to someone else that he had such a plan in mind." Parrish chuckled. "I mean, can you imagine telling someone you can get another person out of the way and then, two weeks later—?"

"I object," Masters said angrily. "Mr. Parrish is supposed to conduct a cross-examination, not give a dissertation."

Parrish was the soul of blandness turning to the judge. "Your Honor, this witness, this *prosecution* witness, has been seriously upset by the prosecution's direct examination. She's not my witness, she's his witness, mind you. All I'm trying to do is steady her so that she can answer my own questions."

Simms said, amazing himself at his temerity, "I have no objection to your soothing the witness, Mr. Parrish, but I should like to remind you that this is not the time for your summation."

Laughter exploded and Parrish arched an appreciative eyebrow. Simms sat back, flushing with pleasure. He had amused the court with a clever *bon mot*. More than that, he had jibed at the great man and not been excoriated. In fact, Parrish seemed to enjoy the sally. He wasn't so fearful after all, quite a decent chap, really. Not at all like those screaming and yelling lawyers who committed constant contempt of court.

The laughter eased courtroom tensions and helped to relax Katherine Lord. She put away the handkerchief and Parrish said to the judge, "I see your cure is faster than mine," which got another laugh. Then he got to work. Would Miss Lord relate those other schemes of Jerry's to eliminate Sally as a barrier between them?

Masters tried to object on grounds it was irrelevant and immaterial, but since the prosecution had brought up the subject, it was available to be pursued and Parrish had his way. The judge directed Miss Lord to answer.

One such scheme, she explained, was to refuse to pay her bills, give her money, or in any other way support her. Another was to refuse to go anywhere with her or speak to her or have any thing to do with her. Then, however, he found out about Sally's affair with Costaine and decided those schemes wouldn't do any good.

"Did you ever suggest to him that he use his wife's affair as grounds for divorce?"

"No."

"Why not?"

"He's too much of a gentleman to do something like that."

"Did he ever suggest it himself?"

"No. For the same reason."

"You would have us believe, Miss Lord, that you and Dr. Whittaker were desperately in love, so desperately that he would do anything to get the chance to marry you, but he wouldn't do that?"

"Of course he wouldn't."

"The prosecution would have us all believe that he'd kill her to get her out of the way, but you tell us he wouldn't even expose her to get her out of the way?"

"That's right, he wouldn't. He wouldn't kill her either."

"It appears, doesn't it, Miss Lord, that despite all his talk and despite this supposed great love he had for you, he wouldn't really do *anything* to get his wife out of the way?"

"He wouldn't do anything sordid."

"The fact remains, doesn't it, that he didn't do *anything*, sordid or not sordid?"

She flushed and he had to prompt her to get her to concede the point.

"What sacrifices has Dr. Whittaker actually made for this supposedly great love he bears for you?"

Masters objected that she wasn't qualified to know and Parrish rephrased the question. "Are you aware of any sacrifices the doctor has made for you—any at all?"

The girl pondered but all she could come up with was some extra expenses, paying a share of the rent, taking her out sometimes, buying her things, perfume, undergarments, and the like.

Parrish's voice had a drop of acid in it. "That's your idea of a sacrifice?"

"Well, he would have had that much more money if he hadn't."

"In the same way that one can have that much more money if he doesn't go to the movies? That's your definition of sacrifice?"

She flushed again and murmured a yes.

"And while we're on the subject, what sacrifices have you made for him?"

She was at a loss. She couldn't think of any.

Parrish switched subjects abruptly and hit her from a different angle. "Miss Lord, had you ever had sexual intercourse with a man before you met Dr. Whittaker?"

"Yes. I was married."

"That's right." Parrish acted as if that part of her testimony had slipped his mind. "You were briefly married, weren't you? Tell me, did you ever have sexual relations with any man other than your husband before you met Dr. Whittaker?"

She bit her lip and nodded quickly. Parrish reminded her that she must answer and she murmured assent.

"You did have sexual relations with someone other than your husband before—"

"Yes. You see, back when I—"

"Please, Miss Lord, may I remind you—" and he looked at her warningly, "—that a yes or no will do! Make it yes or no, will you, please?"

Simms leaned forward, hesitating. It was his duty to lecture the witnesses or explain their roles and he really shouldn't let the defense attorney run the court. He was going to speak but already Parrish was back to his questioning and Simms let it go.

"You said you did have sexual relations with a man or men

before you met Dr. Whittaker? Did you have sexual relations with a man before you got married?"

Katherine was remembering what she was there for. She was saving Jerry. Cleve would get rough. He'd told her he would. But she didn't care so long as it protected her beloved. She was no longer flushed and her voice was no longer faint. "Yes," she said. (It was her fiancé, before he went to Vietnam, but she wasn't supposed to volunteer anything and she wasn't going to.)

"Did you have sex relations with any men between the time of your divorce and your meeting with Dr. Whittaker?"

"Yes."

"And is Dr. Whittaker aware of this?"

She nodded. "Of course. We have no secrets."

"Yes or no."

"Yes."

So far so good, except he'd better lock her in with a couple more yes or no questions. "You did have sexual relations before your marriage?"

"Yes."

"You were not a virgin, then, on your wedding night?"

"No."

She had flushed when she said it but she hadn't attempted to explain. That was to the good. Let's try another. "And you went to bed with a man or men between your divorce and your relationship with Dr. Whittaker?"

This time she didn't even nod. She issued a flat, "Yes."

"And Dr. Whittaker is aware of this?"

"Yes."

She was remembering. She was conditioned. Hopefully she was conditioned for what would come next. Cleve mentally crossed his fingers. "That's good," he said. "And now, Miss Lord," he said carefully, "would you tell me: Have you had sex relations with any other man *since* you met Dr. Whittaker?"

Katherine's eyes widened in horror, shock and disbelief. What was Cleve's game? Did he want to announce, publicly and in open court, that they'd been to bed together? He wouldn't let her tell Jerry, and now—? What did he want? She couldn't understand. Her senses swam and her eyes brimmed.

Parrish's heart almost stopped. "Yes or no," he said desperately.

276

"Have you had sex relations with a man or men since you met Dr. Whittaker? Yes or no?"

She tried to concentrate. He was telling her something. She was supposed to do something. What was it? She had to answer but she couldn't think. She said the only word she could say, staring at her lap and mumbling so brokenly that the court recorder had to ask what she'd said and then the judge had to ask her to speak a third time so the court could hear.

"Yes." Without lifting her head she shot a quick glance at Jerry. He was in shock, white, stunned and staring.

Parrish's knees steadied and his heart started to beat again. This girl didn't run to any form and it was impossible to predict her responses. He was walking a wobbly tightrope in a hurricane. "You say you *have* had relations? This is correct?"

Her yes was a little more forceful, as if she were remembering now what she had to say and what to be prepared for.

Cleve reinforced her with another such question before opening new ground. Outwardly his demeanor was smooth and effortless, but Melody could tell his torture. Only she could interpret the extra paleness in his cheeks, the tense working of his fingers. "And, Miss Lord," he said, "have you had sex relations with one or more men since Dr. Whittaker has been in jail?"

She was shaken anew and sat very still. What did he want her to do? How much did he want her to tell? It was coming back. Yes and no was what he wanted. The truth, but in short answers. She mustn't volunteer. She mustn't volunteer. She must only say yes or no. It was for Jerry. She looked up and her voice was firmer. "Yes, I have. I mean—yes."

"Did Dr. Whittaker approve of these—ah—carryings-on?"

Katherine trembled. It wasn't a yes or no question. What was she to do now? "I—ah—he didn't know about them."

"He didn't know about them?" (arched eyebrow).

That was an easy one. "No."

"You mean, you didn't tell him about these—ah—sexual escapades?"

"No."

Parrish was feeling better. She was getting the hang of it. But there was always the danger she would slip and add a sentence or two in explanation. Just then he'd been holding his breath lest she answer, "No, you told me not to."

He restated the question to get the "No," again and reinforce it

277

in her mind and in the jury's. Then he said, "So you *do* have a few secrets from Dr. Whittaker after all, isn't that right?"

She bit her lip and muttered a yes.

"And you aren't as honest and honorable as we've been led to believe, isn't that so?"

She nodded, her head lowered.

"The court reporter can't see you, Miss Lord. Will you answer, please?"

"Yes."

"Under the circumstances, would you say that a girl who cheats on her lover the minute his back is turned would make a good wife?"

She was beginning to see the great man's plan. He wanted to discredit the all-consuming love affair Masters had established. All right, she could do that. She shook her head and said, "No."

Color began to return to Parrish's cheeks and the working fingers began to relax. "Did you receive any money for these sex relations you had while Dr. Whittaker was in jail?"

"No."

"You're not a professional prostitute?"

"No, I am not."

Parrish could even begin to enjoy the proceedings. "Are you sorry that you have been made to reveal these sex acts on this witness stand in the doctor's presence?"

She looked at Jerry but he looked away. "I am," she whispered.

"Do you think it will change anything in your relationship?"

"Probably."

(It damn well is going to, sister. Dream of him when you're in my arms, will you?) "Do you think it might lessen his supposed eagerness to marry you?"

She kept her eyes averted. "I don't know."

"Do you think the doctor should be surprised at your behavior, considering the way you threw yourself at him in the first place?"

"I suppose—I mean, no."

Parrish was feeling confident now. "Miss Lord, would you call yourself a whore?" (Ah, see the way her cheeks turn pink, see the way she shrivels.)

"I don't think so."

(You don't, eh, you slut? Spurn my advances, will you?) "How would you define a whore, Miss Lord?"

She wasn't sure and she fumbled. Parrish had said he might get

278

rough, but she wasn't expecting anything like this. (But it was for Jerry!)

Parrish went on with it. "The dictionary defines the word as, 'one who has unlawful sexual intercourse, who is promiscuously lewd.' Would you accept that definition, Miss Lord?"

"Yes."

"Do you think that definition would apply to you?"

"I—uh—"

"Have you not had unlawful sexual intercourse?"

"Yes." (He wanted me to say yes to the last question. That's what he was after.) "Yes. The definition applies to me."

"You could call yourself a whore, then?"

She swallowed. "Yes."

"Tell the jury, then, exactly what you would call yourself!"

Masters, numb from shock, finally pulled himself together. "I object, Your Honor. Counsel is badgering the witness."

"No, Your Honor. I am only trying to develop the true picture of this woman, this woman who appears before the jury in demure clothes, who has been foisted off on the jury by the prosecution as a great love of Gerald Whittaker's. The prosecution is trying to establish motive for murder through this girl and I am entitled to show the jury that such a motive does not exist. A man's future life is at stake here, Your Honor, and he is entitled to have the jury know the facts." (Come on, you son of a bitch judge, let me make her say it. She kicked me out of her bed and she's going to pay.)

"Objection overruled. The witness will answer the question."

"I—ah—what was the question?"

"Let's have the question again." Parrish paced back and forth while the stenographer retraced his notes.

"Question: 'Tell the jury, then, exactly what you would call yourself.'"

She was squirming and even though it was for Jerry, she choked on the word. "A whore."

(Look at her writhe, but that's only the beginning. It's for Jerry, all right. It's going to beat the rap for him but she's going through the muck doing it. Murder is illegal, but this isn't.) "All right, Miss Lord, we have established that you are a whore. Now let us consider the subject of faithlessness. The prosecution would have the jury believe you and the defendant were possessed of a great and glorious love for each other. Now let us see how long, once Jerry was out of your life, you remained true to him."

The degredation of Katherine took the rest of the afternoon. There was plenty of time and Parrish wanted to savor every moment. What added spice and relish was that she had to help him do it. The worse she was smeared, the better for Jerry. The greater the agony of her public humiliation, the greater his redemption. And Parrish made it great indeed.

Through it all, stunned and shattered, sat Vincent Masters. How on earth, in his interviews with Katherine, could he have failed to ask about her sex life now that Jerry was in jail? He had been so taken in, he decided, by her romantic vision of the Great Love that it never occurred to him she would look at another man so long as Jerry lived, even if that life were spent behind bars. But Cleveland Parrish had thought to ask her about men and he had turned up a treasure trove. He had revealed her as a wanton and who on the jury could now believe Jerry wanted to marry the girl?

Cleveland Parrish had so totally destroyed the Great Love concept that Vincent Masters, outwitted and helpless, made a second mistake and didn't re-examine Miss Katherine Lord. He couldn't wait to see her gone.

CHAPTER 60

Parrish had Pete waiting outside the courtroom and rode to the jail the moment the trial recessed, arriving at the visitors' cage almost before Jerry got back to his cell. As soon as the taut, angry doctor was brought forth and locked in the visiting room with him, Parrish started to straighten him up. "I know how you feel," he said, leaning forward at the table to grip the other man's arm. "It's a shock. You're rattled. You can't believe your senses. Well, believe me, Jerry, I wouldn't have stripped her mask off like that if it wasn't absolutely necessary. I would have let you go back to her after the trial in total ignorance. It's none of my business. But I've got a job to do and that job is to get that jury to understand that you didn't kill Sally. Nothing is more important than that!"

Whittaker shook his head numbly. "I know," he mumbled. "I'm not blaming you. But I just can't believe Katherine—that she would —I would have bet my life on her love."

"And that's why I had to expose her." Parrish shook the doctor's arm, trying to get through those blank, hurt, disbelieving eyes. "You saw what Masters was trying to do, didn't you?"

Whittaker looked at him vaguely. "No. What?"

"He was trying to establish an infatuation between the two of you that was so great you'd kill Sally to get to Katherine. And Katherine was playing right along with it. I don't mean to suggest she was doing this deliberately. I believe she really does love you— in her fashion."

"Some fashion," Jerry said bitterly.

"Well, I will admit, any girl who will sleep around just because her steady boyfriend isn't available—well, I guess I wouldn't call that a Grand Passion. But you can be damned lucky it wasn't. You can be damned lucky the jury knows what you and Katherine felt for each other was too shallow to kill for."

Whittaker buried his face in his hands. "Oh, God."

"All right, straighten up. Pull yourself together. Life goes on." Parrish rose from his chair. "At least it *will* go on if the jury keeps seeing that your relationship with Katherine was the ordinary garden variety of relationship and not something you'd lose your head about. And up till now we're succeeding."

Whittaker moaned, "But at what cost?"

"Ignorance is bliss, huh? Well, we can't live in ignorance all our lives. Sometimes we're going to find out things no matter how much we don't want to."

Parrish looked at his watch, clapped the broken man on the shoulder and called for the guard. He returned down the hall to the entrance lobby just as Katherine came flying through the front door. She was so haggard and distraught she didn't even see Cleve until he caught her by the arms and turned her around.

"I thought you'd be showing up about now," he told her, opening the door and marching her outside again. "I guessed this was just how long it would take you to pick up your car and drive over. How about dropping me off at my hotel on your way home?"

"Cleve, stop," she cried. "I've got to see Jerry."

"No you don't."

"Cleve, I've got to. He must be frantic. I've got to explain to him. I've got to try to make him understand what happened—I mean with you and me. I don't even understand it myself. But I can't let him think—"

"Oh yes you can."

"Cleve, you don't understand!"

He had her at the car door. "Get in," he said. "We're going to talk."

She was almost in tears but she got behind the wheel. He circled to the passenger side and signaled Pete in the mauve Cadillac to go home. He got in with her and said, "Let's go."

"Cleve, please." She was starting to cry.

"We're going for a ride. You've got to learn the facts of life."

She started up, backed into the narrow street and headed for town. She was dutiful, but desperate. "Please, Cleve," she pleaded. "I've got to talk to him. I know what you were doing. I know you were deliberately making me look cheap and low and I don't blame you. It was the right thing to do. It'll help save Jerry. But I've got to let him know I'm not that way. I've got to tell him why you did it."

Parrish, staring grimly through the windshield, shook his head. "Oh no you don't. You can tell him anything and everything once the trial is over. But you are not to see him or speak to him or write to him or have any contact with him from now *until* the trial is over."

She turned. "But why? He must be going crazy."

"He is. That's exactly what he's doing. And that's exactly what I want."

"You want him to be frantic? You want him to believe those lies about me?"

"Yes."

She shook her head. "But why? I just don't see it. I don't see why you want him to suffer needlessly."

He gave her knee a momentary pat. "I don't want him to suffer, Katherine," he said in a kind and gentle voice, "and I certainly wouldn't want him to suffer needlessly. But we've got to put first things first. We must remember our priorities. You know what comes first, don't you?"

She nodded. "Getting him out of jail."

"Getting him acquitted. That's right. Now, he's got to take the stand in the next few days and fight for his life. Do you think he could do a good job if he knew about us? If you told him that, he'd be more upset than ever."

"But, Cleve, I can't let him think what he's thinking—that I'm just a cheap floozy, that I really am—a—whore."

"Yes you can, and you're going to. Because that's exactly what I want him to think when he's up there on that witness stand."

"Why?"

"Because he'll do a better job of convincing the jury he never would kill for you."

She was silent for a moment. The tears stopped rolling down her cheeks, but her face was still miserable. Cleve said, "Do you understand why you've got to keep quiet?"

"Yes," she moaned. "But I ache for him. The torment he's suffering. Oh, I wish we'd never done what we did. I don't know what got into me. How can I ever make it up to him?"

God, she could be insulting! "What's his kick?" Parrish answered irritably. "He didn't stop sleeping with Sally when you came along. His love for you didn't stop him from that, did it?"

"But it's different with a woman. If only we hadn't done it, Jerry wouldn't be suffering and I wouldn't be suffering."

There it was again, another slap at his prowess. "Be damned glad we *did* do it," he snapped. "It stopped Masters' plan. We pulled the rug out from under him on that one."

She looked at him quickly. "Did you—is that why you—did it? So that you could put me on the stand and blacken me and spoil Masters' plan?"

Even Cleveland Parrish's scheming mind wasn't able to conceive a plan that esoteric, and certainly his sexual appetites could not have played such a subsidiary role. No, his desire for her was all too real.

But what he said was, "Just be glad one of us was thinking about Jerry."

CHAPTER 61

While Cleveland Parrish might have spiked his biggest guns, Masters was still not without recourse and he sprung his final ace after the weekend break. This was Dr. Marvin Liebman, a youngish, vigorously aggressive pathologist connected with Yale-New Haven Hospital. Liebman's testimony, Parrish well knew, could dig a grave for his client, but Jerry had been so shocked and sunken by the previous day's revelations that, despite Cleve's urgent whisperings, he could not be made to care. He sat with his head on his chest, staring dully at the worn dark tabletop in front of him.

Liebman, whose training had helped the State in the past, testified that he had been called by Detective William Coyne at quarter of six on the morning of November first, told of the murder and of the need to establish a time of death. Recognizing the need for haste, he drove to the hospital immediately, arriving forty minutes after the body. He took the body's temperature by means of a rectal thermometer and examined the degree of blood clotting. On the basis of his findings, which were conducted at quarter of seven that morning (or eight hours before the medical examiner arrived), he estimated that the woman had been dead for about four hours.

"Four hours?" Masters said. "Subtracting four hours from quarter of seven, when you examined the body, would give us a time of death of about quarter of three. Is that right?"

At the defense table, Balin shifted uneasily and Jerry Whittaker looked up. For the first time he began to note proceedings.

"That's right," Liebman said. "I'd put the time of death between two-thirty and three o'clock."

Masters turned the doctor over to Cleveland Parrish and it was up to Parrish to shake the doctor's testimony, a matter of vital consequence since a three o'clock time of death would be fatal to Jerry.

But Marvin Liebman was self-assertive and positive and would not be shaken. The absolute latest he would concede that death could have occurred was quarter past three and, mind you, that was the latest, which meant it had unquestionably occurred before that.

What was the body temperature, Parrish wanted to know.

Liebman said, "Ninety-three point three degrees."

"That's rectal temperature, which is roughly one degree higher than oral temperature?"

"Roughly."

"So the body had cooled about six degrees?"

"Six point three degrees."

"You know the rule of thumb that body temperature drops a degree an hour, Centigrade?"

"That's just a rule of thumb, yes."

"Since a Centigrade degree is nearly two Fahrenheit degrees, we should expect a drop of about eight Fahrenheit degrees in four hours, shouldn't we, Doctor?"

Liebman was a stickler for accuracy. "A Centigrade degree is nine fifths a Fahrenheit degree, sir, not twice. We can expect the difference to be closer to seven degrees."

"Which is still well below the actual temperature."

"Not so much below. But, as I remarked, that is only a rule of thumb. There are other factors affecting the temperature loss, including room temperature. And the room was a warm one. Detective Coyne gave me a reading of seventy-four degrees, which I took into consideration in making my analysis."

Parrish pursued the matter further but could not shake the man on the matter, though he kept trying. Dr. Liebman was arrogantly sure of himself. Sally was killed around quarter of three and that was that.

Parrish pointed out that the last guest had left at half past two, that Sally was still in her costume, that she thereafter had changed clothes, that she had to have come downstairs and that obviously some kind of altercation had taken place with someone who got sufficiently enraged to seize a poker, chase her around and beat her to death. Did Dr. Liebman really think all this could have taken place in only fifteen minutes?

Liebman didn't budge. He had picked quarter of three as a central time. According to his analysis of the body, death could have occurred as early as half past two or as late as three, with three-fifteen as the absolute outside limit. So if Mr. Parrish found the suggested time of two forty-five objectionable, he was at liberty to pick a more satisfactory one. "Make it three o'clock if you want," Liebman said.

The doctor was obviously a favorite with Coyne and Masters for more reasons than his medical knowledge. He was forceful and he was blunt. He didn't quibble or vacillate. His answers were unequivocal and that went down well with juries. Jurors were impressed by experts who knew their business and didn't hem and haw and come out with a lot of, "in my opinion"s. This man knew what he knew and nobody, including Cleveland Parrish, was going to talk him out of it. In fact, the more Parrish tried, the more dogmatic he became. And by the time the defense lawyer finally gave up, Marvin Liebman was dogmatic indeed.

Simms called the midmorning break and Jerry and Ed Balin huddled with Parrish in the prisoners' room. "He's lying," Jerry said, as if it didn't matter much. "It was quarter after four."

Balin said, "That's damaging, Cleve, his insisting on three o'clock like that."

"He's rigid," Parrish agreed. "That's what the prosecution likes about him. If he goes their way, he'll go right down the line. I could see that the first time I met him."

"You met him? You knew what he was like before he took the stand?"

Parrish flicked cigarette ashes on the floor irritably. "Of course I knew what he was like. Do you think I walk into a courtroom cold?"

Balin was unusually bold. "But if you knew, what did you push him for? You made him say it over and over again. Three! Three! Three! That's going to impress it on the jury's memory. I mean, Cleve, it seems to me—"

"And it seems to me you'd do a lot more good worrying about our client than about the jury. The jury's going to be a damned sight more impressed by Jerry's hangdog, down-in-the-dumps attitude than the irresponsible testimony of a cocky son of a bitch thermometer reader." He shook the doctor. "Now I'm going to tell you, Jerry, when you're out in that courtroom you're on stage and if you don't shape up and look alert, nothing's going to save you. If you want to moon over a lost piece of ass, you do it in private!"

CHAPTER 62

Masters' last witness for the prosecution was the huge, reddish-haired county detective, Bill Coyne. Like Liebman he was good on the stand. He'd sat in witness chairs a hundred times and given testimony in the most bizarre or cruel, or heinous cases. There was little his eyes had not seen and little that his talents had not investigated, little of human nature that he had not encountered.

He was an easygoing, sloppy type; easygoing because he made himself comfortable, and sloppy because his size was so great that he gave the impression of spilling over. In the confines of the witness chair, he literally did.

Unlike Liebman, who was aggressively assertive, Coyne was low-key assertive. If Liebman feared hesitation or reflection betokened uncertainty, Coyne's answers were as casual as his shifting positions in the chair, but what he said came from the depths of experience and had the rumble of authority.

He described his actions at the scene, his call to Liebman, his confidence in the pathologist's opinion, his study and analysis of the murder room. He was so matter-of-factly clinical in his description of the body that he lent it a gruesomeness that attempted gruesomeness wouldn't have achieved.

His testimony, coming at the end as it did, recalled the murder to the jury's mind, recalled the fact that Sally Whittaker had, shortly before that moment, been a living, breathing, active human being with her own particular life-style, her own experiences and memories, habits, quirks, joys and sorrows. The method of his testimony reminded the jury that this young girl had had her life taken from her, had been robbed of the one thing that could never be given back, that she had been unfairly deprived of existence.

The method and manner of Bill Coyne's testimony revealed that in his own mind—his experienced and knowledgeable mind—he was convinced that the person who had so unfairly deprived her was her husband. Nor was it what he said so much as how he said it, the calm conviction in his voice.

The things he saw were damaging too. There was his description of setting up the search for the poker: the first place he wanted searched was the deep grass in back of the house. That was because it was dark out back and because he thought, despite Whittaker's story, that a back door would be a more tempting exit for a murderer than a front door.

How had he organized the search? He had focused his searchers in areas that he estimated were a poker's throw from: (1) the back patio of the doctor's house; (2) the edge of the grass; (3) the corners of the house.

Which of these areas was Joe Durkin, who found the poker, investigating?

He was investigating area one—where Coyne estimated the poker would land if flung from the back patio of the house!

"Did you at that time think that the doctor had done it?"

"Objection. The witness is on the stand to attest to what he did, not what he thought."

"Sustained."

Masters wasn't able to get direct testimony that Coyne believed Whittaker guilty, or what led him to that conclusion, but what he did get was almost as good. The jury knew Coyne's convictions even if he couldn't profess them.

Parrish, in cross-examination, didn't challenge Coyne as he had Liebman. He limited himself to queries about the search for the poker. How long had the search lasted?

Five to seven minutes, said Coyne.

"And you testified that you positioned the men where you thought it might have landed?"

"That's right."

"And Mr. Durkin was positioned where you thought the poker would land if thrown by a man from the patio?"

"That's right."

"So the poker was actually located *not* where it would land if thrown from the patio."

"It wasn't at the exact spot I started him searching from, but it was within throwing range of the patio."

"But not where you thought it would most likely land—if thrown from the patio?"

"It was in the same area."

"It was not where he started to search, was it?"

"No, sir."

"Which was where you positioned him?"

"Roughly speaking."

"Don't say, 'Roughly speaking.' You told him where you wanted him to start looking, didn't you?"

"Yes."

"Which spot was regarded by you as the most likely place for the poker to land—that is, if it had been thrown from the patio?"

"In general—"

"Yes, or no? You just testified that was what you had done when Mr. Masters asked you the question. Do you want to alter your testimony now?"

"No."

"Then your answer to my question is, yes, you did station Mr.

Durkin where you thought a poker thrown from the patio would be most likely to land, is that right?"

"Yes."

"And, starting from the spot where you thought the poker would land—*if* it had been thrown from the patio—he nevertheless had to search for five or seven minutes before he found the spot where the poker actually lay?"

"Yes, but—"

"Yes or no? It's a simple question. A simple yes or no will answer it."

"Yes."

"No further questions."

Masters tried to re-establish the connection between the location of the poker and the patio of the house on redirect but Parrish wasn't letting him and hammered the point again that the poker had actually been found a seven-minute search away from the spot Coyne had considered the most logical one for a patio-tossed poker. He was using Coyne's own experience against him and was not going to accept, or let the jury accept, a seven-minute search as a reasonable error.

Masters finally abandoned the issue, feeling he was losing more than he was gaining, and thereupon announced to the judge that the prosecution rested.

It was midafternoon and Judge Simms was willing to let Parrish start his defense on the morrow. Parrish, however, wanted to start at once.

It wasn't only because he had witnesses in the wings—Whittaker's horde of devoted patients ready to sing his praises—which he wanted to get started on. The real reason was he had no intention of leaving the State's case as the last thing on the jury's collective mind.

CHAPTER 63

Melody Stevens, kneeling on the couch, leaned on the back and looked through the windows of Cleve's suite at the courthouse across the green. It was nine o'clock and dark, but the stately old edifice gleamed in the mercury vapor streetlights. There was something solid in the way the building held the ground, something calm and great in the way it imposed upon the green. It stood for justice—not justice as imperfectly rendered by the humans who dealt with it, but the concept itself, the essence of law, the meaning of the social compact, the sense that man could not live without law any more than civilization could live without law. As the three churches, gleaming in the floodlights, reminded men of the presence of God and stood as so many repositories of God, so the courthouse served as a reminder of justice and stood as a repository of justice.

She sipped from the brandy snifter Cleve had given her. He was on the phone catching up on calls, and she could hear the shadings and nuances of his voice. There'd been a long conversation with Claude Decker on the cannibalism case. Now he was talking with Art Canaris, his real estate agent, arguing about the Whittaker house. Canaris had an offer of seventy-two thousand and Cleve was holding out for seventy-eight. Melody didn't know how he could conduct business at a time like this. She would never, repeat never, attend another trial. Her heart wouldn't stand it.

The phone rang almost as Cleve put it down and he picked it up again. Melody watched a Temple Street bus take on passengers in front of the farthest church and move toward the corner of Chapel. Then she became aware that Cleve was being very silent and there was an ominous air in the room. She turned. He had the phone at his ear, his shoulder against the wall, and he was scowling in a way that frightened her.

Finally, after a long, long time, he said in the quietest, most malevolent tone she had ever heard, "What did you say your name was?" Then he said, "It doesn't matter. I'll be waiting for you," and hung up.

Some of the tension cracked with the click of the phone and Melody could breathe again. Parrish looked up and saw the question in her eyes. He snorted and shrugged it off. "Just a little blackmail," he said. "Let him try it."

"Who? What?"

"I don't know who. He gave me a name I didn't catch. He says he can prove Walter Costaine was in his motel room when Sally was murdered but he'll be willing not to testify to that if I'll pay him a thousand dollars." Parrish put the phone aside and uttered a four-letter word.

"Somebody who was registered at the motel that night?" Melody suggested. She rose from the couch. "I'll get the list."

Parrish shook his head. "Forget it. I didn't get the name but there was nothing like it on the list." He picked up the phone book and thumbed through the pages.

"Who are you going to call?"

"Masters. If he doesn't know about this guy, he should."

In the East River Motel on the borders of Guilford, Gary Stevens put the phone down and shakily picked up the stub of his cigarette. He had tried to make his voice as deep and authoritative as possible, but it didn't even begin to pry a thousand dollars out of Cleveland Parrish. Cleveland Parrish didn't even ask him what it was he had to save Costaine with. He just asked him to repeat his name—the phony name he had given—and it was Gary who went to pieces. Like Cleve knew it wasn't a right name, that Cleve only wanted to listen to his voice some more. God, Cleve couldn't have recognized it, could he? No, Cleve only saw him that once. He'd never know him now, not with the beard and long hair and the glasses. And he wouldn't know his voice either, not if he was speaking from the witness chair and remembering to keep it husky.

But he couldn't stop shaking. What he had to have was a drink. He couldn't hardly stand now without a drink.

He mashed out the cigarette, pulled himself to his feet and left the small room, closing the door behind and knocking on the one beside it. He didn't wait for permission, but twisted the knob and pushed it open.

Walter Costaine was lying on his bed watching television listlessly. He held a can of beer and a cigarette, but the open bottle of rye was on the table between the beds.

Gary didn't ask permission. He grabbed the bottle and poured an inch into the nearby tumbler, then downed half of it in a gulp. He hadn't even liked alcoholic beverages before Rita and Morelle, and now look at him.

Costaine frowned at the inroads on his liquor, but he had to be careful. "What'd Masters say?"

"The line was busy." Gary sat down on the opposite bed. He was sweating and he wondered if it showed. "I been thinking," he said, concentrating on keeping his glass steady. "Three hundred dollars isn't going to be enough. It's got to be five."

Walter Costaine slowly swung around and got off the bed. It was a threatening move that brought the bearded young man to his own feet, but Walter had no plan for attack in mind. All he knew was he couldn't pay five hundred. He really couldn't pay three. "Listen, Mr. Rumpleman," he said, "you told me three hundred. That's all I'm going to pay you."

Gary tossed off the rest of the rye and felt his tongue thicken. "Now you listen, Mr. Costaine. You need me. I'm the only one who can save you. You know Mr. Parrish is trying to stick you with the murder. You know the doctor did it. If I testify, it's the doctor. If I don't, it might be you."

"Three hundred," Costaine begged. "I haven't got five hundred. You can't change your price on me right in the middle." He gestured helplessly with the beer, but his brain was working. Once Masters knew Joseph Rumpleman existed, maybe he could subpoena him and Costaine wouldn't have to pay him anything. "Try him again. Maybe his line isn't busy now."

"Yeah, all right."

Costaine offered the use of his own phone but Rumpleman wouldn't take it, worse luck. Well, Costaine wouldn't pay off unless Masters verified that he would put Rumpleman on the stand.

"Joe Rumpleman" closed himself into his own room again. Dammit, even being with Costaine made him scared he'd be found out. Now the liquor made him woozy and he had stupidly brought the glass along with him. He put the glass down and repeated the words, "Hello, Mr. Masters, my name is Joe Rumpleman," three times, enunciating clearly. He told himself the thousand dollars from Parrish was nothing but a flier. What did he have to lose? Now he'd better quit fooling around, though, and tie up the three hundred. And, if Masters really went for it, he might be able to squeeze out five. Costaine should be willing to pay that much to save his crinkly old skin.

He sat down on his bed, pulled the phone onto his lap and put the call through the motel office. There was a lot of ringing and finally he heard the calm, solid voice of Vincent Masters in his ear. He went through his carefully enunciated, but slightly rapid, Joe Rumpleman introduction.

"I beg your pardon, will you spell that, please?"

Gary screwed up his courage. After all, it was a phony name and couldn't be traced. He spelled it and went on hastily. Wasn't it true that Cleveland Parrish was accusing Mr. Walter Costaine of the murder of Sally Whittaker? . . . or something like that. Well, he could prove Costaine was innocent. . . . That's right, absolutely innocent. How? Easy. It so happened that on the night of October thirty-first he rented room two in the East River Motel in Guilford. He was a salesman and was on his way home to wife and family in Boston. And while he was at the motel he entertained a young lady. You know how it is. (That's a good touch. That makes the alibi sound really authentic!) And he went to take the young lady home at precisely quarter past four and he noticed that the old white Chevy next to his car had a paper cup on the hood.

Why had he waited so long to come forward?

He hadn't really paid much attention to the case, to tell the truth. He was on the road so much. But then he happened to read that Costaine had a white Chevy and a cup had been left on it and what with Costaine being falsely accused and all, why he thought he ought to come forward. But, of course (heh, heh), he'd like to keep it quiet about that young lady.

Where was he now?

Oh, around.

Near enough to come talk about it? Why, of course. Let's say, half an hour?

Gary only delayed long enough to relay the good news to Costaine. "Better get your money ready. I'm going to Masters' house right now!" Then he was in the car, racing west on the turnpike for New Haven.

The state's attorney's house was on Edwards Street, parallel to Whitney Avenue, and Gary knew just how to get there. You couldn't say Gary Stevens didn't do his homework. And if he chose to claim he'd seen a paper cup on Costaine's car, even the great Cleveland Parrish couldn't prove he hadn't.

He took the Trumbull Street exit, picked up Edwards Street at its beginnings, and crawled along. Second block, midway on the right. There it was, the front light glowing invitingly, a driveway to a back yard garage near the front walk.

He swung in the drive and his headlights picked out another car deep to the rear, empty and quiet, with a dome light on the top and the word POLICE on the back.

Gary didn't stop to analyze. His instincts shouted, "Trap!" and his eyes saw jail.

He jammed the shift into reverse, rammed the car back into the street and hit the gas. He'd have to sneak back for his suitcase so he couldn't be traced, but then he was going to put a night's drive between him and the motel. And maybe, while he was piling up the miles, he'd think up another scheme to make money.

CHAPTER 64

After two days of testimonials from Whittaker's patients, replete with examples of his kindness, tenderness, and his predilection to heal, not hurt, Parrish finished off the third week of the trial with a salvo of heavy artillery. He introduced first the ambulance driver who had taken Sally Whittaker's body to New Haven, then one of the stretcher bearers and, over prosecution objections, got agreement from both that the ride from the Whittaker home to Yale-New

Haven Hospital took between thirty and thirty-five minutes, that the actual door-to-door time was forty-five minutes. The estimated temperature in the back of the ambulance, since it bore a body and not a patient, was a cool fifty degrees. There followed a witness from the weather department to testify that the temperature in the New Haven area between five and six on the morning of November first was thirty-eight degrees.

With that data on record, Parrish put two expert pathologists on the stand, one from New York, one from Boston, asked the same questions of each and received the same answers:

"Consider a hypothetical situation," Parrish said to them, "wherein a woman, age thirty-one and a half, height five-six, weight one hundred and twenty pounds, wearing nothing but a light wool miniskirted dress, has been killed in a room registering seventy-four degrees Fahrenheit. Now then, at five-fifteen in the morning, an unknown length of time after she has been killed, she is removed from that room on a stretcher covered with a sheet. For the next three quarters of an hour she spends thirty to thirty-five minutes in fifty-degree temperature and the balance in a temperature of thirty-eight degrees.

"From six till six forty-five she is in seventy-degree surroundings, at which time her rectal temperature is recorded as ninety-three point three degrees. Given these factors, could you estimate a time of death?"

Each doctor guessed a maximum of three hours, an absolute minimum of two.

"Would you consider," Parrish asked each one, "two and a half hours as a good mean, the most likely time?"

"I wouldn't say the *most* likely time, though it's *as* likely as any other. But it is a good mean."

"Then you're saying that quarter past four in the morning is a good mean?"

"In my opinion that would be good, yes."

Masters, in desperate cross-examination, got them to concede that estimating time of death by body temperature was, at best, a rough way of doing it. So many variables were involved. He got them to admit their estimates could be wrong but he couldn't get them to concede, given the hypothetical conditions, that they were likely to be wrong. They were doing their estimation on the assumption that the factors given them were the only factors involved.

The admissions were Masters' only solace for he was helpless. What could he do: put Liebman back on the stand to state that he too had, of course, taken into consideration the time the body was not in seventy-four-degree temperatures in arriving at his conclusions? It would be lame in the first place, and insufficient in the second. For Liebman had never acquired the outdoor temperature data Parrish had so assiduously collected for his own experts. Thus, no matter what Liebman said, the jury would regard it as face saving.

Masters went grimly back to his seat after cross-examination, knowing he'd been had. And it was his own fault. He hadn't questioned Liebman in enough depth. He'd left that hole. And then Parrish, in cross-examination, had cleverly elicited from Liebman the fact he'd taken room temperature into consideration, had got him to say it arrogantly, in fact. Then he had changed the subject and led Liebman away from announcing what other temperatures he had also considered. Then he brought in his experts to plug up the hole his way. It was Parrish's meticulous attention to detail and it had paid off. The victory was clearly his.

Parrish went on from there in the same detailed way. He had a surveyor introduce into evidence a diagram of the Whittaker property including an X marking the spot where the poker had been found. Then, in front of the jury, he had the surveyor draw a semicircle through Whittaker's back yard with the X as the center and the distance to the patio as the radius. If the poker could have been thrown to that spot from the patio, then it could have been thrown there from any other point on the arc.

It was Parrish himself who then drew a straight line from the rear of the house through the woods to Neck Road. It intersected the semicircle at two points and the jury was left to wonder if the poker hadn't been thrown from one of them rather than the patio.

CHAPTER 65

The headlines on the Saturday night papers said, "Whittaker to Take Stand Tuesday." It was the next sensation in the trial and the type size was large.

It was large enough to catch Walter Costaine's eye as he roamed his Forty-second Street stamping ground once more. He was in search of a hooker—if he could find one who would come to terms. He had to strike bargains for he couldn't afford the price any more.

He had thought that once he testified he would become rich. Certainly, in the pre-trial days he was golden enough. His name was everywhere, the story of his seduction on everyone's lips. He was the very heart of a crime *célèbre*. Surely, after he told his story, he would be a full-fledged celebrity with interviews, ghost-written reminiscences, and television talk shows.

Except for Cleveland Parrish. Cleveland Parrish had torn him limb from limb on the witness stand. Cleveland Parrish had destroyed his Casanova image, had bereft him of dignity. Worse than that, Cleveland Parrish had wrecked his alibi and created a public suspicion that he, himself, might be Sally's murderer. Walter Costaine did not step down into a cherry bowl of monetary offers, it was into the startling abyss of oblivion.

At least that was what he thought it was until the sour day when Joe Rumpleman had appeared. It was Rumpleman who reminded him that oblivion was better than suspicion and pointed out the flimsiness of his alibi. It was Rumpleman who showed him the danger of his position. Let Gerald Whittaker be found not guilty and the finger of justice would inevitably point in Walter Costaine's direction. And what protection would his alibi be then, without the backup testimony of Rumpleman himself? Only Joe Rumpleman could save him! Only Joe Rumpleman could prove he never moved his car! And Joe Rumpleman would provide the rescue for only $300. Who could complain about that?

Walter hadn't complained, but he would have had to hock everything he owned. It would have been worth it, though, to be free of the fear. But Rumpleman had mysteriously disappeared and now Walter walked in panic. It was a scheme, a plot. He had only sought to finger a murderer. Would he find himself sacrificed in the murderer's stead?

He had fled his motel, but what would he do now? He was broke and without prospects. There was less than a twenty in his wallet and his suitcase sat in a Greyhound locker while he marked time searching for the sedation of a woman.

What he really wanted was to befriend some kindhearted whore who'd take him home and mother him and support him for a while until he got his feet back on the ground. But, of course, that was only a daydream. Professional prostitutes weren't much on motherhood and they didn't give favors to strangers. The only men they kept were their pimps, and newcomers beware.

An even wilder daydream was that some rich woman—young and beautiful preferred, but old and fat acceptable—would be taken by his charm and move him in with her. There was a time when such a possibility was not too unbelievable. Hadn't he accomplished much the same thing with Sally? But his charm wasn't working so well any more. His hair was turning white, his face looked old and his clothes were threadbare. The Old World charm wasn't quite coming off.

Meanwhile, it was getting late and he had to do something for himself if he didn't want to sleep under the bushes in the library park or bed down in some doorway. He wandered away from Forty-second Street, away from the lights and the throngs to a quiet side street. He was going to have to make a phone call. He'd put it off as long as he could, but he knew the moment would come.

He stepped into a dimly lighted bar. Booths were along one wall, the bar along the other, with phone cubicles at the rear. There were twenty people in the place, men and women, animated but not loud, and business was prospering.

Walter looked at the bottles in back of the bar and thought of the small sum still in his wallet. There was enough. He stepped to a vacant space at the counter and ordered rye with a water chaser. A man beside him jostled him slightly and said in elaborate, tenor tones, "Oh, exCUSE me."

"S'all right." Walter turned. The man was young, with a very good-looking gray velvet jacket and a red open-necked shirt. Oh, Christ, thought Costaine. It's a fag on the make.

"You're new here," the man continued. He had dark, wavy hair down to his collar, he smiled a lot and sent messages with his eyes.

"Yeah," Costaine answered. "I came to make a phone call." He turned to pay for his drink and picked it up.

"The phones are right there at the back," the other man said and pointed artistically. He smiled and added, "I hope she's busy."

Costaine grunted, pulled out and threaded his way to the rear. The women looked old and tired; the men, lax-eyed and weary. The guy in the gray velvet jacket was the only fag in the place.

In the booth he closed the door against the talk, dialed his number, and tossed off his rye when he got an answer. "Morelle," he said and tried to put cheer in his voice. "This is Walter."

He wasn't expecting to excite unbearable enthusiasm in his former wife's breast but he did hope she might be docile enough to consider taking in a non-paying boarder on a temporary basis. That, at least, was the hope he was reduced to.

Her reply dashed it completely. "Why, you son of a bitch," she snarled in withering tones. "You goddamned clap-ridden son of a bitch!"

Costaine managed a smile but sweat was coming out on his face. "Not any more."

She was screaming at him now. "But long enough!" She was maniacal. "You stayed with us while you got cured, and you didn't tell me? And you conned me—you conned me—!" She went into a torrent of four-letter words; Costaine couldn't follow them they came so shrill and fast. "I'm going to the doctor right now," she shouted. "Because of you!" She went into another wild stream of incoherent, violent language, screamed at him never to call again, and slammed down the phone so hard it exploded in Costaine's ear.

He stayed there, staring at nothing, the smile fixed on his face, the sweat running down his cheeks, the phone still nearly at his ear. He looked around. Nobody outside the booth was paying attention. He hung up the receiver slowly and swallowed. Now what was he going to do? Maybe there was a flophouse?

He opened the door of the booth, took out a handkerchief and wiped his face. It really was hot in there. He felt like he was sweating blood.

He stepped out and started to make his way back down the length of the bar. At the end the smiling man in the velvet jacket said, "Hello, again."

"Hullo."

The man moved a half step from the bar, his face sympathetic. "You look terrible." He cocked his head. "Did she stand you up?"

"In a manner of speaking."

"Here, can I buy you a drink?"

There was nothing in the world Costaine needed more at that moment. The first one had done nothing at all. "Yeah, sure," he said. "Thanks."

The young man ordered and seemed to know the bartender well. "My name's Eric," he told Costaine and held out a limp hand.

Walter said his name was Walter and Eric made conversation in the form of questions. What was Walter doing? Where did he live? Where was he going? The man sensed that Costaine was lost and uncertain and his questions were gauged accordingly. When he found out Costaine didn't have a bed for the night, he said, "Would you like to come to my apartment? I have a very nice place only a block from here. I think we could have a very nice time together."

The bartender served the shot of rye and a small glass of water and Costaine picked up the rye to make sure it couldn't be taken away from him after he set the young man straight. "Thanks," he said, "but there wouldn't be anything in it for you. I'm not—that way."

Eric didn't seem surprised or put out. "Have you ever tried it?" he said. "You might find you'd like it."

Walter tossed off the rye neat and sipped the water. "No. Sorry. I'm not interested."

"I'd pay you well."

Walter hesitated before he put down his glass.

"Would you like another drink?"

The young man was persisting. His eyes were eager and hung on Costaine's every move.

Costaine tried to sound offhand. "How much?"

"Twenty dollars."

For twenty bucks he could get himself a broad. "What would I have to do?"

The young man shook his head. "Oh, I wouldn't want to put it on that kind of a basis. That's too businesslike. It's no fun. That's too much like, 'Sorry, your time is up.'" He leaned closer. "I like experiences to be mutually shared. The pleasure comes from the sharing. How about thirty-five dollars and you'll stay all night and we'll have a grand time. You'll find that I'm very easy to accommodate. I wouldn't make any extraordinary demands on you. I'll make you like it. You just wait and see."

Thirty-five dollars and a bed. That's what it boiled down to. Sort of a male variation of that dream of being picked up and supported by a well-to-do and beautiful young woman. It was either that or— or what?

Eric moved closer, so that his shoulder was against Costaine's arm. "How about it, Walter? What have you got to lose?"

Walter shrugged. "Nothing, I guess."

Eric was beaming. "Good. I could tell the moment you came in you were the kind who's eager for new experiences. I have a thing about people. I'm very good at character analysis." He took Walter's arm and led him to the door. "You know something, Walter? I think you and I are going to become very good friends. I think we're going to relate in a very beautiful way. I really do."

Outside, Eric took Walter's hand and gave it squeezes of excitement. Walter had never held hands with a boy before. He fought down the sickness in his stomach and tried to think about women.

CHAPTER 66

For the first day of his ordeal on the stand, Gerald Whittaker wore a freshly pressed suit, a necktie purchased by Melody Stevens, shoes that shone, and a shirt that dazzled. He'd had a haircut, he'd shaved extra close, and he'd undergone a weekend of intensive drilling. That was the Parrish preparation: rehearse and rehearse until the student is letter-perfect, until his responses are programmed.

Whittaker, in answer to his name, came forward before an electric silence and a packed room. He must not think of Katherine, he must remember to walk modestly, not hangdog, not arrogant. He must— what else must he do? How could anyone walk arrogantly anyway? How could anyone help but tremble when he passed those twelve men and women in the jury box? For all the anonymity of their lives, for all their inconsequence upon his own past, those twelve would have more to say about his future than his closest relatives or dearest friends. Economics, business opportunities, climate, or matters of health would not determine where he went from here. These twelve people would.

Did they care what happened to him? They weren't supposed to. Who or what he was shouldn't weigh in the scales. He was to be an object, a non-person. All that motivated, or was supposed to motivate the jury was the question: had he, beyond a reasonable doubt, killed his wife? Or hadn't he?

Reasonable doubt. That was all that counted.

Of course, lawyers would try to make the jury think of the defendant as a human being, as a Dr. Jekyll on the one hand, Mr. Hyde on the other. Defense attorneys would break the jurors' hearts if they could. Prosecutors would paint the defendant as evil incarnate. But the wishes, whims, hopes, fears, past, present, future of the defendant weren't supposed to matter. In the eyes of the law, man was a collective noun, devoid of individuality, of personality, of feeling. The law spoke and the dehumanized being was acted upon accordingly, moved here or there, set free, imprisoned, expunged.

Gerald Whittaker turned in front of the chair, faced the clerk, raised his right hand and never heard the oath being administered. His eyes felt glassy. The sea of watching faces swam before him and his knees started to shake. The clerk finished speaking; Whittaker, with an effort, said, "I do," steadied himself, and kept from collapsing in the chair. He grasped the arms and sat down slowly. The room settled and he decided he wasn't going to be sick after all.

The last six months had been almost beyond endurance, but taking the witness stand in front of those twelve attentive, unfeeling faces, was the worst thing of all. He hoped he hadn't revealed his terror. He hoped he hadn't made a bad impression.

Cleveland Parrish approached, radiating confidence and encouragement, the one face to seize on, the mentor, the savior, the hope. He read Jerry's distress, the inability of his mind to function, and he asked simple questions to unlock him; questions about his background, where he was brought up, where he went to school.

Gradually Jerry came alive again and began to orient. Coming back were the endless repetitions of his story, developed from the whip-crack mind of Parrish which could seize each and every variation from tale to tale. Any details that varied a hair in the retelling were caught by the lawyer for re-analysis, any contradiction of prosecution testimony had to be explained.

If it had been memory and recollection in the beginning, it was rote at the end. Whittaker was detail-perfect. He had it down cold, the exact sequence of events, where each person had been, who had said what to whom. Gerald Whittaker, once done with his stage fright, would tell his story his way and nothing Masters might do would shake him.

Parrish, when he sensed the doctor was ready, brought him around to it. Skipping the nature of their marital life, Parrish asked for the events of the fatal day. Would the doctor describe the activities of that occasion?

Jerry was on well-rehearsed ground now and, under Parrish's guidance, felt a growing confidence. The ordeal was almost over: this last difficult period and then he'd be free. Don't think about Katherine. He'd be free.

He began his tale, describing the tailgate picnic at the Bowl, the return to his place and the preparations for the costume party and dinner, his version agreeing with the tale the Magnusons had told. He described the Bakewells' dinner party and Parrish interrupted to say that other witnesses had indicated he and Sally seemed to be fighting. Was that true? Whittaker said, yes, it was.

"What were you fighting about?"

"Money."

"Money?"

"That was what we were usually fighting about."

"You weren't fighting about Walter Costaine?"

"No. He hadn't been around for weeks."

Parrish drew him out on the constant fighting over money. The problem, Whittaker explained, was that he wanted Sally to live on his income.

"You wanted her to live on your income, you say?"

"Yes, I wanted us both to live in the style of a comfortably well-off doctor with a growing practice. I felt that befitted our position in the community."

"She didn't agree?"

"Well, you see, the difficulty was that Sally was accustomed to a much higher standard of living. Not only was she used to it, she could afford it. She wanted to contribute some of her funds toward the combination but I didn't want that. I did not even want her to spend her money on herself. It might have been selfish of me, but I felt I should be the provider. Sally, however, would not accept such a deprivation and she went ahead buying articles for herself that I couldn't possibly afford, elegant things, flaunting things, showy things. I expressed my opposition, but she was not the kind who would knuckle under."

"Do you think it was right to object to her spending her own money on herself?"

"I don't know. I was probably wrong in insisting. But it was a matter of pride. I wanted to buy her the things she wore. I wanted her life-style to be a reflection of my ability to support her, of *my* style, I suppose. Of *me*. Anything she bought for herself, jewelry and other impossibly expensive items, would create the wrong impression. People would either think I was making far more than I did, or would think I condoned her spending her own money. They might even think I was not above spending her money too. I think the one flaw in our marriage, the factor that caused the lion's share of our problems together was that she had too much money."

Parrish lingered over this analysis. He didn't flaunt it and say to the jury, "So the prosecution thinks he married Sally for her money? See how wrong they are!" He just went over this running quarrel that Whittaker said had fractured their marriage, going into it at great length, getting Whittaker to relate incidents that produced quarrels.

This particular quarrel, Whittaker said, was because Sally wanted a bigger boat. She wanted a cabin cruiser for weekending with other couples, rather than the whaler they had. He was claiming he couldn't swing it and didn't have enough time to make even owning the whaler worthwhile. She'd told him she'd make up the difference, but he wouldn't hear of it and she was, in turn, getting very bitchy.

"You wouldn't have liked a bigger boat?"

"It's not that. I don't like not getting my money's worth. I come from a poor family and that's been ingrained in me. No matter how much money I had, I could never spend it foolishly or recklessly. I think Sally could."

Parrish led him on to the dance and the costume contest Sally had won. She had made the dress, was that right?

"Well, yes and no. The material cost nearly fifty dollars and a dressmaker helped her with it and the whole thing came to better than a hundred dollars. Just a simple costume. But that's what I mean. Madison might be a well-to-do town, but nobody else at that dance spent over a hundred dollars for a costume. She won the prize, which was what she was after, but it was a damned expensive bottle of champagne she bought."

"She shared the champagne at the table, I understand. Then what?"

"The next I knew she was out dancing with Walter Costaine."

"What was your reaction, Doctor?"

"I'd been hoping he'd never come back. That was something else we'd fought about. But not since he'd gone away. I thought maybe she'd gotten him out of her system, but there they were, just as if he'd never gone. I guess I saw red. I stormed over and pulled Sally away from him and I said something like, 'Keep your damned paws off of her.' But she'd been trying to get my goat and she tried some more. 'See you later,' she told him when I was marching her away. That was meant to burn me up, and it did."

"What do you think she meant by that remark?"

"I thought she was trying to indicate to me that she wasn't going to quit seeing him."

"Did you expect her to see him right away?"

"No. I really was pretty sure she wouldn't see him at all. I thought she was only saying that for effect."

"You thought she wouldn't see him at all?"

Whittaker nodded. "I thought after six weeks away from him the novelty would have worn off and she'd take a look at him and at herself and decide if she wanted to play around she could at least find somebody more appealing."

"Did you think she had, perhaps, found such a person?"

"I wouldn't know. I didn't know she'd found *him* until Barbara Costaine told me. I'm so busy with my work."

"And there was Katherine?"

"Yes. There was Katherine."

"Getting back to the party, to your taking Sally away from Costaine, were you aware when you did it that Sally had made a date to see Costaine later that same night?"

"I not only was unaware of it, I wouldn't have believed it if she'd told me."

"What would you have believed if she'd told you?"

"That she was saying it to get back at me because I wouldn't give in about the boat."

"Did she, at any time, indicate to you that she planned to visit Costaine after the dance?"

"Never."

Parrish went from there to the idea for a post-dance party back at his house. Whittaker explained that the Magnusons couldn't return to Trumbull directly from the Summer Club since their clothes and Bowl gear were at the Whittakers'. It seemed a good chance, too, to repay his hosts for the dinner party by having everybody come back for a nightcap.

In fact, he went on, he couldn't understand the special emphasis the prosecution was trying to put on the party. In the circles in which he moved, people almost never split up right after the movies or the theater or whatever they did together. It was customary to go to someone's house for a nightcap afterwards. And, since the Magnusons were his guests, it was the natural thing for him to be the one issuing the invitation.

CHAPTER 67

After the midmorning break, Whittaker described the post-dance party, admitting he had a lot to drink, but denying it was more than usual. The hour was late, he'd been working hard, and he was going mostly on nerve. The guests were adrenaline. He was tired but he didn't want them to go lest Sally start in on him again about the boat.

When the guests did leave, suddenly he could hardly keep his eyes open. It was all he could do to see them out the door. Sally and Henrietta Bakewell got gabbing in the doorway and he didn't wait for them to finish. He went up to bed. In fact, he was getting into his pajamas when he heard Sally close the front door. She didn't come upstairs, though. Probably she stayed down to clean up. That was Sally. She never could let it go till the next day. She was a compulsive cleaner.

Jerry was glad. He could escape her berating tongue. He got into bed, left the light on and went to sleep.

"That was all I knew," he said, "until her screams woke me up around quarter past four."

"Screams?" Parrish asked. "Tell us about those screams. Tell us what happened at quarter past four."

The courtroom was morgue still. Jurors and spectators leaned forward, hanging on the doctor's every resonant, measured word. He was almost as good as Cleveland Parrish himself as he told about the fleeing figure he witnessed from the head of the stairs, his horror at discovering Sally's body, how he cradled her smashed head and staggered to the telephone, not knowing where to turn, finally deciding on a friend who was a lawyer.

"Why didn't you call the police?"

Whittaker shook his head. "I don't know," he said. "Except I've

308

never called the police before in my life. Maybe if I'd been able to think rationally— But as it was, it just never occurred to me. All I could think was, 'Who do I know who might know what to do in such an emergency?' That's why I turned to Ed Balin."

That was his story and once it had been laid out for inspection, Parrish went about nailing down the corners, getting answers to any and all odd things that didn't fit, all the aspects the prosecution would seek to tear apart.

"Mrs. Whittaker's costume was found hanging in her closet and she was wearing a dress when she died. Are you familiar with the dress?"

"Yes, it's one of her old ones."

"One of her old ones?"

"Yes. To wear around the house."

"It's reported that she wasn't wearing anything underneath."

Whittaker said he wasn't surprised and, under further questioning, revealed that Sally had a dislike of feeling hampered, wore as little clothing as she could, went barefoot indoors, tried to get dresses that fit her snugly enough so she wouldn't have to wear a bra. He hadn't seen her prepare for the dance but believed she didn't wear anything under the costume and, when she switched from that to the minidress, it wasn't likely that she'd then don underclothes, especially alone in her own home.

"Why would she get into a minidress rather than a nightgown or robe of some kind?"

"Objection. The witness can't read the deceased's mind."

"Sustained."

"Would she customarily change from an evening costume to a minidress at that hour rather than a nightgown or robe of some kind?"

"She didn't own any nightgowns. She slept raw. As for robes, well, I suppose she could have gotten into a robe but they're more cumbersome than the costume she had on. She might have—"

"Objection. He's speculating again."

Parrish asked another question. "Did she own slippers?"

"Yes, but she didn't wear them much. She preferred going around barefoot."

"Would she go barefoot outdoors?"

"Not out of the yard. And certainly not in November."

"Why not out of the yard?"

"She was old-fashioned that way. She believed women should dress up if they went out in public. She believed they should look their best. She'd never go shopping in curlers, for example."

"Would that minidress costume be the sort of thing she'd wear if she were expecting a visitor?"

"It might be. It would depend on who the visitor was."

"Would she go barefoot if she was expecting a visitor?"

"Again that would depend on the visitor."

"Suppose it was your mother and father, or her mother and father?"

"No, she would not be barefoot. And she'd be wearing a nicer dress."

"How about a lover?"

"If she was waiting for a lover, I don't know why she'd be wearing anything."

"Would she open the door wearing nothing?"

"No, that's right. She'd never do that."

"So her costume would be completely in keeping with entertaining a lover late at night?"

"Objection. This is all speculation. There has been no evidence that Mrs. Whittaker had any lovers other than Walter Costaine, who was expecting her to come to his motel."

Parrish fought back. "Your Honor, because no evidence has been put forth indicating the existence of a second lover doesn't mean there can't be one. Remember, Dr. Whittaker would never have found out about the first lover without outside help. He didn't know Costaine existed, but Costaine has proved to be real enough. Now, Mr. Costaine was away for a period of six weeks. I intend to explore with Dr. Whittaker the matter of his wife's behavior during that period. And I intend to introduce evidence that there was, indeed, at least one additional lover involved."

Judge Simms compressed his lips. He hoped the papers would quote him exactly. "When you have produced evidence of a second lover, Mr. Parrish, the court will give you ample leeway to make what suggestions and draw whatever conclusions you wish regarding the purpose of Mrs. Whittaker's mode of dress. In the meantime, however, I must sustain the objection."

Rebuffed, Parish changed his attack. "All right, we'll not discuss whom she might receive in such a costume. Let us concern ourselves with where she might go in such a costume. You say she would not go shopping barefoot. Would she call on Walter Costaine barefoot?"

"Absolutely not."

"How about with nothing on under a minidress?"

"No. She wouldn't go out in public like that."

"But you believe she wore nothing under her costume at the dance."

"That's true, but nobody would know. That's the key point. In a minidress she might reveal the fact. She was a very fastidious girl, really. She wasn't particularly modest, but she was fastidious. She would reveal only what she chose to reveal and she would never reveal everything. I mean, to the public, of course. She knew the value of mystery."

The next point Parrish put on the record was that Whittaker noticed no difference in Sally's behavior while Costaine was away. Let the jury wonder if she weren't, therefore, getting sex somewhere else. Certainly, it wasn't from Jerry. He frankly said they had not had sex relations since he found her in the motel room with Costaine.

From there, Parrish moved to the Katherine Lord affair and got Whittaker to admit that by the time Katherine appeared on the scene, his marriage to Sally had pretty well ceased to be a marriage. "I'm not using that as an excuse for me and Katherine, except that I regard myself as a healthy, normal male with normal male appetites. Had my marriage been a going thing, I might have been able to resist Katherine. I don't know. As it was, I found her overwhelmingly appealing. Maybe I should have looked the other way but, to be perfectly honest, I didn't want to."

Parrish had him describe the development of the relationship and Katherine's resulting move to Clinton.

"What about marriage?" Parrish asked. "Were you really serious when you told her you wanted to marry her?"

Whittaker lowered his eyes and his voice. His fingers worked nervously. "You know how it is," he murmured, and had to be told to speak louder. He looked around as if trying to spot Katherine in the spectators' section. "You know, when you're going with a girl, when you're keeping a girl, well, you do have to talk some of the time. You do have to discuss the relationship and where it's going. Women expect some, er, kind of commitment. You, ah, practically *have* to talk marriage."

"Meaning you have to talk about getting married, or why you can't get married?"

"Ah, why you can't get married is, er, the way it's usually done," he said lamely. "I guess I'm not the only one."

"And Miss Lord believed your reasons why you couldn't marry her?"

Whittaker flushed. "Yes. I, ah, think so at any rate."

"I believe her testimony was to that effect. In fact, she seemed to agree with your reasons. She didn't want to marry you?"

"She thought the reasons I gave her were so valid that she agreed with them."

"The reasons you gave her were?"

"That Sally would fight a divorce and make a nasty scene and I'd have to leave town and start my career all over again. That was, ah, the essence of it, I guess."

"Would Sally really have contested a divorce, Doctor?"

"She, er, claimed she would. I mean, when we talked about it—before Katherine, that is. When it was the two of us." He was flushed and nervous. "I don't know if she really would have—if I'd pressed it."

"Would you have gotten a divorce if Sally wouldn't contest it?"

"I don't know. I might have."

"If you and Sally had gotten a divorce, would you have married Katherine?"

His face turned an even brighter red. "I, ah, I'm not sure. I might have. I might not."

"Were you in love with Katherine?"

"I, ah, yes, I suppose you could call it love."

"Would you call it anything else?"

"Well, there was, ah, physical attraction. We were attracted to each other. And it—was—I had peace of mind there, with her."

"And no responsibilities? As you would have responsibilities if you and she were married?"

"Yes."

"Would you kill for Katherine Lord, Doctor?"

"Kill for her?"

"Is your feeling for her so strong that you would kill to have her or keep her or protect her?"

He shook his head and said firmly, "No, of course not. I wouldn't kill for anybody. I'm against killing. My job is to heal, not destroy."

"Thank you, Doctor." Parrish turned away to let Masters cross-examine.

CHAPTER 68

Masters came forward slowly, his midday meal an indigestible lump in a nervous stomach. The fate of the case could well hang on his handling of this cross-examination and no one knew it better than he. Throughout Parrish's two-and-a-half-day examination of Whittaker, he'd been taking copious notes, plotting and shaping his rebuttal. He knew, however, it would be futile to counterattack across the whole board. Better to home in on the weaknesses and the important strengths and destroy the doctor's credibility there.

He first tackled Whittaker's claim that Sally had shown no signs of missing Costaine during his lengthy absence. Parrish was building a mythical lover as a stand-in killer and Masters had to squash that idea wherever it came up.

He started with brief, incisive questions and in short order drew the admission from Whittaker that he was busy at the office most of the time and with Katherine when he was free.

Q: So you weren't really paying much attention to your wife, were you?

A: No.

Q: If she had wanted sex, would she have approached you?

A: No.

Q: If she had been *dying* for sex, do you think she would have approached you?

A: No.

Q: And you have testified that you were so busy and involved with your work and with Katherine, and so uninvolved with your wife, that you had no idea she was having an affair with Costaine until his wife told you, isn't that correct?

A: Yes.

Q: And you were equally involved with your work and with Katherine, and uninvolved with your wife while Costaine was away?

A: Yes.

Q: Which means you were hardly in a position to judge how satisfied with life your wife was during his absence, isn't that so?

A: Yes.

Then Masters gave him the *coup de grace:*

"Has there ever been any hint in anything your wife ever said to you or anything she did that led you to suspect she had more than one lover, that one lover being Walter Costaine?"

And Whittaker had to answer, "No," for to say yes would require producing the statement or action in question and, had there been such evidence, he and Parrish would already have gained maximum mileage from it.

Vincent Masters took time out to pour and sip a small cup of water, letting Whittaker's answer build in the jurors' minds. So far so good. He set down the glass, patted his lips with a handkerchief and turned back to the defendant. He said, "What did you do with Sally's shoes that night?"

Whittaker was startled. "Shoes? What shoes?"

"The shoes she was going to wear to Costaine's motel room."

"I object!" Parrish said, rushing to the rescue lest Whittaker become rattled. "There has not been one shred of evidence introduced in this trial that there were any shoes."

"Sustained."

Masters sorted through the exhibits on the table in front of the bench and showed the witness a photograph of the body taken from the living room entrance. "Observe her feet, Doctor. Observe how clean they are. Do you know what that means, Doctor? Either she was killed very shortly after she changed her clothes, or she was wearing something on her feet: shoes or slippers. Which is it?"

"I object," Parrish said again. "Counsel has not been shown qualified to judge how dirty Mrs. Whittaker's feet would get in a given length of time."

There was laughter and the judge sustained the objection.

Masters abandoned the subject, but he'd made the jury aware of shoes and of what he was going after next. That was the minidress with nothing underneath that Whittaker had so assiduously claimed she'd not wear outside the house. Masters asked him about Sally's fastidiousness and said he appreciated the quality, he felt the same way. He liked his wife to look well when she appeared in public. It was all right to relax among friends, but a well-brought-up girl wanted to be at her best in front of strangers.

"But pray tell, Doctor, what strangers could she possibly expect to meet driving to Costaine's motel room at three o'clock in the morning?"

Whittaker was hard pressed. "I don't know. But you never can tell."

"It's three o'clock in the morning. It's late. She's tired. She's going to see Costaine for one purpose. They're going to bed together. It does not require any great stretch of my imagination to picture a woman on such an errand being nude when she steps out of her dress; not bothering to put anything on except that dress. But you, Doctor, believe that your late wife, who, according to you, didn't like wearing more clothes than necessary, whom you suspect of being nude under her Hallowe'en costume, would put on underpants and shoes just because someone might peek out a motel window when she crossed from her car to Costaine's door?"

He made it sound ridiculous and Whittaker felt ridiculous, knowing he would have to answer, yes. Parrish tried to save him by objecting. Whittaker, he said, couldn't be called upon to judge what his wife would do in such a situation.

But this time Masters had him. "Your Honor," he said, "defense counsel has questioned this witness at some length as to what his wife would do and wear in various circumstances, including the trip to Costaine's motel."

It was true and Simms overruled the objection. Gerald Whittaker was made to say his "yes."

Then Masters hit him again. "Why didn't your wife keep her date with Walter Costaine?"

Whittaker blinked. "What?"

Masters: Your wife had a late date with Walter Costaine. She changed from her costume into a dress. According to your story, Doctor, she was murdered at quarter past four, nearly two hours after the party was over. But she was supposed to go to Walter Costaine's motel. Why didn't she?"

Parrish: Objection. Defendant can't be expected to know what his wife was doing or thinking while he was asleep.

Simms: Sustained. That is not a proper question.

Masters: You are correct, sir. It was not a proper question. I only put it to the witness in hopes that he might possibly be able to give me an answer to the strange question of why a woman, who has a date somewhere else, is still at home when a murderer arrives two hours later. I must confess I have no answer to that question and I thought perhaps he might.

Parrish, on redirect, tried to take the sting out of Masters' ridicule. He got Whittaker to explain that while Sally might not anticipate encountering strangers on her way to the motel, there was always the risk of an auto accident and Sally, who believed in being prepared for all eventualities, would have been dressed for it.

After that, the defense rested.

CHAPTER 69

Tuesday, June first, was given over to rebuttal witnesses, but the day the crowds were waiting for was Wednesday. That was the day for which Judge Simms had scheduled the summations.

Vincent Masters' summation took all morning. He and his aides had worked on it through half a night and he had it well polished and rehearsed when he rose in front of another packed courtroom.

Step by step he reviewed testimony pointing to evidence of Whittaker's temper. Take the time he had slapped Sally: he had called her a whore and she struck him, surely a justifiable act. That he then hit her in return meant one thing: despite the milk of human kindness his patients swore flowed in his veins, he could physically—repeat, physically—assault a woman in a fit of rage.

Look next at his fight with Costaine at the motel and later, on the dance floor, both occurring well after he started keeping a mistress on the side. "You will note," he said to the jury, "Gerald Whittaker *does* take action when he's angry. He struck his wife. He attacked Costaine. He caused a scene at the Hallowe'en dance."

Then he pointed out that in each case his anger was aroused by a threat by his wife, (1) to his physical safety, (2) to his reputation, (3) to his ego. That's what it was, Masters insisted. His ego! He could not let it be threatened.

But Sally was threatening it as it had never been threatened before. She not only was cuckolding him, she was doing it in front of his face. She was affronting him with it, daring him. Of course she told him she was going to the motel after the dance. They were fighting and she wanted to hurt him. That's why she danced with Costaine in the first place—to get Whittaker's goat; to bait him and hurt him.

But she made the mistake of driving him too far. He must have watched her change clothes. He knew she had nothing on under her dress. She'd want him to know that. He probably chased her down the stairs before she got her shoes on, chased her to stop her, grabbed the poker in his frenzy and did stop her, killed her and spent himself beating her dead body until he was exhausted and his sense of vengeance assuaged.

That would have been near three o'clock, as the expert who had viewed the body and taken its temperature himself—not someone discussing a hypothetical situation—had testified.

And why had he beaten her so much? Was there more to it than her unfaithfulness? They had been battling over money by Whittaker's own testimony. She wanted more than he could give her. That was his ego too. Would he not, therefore, have struck a few blows over that? No more quarreling over money. No more nagging, frigid wife. Six years of misery were going into that beating.

Then, drained of emotion, with awareness of his deed beginning to assail him, he put his brain to work, went out the back door and flung the poker as far as he could into the deep grass. Next, he got rid of his bloodstained pajamas, perhaps by cutting them into pieces and flushing them down the john, or by burning them and washing the buttons and ashes down the dispose-all unit in the sink. He changed into a clean pair, picked up the party glasses and ran them through the dishwasher to make it appear Sally had done it, took her shoes back to the bedroom—if she'd been wearing shoes—rehearsed the story he would tell until he had it letter-perfect, then called his lawyer and the police.

All the evidence pointed to this. There was no other explanation possible. The defense was trying to lay the crime on the doorstep of some unknown lover. But the defense had produced not a single piece of evidence that would indicate she had an unknown lover. The defense might as well claim it was an unknown stranger, or a man from Mars. They were myths, all of them. Sally had a date with Walter Costaine for as soon as she could make it. She should have been in Costaine's motel room at three o'clock. The fact that she wasn't meant that she was detained—forcibly detained. And the only person who could have detained her was her husband. There was no lover, no stranger, no rape-murderer. Nobody came in and killed her at four-fifteen because, if she weren't dead already, she wouldn't have been around to be killed. She would have been in Costaine's motel room.

It was an impressive performance and when the lunch break followed, newsmen swarmed around the prosecutor.

"You never mentioned Katherine Lord, Mr. Masters. Any particular reason?"

Masters showed no emotion, but the name could make him wince. Katherine, next to Costaine, was to be his star witness, but Parrish had laid her equally to rest. "I didn't think it was necessary," he answered. "The jury heard her. They can judge for themselves."

"This thing about ego, that's a new wrinkle, isn't it?"

"No, it's been there all the time. It's the key to the man and what he did."

"You didn't put any psychiatrists on the stand to talk about his ego. Was there a reason?"

"Yes. The defense wouldn't let us give him a psychiatric examination."

"You don't think Sally's money was a factor, I gather."

That was another angle that Cleve had closed off. Masters said, "I think her money was a factor. If nothing else, it got in the way of their marriage."

After the lunch break it was Cleve Parrish's turn. His summation was not as long or as detailed as the state's attorney's for Parrish believed in hitting at only a few main points, those areas wherein reasonable doubt could be established. Reasonable doubt was the gateway to freedom, why bother with anything else.

He reminded the jury of Costaine. "Here we have an admitted liar, a fraud, a deceiver. Nowhere in his whole self-history does he disclose a single redeeming feature. When given his choice to stay with his family and be a father to his children or continue betraying Jerry Whittaker through his wife, he can't even choose the right course there. What is worse, if anything can be worse, is that even while he pretends to righteousness on the witness stand in his great confession of past lies, he is even then, under oath, telling more lies. I have to ask you, members of the jury. Would you really send a man to prison for twenty years, perhaps even to the electric chair, on nothing more than the testimony of a man like that? Wouldn't you want corroboration for any story he told you? Wouldn't you want outside evidence and lots of it before you believed any word he said? If he offered you a ring for twenty-five dollars that he claimed was a three-carat diamond, wouldn't you insist on having the ring appraised before you parted with that twenty-five dollars? Would any of you twelve people bet twenty-five dollars on that man's unsubstantiated word?

"But, ladies and gentlemen, the state's attorney would like you to bet more than twenty-five dollars on his unsubstantiated word. The state's attorney is asking you to bet a man's future, bet even his life, on Walter Costaine's unsubstantiated word. Because that's all the case they've got against Gerald Whittaker: Walter Costaine's *unsubstantiated* word."

He stopped for a sip of water, and then recounted briefly the theory the prosecutor had woven that morning. "That's a very nice story, ladies and gentlemen. We could even call it a nifty story. Very slick. Very sophisticated. We might even call it elegant. It would make a great movie. And, what's more, it happens in real life. Real people do such things. That's the devilish part of that whole beautiful tale. It can really happen. And the prosecutor wants you to believe that it really did happen over in Madison last November first.

"There's only one trouble with his wanting you to believe this. His whole, wonderfully woven tale depends upon one single key point. That key point is that Sally Whittaker was planning to go to Walter Costaine's motel room. Take that key out of the story and it falls apart. It shatters into pieces. Remove that key and there is no story. There's no so-called threat to Whittaker's ego; there's no baiting—and, indeed, what wife would bait her husband in such a manner? She'd know he'd stop her by whatever means necessary. Think about it. A woman who really had a late date would remain quiet about it so she could keep it. But see? The story, even with the key in place, is weak. It crumbles at the touch. Without the key, it is nothing. Without the key, we have a woman who changed into

319

something more comfortable after her husband went to bed, cleaned up the party things and ran them through the dishwasher, and then—? What then? We don't know. Someone came, and someone killed her. But not Jerry. Without that key it couldn't have been Jerry.

"And who is it who supplied that key, that one vital bit of information without which Dr. Whittaker would never have been brought to trial? Why, Walter Costaine supplied it. By saying he had a late date with Sally Whittaker.

"Is there anyone else in the whole world who can say that it's true? Can anyone else say the diamond is real?

"There is no one. The State can't produce a single soul to substantiate Walter Costaine's word. The State wants you to believe only him. The State puts a self-confessed liar on the witness stand and then asks you, the jury, to believe him. That's the position that you're in, ladies and gentlemen. You are to decide a man's future on the word of another man, who doesn't like him and who is an admitted liar."

Parrish paused to adjust papers and then spoke again. "As an aside, ladies and gentlemen, do you know what Walter Costaine is doing these days? Do you know where he lives and how he lives? No, he's no longer at the infamous motel. He left there without paying his bill. He is now living in New York. He is being kept by another man. He is presently serving as a male prostitute for other males. And this is not a make-believe story, ladies and gentlemen. I have notarized sworn statements on all of this." He shook his head. "I don't tell you this to shock you," he said softly. "I only tell it to you to show that Walter Costaine on the witness stand wasn't undergoing a change of personality, confessing his sins and becoming a purged and honorable man. He is still the same Walter Costaine he's always been. He'll do whatever he has to to get whatever he wants. He was that same kind of man when he sat in that chair there and swore that Sally had said she'd come to him that fatal night."

Parrish went on to list the support for his alternative story, that she never had had any intention of going anywhere, and that her husband had no inclination to kill her.

In this version, Whittaker was having trouble with his wife. She was demanding more than he could give. She had been having an affair and Whittaker was understandably bitter. He might be reluctant to give her much. Her demands, for all we know, might have been within reason, but he was bitter. She also was bitter. They were scarcely speaking that day. But the fight could not have been out of hand. They didn't cancel the Magnusons' visit, the football game, and the dance. It was just another of their fights.

"They went to the dance and who, ladies and gentlemen, should appear, but Walter Costaine, whom Sally had not seen for eight full weeks. Not knowing the real reason for his absence, naturally she was glad to see him again and more than willing to dance with him, especially in view of her fight with Jerry. And Jerry responded as she knew he would. He broke it up and pulled her away. And she reacted as could also be expected. She said, so Jerry could hear, 'See you later.'

"She didn't mean later that night, or any other specific time. She wasn't even talking for Costaine's benefit, only for Jerry's. She was getting back at him by saying, 'I'm going to keep right on seeing Walter, put that in your pipe and smoke it.'

"She might, in fact, have had no intention of ever visiting Costaine again. She might perfectly well have found someone new, someone whom she was *really* keeping secret from Jerry. For, after all, let's face it: Costaine had gone off and left her with no definite plans for a reunion and Sally wasn't the kind of girl who needed to be at a loss for men—especially once the ice had been broken. In any event, all the things she said and did were obviously aimed at getting Jerry's goat. Jerry was the man she centered on, not Costaine.

"As for the rest, it is too ordinary to waste time on. What is more natural than for Jerry to invite the group back to his house for a nightcap, especially if he wants to avoid a confrontation with his wife? And when the guests depart, what do Sally and Mrs. Bakewell talk about in the doorway? A place to buy fabrics at a discount! Can you imagine a woman, panting to be with her lover, discussing anything so prosaic?

"We don't know what happened after Jerry went to bed. We don't know why Sally changed her clothes, we don't know whom she might have telephoned or why. We don't even know what Walter Costaine himself was doing during this time.

"But we do know one thing. We know that a man cannot be declared guilty of a crime unless you, the jury, are convinced beyond reasonable doubt that he has committed that crime. And the doubts that Jerry Whittaker killed his wife, ladies and gentlemen, are not reasonable, they are inescapable.

"Under the circumstances, not just reasonable doubt, but certain doubt has been established, and I ask you to bring in the only verdict allowable under the circumstances. I ask that you judge the defendant not guilty."

Parrish spoke for just under an hour and his appeal was to reason rather than emotion. Emotion was what you went after when the evidence was against you and you had nothing else to fall back on. Parrish thought he was in a better position than that.

After a brief recess, Judge Simms delivered himself of his charge to the jury, a charge he had written and rewritten and polished over the days to make it memorable, to make it, hopefully, a monument. It dealt with the jury's responsibilities and obligations and took fifty-five minutes to read.

When he was through, the twelve members of the panel left the jury box and entered the jury room, the time being twenty minutes of five on that Wednesday afternoon, the second of June. The door was closed and locked behind them.

Now there was nothing to do but wait.

CHAPTER 70

When her phone rang, Melody left the typewriter in relief. It was two o'clock in the afternoon, the jury was still out, and she couldn't get anything done. Cleve was chewing marble off the walls at the courthouse, but the suspense was just as bad at the hotel.

She picked up on the third ring, expecting a reverse-charge call from Ma and wondering if she could hide her impatience. Ma would go on and on about Priscilla, the baby, and the breakup with Gary, when poor innocent Jerry Whittaker's future was all that mattered.

It was Gary Stevens himself, instead, the goddam bad penny. She felt positively ill. "What do you want?" she said. "I mean, how *much* do you want?"

He was penitent. "Sis, you've got it all wrong."

"I thought you were going to come up and tell Cleve on me."

"You know I'd never do that."

"Sure I do."

"Sis, you've always been the greatest. Haven't I always turned to you when I needed help? Ma 'n' Pa, they don't understand life. They're like children. They're not worldly like us. We're alike, you and me—the first and the last, brother and sister—"

She could imagine the warm, gushy smile on his face. The con artist, the cute one in the family. He had everybody snowed. But not her. Not any more. Not for a long time now. "Listen," she said, "if you think I'm going to try to patch things up between you and Priscilla—"

"No, no. I wouldn't ask you to do anything like that. I'm through with her. I'm going places, Sis, like you. She couldn't keep up."

"What is it you want? I'm busy."

"All right, I'll lay it on the line for you, Sis. I've got a deal going that will double our money in six months. It's a can't-miss thing. I've got everything I own in it, but it's not quite enough. I need a little more. Just one more thousand."

"You haven't paid me back the last thousand."

"I know. That's what I mean. This way you get your thousand back and the one I owe you. Whaddya say, Sis? It's only a gee and it'll make or break me."

"Go to hell."

He started to plead. "Sis, it means the world to me. You've got to understand that. I'm doing it for us! For us, kid."

The whining note in his voice irritated her. She was enough on edge already. "I don't want you doing anything for me and I don't want any part of your lousy deals. Get off my back."

"Sis, I'm desperate." For once he sounded sincere.

Cleve slammed into the presidential suite, swearing violently. All she could think of was Jerry Whittaker and she panicked. "Go to hell," she told Gary to be rid of him. "You've conned your last nickel out of me." She slammed the phone down in his ear and rushed into the next room. "Cleve, what is it? Did the jury—"

Cleve stormed around the living area. "The jury is still out. They're asking to see some of the exhibits. What's the matter with those goddam monsters? Don't they know what they're doing to me?" He came back to the dining table, picked up letters Melody had tried to type, threw them down and stalked off again. "I wonder if I overdressed him. Maybe the jury thought I was trying to phony him up!"

Melody gave one last thought to Gary, a wonder what his game was. But he couldn't touch her. He had lost his power. What happened to Jerry Whittaker was what mattered. That, and soothing Cleve.

"No, no. He was perfectly dressed. Don't be silly."

He lighted a cigarette, went to the windows and came back again. "Was I too cocky in my summation? I wonder if I sounded too sure!"

He was always wrought up over delayed verdicts, analyzing his performance. But this time she had been there and could judge. "No, Cleve. Your summation was brilliant. It left the jury with no alternative. It really did."

That kind of conciliation only enraged him. "Don't talk stupid. Juries always have alternatives! Why do you think they haven't reached a verdict? Why do you think the prosecutor winked at juror number five?"

She sipped cold coffee from the lunch tray by her typewriter. "Oh, Cleve, you're imagining things. By the way, Claude Decker phoned." That was one way to change the subject. "He wants you to call back right away."

Parrish wasn't moved. "He can goddam well wait. I can't get *his* son out of jail until I get Jerry out of jail. One goddam thing at a time."

Another approach was needed. Melody took a bite of half-eaten sandwich. "For heaven's sake, Cleve, you talk as if you've never won a case before. You have a fantastic success ratio. You don't lose one case in twenty."

"But this might be the one. That's the hell of it." He circled in front of the couches. "I wonder if the blacks on that jury know what I did for the Turner kid. Damn, I hate niggers and spics on juries. They've got it in for whitey. A white jury with black defendants—that's a piece of cake. But a black jury with white defendants—they'll kill you. They'd just love to bring down some nice, reputable guy like Whittaker. Clap him in the can, step on him, spit on him, ruin his life. Just because he's got white skin and making a good living!"

He turned and stared at walls. "But if they know I got Turner off, they might decide to give my client a break—do me a favor. Damn it, I've earned it from them!"

"Oh, Cleve," Melody said, "the jury isn't going to think that way. They're going to be judging the evidence."

"How do you know?" he said, wheeling on her. "You've never been on a jury. You don't know what goes on behind those doors."

"But there are only three blacks on the jury, Cleve. They can't determine the verdict all by themselves."

"They can if they get the whites feeling guilty. You know how this stupid society is these days—people with white skin blaming themselves because people with black skin got sold into slavery two hundred years before they were even born. Just because the slave traders had white skin. Those three blacks in there—they'll dominate that jury."

He went to the portable bar and poured himself a stiff belt of brandy. "I didn't want any blacks," he complained. "If only I'd had enough challenges."

Melody watched as he downed the drink in two quick gulps. It was more than three shots. "Well," she said, finishing her sandwich and sipping coffee, "if you get a bum verdict, you could use that as the basis of an appeal."

"That won't buy me anything. The Black Panthers went through the whole bit, challenging the method of jury selection, and it was upheld."

She'd go to pieces herself if he kept on like that. "Why don't you go back there and wait? It probably won't be much longer."

He shook his head. "I can't stand it over there. And that jury isn't going to reach a verdict today anyway. I can feel it. They're going to kick it around tomorrow and all weekend while we sweat." He looked into his glass and put it down. He turned and eyed Melody. "C'mere."

"What?"

He gestured perfunctorily. "C'mere."

She set aside her coffee. "What's the trouble?" She approached him wonderingly.

He put one hand around her waist and pulled her close. The other went for her breast.

It was totally unexpected and she felt outraged. "Now, just a minute."

He tried to kiss her. "I want you. Forget your work and come into the bedroom."

The arrogance! She twisted her face to avoid his lips but she couldn't get away. The arm around her waist was like a clamp and his hand was kneading her breast painfully. "If you want sex, get Katherine Lord," she gasped, fighting for breath.

His lips were on her throat. "Don't you understand yet?" he growled. "I only went to bed with her so I could show her up on the stand."

Melody didn't believe him. She didn't disbelieve him either. He was quite capable of such a tactic. There was nothing he wouldn't do to get a client off—except cheat. And that was only because he wouldn't risk his own neck for anybody.

"I don't care," Melody said. "Let me go. Find another woman for your whoring."

"God damn it, you're the only woman and you know it."

She struggled. She tried to tell him it was different now. She had only agreed to stay with him through the Whittaker case, and this wasn't part of it. He wasn't listening.

"Cleve! You're tearing my blouse."

"Then unbutton it." He loosened his grip and pushed her toward the bedroom.

He'll rape me, she thought incredulously. He'll really rape me. She was certain of it. He would beat her, hurt her, do what he had to do to force her. He was wild and frantic. Not with desire for her; she knew better than that. He had to unwind, to escape the tension and torment of waiting for that jury. He would rape her, if need be, to forget.

She stumbled toward the bedroom, held and maneuvered by the all-powerful lawyer. She was going to be laid—willingly or unwillingly. Parrish had made the decision and it was final.

There was the bed, the one against the wall, the one she had found him and Katherine on. That was the one for her as well—not the nearer bed, the bed he slept on. This was the bed he screwed on.

What was that old "Confucius say" line? "If rape inevitable, relax and enjoy."

Gary Stevens looked up when the door of his cell was opened. A bushy-haired and bearded young man, wearing a jacket and tie, came in. "Your name is Stevens?"

Gary nodded but remained seated on the side of the bunk.

The man made no move to shake hands. He said his name was Bonner and that he was the public defender. "You have a lawyer of your own?"

"No."

"Have you got bail money?"

"Where do you think I can lay my hands on a thousand bucks in a hurry?"

"No family or friends?"

"Nobody I can hit for that kind of money."

The man named Bonner asked him other questions: about whether he had ever been in trouble before, what his educational background was, where he had worked, and what positions he'd held. Gary told him the truth most of the time. Then the man told him he'd been charged with breaking and entering this gas station in this small town in Pennsylvania and how did he wish to plead?

Gary shrugged. "Not guilty."

"The two policemen who arrested you say they found a broken window and you inside. How are you going to explain that?"

"I wanted some gas."

"There were a lot of stations still open."

"Look, what do you want from me?"

"Help in getting you the best break we can. You have no prior arrest record so the chances are they'll go easy with you. You didn't have any money, you were desperate—"

"Well, what the hell am I supposed to do when I'm outta dough, starve?"

CHAPTER 71

The jury did not stay out over the weekend. It reached its decision at eleven-thirty Friday morning. The word was relayed to the proper parties and from there it radiated by grapevine throughout not only the courthouse but the whole of downtown New Haven.

By the time Parrish and Balin were mustered and ready, the courtroom was jammed with press and spectators. Vince Masters and Jeff Kelly toyed with papers at their desk and the big room groaned under the weight of people while its air sparkled with the excited hum of anticipation.

Parrish and Balin took seats at the defense table and now, with them on hand, all was ready. Whittaker was led in to take his chair and Judge Simms appeared from the opposite side. The room was abuzz with excitement and everyone leaped to his feet when Simms came into view. It was a response programmed by expectancy.

Then the judge was seated and the rest followed suit. Simms adjusted the pad before him and said, "Bailiff, you may summon the jury."

When the door opened, the first juror out was the young, twenty-nine-year-old Negro, Edgar Milford. So he was the foreman! Parrish thought surely it would be the retired history professor. What had he told Melody about blacks infesting whites with guilt? Maybe it was really true!

Milford solemnly led the way into the first row of seats, taking the end one nearest the witness stand. The others followed, filling the remaining chairs. Kitty Haus and Marline Bender looked at Whittaker. The others did not. The claim is that if the jury looks at the defendant, the verdict is innocent, if they look away, the

328

verdict is guilty. Parrish was too experienced to believe juries ran that true to form. He knew it was impossible to guess the verdict by the faces and actions of the jurors, yet that was exactly what he was doing. It was what he always did. And, as always, he couldn't be sure of anything.

"Has the jury reached a verdict?"

Milford said, "We have."

"Would you stand and face the prisoner?"

Milford rose and looked soberly at Whittaker for a moment, but turned when the clerk started to read the charge and to ask whether the jury found the defendant guilty or not guilty of the charge of murder in the first degree.

Edgar Milford spoke in a steady voice. "We find the defendant not guilty of that charge." He paused and there was an incompleteness about it. He seemed to be waiting for a cue.

The clerk said, "Do you have anything further?"

"Yes," Milford replied. "We find the defendant guilty of murder in the second degree."

CHAPTER 72

There was pandemonium. Three reporters broke from the room. The bailiff pounded his gavel and kept pounding.

Balin was open-mouthed; Whittaker sat stunned and shrunken, a little old man; and Cleveland Parrish stared as if struck by lightning. Milford remained standing, his eyes on the clerk. The other jurors were statues, their faces fixed, devoid of expression, showing no response to the verdict or to the commotion it caused. Two spectators rose and bent over someone on the floor. A bailiff hurried to the spot. Katherine Lord had fainted.

Simms, sounding faintly stern, threatened to clear the courtroom and a semblance of quiet was restored. Those who had risen from their chairs sat down again, except for the ones reviving the attractive Miss Lord and assisting her from the room.

Finally the clerk could make himself heard. "So say you all?" he asked of the jury and they chorused assent as Milford sat down.

Cleveland Parrish, still in shock, pushed himself to his feet. It was beyond belief! He worried and he sweated. He was always pessimistic about outcomes, but that was only surface. Deep down he was ever certain he would win, and never more so than on the present occasion. The State had no case! The State had nothing!

"Your Honor," he said, "I request that the jury be polled." That would do it. Make all twelve of them say "second degree." It was a put-up job. It was a crazy verdict. Sally Whittaker had been murdered deliberately and with malice aforethought. Nothing could be plainer than that. So whoever had killed her was guilty of murder in the first degree. If Whittaker was the killer, then the verdict should be first degree. If someone else had killed her, then the verdict should be innocent. It was all or nothing.

But this jury had come in with something else. It was a compromise verdict. Some members of that jury weren't happy with it. And if they were made to state, loud and clear, in open court, that they supported that verdict, they just might recant. Then Parrish could claim a mistrial.

The clerk was saying, "Number six. Gilbert Muncy. Is that your verdict; murder in the second degree?"

"It is."

The bailiff tolled, "One."

"Number nine. Kitty Haus. Is that your verdict: murder in the second degree?"

"It is."

"Two."

Parrish searched their faces. All looked firm. Every one of them would say, "It is." He knew it. The crazy, stupid, incomprehensible verdict was going to stand. He looked at Whittaker, beside him. The doctor was staring at the jurors as the poll was taken and tears were in his eyes. Parrish put a firm hand on his forearm and leaned close. "This is the most incredible miscarriage of justice I've seen in all my years in court!"

Whittaker nodded numbly and a tear ran down his cheek.

"Number sixty. Shirley Rogers. Is that your verdict: murder in the second degree?"

She nodded. "It is."

"Eight."

"Number seventy-one. William Sturgess—"

Parrish looked around. The spectator sections remained jammed but an uneasy quiet had fallen. The eyes were on him. "They figure the city slicker got taken by the hicks," Parrish thought bitterly. "The sons of bitches, the lot of them. And what about the case of that kid—the cannibal? His old man won't be happy at my losing this one. But I've got his fifty grand. He's stuck with me. But I'll get the kid off. I don't care if they find a human arm in his stomach, I'll get the son of a bitch off."

"It is," said juror 107, Marline Bender.

"Twelve," said the bailiff.

That was it. Nobody reneged. Nobody even hesitated. Not one in the whole goddam twelve of them, the stupid jerks. Who in God's green earth got the idea of entrusting human lives and human fortunes to the whims of other humans—of motley arrays of other humans—of motley arrays of dumb, stupid, prejudiced, ignorant, brainless humans? Even that goddam Yale history professor. Does he fancy himself an intellectual? He's a spineless nothing. He should have led them, and all he did was follow.

The judge thanked the jury and said he couldn't remark on the verdict because certain motions might be made and he could not show bias. Parrish, watching, felt that Simms didn't seem appalled by the verdict. Even so, he rose and made the obvious motion. "Your Honor," he said, careful not to sound undone, "I move that the court set aside the verdict."

Of course it didn't work. Judge Simms denied the motion firmly and without hesitation. Parrish sat down again. What else could he have expected? Simms and his pious preachings about law and the American judicial system. You could damned well bet he'd never take exception to a jury verdict. Twelve good men and true: that was what Simms set his course by. Anybody else could see what a faulty, inept, totally wrong verdict it was. But not Simms. If the verdict had been to cut off Whittaker's big toe, Simms would have salaamed and said, "Thank you, O Great and Glorious Jury."

Now it was over. The jury was excused, the judge left, Jerry Whittaker was taken away, and spectators began scraping chairs and departing. A date for sentencing would be set but it was a formality. The automatic sentence for second degree was life imprisonment, which meant a minimum of twenty years before one could apply for parole.

Balin turned and shook his head. "I just don't understand juries," he said. "You were magnificent."

"Yeah."

"Say, how about us having a drink and working something out? My club is right around the corner."

It was bad enough losing the verdict. Parrish was goddamned if he was going to get stuck with Balin to boot. Besides, he had his eye on that history prof, Ellsworth Deming. He wanted to corner him and say, "Just what the hell did you people do in that jury room?"

"Sorry," he said, getting up. "I've got some calls to make." He put a hand on Balin's shoulder to keep him down. "I'll see you later."

At the door, two reporters cornered him. Was he surprised at the verdict?

"Could anybody not be?"

"What do you think of the verdict?"

"It has as much relevance to the case at hand as finding him guilty of cattle rustling."

"Are you going to appeal?"

"To the Supreme Court." He craned his neck. Deming was getting away. He was across the corridor heading for the exit.

"If you had it to do over, would you handle the defense any differently?"

"I don't know. I can't answer that off the top of my head. Look, I have to see someone." He was always the soul of politeness with the press. "Can I talk to you later?"

He moved on quickly across the corridor, past the elevators and out the front door. He looked around but Deming wasn't in sight. Damn, damn, damn. This was one of those days. Nothing went right.

He turned and almost bumped into the mountainous county detective, Bill Coyne. Coyne grinned and called him counselor and edged past. Parrish caught his arm. "Say, tell me one thing. Who the hell tipped Masters off about Katherine Lord?"

Coyne rubbed his massive chin. "Why you did, Counselor."

"I?"

"Yeah. You brought her to a restaurant in Killingworth I and my ma were eating at. I got curious and tagged along to see where you left her and who she was. I couldn't get a line on her, thought she was a friend of Costaine's but that wasn't right. So I sprung Whittaker's name on her and that was punching the right button." He chuckled. "I could see why you were keeping her under wraps."

"She didn't do you a damned bit of good, I suppose you know."

Coyne grinned. "At least we kept you from springing her on us." He went down the steps, the breeze stirring his thinning red hair.

"The nosy son of a bitch," Cleve muttered to himself, but was glad Coyne hadn't found out more about Katherine Lord. The thought of himself being revealed as her lover made him shudder. He still wondered how he'd dared risk the chance in his cross-examination.

He craned, still searching for Deming and, coming out the door, was Marline Bender, juror number 107. "Oh," she said a little awkwardly, "uh, hello." She acted as if she still had to keep arm's distance from the principals in the case. She looked away and started to go around him.

"Mrs. Bender," Parrish said, turning on as much charm as he could muster, "could I speak to you for a minute?"

She was uncertain. She explained she and the other jurors were going to have lunch together. Sort of a final celebration—er—party—er—get-together—and she had to hurry.

"I'm just curious about the verdict."

"Oh," she said. "It's nothing against you. You did a wonderful job. You did the best for him that anyone could have done."

(Why, the damned, patronizing slut.)

"Yes, well, I'm curious. What happened in that jury room to produce that verdict?"

"Oh, I don't know. We took a poll Wednesday afternoon. Young Edgar did, as soon as we elected him foreman. He took a secret ballot. It came out nine guilty, three innocent. So then we each explained what we thought and we talked. That was all day yesterday. And today the other three came around. But they didn't want it first degree. They were insistent about that; all three of them. They didn't want any possibility of a death penalty. They didn't even want to discuss such a matter. So we agreed we'd all go for second. It's just the same, really, because we wouldn't have voted the death penalty for him, even though I personally think he deserves it."

"But what turned you against him? That's what I don't understand. What made you think he did it?"

"Oh," she said. "There were two things, really. One was that girl, that Katherine Lord. She was so attractive. We all liked her. But you made her out as nothing; as—well, practically a streetwalker. And she wasn't. We could tell. We could feel it. So we thought, 'There's something funny here. Otherwise, Mr. Parrish wouldn't do that to her.'

"Then, when the doctor took the stand, he was fine until he started talking about her. Then he changed. He was pretending he didn't really like her and you could tell he was lying.

"We didn't mind their being in love, but when they tried to pretend they weren't, that's when we knew he was guilty. That's what convinced the three who thought he was innocent. If he was innocent, they wouldn't have had to lie.

"But," she said, "that's not your fault. You tried your best to hide it that they were involved with each other."

"I see," he said, trying not to be curt. "Thank you. Well, I won't keep you from your lunch."

He went down the broad front steps away from her, away from people. He didn't want anyone to see the bitterness on his face. You guess. You try. But there's no telling about jurors. That's the whole goddam trouble with the jury system. You're bright. You study law. You know the business. You can talk to judges. You can work on judges, work on other lawyers, manipulate them, move them around the way you want—if you're smart enough and knowledgeable enough. But those stupid, dumb clucks that are called in to serve on juries! You can't read their minds because they haven't got minds. You don't know what to do with them. You don't know what they're going to come up with. You might as well try to guess the weather.

Parrish crossed the green, seething with rage and frustration. He went up in the elevator and into his suite. Melody was there to meet him, her face dismayed. "I was outside," she said. "I heard. Is it true? They really called him guilty?"

"They damned well did. Second degree, if you can believe such a thing!"

"You're going to appeal, aren't you?"

"Yeah. At least I'll make all the right noises."

She sobered. "What's that mean?"

Parrish poured himself a brandy and his mouth set wryly. "The

334

trouble with soft, lenient, wishy-washy judges, my sweet, is that while they're letting you run wild in the courtroom, they're also not giving you anything to complain about. What are you going to appeal a verdict on? It's going to be that your client didn't get a fair shake. So you attack the judge as having kept you from presenting all that you wanted to present. You take exception to the opposition objections that he sustains. But when a judge is as lenient as that stupid ass Simms, we're up a tree. He let me do everything I wanted to do. So if we try to claim my client didn't get a fair shake, I'd have to say *I'm* the one who didn't give it to him."

"But you did!"

"Of course I did. I did everything I could."

"You mean, then, there's nothing you can do for Jerry?"

"I mean I want you to get me what's-his-name on the phone—the father of the cannibal, the alleged cannibal. I haven't been paying enough attention to him."

CHAPTER 73

Parrish talked to Claude Decker for half an hour, getting his mind off the old case and onto the new. Sure, he could save the boy. No question about it.

That was the thing. Never let your lickings shake your confidence. He would have won the Whittaker case too, except for the screwiest imponderables. He eliminates the Whittaker-Lord love affair as a motive and the jury puts it back in as a motive—just because he had eliminated it. If he'd left it in, they'd probably have found Whittaker innocent! There's no figuring juries. But, of course, if Cleve could figure them, his record would read all wins and no losses.

Anyway, with the present case over, except for the technicalities—appeals and such—it was time to move ahead with Decker.

How did the Whittaker case come out? Decker wanted to know.

"Guilty of murder two," Cleve said, and went on to paint the out-come as a victory. After all, the charge was murder one. "I could have gotten him a light sentence on an insanity plea if he'd let me. But he was foolish. He insisted on pleading innocent."

"But he was really guilty?"

"Of course he was. He told me so himself."

After the phone call, Cleve had Pete Tucker drive him to Zack Whittaker's drugstore on Elm Street. If that flea-bitten creep was go-ing to come to the aid of his son, it had better be now.

A plumber's truck was parked in front and renovations were going on inside. A soda fountain was being installed where the old cash register used to be, and a strange young man was behind the glass in the prescription room. A sharp-nosed, toothy man with his hands in his pockets, was rocking on his heels and overseeing the new installa-tions. He seemed to be in charge.

Parrish asked him about Zacharias Whittaker and the toothy man shrugged lackluster shoulders. "He's moved out. I don't know where he's gone."

Parrish explained who he was and his relationship to the Whittaker clan. That made toothface more communicative. "Wraxler's my name. Martin Wraxler. I just bought the old man out."

Aha, Parrish thought. Zacharias had anticipated the need. "Because of his son?"

"Well, that's the funny thing," Wraxler answered, stopping to warn the plumbers against scratching the sink. He peeled a cigar. "It was right after it came out about young Jerry and that mistress he had. The old man called me up that night and said he'd sell. I mentioned something about his son needing the money and the old guy said it wasn't for his son. He and his wife were going to retire to Florida."

"Florida?"

"Yeah, except the last I heard, the wife's in the hospital, doing pretty poorly, so I guess he's still around."

Wraxler didn't know where the old man was, but thought Parrish could trace him through the hospital, or the lawyer who handled the sale. Wraxler had forgotten his name, but could look it up.

Parrish said thanks and got out of there. He'd be following a lost cause trying to get help out of that sanctimonious old Bible-reader. He could read the bastard's mind. His son was a sinner and deserved to be punished. Well, nothing to do but go over and see Jerry.

They sat together at the table in the narrow, screened compart-ment and Whittaker looked sick and discouraged. "I still can't get over it," he said. "I always believed in our system of justice. I always had this naïve faith that nothing could happen to an innocent man. I thought if I obeyed all the laws, did a good deed every day, and kept my nose clean, nothing could happen to me."

"That's the way it usually is," Parrish told him. "But once in a while, like now, everything will go haywire. This is the most flagrant miscarriage of justice I've seen in my whole professional career. I can't believe it myself."

"What did we do wrong?"

"We didn't do anything wrong. It's the jury that did the wrong."

Whittaker sighed dispiritedly and took one of Parrish's cigarettes. "So what do we do next?"

"There isn't much we can do, except possibly appeal."

"How do we do that?"

"The first thing you do is get a lot of money together."

Whittaker laughed mirthlessly. "Yeah, ha ha. Big joke. I don't have any money."

"Well, you're damned well going to have to get some. We can't do anything without money."

Whittaker shook his head dazedly. "But what do we need all this money for?"

"In the first place, we have to pay to have a transcript of the trial typed up. The cost for that is a dollar per page and fifty cents for each carbon and I don't know how many hundreds of pages there'll be. And that's just the beginning. So you'd better start thinking who you can raise money from."

"What about the money I paid you? There must be enough left—"

Parrish's snort was equally mirthless. "Are you kidding? I must be ten thousand dollars out of pocket. Look at your house. I'm going to take a big licking on that. Real estate, especially in that price range, just isn't moving these days. All the agents in the area are crying. I'll be lucky if I can get fifty thousand for it and after the mortgage is paid off, I'm not going to be left with enough—"

"But it's worth seventy-five at least. I paid sixty-five six years ago and land has been going up ever since. If you just hold onto it a while—"

"I can't hold onto it. That's the trouble. I've got creditors to pay. They're not going to sit around waiting for prices to go up. They want their money now." He shook his head sadly. "No, this case has really cost me. I'm up to my neck in debt because of it. I can't go in any deeper."

"If you could just lend me the money—"

When would the stupid jerk grasp the facts of life? "Now, listen, Jerry," Parrish said in a stern tone, "I believe in you. I know you're innocent of any wrongdoing. I know you got stuck with a bum rap. I know it's cost me a hell of a lot of money trying to see justice done. But I don't stake clients. That's not the way I do business. I'm not a charitable organization."

Whittaker seized the lawyer's arm. "But, Cleve, once I'm cleared, I'll be worth over three hundred thousand dollars. I could afford anything then."

"Sorry."

"I'll give you half. I'll give you half of Sally's holdings. I'll give you half of her insurance too."

"Stop it, Jerry. You don't have Sally's holdings or Sally's insurance."

"But when I get a new trial—"

Parrish wished he'd shut up. Didn't he see it was his own fault he was back in jail? He was the one who had blown the case. The jurors convicted him because they thought he was lying and, to their mediocre little minds, an innocent man wouldn't need to lie. Of course, there was a certain merit to that, but the point was that Jerry was responsible for his own predicament and responsible for Cleve losing a case he shouldn't have had to lose. No getting around it. Jerry Whittaker was bad news and the sooner rid of him the better. That cannibal case was beckoning and Parrish wasn't fool enough to underwrite Jerry's delaying tactics.

"Not *when* you get a new trial," he interrupted. "*If* you get a new trial. There's a big difference between those two words."

Jerry stared at him. "You don't mean there's any doubt about it, do you? A miscarriage of justice like that?"

"Let's say, miscarriage, in OUR opinion. I'll lay you odds Vincent Masters doesn't think there's been any miscarriage. And since our view can be considered prejudiced, the Supreme Court of Connecticut isn't going to be impressed. The Supreme Court is going to want tangible evidence that you weren't given a fair trial."

"Well then, let's give them some tangible evidence!"

"I'll be glad to. Do you have any ideas? Is there anything about the trial that strikes you as unfair—other than the verdict?"

Whittaker hesitated and slowly withdrew his hand. "You mean—you mean, I might not get another trial?"

"I mean, if you can raise enough money to get a trial transcript, we can go through it page by page and see if there isn't something somewhere that we can say was prejudicial to your rights. But I'm going to tell you frankly, Jerry, I listen for things like that. All the time a trial is on, I'm listing all errors and all possible errors so that I'll know what to appeal on and how much chance an appeal has got if we get the wrong verdict. And I have to say, there is nothing sensible—nothing that realistically has much of a chance of altering the verdict or giving you another trial."

Whittaker's eyes widened slowly. "What you're doing is telling me to forget it? To sit here in jail for twenty years?"

Parrish was quick in his reply. "No, I'm not telling you to forget it. For Christ's sake, what do you think? No, I'm telling you to go ahead, raise the money, get the transcript, and we'll see what we've got. But I'd also be less than honest with you if I didn't tell you to be prepared for the possibility that there's going to be nothing you can do. I'm telling you you just may have to spend the next twenty years in jail." He patted his arm. "It's not a foregone conclusion, mind you. I'm not telling you it's going to happen. But you'd be smart to get yourself psychologically adjusted so that if that's the way the ball bounces, you won't be caught unprepared."

"Yeah," Whittaker said bitterly. "Unprepared!"

"But you're going to fight. You've got everything to gain and nothing to lose. Get some money together and we'll get the transcript and we'll find something in there we can complain about and if we get a sympathetic judge—"

Whittaker was angry now. "Money, money! Damn it, I keep telling you I haven't got any money and I can't get any money!"

"What about Katherine? She'll stake you."

"I can't take money from her."

"If you're going to let false pride or anything else keep you from grabbing money anywhere you can get it, you're a damned fool. You'll be buying yourself twenty years in prison, do you understand that?"

"Katherine doesn't have any money, to begin with. And even if she did, I can't ask her for anything now. Not after what I said and she said on the stand."

"Oh, for Christ's sake, forget the trial. She's nuts about you. She'll give you the money."

"She doesn't have any money, I tell you. I helped her with the rent. Don't you know that? She might not even be able to keep the place now."

"Well, then, try a bank. Try your wealthy friends. Try your patients. Make them the offer you made me. You'll give them half of Sally's estate, if you can collect her estate."

"Fat chance," the doctor said glumly. "If you wouldn't do it, nobody else will."

"Lots of people would jump at the chance. Most people are born gamblers. I'm not, but most of the rest of mankind is." Parrish rose and put a hand on the doctor's shoulder in a parting gesture. "That's what you're going to do, Jerry. Draw up a list of potential contributors to the Gerald Whittaker Defense Fund: people who want to gamble for a share of future treasure. You're going to list everybody you can think of and send them a form letter and when you get twenty thousand dollars in contributions, kiddo, we're in business." Cleve looked at his watch and said he had to run. "I'll drop in and see you tomorrow before I go back to New York. Have that list ready."

CHAPTER 74

In his dreary steel and stone cell, Dr. Gerald Whittaker, former internist, now a convicted murderer, sat on his bunk and sobbed as he had not sobbed since he was ten. The tears were not only of frustration and bewilderment, but hopelessness and despair. Parrish so glibly talked of canvassing friends for money. There were no friends. There was no money.

He didn't even have parents any more. His father had not come to see him since the Katherine Lord affair and Jerry knew why. His father would not interfere with the Lord's vengeance.

Jerry looked around at the bleak, hard horror of his surroundings. He had borne it for six months because he had believed he would go free. He had believed that, at this particular moment, he would be out in Madison, gathering together the remnants of his life for a new beginning. Now, twenty years of existence in a cell stretched before him, and he could not harbor the thought.

He lifted his head. His name was being called. He had another visitor.

The guard came through the narrow corridor and opened his door. Yes, he was the anointed one. There was someone to see him, to break the endless monotony of prison, someone to breathe to him the air of freedom, someone who could come and go, as he could not.

His thought, as he followed the guard down the way, was that Parrish had returned—with hope. He believed in Parrish. Parrish saved the innocent. Parrish never lost cases. Parrish insured that justice was done. And Parrish would save him in the end. Parrish would never let lack of money stop him. Parrish was good and pure and true, the knight in white armor, battling to the death.

When he got to the cage, he saw that it wasn't Parrish who had come. The visitor was outside the grilled metal screen and would have to communicate from there, as she had on all the other occasions. It was Katherine.

Gerald hadn't seen her since the trial began, since long before their testimony and the horrible answers they each had given to Parrish's terrible questions. He wondered now why he had spoken that way. Was it only in self-defense? Or was there vengeance involved?

He looked at her and his breath caught, but he didn't know what he felt. Was he glad or sorry she had come?

"Hello, Katherine."

He moved to the screen and didn't wait for the guard to depart. It didn't matter if the guard overheard. Nothing mattered any longer.

"Jerry!" Katherine was behind the iron rail that kept her from standing as close to the screen as he. Her eyes were swimming and a million years of suffering were in her face. It was a beautiful face. It said she was his. Everything about her said she was his. But, of course, she wasn't his. She had turned from him and gone with other men. Perhaps she couldn't be blamed, but he had thought—he had believed—

"How are you?" Jerry answered and wondered if his eyes stared at her as hers did at him, as if to melt distance.

"I have to talk to you, Jerry. I have to explain."

He shook his head not to hear. No one could explain such things. The fact that one tried meant that one could not. "No," he whispered. "It's all right. I don't blame you." He lifted his hands. "I'm here and—"

341

Tears started down her cheeks. She closed her eyes and rocked her head from side to side. "You don't understand. There was never anyone else. There never could be. You must know that."

He nodded. "I do." He could almost believe it. When she was this close, talking in this manner, what could he do but believe?

Yet she had gone with other men. Whether or not they meant anything to her, she had gone with them. And that made it different. She was different. He could see that now. Was there not a harder look in her face than he had noted before?

Or was he bemused?

It didn't matter, really. What mattered was that he looked for these things. That made it different. All of it was different and no one could turn back the clock. Their relationship could never be what it had been, even if they both wanted it to be. They had found out too much about each other.

"I had to say those things," she told him. "It was to help you. That was why Cleve asked those questions."

"He knew about you—you and other men?"

"One other man. Only one. And he—"

Whittaker broke in tightly. "I don't want to know about him, Katherine. One or twenty-one, it's all the same. I'll believe you were lonely, that he took advantage. I believe all those things. I forgive them too."

Her tears were blinding her. They ran down her face and throat, into her collar. "But I don't forgive myself."

"It doesn't matter."

"It matters terribly."

"I mean, it doesn't matter, because I've done just as bad."

"You haven't done anything."

"You heard me. I lied on the stand."

"No, you didn't."

"I lied. I said I led you on, that I didn't really love you, that I only said I couldn't marry you because I didn't want to. And I wanted to more than anything in the world."

"I believe you."

"But I betrayed you. Do you know what Judas did to Christ? He denied him, to save his own life. And I did it too. I sold you out and I repent too late."

She shook her head. "But you had to. After what I said, you had no choice."

"I did have a choice. And I made the wrong one. And I must pay the penalty."

"It's not too late." She leaned forward. "You're going to get out. I'm going to get you out. No matter what, I'm going to get you out. Believe in me, darling."

He nodded. He said, "I believe," but he didn't believe. She had no weapons, she had no money, she had nothing but desire—and he could no longer be absolutely sure she had that. If he could fly over prison walls to her little bungalow in the Clinton woods, would he find an empty home? Or would another man's clothes hang in the closet where his used to hang?

The thought wrenched him and he thrust it away. He could trust her. He knew her, didn't he? If he had ever known another human being, didn't he know her? Could it all be false?

But again, the fact that he could question was the fact that damned. There was no hope, there was nothing. They could talk, she could cry, and both could promise the world. But today was not yesterday and could never be.

He looked at the tears on her fresh young cheeks. He impressed her features on his memory, the short nose, the dark, flowing hair, the enormous open-hearted eyes, the full lips, and told himself to etch every detail on his brain to make it last. Because he knew he would never see her again.

CHAPTER 75

Cleve Parrish, in bathrobe and slippers, let the bellhop in with the breakfast cart and a meal for two. When the boy had gone, he called Melody and she appeared from his bedroom in a powder blue dress and pink scarf. He had screwed hell out of her last night and felt better toward the world. She had been pliant, even willing, which was an improvement on the hard time she'd given him Thursday afternoon.

That was what he needed her for. Sex was his solace, as much so now as it had been in his riotous school days when he could forget failing grades in the exploration of girls' bodies. Now, in the morning light, his values were reordered, the horrors of the case were receding. He could even look out on the green and that lousy, goddam courthouse without wincing.

They sat down to breakfast together and Melody opened the accompanying newspaper.

She screamed. She put her hands to her face and screamed again. Then she was upsetting the chair and fleeing to the bedroom, her cries of hysteria reverberating throughout the suite.

Cleve, up on his feet, stared after her. He looked down at the open paper. Even inverted the huge headlines were unmistakable. "WHITTAKER SUICIDE IN CELL."

He picked up and skimmed the article. Dr. Gerald Whittaker had hanged himself with his shirt. There was no note and no other explanation than his being found guilty of murder. Two visitors had called on him after the verdict: his lawyer, Cleveland Parrish, and his mistress, Katherine Lord.

Parrish snarled in rage, crumpled the paper and threw it at the couch. In the bedroom, Melody's screams had degenerated into torn and broken sobbing. He moved to the door and pushed it open. She lay on the rumpled bed they had used for love.

"Crying isn't going to help," he said. "What are you taking it so hard for?"

"I feel so guilty."

"Guilty about what?"

She rolled over, sobbing, and sat up. "It's such a shock," she moaned. She blotted her eyes with her napkin. "I feel so awful. I feel as if we could have helped him. We could have done something for him."

"I did do something for him," Parrish answered. "I did everything I could. I was very encouraging about an appeal. I told him we'd give it the old college try. I don't know what the hell got into him."

The phone rang and it was Balin. He'd just heard the news. "I was going to see him today," he said. "I was going to tell him not to be discouraged, not to give up hope. I was going to tell him there were all kinds of things we could do."

"Yeah. Good try, Balin. But I told him the same thing yesterday. I don't know what got into him."

"I drew up his will, you know. He named me executor of his estate."

Parrish all but snorted. Whittaker didn't have an estate. Out of curiosity he said, "Who inherits?"

"Sally. I drew it up several years ago. He didn't change it."

Balin went on about the funeral home and when and where the funeral would be. Tuesday, in Madison, he said. Perhaps Cleve would serve as a pallbearer?

Like hell Cleve Parrish would be a pallbearer. He wasn't hanging around New Haven past noon today—in fact, *until* noon, since now he wouldn't have to visit Whittaker—and he wasn't going to have anything more to do with that idiot Balin. And he certainly wasn't going to permit any further unnecessary linking of his name with Whittaker's. God damn it, such publicity was damaging.

Cleve told Balin he couldn't possibly be a pallbearer, much as he'd give a right arm to. He had commitments in New York that he simply could not get out of. But thanks for asking him. He felt signally honored.

He hung up and the phone rang again. This time it was a reporter wanting a comment. Cleve told him it was one of the greatest tragedies of our judicial system. He himself stood foursquare behind the structure and operation of the system, but human error does occasionally produce a miscarriage of justice. Such a miscarriage had happened to Whittaker, and while there was every expectation that the wrong would be righted, and he had told Whittaker exactly that the preceding afternoon, apparently the doctor's mind gave way beneath the strain and stress he'd been living under for the past six months. As for Parrish, no, he had not discerned anything in the doctor's manner that led him to suspect such a thing would happen. If he'd had the slightest inkling, why he would have taken immediate steps to protect the poor man and give him psychiatric help.

Melody came out and sat down at the breakfast table. She was in shock but under control. Cleve sat down opposite her, both toyed with their scrambled eggs, and the buzzer rang. Cleve swore and Melody went to answer.

He could see a touch of scarf under her well-set hair as she stood in the partly opened doorway framed between the jamb and the panel. One hand fondled the knob and she shifted her weight from foot to foot. She was talking to someone but he couldn't hear. Then she said, "No, you can't come in, he's busy." She started to close the door but suddenly she leaped back. "Cleve! It's a gun!"

Parrish sprang to his feet, his heart pounding. Melody retreated past the portable bar to the far side of the breakfast table. Following her, holding a newspaper in one hand and a gun in the other, was Katherine Lord.

Cleve took a half step to the side of the table. He could get to the living room, but there was no way out. "Katherine," he said, but his voice lacked its customary authority.

She stopped and held out the paper with its giant headlines. "Look what you've done," she cried out. "The dearest, kindest, noblest man alive. And you killed him!"

"I?" Cleve pretended shock. He had to dissuade her, to disarm her with talk. There were eight feet between them. It was point-blank range and he didn't want to die. "I didn't kill him."

"You did! He didn't kill himself. You did it to him!" Her voice grew alarmingly wild. "Murderer! Murderer!"

The gun waved menacingly and Cleve's knees trembled. He gripped the chair back and pleaded. "Katherine, you're distraught. I know how much you loved Jerry and what a shock this is, but you mustn't let it derange you. You must keep control of yourself!"

"You're a bloodsucker! You suck people's blood. You drained him. You took away everything he owned. You took me. You even took his pride. He didn't kill himself. He was already dead."

Parrish made soothing noises, but he could not move. His face was wet, his skin was gray, and his legs weighed tons. What would she do to him?

"You're the one who ought to be dead," she said in bitter tones. "Not him!"

He tried to swallow. "Katherine, Katherine, you've got it all wrong."

She was looking at him with steadfast hate. The knuckles of her gun hand were white. Cleve tried to pray. She took a little step.

Melody sprang. She was like a cat, quick and deadly, and Katherine almost left her feet from the unexpected impact. Katherine snarled and struggled, but Melody had her wrist and was clawing for the gun. She was lithe, desperate, and strong; Katherine, weak and uncertain.

"Yes, yes," Cleve cried. "Get the gun, Melody." He started forward at last, but he wasn't needed. Melody, panting, had won the fight, and Katherine stood disarmed and sobbing.

"My God," Melody said, staring at the instrument in her hand. "It's a toy."

"Of course it is," Katherine cried. "If I had a real gun I wouldn't have talked to him, I would have killed him." She put her face in her hands and wept.

Parrish was once more the master of the situation. Inside, he wanted to kill her with an equal passion. He had never been so tortured and terrified. She had almost made him wet his pants.

He controlled himself. "Now, you listen to me," he said, letting his ferocity breed justification. "It's Jerry's own fault he got convicted. I gave him the best defense there was."

"You gave him nothing," she cried out. "All you did was take. You took everything. Even his girl. And you rubbed his nose in it."

Parrish said through his teeth, "Listen, if you were fool enough to tell him about us, then his death—"

"I didn't tell him *who*," she sobbed in rage. "But I didn't lie to him. I told him it happened. I had to tell him that because you made me say it in court. I tried to tell him it didn't matter. I tried to tell him I'd save him." Her voice broke into sobs again. "But what could he believe then? What could it matter? You had destroyed what he and I had together. We couldn't get it back again. I tried, but we couldn't. And he went and killed himself."

Parrish stepped close, making her draw back. "Don't be such a stupid ass," he snapped at her. He was in full control now. "Jerry didn't kill himself because of you—or me. He killed himself because he lost the game."

"Lost the game?" she flared back. "He didn't lose a game. He lost the world."

"That's right—his world. He thought he could have it all, but society wouldn't buy it for him."

She backed away from his leering face. "What are you talking about?"

"He killed his wife and he got what was coming to him. And when he saw he was going to have to pay the piper, he took the coward's way out."

"Killed his wife? He *didn't* kill his wife!"

"Grow up, will you? Of course he killed her. He killed her as surely as the sun is going to rise tomorrow."

"He did not. I know!"

"You don't know anything! I'm the one who knows. What kind of a fool do you take me for? You think I couldn't read that pip-squeak of a man like a book? I could tell what he was going to think before he ever thought it. I've been around too damned long, sister, to be fooled by his baby-faced, innocent look. He killed his wife and he thought I could save him from hanging for it. It's as simple and cold-blooded as that. He gave me everything he owned because he thought he was

347

going to collect everything Sally owned. But it didn't work out and he couldn't face the music."

"No," she said, her voice calming and becoming steady. "That's what you think because that's the *way* you think. That's what you'd do if you were Jerry." She shook her head. "But you aren't Jerry. You couldn't be Jerry. You didn't know him at all. You couldn't understand him because you aren't capable. You think the worst of men because the worst of men is you."

Parrish raised the back of his hand. How he wanted to slash her face! "You ignorant hag," he snarled. "Outgrow that 'shining knight' complex, will you? Do you really think he's going to take a beating from Costaine and turn the other cheek? Do you think he's going to laugh at being cuckolded? Do you think nothing rankles? Do you think the picture of his wife in Costaine's arms didn't bug him, even when he was in yours? Wake up to what's going on!"

Katherine started to laugh. It grew wild, maniacal. "You fool!" she shrieked. "You dumb, ignorant fool! Don't you know anything? You, who think you're so goddam, Godalmighty smart? Haven't you figured it out yet?"

"What are you raving about?"

"About who killed Sally." She screamed it at him. "Who the hell do you think did it? It wasn't Jerry. Didn't I tell you it wasn't Jerry? So how the hell did you think I knew? Didn't it dawn on you? It's so goddam obvious!" She leaned forward and raised her voice higher. "I killed her! I did it!" She jabbed at her chest. "I—I—I—I!"

Parrish was taken aback. He shrank from her, but only for a moment. "You goddam liar." He moved in again. "You goddam bitch of a liar! You wouldn't even know how—"

She was hysterical. "Wouldn't I? It was easy! I waited till the party was over. I rang the doorbell. We talked. We argued. We fought. And I killed her. Just like that." The wildness turned to wails. "And I would have saved him," she sobbed, "but you killed him too soon."

He seized her by the neck of her coat. "You maniac," he snarled. "You go around confessing to crimes you didn't do and you won't end up in a cell, you'll end up in the asylum. That's where the crackpots go!" He turned her to the door and opened it. "Get out of here while I still let you," he warned, twisting the coat against her throat. "Go back to your broomstick or I'll have you committed. Do you hear me? I won't bury you in the ground, I'll bury you with the

348

freaks. I'll make you wish you're as dead as Jerry is. If I ever see you again, you'll curse the day."

He thrust her into the hall and double-locked the door.

CHAPTER 76

Parrish came away sweaty and shaken. Never had he been so terrified. But it was not without value. Melody had tackled the girl with the gun. She had risked herself for him and that was precious information to have. He returned to the table, carefully controlling himself. "God," he said in exasperation as he sat down and picked up his coffee, "why is it all the nuts in the world end up on *my* doorstep?"

Melody took her place opposite, stricken and withdrawn. She looked at the nearby cap pistol, made a face and pushed it away.

Cleve gulped the coffee, jabbed at the eggs and put down his fork. "I'm not hungry," he said petulantly. "That goddam witch has spoiled my appetite." He rose, threw his napkin on the table and strode to the windows. Across the green stood the shining marble courthouse, a mocking reminder of his defeat.

He flung himself away from the view. "Damn it," he said, "what are we waiting for? Get Pete on the phone and tell him to move his ass up here for our things. I want to get the hell out of this stinking city."

Melody went obediently to the phone and called Pete's room, down on a lower floor—the least costly location Cleve could get. That was the way Cleveland Parrish worked. Spend money where it shows. But to spend it where it doesn't show is throwing it down the drain. And Parrish never threw anything down drains. He never threw anything away anywhere so long as some value could be gained from it.

The phone in Pete's room buzzed and Melody found she was like Cleve. She had no appetite either and she wanted to get back to New

349

York just as fast as he did. New Haven was a lousy city. Like that cruddy little town in Tennessee where the Turner trial was held, it was a city full of hate. Or was it that hate lay only where Cleveland Parrish trod? He took unpopular causes and he achieved unpopular results, but was that all there was to it? Could the hate that dogged them both only rise from that?

Melody didn't know. It was too much beyond her. All she knew was that the isolation, the hate, and the rest of it gave her those awful pangs. She wouldn't get one now. There were too many things to do. And Cleve was there. But sometime, when she was alone and there was no way of turning off, the sound of Katherine's voice confessing to murder would haunt her mind and the terrifying black depths would yawn.

But Katherine was lying. Melody could see that. Cleve had opened her eyes. Jerry was guilty. She had wept for his death because she had believed in his innocence. But Cleve called him guilty and Cleve was smart. He knew. His arguments were impeccable. Katherine couldn't have done it. She didn't have the temperament. Besides, she wasn't strong enough. No! If there were a just God in heaven, Cleveland Parrish was right. Jerry Whittaker only got what he deserved.

Pete Tucker answered the phone in his usual laconic fashion. He knew it would be she and the contempt was in his voice. It stung her. It was more of the hate she had to live with. And she was filled with sudden hate herself. Who the hell was Pete Tucker to sit in judgment on her? She was trapped in the job. She couldn't escape it. She was spoiled for anything else—by the money, the excitement, the big-time quality of her life. Cleve needed her. He couldn't get along without her. He wouldn't let her go anyway. He could blackball her so she could never get another job.

But Pete Tucker? He wasn't beholden to Parrish. Who was he to sneer at her for catering to the big man, for working for someone who, as Katherine would have it, was a bloodsucker who drained everyone dry? Pete could get a job anywhere. Pete was quite beyond Cleve's reach. Pete was one man Cleve couldn't touch. So why the hell was Pete working for him if he had such contempt for the man? Talk about hypocrites! Melody at least had the excuse she had no-where else to go. But not Pete. So who was he to take that tone of voice with her?

"Cleve says get your ass up here for our bags," she snapped. "And be quick about it."